EXPIATION

Persephone Book N° 133
Published by Persephone Books Ltd 2019

Reprinted 2021

Preface © Valerie Grove

First published in 1929

Endpapers taken from a 1924–5 silk and rayon used
on a day dress, fabric in a private collection.

Typeset in ITC Baskerville by
KSPM, Wolverhampton

Printed and bound in Germany by
GGP Media GmbH, Poessneck

978 191 0263 235

Persephone Books Ltd
8 Edgar Buildings
Bath BA1 2EE
01225 425050

www.persephonebooks.co.uk

EXPIATION

by

ELIZABETH VON ARNIM

✳✳✳✳✳✳✳

with a new preface by

VALERIE GROVE

PERSEPHONE BOOKS
BATH

PREFACE

****

Elizabeth von Arnim blew into my life in 1991 when someone from the film company making *The Enchanted April*, her most popular novel, arrived on the doorstep looking for a location. Our Victorian redbrick semi (commonplace in North London) could be just the house lived in by Mrs Arbuthnot – one of the four ladies who respond to an advertisement in *The Times* offering 'to Those Who Appreciate Wistaria and Sunshine' a month's escape from the dull English spring to a medieval castle in Italy. So naturally I read *The Enchanted April* (1922) and was captivated by it. And later, by the film, directed by Mike Newell. And in between, by having Miranda Richardson (Mrs Arbuthnot) use my bedroom as a dressing room, and seeing Jim Broadbent (playing her husband, home late) creeping up our staircase. Plus the bonus of a catering van outside, serving full English breakfasts and profiteroles. It was their first day of shooting, 21 April – but it actually snowed, briefly, so we all shivered and huddled, and longed to get away ourselves to the Italian Riviera.

No film could quite capture the subtlety of Elizabeth von Arnim's probing of the inner thoughts of her characters. But visually, the benign, life-changing effect of San Salvatore on Miss Richardson, Joan Plowright, Josie Lawrence and Polly Walker was soothingly reflected. The author had once stayed at the very *castello* chosen for filming, near Portofino: she had known those 'heavenly blue mornings' and 'the sea like a liquid pearl'. Of course: Elizabeth was a privileged, much-travelled woman who owned and stayed at many such charmed places – she built two, named Chateau Soleil and Le Mas des Roses – offering balm to the soul in peaceful, thyme-scented walks, and umbrella pines, and gardens overflowing with sunshine and roses.

By the time she wrote *Expiation*, her thirteenth novel, the twice-married Elizabeth had brought up five children: an almost unique achievement among women novelists, rivalled only by Elizabeth Gaskell. It was 1929 and she was filled with trepidation that her affair with A S Frere (the Cambridge undergraduate who had come to catalogue her books and stayed to be her lover) was fading. Indeed, readers might suspect that she must already have experienced the pain of the end of an adulterous affair. She had certainly experienced a husband of the type to exact revenge on his wife, and had exposed him in a previous novel, *Vera*. Plundering her emotionally-charged life in her novels was what she did, coolly and unsentimentally.

At *Expiation*'s opening, Elizabeth presents Milly, her hero-ine, who sits, apparently calm and detached, not weeping, pondering on the sudden death of her husband. At forty-five, she is 'a little cushiony woman, fair-skinned and dove-eyed, with dimples on her plump hands where other people have knuckles'. She embodies propriety. No children have resulted from her marriage to Ernest Bott, scion of the wealthy and public-spirited family of Botts who are highly valued in Titford, 'that important south London suburb'. Instantly, Elizabeth shares with us her amused, gentle mockery of self-importance – of both the unfortunately-named Bott family and Titford the suburb. The Bott husbands (of the five Bott daughters) admire Milly's round softness, so much preferable to boniness. 'The bones of wives got into their characters,' those Botts thought, 'whose wives were thin and had recently been angry.' One, Bertie Bott's wife, is 'a positive toothpick'.

But then the reading of the Will reveals that Ernest Bott has disinherited Milly. 'My wife will know why,' he had dictated. Why so? Even Milly's hair is 'the colour of respectability'. Only Mrs Bott, Ernest's wise old mother, the materfamilias, seems to have an inkling of what might be afoot here. Once, she had heard Milly declare feelingly that 'she might soon be rather tired of "Everything, *everything*!"' and Mrs Bott had wondered about the cause of this outburst: was it Ernest, or some new man? But that suspicion had passed. Like any mother of a large family, she had other children to concern her. Her eldest daughter had recently got married at last, to her relief: 'for till a woman had been through a husband, the old lady held, she didn't really know what God could do to her.'

And how true this is, when a husband may consign his widow to total penury.

There are echoes of Jane Austen in the Bott family's discussions of what is to be done to help Milly. Shades of Lady Bertram and Mrs Norris in *Mansfield Park*, downgrading the

****

needs of their poor niece Fanny; or even of Lear's elder daughters reducing his retinue, reasoning his paltry needs.

The Botts discuss how many pounds per year each sibling-in-law might spare for Milly. 'Fifty each? Oh no – much too much – and nothing whatever for her to spend it on.' By the time they set forth to inform her of their magnanimous plans for her – that Milly should spend six months in each household – Milly, they discover, has vanished.

Here is the nub of the plot. 'For Milly had sinned.' Hence the title, and the theme: how is Milly to bring about the expiation of her adulterous secret? Ernest had been a repressive man. Only by defiance had she managed to keep surreptitiously in touch with her only sister Agatha, who had, when young, caused a scandal ('and who can be responsible for what sisters do?'). Ernest had forbidden her to correspond with Agatha. The solace Milly had found elsewhere twenty years ago had once been a love affair, but that has by now dwindled into companionship.

Here are questions: of morality, of principles. Should Milly be obliged to cleave to a husband who 'had vowed to make her happy for ever and ever, but had not'? In 1929 divorce was still rare, and shocking. And as Elizabeth asks: 'Was anybody or anything in the world worth leaving off being good for?'

There is much disillusion ahead for Milly, who had trusted her sister to 'fold her to her heart', not to condemn her. (In life, Elizabeth and her sister Charlotte were starting to have their differences.) Agatha has been through much hardship in her Swiss marriage, but spurred on by pride and youthful determination has never divulged this in letters to her 'plump, smug, expensive looking' sister.

When young, Agatha had personified grace and charity, but poverty had ground it away. Now she has grit. 'Grit was good, and she admired it,' writes Elizabeth of Milly, 'but not such quantities of it.' And Milly's obdurate search for expiation will involve exercising grace and charity. She becomes a Mary Poppins, a Pollyanna, sorting out the Botts' problems and predicaments, wreaking goodness and mercy on their households. Until her intercessions, the five Bott husbands were hopeless at fathoming their wives, or even talking to them. One is 'no good at all at working out what women . . . were feeling'. Another has never noticed his wife's extreme possessiveness, 'uncontrolled by the very smallest amount of intelligence'. They were such busy men. Too busy for 'the discomfort of quarrels at home'.

For Milly herself, there is a new realisation: that there is no escape from herself, nor from the relentless routines of life. As for women's dependency on men, allowing them to be God almighty, 'could idiocy go farther?' Beneath the meek little suburban wife seethes a formidable feminist. In the same year as *Expiation*, ninety years ago, Virginia Woolf published *A Room of One's Own* (now Persephone Book No. 134).

Elizabeth von Arnim is admired for her beady-eyed female perspective on men and families, and it is no wonder. Her life gave her ample opportunity for that. As a girl, Mary Annette Beauchamp – 'May' to her family – learned 'sweet twining ways' with men from her mother, Louey, and grew up to be like her: small, vivacious and flirtatious. Louey could always win her husband round when he was angered by a £100 bill for ribbons. Henry Beauchamp, previously rich but now less so, remained Micawberishly cavalier about their precarious finances. He still travelled extravagantly, and despite his ambivalence about the disruption of five noisy children, took them – with maids and friends, a party of fourteen – to the Swiss Alps when Elizabeth was six. At other times he absented himself abroad for years at a stretch, during which family life became 'sprightly, roomy', liberated from restraint. Elizabeth's was a happy childhood in Lausanne and London, with expeditions, games and lots of music. Unlike her beautiful sister Charlotte, who (astonishingly) had an illegitimate child at fifteen, but later married well. Elizabeth was not presented at court. But her father thought her 'bright, industrious and good'. Failing to be accepted at Cambridge (she was ill), she studied the organ at the Royal College of Music and could perform for the Wagners when in Bayreuth, in 1889, during a Grand Tour with her father whose purpose was to find her an eligible husband.

Playing the organ in St Peter's in Rome, she caught the eye of Graf Henning von Arnim-Schlagenthin – officer and widower, large and bald, fifteen years her senior. Henning's proposal was boldly Teutonic. 'All girls like love. It is very agreeable. You will like it too. You shall marry me and see.' But after their wedding in London in 1891, she found life in Berlin among the absurdly stiff Junker society a trial: the language, the servants, the embassy receptions, the loneliness (also described in the 1895 *Effi Briest* by Theodor Fontane, Persephone Book No. 121). Henning gave Elizabeth a small dachshund that had belonged to his first wife, although he forbade her to kiss it: 'I have provided you, for kissing purposes, with myself.'

Elizabeth endured three difficult pregnancies in as many years. Henning had only to blow his nose in the same room, she said, and she was pregnant. Long hard labours produced three daughters, on whom she bestowed an idyllic childhood replicating her own, at Henning's beautiful but neglected 8000-acre Pomeranian estate, Nassenheide. In its wild garden she could spend whole days in solitude, losing herself in Keats, Goethe, Walt Whitman, Boswell and a new discovery, Henry David Thoreau, who must be read out of doors. In the seventeenth century house she created a welcoming library of lamplit warmth. 'What a blessing it is to love books,' as she wrote. To Nassenheide came a succession of clever young men to tutor her children: E M Forster was the one they liked best. Another was Hugh Walpole, who said Elizabeth had three moods – charming, ragging ('until you are reduced to idiocy') and silence.

Here she wrote her first novel – inspired by Alfred Austin's 'The Garden that I Love' – *Elizabeth and Her German Garden* (1898). 'May 7th – I love my garden' was its opening line. Getting this book published gave her 'the most purely happy moment of my life'. It was reprinted eleven times within the year, earning her at least £10,000 (three-quarters of a million pounds in today's money) which helped pay off Henning's debts. Her cousin Katherine Mansfield, aged ten, read it and resolved to be a writer herself. In 1898 'Elizabeth' (surname-less) became famous, despite her anonymity.

****

A fourth daughter arrived the next year, coinciding with her husband's imprisonment for fraud. A fifth pregnancy filled her with dread – another daughter? – but her doctor refused to intervene, and it was a son, Henning Berndt, 'H B'. Some suspected that the then slim and personable Lord Francis Russell, elder brother of Bertrand, might be the father. He and Elizabeth certainly went about together during her visits home, and even travelled to Venice, despite his entanglements with his previous wives: Mabel, who lasted only three months; and Mollie, 'a fat florid Irishwoman of forty'. For marrying Mollie (in the US in 1900), Russell had served three months for bigamy.

Count von Arnim – who faced financial ruin, and stayed behind when Elizabeth and her German family became refugees in Devonshire – died in 1910. The elder daughters went off to Girton College, Cambridge. Elizabeth, sole provider and dispenser of largesse, was hoping for a new life with her married lover, H G Wells – until she was ousted by the much younger (and handsome and clever) Rebecca West, who was pregnant by Wells.

It still remains a mystery that as the Great War loomed, Elizabeth was infatuated enough to marry Francis Russell. But he was violently and overbearingly in love with her, and he would make her a Countess again. The consolation for this regretted marriage – her misgivings began in 1913 at the wedding and will-signing, when she angered him by bequeathing her money to her children – is that it inspired *Vera* (1921), Elizabeth's eleventh novel.

In it, we see Lucy, newly orphaned at eighteen, succumbing almost hypnotically to the courtship of Everard Wemyss,

****

a man of substance, whose first wife Vera has fallen, or thrown herself, out of the study window at their home. The house in the book represents Telegraph House, the redbrick villa Francis had just built in a splendid position, on the summit of the Sussex Downs in 250 acres of park. Elizabeth was never happy here. (It was later occupied by his brother Bertrand and his second wife Dora, who ran a progressive school, Beacon Hill, there in the 1920s.)

In *Vera*, we get a vivid account of Lucy's post-honeymoon arrival at 'The Meadows': a scene that prefigures Daphne du Maurier's *Rebecca*, when an innocent bride is brought to a house dominated by the spirit of a dead first wife. Lucy is appalled to watch her adored husband scold and bully the servants, and quickly realises that he is crushing her spirit too, mocking her every utterance, punishing her for catching a cold, sadistically denying her any comfort, being utterly impossible, filling her with fear. 'The assertion of the Scriptures that perfect love casteth out fear only showed' (thought Lucy) 'how little the Scriptures knew what they were talking about.' Wemyss is so exact a portrayal of the by now burly and florid Russell that his brother Bertie, who got on famously with Elizabeth, advised his sons 'never marry a novelist'. Readers today are familiar with marital tyranny – 'coercive control' now being an accepted provocation to murder, and 'gaslighting' (making a spouse believe she is deluded) a familiar form of subjugation. It's even been a storyline in *The Archers*.

Elizabeth and Russell never divorced, but when she fled from his house in 1919 Russell sued Shoolbred's, the removal

****

firm that carried away her chattels, claiming back things he considered his – including electric light fixtures, a hammock and 'tennis balls, both old and new'. The great advocate Edward Marshall Hall was Elizabeth's counsel, and when cross-examined she acquitted herself with wit and aplomb.

After this novel dredged from bitter experience, she thought she would never write anything as good. The next novel, *Introduction to Sally*, was light-hearted. But then in 1929 came her best work, *Expiation*: darker, very funny, but despite its humour painful to write. For all her seeming indifference to social disapproval of affairs, including with married men, she did feel something akin to Milly's guilt. She celebrated its publication with A S Frere, her former lover who was newly married. Most reviewers welcomed the book's 'familiar charm'. The *Times Literary Supplement* praised the colour and distinction of her prose, and the *Evening Standard* critic said, 'How wise Elizabeth is about men and women.' There were, however, dissenting voices, including L P Hartley who was not convinced by Milly.

Elizabeth waited until 1936 to produce a memoir, and did so from an ingeniously oblique viewpoint. 'I would like, to begin with,' declared the opening line of *All the Dogs of My Life* (1936) 'to say that though parents, husbands, children, lovers and friends are all very well, they are not dogs.' One could measure out one's life in dogs, she decided, having loved fourteen; and since her second marriage was dog-less it could be dispensed with in a sentence. Her canine relationships could be oddly inconsistent. The arrival of her first baby distracted her from Cornelia, her adored dachshund companion, who then fell into a decline. There was a heart-breaking reunion with her favourite dog Coco – left behind in Switzerland during the Great War; Coco died before her eyes upon her return five years later. When she started her affair with A S Frere, he sent her – through the post! – a woolly mongrel puppy that she did not care for when he got fat and lethargic, and later a fox-terrier. For dog-walking purposes she even built a new house in Virginia Water in stockbroker-belt Surrey, for their sake.

Elizabeth was worshipped by her children, but inexplicably dealt a terrible retribution to her youngest daughter, Felicitas, for misbehaving at school. Depriving the child of her beloved piano was the prelude to a tragic ending: the death of Felicitas (of double pneumonia) at sixteen. And there were other contradictions in Elizabeth. She could be reclusive, craving solitude, silence and the simple life – 'happiest when I never go anywhere and never see anybody' – but revert to a frivolous, party-going Riviera social life, when her diaries bristle with names: Somerset Maugham, Ottoline Morrell, Chaliapin, Max Beerbohm, Charlie Chaplin, the Aga Khan.

But what was constant was her lively, caustic wit, her perception of human folly. She is like an old friend in whose company there are no dull or banal moments, who tells stories against herself and never takes anything too seriously. 'Chanterai ma chanson' – I will sing my song – was the motto on her bookplate; and when she died in South Carolina, in 1941, aged 75, 'Parva sed apta', small but effective, was the motto on her gravestone.

Valerie Grove
London, 2019

EXPIATION

EXPIATION

MILLY sat in her chair without moving. Her round, pale face was empty of expression. Her eyes were fixed on her hands, lying as if they didn't belong to her, folded, plump and passive, on her black lap. She had been like that, sitting quiet, looking at her hands, ever since it happened.

"Rouse her," the doctor had said, when poor Ernest's relations drew his attention to this conduct. But in vain did the clustered sisters-in-law try to; she remained silent, motionless, looking down at her hands folded on her black lap.

"If only she would cry," the Botts said to each other.

"A good cry would make all the difference," they agreed.

But Milly didn't cry; nor did she speak, except to murmur in her gentle voice, each time a sympathetic and condoling relative stroked her arm, or, from behind her chair, patted her bowed head, "How kind you all are."

Who wouldn't be kind to poor little Milly in her sorrow? Not only were the Botts kind, but the whole of Titford was kind. That important south London suburb appreciated the Botts, so financially sound, so continually increasing in prosperity. They were its backbone. They

subscribed, presided, spoke, opened. Titford was full of
Botts, and every one of them a credit to it. Whenever
they married, which they did punctually on arriving at
the proper age, or gave birth, which they also did
punctually, once married—except Ernest, who had
been childless,—Titford genuinely rejoiced; and whenever they died, which they did on achieving ripeness and
not before—except Ernest, who had been cut off
in a street accident,—Titford genuinely mourned, and
genuinely sympathized with the survivor; usually, by
that strange law of nature which makes the frailer
vessel to begin with yet ultimately the tougher, a
widow.

In this case the sympathy was particularly warm,
for Milly had always been popular. Long ago Titford
had decided that Mrs. Ernest Bott was a very ladylike
woman, and had taken her to its heart. Twenty-five
years almost to a month, it recollected, since poor
Ernest Bott brought his bride to the handsome red
brick house in Mandeville Park Road,—a slip of a girl
she was then, hardly more than a flapper, and looking
absurdly young to be the wife of a man nearing middle-
age, but from the very beginning behaving as a lady in
her position should, and going on behaving as she
should, in spite of what her sister did from that very
house only three months later. And so she had gone on
behaving ever since. The years rolled along, round,
comfortable, blameless years, the sister didn't reappear
and was forgotten, except deep down in the heart of the
Botts, who were slow to forget disgrace, and of all the
men in that numerous family Ernest was held to have
been the most fortunate in his marriage. Long since had
Mrs. Ernest ceased to be a slip. Long since had the
increasingly solid comfort Ernest was able to provide
had its way with her. And here she was at forty-five,

a little cushiony woman, fair-skinned and dove-eyed, with dimples on her plump hands where other people have knuckles, and a smooth head, sleekly covered with agreeable hair the colour of respectability. Her life, except for that one scandal of her sister—and who can be responsible for what sisters do?—had been blameless. Gossip had nothing to say about her; criticism let her alone. She was just simply a credit to the family and the place,—normal, well mannered, never saying anything particular or much, ready at any time to do a kindness, pleasantly smiling, nicely dressed, abundantly nourished, returning calls punctually, at first in a neat brougham with one horse which presently developed into a pair, and later on in a car that kept on becoming bigger, going to dinners in her velvets, going to church in her furs or feathers, having an At Home day once a month, amiably receiving visitors in her handsome drawing-room, listening nicely, never contradicting, never being clever, never asserting, at the most gently suggesting, and ready smilingly to withdraw her suggestion if it seemed to be in the least degree unwelcome.

What a wife. What a nice place the world would be if all wives were more like Milly, the male Botts had frequently thought—whispering it to themselves, for it wouldn't do to say it out loud—when they had been having trouble with their own. Ernest hadn't had a day's trouble, an hour's bother, with Milly. Sweet little Milly. Dear, easy-going little woman. One would do anything for a woman like that. And so pleasant to look at, too—so round and soft. All wives should be round and soft, if only because one had to sleep with them. As well ask at Whiteley's or Shoolbred's, thought the Bott brothers, for a bony bed and expect to be comfortable in it, as expect to be comfortable, lastingly comfortable, with a bony wife. The bones of wives got into their characters, thought those upset Botts whose wives were thin and had recently been angry. But only secretly were they upset. Outwardly, each was an affectionate and contented husband. One has to be.

§

And here was Milly a widow, and a rich widow, and not one of the brothers a widower at the same moment and able to marry her, and keep her and poor old Ernest's money in the family. She would be snapped up at once—on the very day year. Bound to be. What man in his senses wouldn't wish to snap up Milly, even if she were poor? What man wouldn't wish, wouldn't most earnestly wish, to be gathered for the rest of his life to that soft, kind, pillowy bosom, and remain for ever safe in it from quarrels and angry words?

But the sisters-in-law, thinking of all the good Bott money, said, "Of course she won't dream of marrying again. Why should she, now that she will be so well off, and can do as she pleases?"

And that one of the sisters-in-law who had a temperament, and prided herself on it, and told her husband, when he remonstrated, that he ought to thank God on his knees that he had married a real woman and not the usual fish, said, "It isn't as if she had any sort of *go* in her. What does poor Milly, of all women, want with a man?"

And the old lady in whose house these things were being talked of, the oldest of anybody, the original old Mrs. Bott, who was many times a grandmother and a great-grandmother, and had even begun to be a great-great-grandmother, and who lived benignly on the top of Denmark Hill so as to be within easy reach, as she often said, of all her dear children in case they needed

her, and yet not so close as to oppress them—the old
lady recalled in silence, as she sat slowly shaking her
head because of this speech of George's wife, who was
more of a gipsy than a gentlewoman, old Mrs. Bott
sometimes thought, but refrained from saying because
she long had known that in families the more you re-
frain from saying the better,—the old lady recalled in
silence an odd scene ten years before in that very room,
when Milly, so quiet and well-behaved till then, had
walked in one warm spring morning (it must have been
spring and warm, for she remembered the French
window was wide open and the gardener was mowing the
lawn, which had suddenly become a field of daisies),
and then had gone to the window and watched what was
being done for a time, and then had turned round with a
jerk, looking queer and different and very hot, too,
poor child, after her walk, and said that she was feeling
as if she might soon be rather tired of everything.

"Everything, *everything!*" she had then cried quite
loud, as if she couldn't hold herself in a moment longer,
flinging out both hands in a funny gesture, and crimson
in the face from climbing the hill in the heat; and she
had added, with tears in her eyes, "I can't any longer—
I've come to the end——"

The end? thought old Mrs. Bott. Which end? There
were so many ends to life, and in one's younger years
one was always coming to them, and then finding that
they weren't ends at all.

Well, well. She had given her a nice cup of tea. Poor
Milly. There was a man in *that*, for dead certain, she
decided; either Ernest and tiffs, or some new man and
what these poor, eager, tormented children called love.

Whatever it was, however, it passed. Milly never said
any more, and soon was her own gentle, contented self
again; indeed, a few weeks after this little outburst she

had become much sweeter, if possible, and more contented than ever before. Learning wisdom, thought the old lady. Settling down. One does.

Poor children, old Mrs. Bott often thought, contemplating her posterity,—so hard for them sometimes. And they didn't know, and nobody could tell them, because they wouldn't believe, how quiet and comfortable everything was going to be at last, and how little their troubles in the long run would really have mattered. No need to have worried so much, and eaten out their poor hot hearts,—no need, no need at all.

And now ten years later here was Milly bereaved, and so much overwhelmed that nothing roused her from the silent contemplation of her lap. There in the bedroom she sat, the bedroom from which Ernest had issued that last morning, never dreaming he wouldn't come back to it again, and old Mrs. Bott, brought over from Denmark Hill for the funeral, and sitting upstairs with Milly while the Will was being read in the dining-room, vainly tried to comfort her, laying her shaky hand at intervals on the motionless crape-clad shoulder, and saying such words as seemed most likely to be the right ones.

If only the shoulder would heave, thought old Mrs. Bott; if only poor Milly would cry. It was so much more like the very extremity of grief not to heave, not to cry, to sit pale and silent, with her head hanging like that. Who would have thought Milly had loved Ernest so much? The old lady dispassionately recalled her son, and wondered.

"You know, my dear," she quavered, for by this time she was extremely old, and everything about her quavered, "we shall all take such care of you, and see that you are never lonely."

Milly's head hung lower.

"The girls"—so old Mrs. Bott spoke of her daughters and daughters-in-law, by this time every one of them in the forties and fifties and sixties—"have made up their minds that you are to be their special care."

Milly's drooped eyelashes faintly quivered.

"And it isn't as if there were going to be any difference in your style of living, my dear, because Alec tells me"—Alec was the eldest son—"Ernest was even better off than we had been able to guess—I'm sure I don't know why men should be so secretive about what they're making—and you'll have all of it, and stay on in your nice house that you're so fond of."

"I—I don't deserve——" gasped Milly, faintly.

Was that a tear? Something dropped, surely, on her lap.

"There, there," quavered old Mrs. Bott, renewing her patting, her own eyes filling with tears. "There, there. Nobody ever deserved all we can any of us give you more than you, Milly, my dear. There, there. You'll be the better for a little cry—ever so better."

And she cried a little herself; only a little, for the years had dried up most of her tears. But a recollection of the days when Ernest was a baby had come into her mind, and all her hopes of him and all her pride, and how he had had tiny fair curls she used to twist into shape round her fingers—he who for so many, many years had been bald; and it seemed strange and sad to know that he was lying alone now under his wreaths—beautiful wreaths, too, and such a number of them—in the cemetery up the hill, and going to lie like that till kingdom-come, and nothing to show for having been alive at all, except his widow and his money. No children, that is. Ernest, in the matter of posterity, had been a blind alley, a *cul-de-sac*. Strange and sad not to go on in any way, to come to a dead stop. Old Mrs. Bott couldn't help crying a little to think of it. Poor Ernest;

all his tiny fair curls and pretty ways to end in nothing but a widow.

"It's only a dream," she said, drying her eyes and nodding her head wisely. "Life's just a dream." And she added, as through the open side window an un-mistakable smell drifted from the house next door, "Curry, *I'll* be bound, at Glenmorgan to-day for lunch."

Then, laying her hand again on Milly's shoulder, and in her mind's eye gazing down the immense vistas of the years of her own life at all the little black dots strewn along them that were deaths, and seeing how small these dots had become, and how they dwindled smaller till the first ones were almost invisible, and it was quite difficult to sort them out and know which was which and whose was whose, she said, a second time wisely nodding her head, "It's all dreams, my dear. In the long run nothing, Milly my dear, but dreams." And her hand still shaking on Milly's shoulder, she stared with her red old eyes at the house opposite, and thought how queer it was the way the personalities those death-dots represented had disappeared out of her mind—her husband, for instance, dead these fifty years, only now came back with any clearness when she forgot at night to put the lid back on the vaseline. Every night through-out her grown-up life she had rubbed her eyelids with vaseline before going to sleep; and sometimes she had forgotten to cover the pot up again, and when that happened, and in the morning poor Alexander saw it, he used to scold her. He said, she recollected, that it was dirty and insanitary, and he talked of germs and dust getting in. And now, whenever she woke in the morning and saw the lid not on the pot, back he came as distinct and fresh as ever; never else. Queer, thought old Mrs. Bott, mechanically patting Milly's shoulder, and deep

in contemplation of the strangeness of life, that there
should be nothing left at all of poor Alexander except
when a pot of vaseline had its lid off.

She blinked a little. The sun lay very brightly on the
red house opposite, and dazzled her eyes. Life was
certainly just a dream. From that house, too, came a
smell of food; chiefly cauliflowers this time old Mrs.
Bott opined, lifting an interested nose. Life was a
dream, it was true, but a dream with waking moments.
Right up to the very end meals were real and interest-
ing. No doubt, she thought, her nose lifted, those were
the people Ernest had complained of who had fads, he
said, and wouldn't eat meat, and said rude things about
England. "Poor creatures," she thought indulgently,
"they've got to go through with it"—and she wished for
their sakes they would go through with it quickly, for
meanwhile they were missing a good many nice slices
of mutton, and she supposed it would be difficult to
like England or anything else if one were full of nothing
but cauliflowers.

Then, as she was thinking this, the bedroom door
opened a crack, and the head of her youngest son Bertie,
a meat-fed man of fifty-two, was put through so carefully that it was evident the rest of him was on tiptoe.

"Come in, Bertie, and shut the door," quavered old
Mrs. Bott. "No use making draughts."

"Do you," he asked in the half whisper of the occasion, looking at his sister-in-law, "feel equal to a talk?"

"Speak up, Bertie," quavered his mother. "No use
standing there just making faces. Equal to a talk?
Of course she is. Milly is always equal to anything—
aren't you, my dear?" And again she patted the crape-
clad shoulder, for of all her daughters-in-law she was
fondest of this one. Much the fondest. She loved her.

Bertie took a neat, swift step into the room, and deftly

shut the door behind him, without making a sound; and there was such practice in the movement, such a completely noiseless dexterity, very surprising in one so big and heavy, that for the first time it occurred to old Mrs. Bott that perhaps he wasn't a faithful husband. So much skill in the silent shutting of doors. . . . Well, well; poor children; they had to fight it all out. She only hoped Bertie didn't worry too much about it, and make himself miserable with qualms. When he was as old as she was he would see that these things too were dreams, and to have qualms about what turned out afterwards to have been nothing but a dream was a sad waste of time.

"My poor Milly," began Bertie gravely, as one whose tidings were evil.

He seemed strangely moved. Quite upset, in fact, thought old Mrs. Bott, observing him with watery-eyed surprise; and crossing to where his sister-in-law sat he drew up a chair beside her, and put his hand on her arm with such an obvious desire to impart courage that old Mrs. Bott's surprise increased. Courage? What did Milly want with courage, when she was going to inherit several thousands a year?

"Has the Will been read?" she asked.

"He must have been ill," was Bertie's answer, as he cleared his throat.

"Ill?" echoed his mother. "Do you mean when he took that taxi?"

"When he made the Will," said Bertie, looking very uncomfortable. "Or rather, when he added the codicil."

It was evident to old Mrs. Bott now that there was to be a blow. "What codicil, my dear?" she quavered, across Milly's bowed head.

Bertie glanced at Milly. Fancy having to hit anything so gentle, so dove-like and patient, as the round black figure in the chair. Her feet were on a footstool because her legs were so short, and it seemed to Bertie to make his unpleasant job more difficult that poor Milly's legs shouldn't reach the floor. Dear little legs too, he'd be bound. He jerked back his thoughts. This wasn't the moment to think of things like that.

"Poor old Milly," he said, taking her hand.

"Say what you've got to say, Bertie," quavered old Mrs. Bott.

"I'm afraid it's a bad business—a very bad business," said Bertie, shaking his head and extremely reluctant to go on.

"No good beating about the bush, then," said his mother.

And then, holding Milly's hand so tight that it hurt, he burst out that he couldn't understand Ernest—he simply couldn't.

"Why?" quavered old Mrs. Bott, very anxious indeed.

"It's so *unfair*," said Bertie. "It isn't even commonly *decent*."

"But why, my son?" asked old Mrs. Bott, her mouth quivering.

"Why?" repeated Bertie, dropping Milly's hand, which lay inert where it fell, and getting up and going to the window. He stood looking out. He couldn't look at Milly—not while he hit her.

"Why?" he said again, his back to the two women. "That's just what *I* want to know. He's only left Milly a thousand pounds—one beggarly thousand, out of the whole hundred thousand he'd got, and the rest is all to go to a damned charity. Is that the way to behave to a wife who has devoted herself for twenty-five years? And to Milly, of all wives!"

The old lady sat staring at his back, her mouth quivering so much that she could hardly speak.

"Whatever——" she began.

"And everything is to be sold—the house, furniture, every blessed thing—and given to this charity. Such a charity too!" He spun round in his indignation, and faced them. "He must have been stark mad. It's some Home of Rescue in Bloomsbury for fallen women. Why, none of us ever had anything to do with things like that. I didn't know Ernest had ever given such places a thought. It suggests—I'm blest if I know what it doesn't suggest. And for Milly, for the best wife a man ever had, nothing. Not a stick of furniture. Nothing but the bare thousand pounds. To keep her for a bit from starving, I suppose. To keep her out of the nearest gutter. It's the most scandalous——"

Old Mrs. Bott got up. She got up with difficulty, and Bertie had to go and help her. "I'm going downstairs," she said. "I don't believe a word of it. I shall ask Ernest's solicitor for myself."

"You won't get much out of *him*," said Bertie, helping her. "Of all the thin-lipped, cold-blooded——"

But he didn't try to keep her back; on the contrary, he encouraged her to go, leading her to the door by her elbow and assisting her carefully down to the dining-room.

Then he came back. Milly was sitting just as he had left her. He shut the door, swiftly and softly, and stood against it with his hands spread out behind him, as if to prevent anyone from coming in.

"Look here, Milly," he said, "there's something more. Mother'll hear that, too, before she sees you again. I only hope it won't get into the papers—you know how they put in whatever a man says in his Will that's at all out of the way. And what do you think Ernest put in his?"

Milly, her eyes bent on her hands, shook her patient head.

"He said, after leaving you the thousand pounds,

and expressly adding the word 'only,' which in itself is as good as a slap in the face—the whole thing beats me altogether—he said, 'My wife will know why.'"

§

For an instant Milly's mild eyes were veiled by some immediately suppressed emotion. Colour rushed across her face, and left it paler than ever. Her lips dropped apart. She raised her head and looked at Bertie, and her hands, so listless before, tightened in her lap.

Of course, thought Bertie. Naturally. Feeling the slur. What a damned mean thing to have done. Poor little Milly. Kind, sweet little woman, who wouldn't hurt a fly, to be served so. A wife in a thousand Milly had been, and now look at this. He had always supposed Ernest was a decent chap—a bit glum sometimes, when his liver was worrying him, but decent. How unpleasant, seeing that he was dead, to have to realize that he had been nothing but a cad. Some petty quarrel, some impulsive visit to his solicitor, some nursed resentment, and a life's devotion and affection wiped out with a smack in the face. A *post-mortem* smack, too,—of all smacks the meanest, thought Bertie. Not that Bertie for a moment believed Milly would or could ever quarrel. It must have been entirely on Ernest's side. The best one could say for him was that he was ill when he put in the codicil, having probably one of his worst liver attacks. But to let a liver attack turn a man permanently into a scoundrel!

"I've *done* with him—*done* with him," he vehemently declared; just as if there still was anything left of Ernest to be done with.

Milly, however, neither saw him nor heard him. Her eyes, wide open, were fixed now on the window, her hands tight together in her lap.

"How long?" her pale, astonished lips managed to get out, while she stared at the red wall of the house opposite.

"What, my dear? What, my poor little girl?" said Bertie, hurrying across and bending over her. A dear little woman. A dear, dear little woman. And with such pretty dark eyelashes too curling up at their tips. His wife hadn't got any. None visible, that is. Sandy.

"When?" whispered Milly, staring straight in front of her.

"When? Do you mean when he put it in? Two years ago. It's in a codidil. It beats me," said Bertie, his eyes moist with angry sympathy as he felt the warm roundness of the shoulder his hand was resting on, "how he could ever have quarrelled with you. And the worst of it is," he went on indignantly, "I can't let myself go about him because he's dead, and it wouldn't be decent. But I can tell you this, Milly——"

"Hush," she whispered, catching the hand on her shoulder quickly in hers, her eyes on the red wall opposite. So he had known. So Ernest had known. Two years ago. For two whole years he had known. Extraordinary. Incredible. . . .

"I can tell you this," persisted Bertie, refusing to hush, "that we're not going to let you suffer because Ernest chooses to behave like a damned——"

"Oh, don't," gasped Milly. "Please—I can't bear—you mustn't——"

And for the first time since Ernest's death she began really to cry. Laying her cheek in an abandonment of grief on the hand she held in hers, she cried so bitterly that her whole body shook. "Poor Ernest——" she sobbed. "Poor, poor Ernest——"

Bertie was profoundly moved. "Milly, you really are an *angel*," he said.

**٭(*II*)٭

THE other Botts, however, didn't take it like that.

At first they too were indignant with Ernest, and ashamed of him, besides being very cold to the solicitor who had lent himself to the drawing up of such a scandalous codicil; but presently, after he had packed up his attaché case and gone, and they still all lingered there uncertain what to do next, there gradually spread among them an extremely unpleasant word, passed on somehow from one mouth to another, and whispered round till at last it got to George's wife, who said it out loud.

The word was *Fishy*.

The moment it had been said it was recognised as appropriate. There was no getting away from it—fishy was the word. A man didn't do what Ernest had done, and for two years allow it to remain unaltered, without some good, some tremendous reason.

'"Oh, yes, he does, if he's a sneak and a coward," burst out Bertie.

"Bertie!" they cried, shocked; and suggested he should remember that Ernest was dead.

"I can't help that," said Bertie—as if anybody had supposed he could.

His wife looked at him with narrowed eyes. She had long suspected him of being more interested in Milly than brothers-in-law are supposed to be.

Old Mrs. Bott expressed a wish to be taken home. Poor children; they were going to quarrel. And all of no use, if only they could be got to see it—just waste of time and emotions, poor things. But nothing would stop them once they began. She might, then, just as well be at home. Better. Having tea.

"Alec, my dear, will you take me home?" she quavered, trying to attract her eldest son's attention, who was so much confounded and bewildered by what had happened that he didn't hear.

All the Botts were confounded and bewildered, and stood about in the dining-room in confused groups, taking no notice of the refreshments spread ready on the side-table, and shutting the door—Fred thought of that—on the maids who tried to bring in soup and coffee. This wasn't the moment for having maids about, nor for eating and drinking; though George's wife, the one with the temperament, whose eyes were bright with excitement and curiosity, and who after all wasn't by blood a Bott, did furtively nibble chocolates.

"Fancy Milly," she whispered, being the first definitely to fasten the fishiness on her. "That quiet, meek mouse. Just fancy!"

Yes—fancy Milly indeed, the other sisters-in-law thought.

Nothing like this had ever happened to the family before. They stood staring at each other. And there was Titford looming in the background, unconscious for the moment, but sure, unless the most minute precautions were taken, to know soon, as it always did know soon on every occasion when there was anything to know. What was to be done? Certainly, without any doubt whatever, the thing was fishy.

"You remember her sister?" Bertie's wife whispered.

Remember? They remembered as if it were yesterday. The same blood, their eyes said, as they nodded shocked heads, come out again. But blood that comes

out at forty-five is much worse, of course, than blood
that comes out at nineteen.

No, no, said the brothers and brothers-in-law, pulling
themselves together, it couldn't be. Too bad, too bad
to think for a moment that Milly . . . The truth was,
Ernest was a coward, with the deuce of a temper, which
he didn't dare let out because he knew nobody would
believe Milly could possibly give him any reason to be
angry. So he revenged himself like this, he played this
low-down trick on her. It was pretty unpleasant having
to regard him, now that he was dead and all that, as a
cad, but there it was.

Yes, yes, it must be, said the sisters and sisters-in-law
—and how could his brothers speak so of poor Ernest,
who was dead? Unpleasant as it was, they admitted, to
have to think of Milly, who had always been held up to
them as a pattern of what a wife should be—they looked
at their husbands—and what a daughter should be—
they looked at the old lady—unpleasant as it was to
have to think of her as deceiving them, it was much
worse to defame the dead. Clearly Milly had somehow
profoundly injured Ernest. She must have. She had.
That codicil could be explained in no other way. For
two whole years, and probably longer, she had been
taking them all in; she, at her age, and with her figure.

"Look here, you scrag women—you leave Milly's
figure alone," burst out Bertie.

What a thing to say, they thought, indignant and
shocked; what a thing to say on an occasion which had
only just left off being a funeral.

"Alec, my dear——" quavered old Mrs. Bott, again
trying to attract his attention.

"Shut up, Bertie," muttered his brother George, a
quiet, stout man in horn-rimmed spectacles.

He would have liked to say something of the sort

himself, but what was the use? After all, he and his
brothers had to sleep with their wives, and it made a
good deal of a hash up of one's business next day if there
hadn't been quiet in bed. That, thought George, who
was a plain, sensible man with plain, sensible thoughts,
was where wives got one: they could, and did, wear one
down in bed.

"Alec, my dear——"

"It's waste of time to squabble," said Fred, the rich-
est of the family, taking out his watch.

"I should say it's great waste of time forgetting that
one is supposed to be a gentleman," said Alec's wife,
usually of few words but stirred by Bertie's rudeness.

"The question surely is," said Alec, stroking his
beard nervously, "not what Milly has done or not done,
nor even"—he smiled propitiatingly at the assembled
wives—"what the poor little thing's figure is like, but
what steps we must take to keep this quiet. It seems to
me most important that we should keep it quiet."

Yes, they saw that; they were all agreed as to that.
And they shuddered as they pictured to themselves the
sorts of things Titford would say if it heard that Ernest
had disinherited his wife, and left everything, except
that one insulting thousand pounds, to a charity. It
mustn't hear. At all costs it must be prevented hearing.
That charity! The more they thought of it the more
ashamed they were. Indeed, no room had ever before
held so many people being so much ashamed as Ernest's
dining-room that afternoon. They were ashamed of
him, ashamed of the solicitor, ashamed of Milly, but
most of all, they discovered on thinking it over, were
they ashamed of the charity. A Home of Rescue for
Fallen Women? Extraordinary to have chosen such a
thing. Entirely unaccountable, this was, on Ernest's
part..

Then, somehow, it too was accounted for. No one knew who first accounted for it, but the explanation began to drift round among the sisters-in-law, passing from ear to ear in a whisper. A horrible explanation. It was, *He wished to provide for her future.*

There was a shiver, a silence, and then from somebody a faint giggle.

"Alec, my dear——" quavered old Mrs. Bott more insistently. Poor children; bent on being angry and unkind. So much better to have some nice hot soup and a sandwich, and then go quietly home and sleep it all off.

"I wish to *God*——" burst out Bertie a second time, bringing his fist down on the table with such a crash that the cups leapt in their saucers.

But what he wished he didn't say. He stopped, all red, looking as if his collar were going to choke him. No good; better hold on to oneself, he thought, remembering, he too, the importance of his night's rest. And there was that delicate business next day with Palliser and Leeds to fix up. He couldn't afford to go into that with his nerves all in rags.

Fred again looked at his watch. "We're wasting time," he observed.

"Quite," said Alec, nervously stroking his beard. He was the only Bott with a beard, and it was a very beautiful one—silvery, as became his years, and long, and always spotlessly clean, and a great comfort to him whenever he was worried or nervous, for then he stroked it and it soothed him.

"What line are we going to take about Milly?" asked Fred, shutting his watch, a gold hunter bequeathed him by his father, with a click.

"Much more important," said Bertie's wife, "is what line are we going to take about Titford."

"Isn't it the same thing?" one of the brothers-in-law,

a mild man, suggested; and surely, he thought, he hadn't said it aggressively? But Bertie's wife appeared to think he had, for she turned to him with some tartness, and said it wasn't. "At least," she said, "it doesn't seem so to me, but then I'm not as clever, perhaps, as you."

"Poor old Bertie," thought the brother-in-law.

"Poor little children," thought old Mrs. Bott. "Alec, my dear——" she said aloud.

"It *is* the same thing," said Fred. "The same thing to a T."

"I rather think so too," ventured Alec, his hand deep in his beard. How much he dreaded family conclaves. The women, when they got together, seemed to work each other up so. Separately, they were quite nice and good-natured. What was the matter with them, that they should be so unmanageable when they got together? Even Ruth, his quiet wife . . .

Then Walter Walker, of Shadwell and Walker, the great wool-brokers in Threadneedle Street, lifted up his voice and offered the suggestion for what it was worth— "For what it's worth, mind you," he repeated, anxious to show he knew he wasn't really a Bott but only connected, and therefore had little to say in this—that Milly should be taken into each of their homes in turn for three months at a time, perhaps six; taken in, and made much of, poor woman, he added, forcing himself to gaze round courageously through his spectacles at his sisters-in-law. Because, he affirmed, continuing courageous, this was not only the decent attitude, surely, to one who had always deserved well of them and had suddenly lost everything, husband, fortune, and home, and who was childless into the bargain——

"Whose fault is that?" interrupted his wife.

"My dear, you're not going to suggest that it was her fault she lost Ernest?" asked Walter mildly.

"Or that she's childless?" asked Bertie.

"Don't let's be *coarse*, please," said Bertie's wife, narrowing her eyes at him.

"You know perfectly well what I mean," said Walter's wife. "Whose fault is it that she lost her fortune?"

"Ernest's, of course," said Bertie.

"It's a pity, Bertie, that you will persist in taking that line about the dead," said Alec's wife.

Poor children; all so angry. And Ernest himself, over whom they were quarrelling, quite quiet up there on the hill, under his beautiful wreaths. "Alec, my dear——"

"Well, we won't go into that now," said Fred, looking at his watch a third time.

"Shall I finish my sentence?" asked Walter Walker mildly.

"By all means," said Alec, finding comfort in his beard.

"It's not only the decent attitude," continued Walter, clearing his throat, "but the best, quite the best way, of stopping criticism and gossip. In my opinion—I offer it, of course"—he glanced round deprecatingly—"for what it is worth—Milly should be taken in by the family in turn, and rather conspicuously made much of."

"Do you mean taken in for always?" asked his wife.

"Why not?" he said.

"Do you mean for the rest of her days she is to go round visiting us?" asked Bertie's wife incredulously.

"Why not?" said Walter Walker again.

There was a silence. The women looked at each

other. Putting aside the making much of Milly, which was absurd of Walter, for why on earth should she, who had brought such trouble and disgrace on them, be made much of?—putting that aside, taking in was, they felt, a delicate job. In the happiest of circumstances they could imagine it would be a delicate job, unless the person taken in was well enough off not to need it. These weren't happy circumstances. These were most doubtful ones, the Bott wives were sure, and the Bott husbands uneasily suspected. It would be asking rather a good deal of human nature, the wives thought—except George's wife, who was excited and curious, and would have liked to begin taking in Milly at once—to have Milly in their homes, in their very bosoms, among their innocent children and grandchildren, after whatever it was she had done. And to be asked to make much of her into the bargain!

"Walter's quite right," said Fred.

"She certainly has got to live somewhere," said Alec.

"And you can't live on the interest of a thousand pounds," Walter Walker pointed out deprecatingly. "You can die on it, of course, but, even then, only in an attic or a cellar. I'm sure none of us want Milly to die, let alone in an attic or a cellar."

"I pay my typist a hundred and fifty a year," said Fred. "Three times as much as the most we can get safely for Milly. And it doesn't seem to stop her from being a hungry-looking thing."

"Certainly we can't have one of our family either living or dying in an attic or a cellar," said Alec, shocked at the picture Walter's words had conjured up.

No; they couldn't have that, of course, agreed the wives and sisters. The family had always behaved well and generously in regard to money, and it would never do for Titford to suspect them of meanness. It did look

as if Milly might have to be taken in. But how unpleasant; how awkward; how certain to be painful.

"And the sooner the better," said Bertie.

"Beginning with us, I suppose," said his wife, narrowing her eyes at him.

"She's like a toothpick," thought Bertie, glowering
at her. "She's got the figure of a toothpick." Aloud he
said, forcing himself to speak calmly, "The house may
be sold any day over Milly's head. I didn't like the look
in that fellow's eye—that solicitor fellow of Ernest's.
He's got a down on her."

"Perhaps he knows more than we do," said his wife.

Again Bertie glowered at her, and held on to himself.

"Why Ernest should leave us all out, and appoint as
his executors this solicitor, whom none of us know, and
the director of that very unpleasant charity——" began
Alec, clutching his beard.

"Yes. I don't understand," said Walter Walker.

"There's something dashed queer about it," said
Fred.

"Fishy," said George's wife.

Really, the more they considered it, fishy was the
only word.

"But when you say, you men, that we're not only to
take her in but to make much of her——" began Bertie's
wife.

"She *is* a toothpick," thought Bertie, thrusting his
hands into his pockets and walking over to a window
and staring out, "boring away, boring away——"

"Only a man would have an idea like that," said
Walter Walker's wife, looking severely at her husband,
who also went to a window, another one, and gazed
abstractedly at the view, which was a conifer.

"Well, hang it all," said Fred, who, being the most
successful of a successful family, was also the boldest,

"you can't not make much of her. It wouldn't be human. Petting's what she wants."

Petting?

There was a scandalised silence.

"No doubt you men will find it all quite easy," then said Fred's wife unexpectedly, for she usually kept pretty quiet.

"Yes—you've always been absurd, quite absurd about Milly," said the eldest Bott sister.

"You've bored us stiff with her virtues, and Milly this, and Milly that," said another sister.

"Rubbing her in till we got tired of her very name," said another.

"Actually admiring her for having lost her figure," said another; and the four wives of the four Bott brothers nodded their heads in agreement.

The men were amazed at this sudden flare of bitterness. The two at the windows turned round to stare. Why, they had always understood their wives were very fond of Milly, someone was heard to murmur.

"Fond of Milly? Of course we were fond of Milly," they cried. "But that never blinded us to——"

"Besides, you know quite well it's different now——"

"You yourselves admit what has happened is fishy——"

And the room, for the next ten minutes, was a babel of heated and disjointed conversation.

Poor children; poor children; all getting so hot and angry. The old lady could only sit and listen, her shaking hands clutching the top of her stick. No good trying to stop them. They had to go through with it. And presently the room would be quiet again, and the noise and anger have happened yesterday, last month, last year, twenty years ago, and be slid away for ever into silence. And then, before they could turn round, before they had had really time to think, these poor excited children would be quiet too, and asleep as Ernest was asleep. It seemed a pity they didn't realize, and that nobody could make them realize, that in the end it all wouldn't have mattered a bit what Ernest had meant or what Milly had done, and that they might just as well have been kind and happy together on this particular afternoon, as indeed on all their few afternoons, and together comfortably eaten the nice soup and sandwiches. Milly's cook made beautiful soup and sandwiches. Pity to waste everything like this, and all just so as to be angry and say unkind things.

She made a great effort, and by laying hold of the chimney-piece with one hand, and heavily leaning on her stick with the other, pulled herself up out of the chair.

They turned and looked at her, surprised. They had forgotten she was there.

"My dears," quavered the old lady, the stick shaking beneath her weight, "I want to go home."

"Why of course, mother," said Fred, who was nearest. "Tired?" he asked, drawing her arm through his and patting it.

"I'll send for the car," said Alec, ringing the bell.

"Never saw you, mother, you've been sitting so quiet," said George.

"And, my dears—" she looked round at them, "don't quarrel."

"We're discussing," said the eldest daughter, who had married late in life, and it had been a great relief to old Mrs. Bott when she did, because it seemed at one time as if she were never going to, and that would have been a pity; for till a woman had been through a husband, the old lady held, she didn't really know what God could do to her. "Mother," explained this daughter to the others, who were well acquainted with the theory, "always thinks we're quarrelling when we discuss anything."

"And so you usually are, my dears," said the old lady. "And it makes you so hot. Look at your poor hot faces. I wish you'd all have some nice soup. I can smell it through the door. It's waiting ready in the kitchen, I'm sure. It'll do you good."

"Mother," said the eldest daughter, again explaining to the others, who were well acquainted with this theory also, "invariably thinks everything can be settled by soup or a cup of tea."

"And so it usually can, my dear," said the old lady, holding on to Fred's arm.

"Not at all an unsound theory," said the youngest daughter's husband, a Mr. Noakes, of the Welsh Widowers' Life Assurance; and George's wife agreed with him. "Let's have in that soup, Alec—soup, and a glass of sherry, eh?"

"And my dears," the old lady continued, addressing them collectively from Fred's arm, "no need to worry your poor heads about Milly and taking her in, because I would like to take her in myself, please—take her in and make much of her, Walter my dear," she said, nodding her head at her Walker son-in-law.

"You, mother?"

The family stared.

"But you can't afford——" someone began.

"Can't I, my dears?" she interrupted. "Well, I daresay I can't—but you can. You can all subscribe. So much each. Whatever you think will be enough for poor Milly. She won't want much. She's a small eater."

The family now stared at each other. Why, of course; the real, the only solution. And so safe. Out of everybody's way, wrapped round, impenetrably to tongues,

in the mantle of the old lady's affection and respectability—how was it nobody had thought of it before? Fancy
mother, at her age, still being the one to think of things!
And it needn't cost much either, said the portion of the
family described by old Mrs. Bott as the girls, making
rapid calculations; there wouldn't be so very much to
subscribe. The interest on the thousand pounds would
go a long way, and there were nine brothers and sisters,
and if each paid, say, fifty pounds a year——

Fifty each? Oh, no—much too much. Fifty each
would make five hundred a year with her own fifty, and
nothing whatever for her to spend it on.

Thirty each, then.

George's wife said it ought to be fifty, and the other
wives said it was all very well for her, who had only one
child and accordingly hardly anything to spend George's
money on——

Twenty, said somebody. Twenty each would be
ample.

George's wife still persisted it ought to be fifty, and
Alec's wife said she thought perhaps thirty——

So they then decided that best of all would be simply
to pay mother's housekeeping books, and divide whatever they came to.

"Isn't she to have any clothes?" asked Fred.

Clothes? Why, she was a widow, and widows didn't
want clothes—not for at least a year, said the wives.
And after that there were all the clothes she had been
wearing before this happened. Not for years, as far as
they could see, would she need any more clothes.

"Considering that it's our money that's going to pay
for Milly——" began Bertie.

"Not altogether your money," said his eldest sister,
conscious that she and her sisters each had money of
their own; and the old lady, anxious there should be no

more arguing, interrupted again, and said, "I'll take Milly now, if she'll come. Go up and fetch her, Alec my dear. Then we'll be home in time for a nice cup of tea."

§

But Alec brought the message down that Milly was asleep, and had left word asking them to be so kind as not to disturb her.

"Fancy being able to sleep," murmured Bertie's wife.

"Poor child—sleeping it off," said old Mrs. Bott. "To-morrow, then," she added, as she was led out and carefully hoisted into the car by Alec and Fred. "You can bring her over on your way to the City, Alec my dear."

When to-morrow came, however, and a deputation of the brothers went round to Mandeville Park Road to tell Milly what had been arranged, and explain that it was not merely the best but the only thing to do, and that she couldn't possibly stay where she was, because at any moment the house might be sold, they found that she had left that morning before breakfast, and no one knew where she had gone.

✲✿(*III*)✿✲

FOR Milly had sinned.

During the entire length of ten whole years she had been sinning. The suspicions of her sisters-in-law, and the uneasiness of her brothers-in-law, were only too well justified: she had taken the Botts in, and for all those years had been unfaithful to Ernest.

It had begun quite by chance. And what a chance, thought Milly, looking back now with the horrified clear vision which is the portion of the found out, at the beginning. Such small things had made it begin. Five minutes earlier, five minutes later, and she never would have met Arthur. A missed train, a slower taxi, even just a pause to watch the pigeons in the courtyard, or, indeed, even a little decent reserve, and she would have been saved. But the train was caught, the taxi was swift, the pigeons didn't interest her, and in she went; and there, in the British Museum, in the gallery where the busts of the Roman emperors are, she met Arthur Oswestry, and they sinned.

Ultimately, that is. For a long while they hadn't an idea that they were going to. Sin creeps along towards one, she discovered, looking quite good for quite a long while. It had taken weeks of meetings before it really began—meetings again at the British Museum, then at the National Gallery, in tea-shops, in parks, and even once in Westminster Abbey, which did seem peculiarly wrong—weeks of talk, pleasant, comforting, illuminating after the Titford talk, and presently weeks

of doubts, accompanied by tremors and flushing if
Ernest's unconscious eye happened to rest on her more
than usual when she got home, and by starting if he
suddenly spoke—ah, how base, how contemptible this
wretched love-business was, she saw now—and then
weeks of an increasing desire to avoid the Botts and
get out of her engagements, and then weeks of quivering
reluctances and stabbing yearnings, and then weeks of
agonized efforts to stick to her duty, of repeated attempts to keep away from Arthur, not to see him, to
forget him, wipe him out. In fact, it took a long while.
But it did begin ultimately; and they entered into that
condition of doubtful bliss, of continual looking forward
and continual unfulfilled expectation, of wonderful
dreams when they weren't together and acute, knife-
edged reactions when they were, and always terror,
terror, terror of being found out, which is passionate
love. Illicit passionate love, that is; passionate love
except for one's own husband. In other words, as Milly
well knew at the beginning, and now was once more
overwhelmed by knowing, Sin.

Who would ever have suspected, thought Milly at the
time, amazed at the upheaval in her entire nature, that
she should be capable of passionate love? It was the
very last thing she had suspected of herself. She was
thirty-five then, and Arthur was forty-five, and she had
never been in any sort of love before, least of all passionate; and neither, particularly, so he said, had he. As for
him, his kind sister who had lived with him had lately
died, and he was lonely and miserable and cold, and he
found Milly; his life had grown suddenly empty and
thin, and he found this soft, dear, loving little woman,
this sweet, pillowy little thing, with no children and
brimful, as he presently discovered, of thwarted ma-
ternalness. She was crying, too, that day, and he never

could bear to see anyone cry—standing glued, almost, to the cold bust of Marcus Aurelius so that she shouldn't be noticed, her own warm bust heaving. But he noticed. Halting along—he was slightly lame, and what a passion of tenderness this was presently to arouse in Milly—he noticed the heaving and the effort to hide. How did he find courage, who knew so few women, who had lived so much alone with his sister in his rooms in Oxford, where he was classical lecturer at Ebenezer—a cooling calling, and indeed until he met Milly he had never been very warm—how did he find courage to speak to her? But he did; and instantly, though he was unaware of that till later, was plunged up to his ears in a passionate love affair; a passionate love affair with someone else's wife; in other words, Sin.

Compared to herself, though, how much less was he a sinner, thought Milly, staring wide-eyed at the past. He wasn't married. He was betraying no one. Whereas she——

Too awful. Milly, on the night of Ernest's funeral, locked in her bedroom, supposed to be sleeping the sleep of exhausted grief, saw it all. For over nine years —their passion, and with it their fears and conscious-ness of guilt, had lasted only one year—she had been so much used to sinning that she hadn't thought about it any more, either one way or the other. Terrible, terrible, cried out Milly's heart, while her body walked up and down the room distractedly, to have got used to sinning. But there it was—a habit, and a completely regular one. Once a week she spent an afternoon with Arthur in Chelsea, where he had taken a studio—Ernest's office, and accordingly Ernest, was in the City—and was back in time for dinner, refreshed and happy. Refreshed and happy? Refreshed and happy because she had been betraying her husband? "Oh, what shall I *do?*" Milly

cried, twisting her hands together; for, with Ernest
dead, how was she ever to make it up to him, how was
she ever to get forgiven?

There it was, however: she had come back refreshed
and happy. Because, as soon as she and Arthur were
out of the passionate stage of love, and therefore out of
the stage of being sensitive and exacting and of feeling
guilty, which spoilt things a good deal, because it made
them go in deadly fear of being found out, they began
to be quite happy. They settled down, that is; settled
down to sin. Too awful, she now saw. But there it was.

That, she supposed, was what had helped to blind her
to the real nature of those afternoons,—her coming back
from them refreshed and happy. Could that be bad, she
had sometimes in the second year asked herself, and
decided that it couldn't, which made her be so good?
Always after her afternoon with Arthur she was extra
pleasant, extra amiable to Ernest, extra zealous in agreeing, in approving, in apologizing, in promising, with a
kind of radiant good-nature about her that nothing
could dim.

"What a wife," sighed the Bott brothers.

"There's no one like Milly," said old Mrs. Bott.

Titford loved her.

Besides, as time passed there were such numbers of
these afternoons. Could that be wicked, she asked herself after Ernest's death and before the Will had opened
her eyes, as she sat in the bedroom drooping over the
remembrance of what she had done and seeking comfort,
could that be wicked which went on steadily so long?
Didn't time, if there were enough of it, end by trans-
muting everything? Did not the very slang of one
generation—so did her thoughts anxiously wander in
search of reassurance—become the polite language of
the next? They had gone on and on, the afternoons had,

year in and year out, increasingly secure, increasingly
placid, at last indeed almost ordinary and mechanical,
with Arthur long since just a dear, very intimate friend
—really her only one—and the love-making, which had
notably quietened during the second and third years,
and by the fourth was mere affectionate routine, a
rather elaborate but sweet way of saying, How do you
do, after which they composed themselves to tea and
talk on calm things like excavations, which was what
Arthur in his off times was chiefly interested in—the
love-making latterly become quite unidentifiable as
such.

They were pleased to see each other; much pleased.
Arthur would say, when he opened the door on her
arriving, "Well, dear?" and kiss her affectionately, and
tell her about his cold. Generally he had a cold, for he
was delicate. And when she left, he would walk openly
with her to King's Road, and see her into a taxi for
Victoria, and remind her to keep her feet dry, and ask
her if she had enough change, just as if they were comfortably married.

It would have seemed to Milly fantastic, in these
later years, to regard such mild encounters as sin.

No, no—that wasn't sin, she had kept on assuring
herself during the days before the funeral, while the
kind, unconscious Botts patted her and said what they
could to comfort. Of that simple domestic happiness
Ernest, after all, had had the backwash. Because of it
she had been able to go on being a good wife to him.
Strange as it would seem to the Botts, to Titford, to the
whole world, she had been a very good wife to Ernest,
and entirely owing to her having been what the Botts,
and Titford, and the whole world would call a very bad
one. Those quiet afternoons with Arthur had created
a serenity in her that nothing could ruffle, a limitless

readiness to do everything Ernest wished. They had lit up the house in Mandeville Park Road like a lamp; they had warmed its hearth like a fire. Was not love, then, a good thing for a woman if it made her so much nicer all round? Had not her having had this dear, secret friend been for Ernest too sheer gain?

So she had thought, helped by Arthur, in the first weeks of their love, when she felt guilty and scared and was seeking justifications, and so she kept on telling herself she thought during the days before the funeral. Arthur had explained at the beginning the true wholesomeness of the situation to her, pointing out how three people were now content who before had all been unhappy——

"But Ernest wasn't unhappy," she remembered saying.

"In his heart he must have been," Arthur had insisted. "He must have felt you were only doing your duty, and that there wasn't any love in it. I think men must always know."

"Not husbands," Milly had said.

"I think they must," Arthur, who had never been a husband, gently persisted.

Well, perhaps; perhaps. Milly had doubtfully agreed. Ernest was so quiet, one never really knew what he thought about anything. Sometimes she had supposed he didn't think, except about his business; or hardly at all. He certainly never talked to her about anything except his business or the arrangements of his house, and when he was annoyed with her he didn't so much talk as smoulder. She got to know these smoulderings well. They were very punitive in their effect, much more so than a great blaze-up. Nor did he read anything, except newspapers and magazines, and disliked if she, in his presence, read. Their evenings were always the same—

two armchairs; a roaring fire, or, in summer, ferns; she
and he in the armchairs, he with a newspaper, she with
her crochet work, both doped with dinner. For fifteen
years it had been like that each evening, except when
they went to or gave parties; and every year she was a
little fatter, a little heavier, a little more expensively
dressed, and, because she had had another birthday,
with one more bracelet on arms which were thickening,
or one more brooch on a bosom grown rounder.

She was cooped round with comfort. "Will it be
enough," she sometimes anxiously used to wonder,
"when God, at the end, asks me what I have done with
my life, to point to Ernest and say, I saw to it that his
meals were good?"

No, it wouldn't be enough; she knew it wouldn't.
And she, having no children to keep her busy and give
her fresh interests as she grew older and new hopes,
after fifteen years of these evenings, and of days filled
with calling and callers, with visits to and from relations,
with hearing the same things said over and over
again, with smiling the same smiles and expressing the
same agreements, was becoming so intolerably lonely, so
much oppressed by the dreadful repetitions of life, that
she had been on the verge of throwing up the whole
thing, and scandalizing her world and making the Botts
acutely ashamed and miserable, by going off to her disgraced sister—for she was still only in the middle thir-
ties, and not nearly so heavy as she afterwards became—
when, on that aimless day of unhappiness, she met
Arthur, and he saved her.

Saved her? By adultery? Milly shuddered to think
that there had ever been a time when she thought of
adultery as salvation. To what depths of cynicism had
she not, with a light-heartedness that amazed her, de-
scended, and with what comfortable contentment had

she not, during the long quiet years before she was found
out, remained in them! Only now did she see the whole
thing as it really was; only now, in the awful light of
Ernest's dead, accusing eyes.

Terrible what she had done—cheating and smiling
while she cheated, being fed and clothed and trusted by
the person she was cheating; trusted, that is, till two
years ago when he found her out—so easy, seeing how
careless she and Arthur had become, to find out—and
yet went on clothing and feeding her, and letting her
smile. Why, why didn't he stop everything, the clothing,
the feeding, the ghastly cheat-smiling, and turn her out
and have done with it? Perhaps he thought he might as
well in his turn cheat and deceive. Perhaps he thought
he might as well be as base as she was, and having discovered what she was doing not say a word, make no
sign, behave as usual, and accept her eager attentions
and devotions and panderings—all the things one pays
back in, one makes up with—while in his heart he
horribly laughed, as he watched and said nothing, hug-
ging the knowledge of what he had put in his Will.

Ernest behaving like that—*Ernest*. And this too was
her fault. She had made an incredible sneak of him who
probably wouldn't have been a sneak at all if he had
been let alone; she had made a cynical, sardonic, artful
creature of somebody who was naturally, she had always supposed she knew, quite simple and easy to
understand. And she who, during the days before the
funeral, since the awful afternoon when he had slipped
away from her for ever without recovering conscious-
ness, without her even being able to get the word *Forgive* across to him, she who had been so much overwhelmed by the thought that he hadn't known, that all
these years, however difficult he might sometimes be
about details, he yet had loved her and believed in her.

and had died loving and believing in her, was appalled by the knowledge that for at least two years he had been doing nothing of the sort. While strangest and most terrible of all was it to Milly that she only now should see how wicked she had been, now that she had been found out.

§

She spent a dreadful night. She was paralyzed by knowing that the morning was rushing towards her, and with it, inevitably, the Botts. Essential, essential, that in the few hours left to her she should think clearly, decide quickly; and for the life of her she couldn't. The Botts would certainly flock round directly after break-fast, still full of affection and desire to help, for they wouldn't have had time, she thought, to put two and two together and guess what she had done, and what she still must have been doing as recently, obviously, as two years ago when Ernest added the codicil—she, well over forty then, whose figure alone made such conduct ridiculous and revolting; but it was only a question of hours before they did.

Her skin burned with shame. She saw the thing as the Botts and Titford would see it, who didn't know the miserable business had begun ten years ago, when she wasn't middle-aged and wasn't yet so fat, and that it had long become just friendship. How was she to meet that injured family, twice now disgraced because of her, for Agatha, who first disgraced them, couldn't have done so if she, Milly, had not brought her into the family by marrying Ernest, how face them knowing that before the next day was over they would be thinking things of her she didn't dare let her mind even look at—of her, when she was in reality every bit as decent, as settled down, as respectable as they till then had supposed?

She stood in the middle of the room wringing her hands. Had Arthur been worth it? Was anybody or anything in the world worth leaving off being good for? "I'm not the stuff sinners are made of," she cried to herself distractedly. "How, oh how, did I ever become one?" For she could no longer remember, in the turmoil of her spirit, the passion and the wonder of the beginning, and could only think of Arthur as an elderly man who talked of excavations and had a cold. Also, who had got her into this mess. If it hadn't been for him. . . .

No; Milly caught herself up. She wouldn't be unjust. Rather should she say, if it hadn't been for her. What could Arthur have done if she had declined to be a party to it? It is the woman who sets the tone, the Botts, and also their circle, which was the best in Titford, held; and no one can live for twenty-five years in the same atmosphere without soaking up at least a little of it. It is the woman, the Botts considered, on whom the duty has been laid of walking steadfastly along the straight path of virtue, thus persuading man, that natural deviator, to walk along it too. Sometimes he won't, the Botts admitted; and then the woman's duty is to continue along it alone. All she can do in that case is to pray for him; for she, having continued, is a good woman, and he, having deviated, is a bad man, and the good pray for the bad. Such was the creed, not often mentioned but always implicit, of the Bott wives and sisters. What would happen if the bad began to pray for the good, Milly had sometimes wondered but hadn't dared ask.

Ah, but they were right, right, the Botts were. She walked up and down in an agony of acknowledgment and self-accusation. She saw now how right they were. Her life was in ruins because she had departed from their standards. How easy it would have been to induce Arthur to follow her in the way of virtue and honour.

He was a delicate creature; he wasn't one of your charging sheiks; she only needed to keep herself to herself for a little, and not blush, and not quiver, and not be so obviously glad each time to see him again. She knew her face had lit up, for she had seen the swift reflection of it on his, and if hers hadn't his wouldn't have. The guilt had been hers. It was she who had led, and he who had followed. The Botts were right when they said, commenting on such rare cases of scandal as illuminated Titford, "That woman must have led him on." And though she had secretly rebelled against this invariable verdict, and though she had kept, beneath the acquiescent smiles marriage to Ernest had taught her, her heart inviolate from it and kindred condemnations, now that the hour of exposure was upon her, Milly, terrified penitent, was only too ready to agree, to admit, to abase herself, and declare that everything that had happened had been her fault alone.

§

To add to her bewilderment, she found she couldn't pray. At intervals during the night she knelt down by the bed and tried to, passionately seeking help, seeking some gleam of light through her confusion; but no words came. Long since, under Arthur's influence, who was not a praying man, she had parted company with prayer, and now when she so urgently needed guidance, and the kind of calm which comes from lifting up one's heart, her heart wouldn't lift up. Not a word came. Dumbly she knelt, gripping the sheets, and her heart stayed where it was. Also, every time she went on her knees she had a dreadful feeling that Ernest was somewhere quite close, looking on sardonically.

Was she going to be haunted? Had she not done with Ernest after all? Crouched by the bed, a heap of crape, for she was still dressed as she had been all day in the expensive widow's outfit ordered for her by the family with the lavishness befitting a widow considered at the time of ordering to be rich, she tried to shut out this feeling of his immanence by burying her face in the quilt, and making renewed attempts to send some sort of petition for help up out of her frightened heart.

Not the least use. Nothing moved upwards within her; nothing even stirred. Her heart, her mind, her soul, stayed flat inside her body on the ground, all jammed together, it seemed to her, in a hopeless, immovable mass.

Part of her punishment she supposed, slipping down in a sitting position, her cheek against the bed, that she shouldn't be able to pray; part of her punishment that she should be made to feel utterly abandoned. She was abandoned in every sense of the word. The Botts, in a few hours, would be using the word when they talked of her—of her they had always, she knew, thought so much of. How artful she must have been to have produced such an impression of guiltlessness on them, how she must have lied, how she *had* lied. She was sodden with lies. In the very first year of her marriage she had become an active liar, and had so continued fluently ever since. That was when Ernest forbade her, after Agatha's disgrace, either to write or to receive letters from her sister so long as they lived; and she, having briefly struggled to obey him, found she couldn't, because she loved Aggie too much, and, like the young coward she was, didn't dare tell him, but had begun to write and receive the forbidden letters almost at once, and had gone on doing so till as lately as a week ago, artfully smuggling them in and out, growing very skilful in deceit, sometimes even meeting Ernest, if he came into the room unexpectedly, with a serene face while there was a letter at that very moment in her pocket.

Clear to Milly was it that those letters had been the first stones in the great fabric of deceit which had reached its climax in Arthur, and now had fallen on her and crushed her. *Be sure your sin will find you out*, floated through her mind. Was that in the Bible? It was certainly true. Here she was, found out at forty-five—so infinitely more terrible than being found out at twenty—toppled right down from the pinnacle of universal affection and respect one somehow gets put on by the time one is that sort of age, into the mud; and during the next few hours she was going to be exposed as that most distressing and ridiculous, surely, of all sinners, an elderly Magdalen.

Flight, flight, cried Milly at the intolerable thought, clutching the bed-clothes and pulling herself to her feet —never to see any of them again, to get away, away from this place, this house, this room with Ernest looking on sardonically at the success of his punishment. . . . The room was full of Ernest. He had not been, alive, a laugher, but she had an awful feeling that now at last he was amused. Ernest brought to this by her, brought to this evil gloating by her wickedness. . . .

"I'm going to make up—oh, I'm going to make *up* !" she gasped—somehow, someday. . . .

But even this aspiration, like her efforts to pray, fell back upon her, and the words, as they came out on a sob, struck her as suspect, as having a double meaning, as being, perhaps, considered appropriate, by whatever Power sends thoughts into minds, to her condition of Magdalen. Or was it Ernest, close beside her, mocking her by putting them into her head?

Ah, but this was awful—she was being haunted.

Panic-stricken she ran and turned on more lights, all the
lights, and then, hurrying about the room, began pulling
out drawers and snatching together the few things she
couldn't do without. Flight before it was too late. . . .
Flight before the servants were up and saw what she
was doing. . . . Flight before the Botts came round and
caught her, and forced her to stand up before them,
naked in her sins. . . .

§

On the dim landing where there was a smell of shut-
up varnished wood, and linoleum and cigars, the grandfather clock was ticking enormous ticks in the silence,
and the faint light of the new day struggled faintly
through the stained-glass window, when, just after five,
she crept out of her room, clutching her suit-case and
her bag. In the bag was all the money she had till she
should have got her thousand pounds. There was not
much—less than five pounds; but enough, Milly thought,
to hide her in London for a day and a night until she had
been to Ernest's solicitor. That was the first thing to be
done, she saw, and quickly, so as to finish with the past
and get away to Agatha. For it wasn't so much a conscious decision as a homing instinct that was sending
her straight to Agatha. To her sister would she go, who
loved her; to her own flesh and blood. Aggie was the
one person in the world who wouldn't judge, who
wouldn't condemn even if she wanted to—which she
never would—because of what she had done herself.
With her she would be safe.

She gave a little sob of longing, as she crept down the
stairs, to be safe, to be out of all this, to be far away
from everybody connected with the past, among people
who, except Aggie—she would have no secrets from
Aggie, she would tell her everything as freely as she

would tell God—would never know anything about it. Aggie would understand; Aggie would love her—just love her, and not mind anything. . . .

The stairs creaked, and each time they did that she stopped, her heart in her mouth, and listened. How strange and different the house looked. Things that were as familiar to her as her own face—the oak staircase, the suits of armour at the turnings, the sea-scapes in their handsome gilt frames, the hanging terra-cotta baskets with ferns in them—these treasures of Ernest's, that she had lived with so long and knew so well, already looking like ghosts, done with, dead. She crept along among them for the last time, the only living thing in what had suddenly become a mausoleum, taking infinite care to make no sound, patiently undoing her long crape veil—part of the outfit ordered for her—from the knobs it got caught in on the suits of armour, and each time the stairs creaked stopping, and holding her breath to listen for movements in the servants' rooms, her heart seeming to beat as loud as the grandfather clock.

But it was the hour when servants sleep most heavily, and no one heard her go except Ernest's Pomeranian, who slept in the study and began to yap when she got down into the hall—perhaps, by some strange dog in-stinct, knowing she was doing something she oughtn't to. How often, then, if that were so, thought Milly, tremblingly unfastening the bolts of the front door, should he in the past have yapped at her. But he hadn't. He had been cool to her and silent, sniffing at her shoes distrustfully, saving up his noises for now; so that the last sound she heard from her old home as she left it for ever was a shrill, violent yapping.

Was it derision? Was it vindictiveness on behalf of his master? She hurried away pursued by the sound;

and it seemed to Milly, in her collapsed condition, that it was the voice of Ernest, using the dog as his mouthpiece, and in this manner saying good-bye.

"*You can't escape—you'll never escape,*" the yapping seemed to call after her.

"Oh, but I *can*—I'm *going* to!" Milly's heart cried back, as she fled down the drive and out into the road.

§

Not till she had turned the corner did the shrill persistent yapping fade away, and leave the dawn in peace. Titford slept. Its blinds were carefully drawn, and its aspect was one of deep repose. No one saw the surprising spectacle of Mrs. Ernest Bott, so well known and so much appreciated as a kind, little well-off woman who gave no trouble, swathed in her new mourning, hurrying along at a pace most unusual, and carrying things a person of her age and standing didn't carry. Yet the very emptiness of the streets made Milly stand out immensely conspicuous, a round black splodge on the pale clearness of the morning, had anyone been peeping from behind those closed blinds; and as she approached the vicarage of St. Timothy and All Spirits, whose inhabitants, she knew, were addicted to pious practices at strange hours, she pulled the crape veil which hung from her bonnet forward over her face, taking cover behind it from the possible eye of some early Christian, who should be preparing, by opening a window, to let in God's air on his orisons.

This made her hot. She was hot already, from the run to the gate and the scared hurrying along Mandeville Park Road, and the crape veil made her hotter. By the time she was out of the residential part of Titford, where in nearly every house people whose names were on her visiting list lay sleeping, and had reached a path that led northwards through some small holdings in the direction of London, she was in a state of extreme melting warmth. Her crape stuck to her. Beneath her widow's bonnet—the Bott tradition dressed its widows for their first six months rather like Queen Victoria—little drops of perspiration slid down her temples into her muslin collar; under her heavy cloak all seemed liquefaction.

But she hardly noticed. Her heart was thumping with relief, as well as exertion. Every yard put between herself and Titford increased her relief, as well as her breathlessness. That haunted bedroom in Mandeville Park Road was behind her. Ernest hadn't come with her, she felt, beyond the hall door. She had escaped. And she had escaped from the really intolerable shame of meeting the Botts. Presently, long before they were waking up, she would be in a workmen's train, disappearing into the all-engulfing privacy of London. No one would find her during her few hours there. She would call on the solicitor, and get her thousand pounds —unversed in the law's delays, Milly supposed she had but to apply in order to receive—and immediately vanish into obscurity; and then, while the family was perhaps trying to look for her, though surely it wouldn't, surely it would be only too thankful to let her go and forget her, she would be far away beyond its reach, on her way to Switzerland and Agatha.

Agatha. Hurrying across the allotments, her back to the past, her face to the future, Milly kept her thoughts passionately concentrated on Agatha. If she didn't, Arthur obtruded; and from the thought of Arthur she turned with a shudder. She wouldn't, she couldn't, think of him. This was no moment for Arthur. Directly Ernest had his accident she began to shudder away from Arthur almost as if it were somehow his fault that the awful thing should have happened—from Arthur, away on his Easter holiday in Rome, whole and alive anyhow, if not actually robust, enjoying himself poking about among excavations, while Ernest, the wronged, lay helpless and broken on the bed he was to die on; and then, after his death, when the sympathizing Botts were comforting her in that bedroom and imagining her good, the thought of Arthur, when it did manage to creep into her mind, made her quite sick. Her fellow-sinner; who would now suppose he had got to marry her. Suppose he had got to marry her! Her head drooped lower in shame. ("There, there,—poor little Milly," said the Botts, patting.) She had brushed the humiliating thought aside. That was what love came to in the end, however splendidly it flamed in the beginning: to supposing one had got to marry her. *Got* to. As though two blacks could ever make a white; as though, if she and Arthur did marry, there could ever be any happiness, with Ernest between them, and his dead, accusing eyes.

No, no—only legitimacy for Milly now; perfect open-and-above-boardness, complete absence, for the rest of her life, of holes and corners, of plots and lies. Legitimacy, legitimacy . . . her spirit, raw with the sudden descent of the punishment that sooner or later, she now saw, overtakes the other thing, craved for its pure clear safety. Even if it were dull, legitimacy was better, she now abundantly realized, than any flashes of apparent delight its opposite might produce; while as for when it also meant love, and the knowledge that one wouldn't be judged, what could the love and necessary absence of judging that Arthur would provide, offer? Besides, she desperately wanted to tell someone she trusted all she had done, and, in telling, free herself of part, at least, of the burden. She couldn't tell Arthur; he knew already. He would say, on hearing of Ernest's death and the Will, "Well, now we must be married——" and then explain that he was afraid he had caught another cold.

For Milly, Agatha had become salvation. She longed for her, as the thirsty long for water; she panted after her, as the soul of the Psalmist panted after God. Always Agatha had been affection, and close blood-loyalty and shared memories of childhood, but now she was also salvation. Only Agatha could take her by the hand, and pull her up out of the swamp of shame she was floundering in, only she could help her to a new, cleared-out life. Since that hasty secret departure from Mandeville Park Road a quarter of a century ago—what nonsense, Milly had long thought, who had done such much worse things later herself, for Ernest and the Botts to make such a fuss about it; yet she too, at the beginning, had been appalled—they had never set eyes on each other. But their letters, after a slight preliminary coolness on Agatha's part, who had resented the way Milly, still trying to obey Ernest, hadn't at first written back, became gradually warmer and warmer, as letters easily will when the writers do not meet, developing at last, each more and more needing an outlet, into real outpourings. Every thought of their hearts had presently been poured into these letters, except, in Milly's case, those thoughts of her heart which had to do with Arthur. Of these she had not written; Agatha was unaware of Arthur. And since, after the first few years, they began to be dissatisfied with such photographs and snapshots of themselves as were taken, and felt they would be misleading, they left off sending any; and then, having nothing to go on when they thought of each other except what they wrote and the recollection of what they used to look like, they began unconsciously to build up images in their minds, increasingly bright and beautiful, and to these in their letters they more and more addressed themselves.

This bright image of Agatha was what Milly now kept
her eyes fixed on, as she hurried along clutching her suit-
case, which seemed to grow heavier with each step.
Towards it she was at last actually going; in a few hours
it would be reality, and at its feet she would have
dropped her sins. Aggie would fold her to her heart,
and understand and love her as much as ever, Milly
knew, for Aggie too had sinned, though only, it was
true, for three weeks, and then only because she couldn't
help it. Compared to Milly's ten years, Aggie's three
weeks were, of course, a mere flea-bite, but even so they
were going to make it easy to tell her about Arthur.
At least she wouldn't be surprised, and couldn't be
shocked. Milly might have worked on a larger canvas,
but on a smaller scale Agatha had done the same thing.
She would utterly understand. And she was the one person in the whole world—except Arthur, who didn't in
the nature of things in this matter count—with whom
Milly would be safe from condemnation.

Safe from condemnation, whispered Milly; hidden in
love; beyond the reach of pointing fingers, or averted
eyes. She sighed. Perhaps it was cowardly to want to
dodge her punishment, to hide from it in Agatha's arms,
perhaps a finer character would have stayed and faced
the Botts. But that was just what was the matter with
her, she thought—she was a coward. She hadn't the
courage either of her repentance or her sins. She hadn't
the courage of anything. In the littlest matters, on the
smallest occasions, hadn't she always searched for the
easiest way out, anxious only to avoid unpleasantness?
What had her acquiescences and smiles been, except,
in miniature, what she was doing now—flight from
black looks, flight from mere disapproval? Beyond
everything she dreaded scenes, and somebody with a
loud voice being angry. She would take, she knew, and

had taken, endless pains to please, to keep everybody happy. Her differences of opinions—and she had many —were all secret. Yes; she was a coward. And such a tactful coward that nobody ever guessed the real reason of the amiability that had made her so popular in Titford, and so much liked by the Botts.

She stopped, and putting down her suit-case wiped the perspiration from her face. No one, she thought, could possibly be more vile. She was in the middle of the allotments, which were quite empty at that hour, and she put up her veil to get her breath. She was very hot. She held her arms away from her warm, damp body, and lifted her uncovered face to the cool morning air, and it seemed to run to meet her with a kiss. Exquisite freshness and newness—the whole world washed clean, thought Milly, her upturned face and swollen eyes caressed by the soft pattings of an uncondemning little breeze. "Oh, how delicious—how sweet—how kind"—she whispered, standing quite still, her eyes shut. Really the morning seemed to be gently kissing her—"Just as if," she thought, "I were somebody good."

§

It was too early for the earliest train, and her idea was to walk towards London, and pick up the first one she could at some station that wasn't Titford. If by chance she were to come across a taxi she would take it, and she would go to Bloomsbury, where her father used to live, and where she had spent her childhood; for she remembered there were many lodgings to let in Bloomsbury, and in one of these, as close as possible to the house where she had been young, she would stay that day and night, see the solicitor, and continue to Agatha next morning. "And when I have slept," thought Milly, picking up the suit-case and going on again, "and when

I have had something to eat, perhaps I shall feel different."

But in spite of her having had no food since the lunch brought up to her bedroom on a tray the day before, and in spite of her not having slept at all, her mind already seemed a little clearer. It was her body at that moment which was chiefly troublesome—so hot, so much out of breath, and with hands and arms aching because they had to carry a suit-case and a bag. Her feet hurt her, too, and she was altogether deplorably out of condition, and a very fit subject, she told herself, angry with her abundant, overfed flesh, for the rigours of expiation. But these very discomforts and difficulties released her mind, detached it awhile from its distress, and by the time she had got as far as Tulse Hill she was in that condition of fatigue which prevents all thought, and only seeks for something to sit down on.

This she found at the station.

A woman, surrounded by bundles and carrying a baby, moved up along the wooden bench with alacrity, solicitously making room for her.

"Don't I know what it is, mum," she said. "Ah dear, ah dear——" and shaking her head at nothing, she jogged the baby, which cried, up and down on her arm.

She was unable to take her eyes off Milly, who, sitting on the edge of the seat because else her feet wouldn't reach the floor, her hands in her new black gloves and neat white wrist-bands tightly holding her bag, kept her gaze carefully fixed on the bit of sky she could see through the top of the window, so as to avoid looking at the woman: for who knew if she mightn't be somebody from Titford?

"'Eaven," thought the woman, respectfully watching this absorption in the sky. "That's what she's thinkin' of, poor dear. Awful the way them real bad bereavements rejuices one."

Some workmen coming in, when they saw the figure of grief so manifestly recent and deep, removed their pipes and left off talking; and the clerk in the booking office, short in his manners as a rule at that hour, on finding his pigeon-hole presently blocked by blackness instead of the usual workman, paused in the act of slapping down the ticket, and handed it to her politely instead, with the air, almost, of offering a condolence.

Everybody seemed sorry for her, and anxious to help. When, having got to Victoria, she wished to cross the street, a policeman briskly stepped forward and held up a fruit barrow, there being nothing else to hold up at the moment; when, having walked as far as the Abbey, she tried to get into it, for she thought that in that great calm place, hallowed by centuries of prayer, gracious with centuries of blessing, she might perhaps be able to find the words which hadn't come in her dreadful bedroom with Ernest at her elbow, and at last send up an appeal for forgiveness, the policeman on duty was quite apologetic, and ashamed of it, whose function was surely to offer consolation to the bereaved, for not being open; and when she approached a taxi, which was lazily taking up its position on an empty rank as though it were only just awake and still yawning, and said to the driver in the gentle, deprecating voice marriage to Ernest had taught her, a voice which long had become second nature to her, turning up a little at the end of its sentences, providing, in its slight final lift, a query to serve as a loop-hole through which she might quickly withdraw whatever it was she had said if anyone showed signs of not liking it, "Taxi?" and the driver looked round languidly, not repudiating, for he knew he was a taxi, but indifferent, the minute he saw her shrouded figure he leapt into instant life, jumping down and opening the door for her, and hoisting her in as if she were not only heavy but precious, and driving her to Bloomsbury with the precautions of one in charge of an ambulance.

"If they only knew," thought Milly, taken aback by all this.

She hadn't been prepared for attention and kindness; they were the last things she wanted. She had hardly glanced at herself in the glass before leaving, intent only on getting away, and was not conscious of what she looked like. Just something black, tying on a bonnet with trembling fingers, and a chalky white face peering out of swathings of crape—this she had seen but not noticed, her whole attention fixed on flight. She now perceived she had been foolish. Only in her oldest, plainest clothes should she have come away. True they would have been an admission to the solicitor that she had no moral right to dress as Ernest's widow, but why not admit what he already for certain knew? As usual, she was getting kindness from everybody by false pretences. Just as in Titford she had skulked behind smiles, now she was skulking behind the solemn appearance of legitimate grief, taking in policemen and honest married women, a Magdalen in widow's clothing.

Odious, thought Milly, shrinking into the corner of the taxi, instinctively trying to shrink away from herself. She would strip off the mourning as soon as she got her money, and buy herself ordinary things in which nobody would look at her twice. Not as a widow would she travel to Agatha. Her weeds, along with the rest of her hypocrisies, should stay behind in England. Perhaps they ought to be returned to the Botts. They were, after all, quite new, and belonged to the family, which would, she supposed, presently get the bill for them. But there were difficulties about sending them back. It might strike the Botts as cynical, as the conclusive proof of loss of shame, if, on opening the enormous parcel, they found it to contain an empty set of widow's weeds.

Well, she would think that out presently, when she had had some sleep. All these thoughts whirling round in her head would settle down then, and sort themselves out, wouldn't they? Oh, yes, they would—she was going to have peace, peace, she whispered, as she watched, heavy-eyed, the increasingly familiar landmarks. A longing to crawl back into the past, into innocence, into a pre-Bott condition, filled her heart. Incredibly beautiful, or so now it seemed, had life been in Bloomsbury; golden, glorious. Along its shining streets—surely they used to shine?—she and Aggie had played with hoops that must have been made of stars. Through its lit, mysterious windows had floated, in the summer evenings, music that drew them out of bed, and held them spell-bound. In the garden of their square marvellous things had happened, and the trees in it had been bright with magic fruits, and the air had quivered with the flash of strange wings. And later when she was older, but still so close, so close to beauty, Milly remembered, in the drawing-room of their house, with its long windows opening on to a little iron balcony, Ernest had courted her—Ernest, the prosperous suitor who could open the gates of ease for her hard-working father and young sister; and she, never courted before, had listened bewitched to his words of love, and had believed every one of them.

What she hadn't known then, thought Milly, as the British Museum with all its memories of her father, who,

had been a librarian there, and later of Arthur, came in
sight, was that people get over love. It was like an illness, she thought, staring at the familiar building, at
the familiar porter at the gate—he seemed to be the
same porter—and at the pgieons, who also were apparently the same ones,—an illness that ran its course.
But, unlike an illness, when it was over, instead of feeling better one felt worse.

She hadn't known that then. How should she? She
was only twenty, and had never had a real lover before,
and for all she knew Ernest was the perfect lover.
Strange to remember his husky, moved voice when he
said good-bye to her the evening before their wedding
and took her in his arms and told her he was going to
make her happy for ever and ever and ever; strange to
remember that he absolutely meant it, Ernest meant it,
who never afterwards said anything the least like it;
and strange to remember how sure-footed she had been
among words right up to her honeymoon, and then the
twenty-five years of learning the right answers. And
within those twenty-five years, because she had not
been able to bear the little that was demanded of her—it
seemed so little now that it was over, such a little time
to have stayed good in—because she was weak, lonely,
and a fool, within those twenty-five years, curled up like
a scarlet snake, lay her ten years of sin.

Milly pulled herself together. Even though she had
had no sleep or food for ages, she mustn't let herself
exaggerate too much, she thought. That word scarlet.
She might have some justification for calling her long,
placid connection with Arthur a snake, for it had been
full of deceit and treachery, but it hadn't been a scarlet
one. Ernest had probably used the word, thinking
inflamed thoughts, as the wronged and imperfectly

informed must; and the Botts, acquainted with the Apocalypse, in their just anger would presently no doubt talk of the Scarlet Woman. But she herself, who knew the details of those afternoons, couldn't. Years ago, perhaps, she might have; just at the beginning; the vivid beginning; like a flame. . . .

She stared out of the window, her lips pressed together to prevent their quivering, as she remembered the beginning, and the terror and wonder and warmth of it. Were all beginnings warm? Were all endings bleak and sorrowful? See how even Ernest at the beginning had been warm, vowing to make her happy for ever and ever. And he was dead, and he hadn't made her happy, and she hadn't made him happy, and it was all over, and here she was come back to the place of her youth alone, middle-aged, disgraced, poor, with nothing left at all, except what yet might be saved of her perishing soul.

Yes—and Aggie. Aggie was still there, still living. So long as there was Aggie, how could she say she had lost everything? Ah, dear, dear sister, whispered Milly, her mouth relaxing, dearest little sister—little only because she was younger, and one felt so motherly towards her, being married and taking her into one's home and all that, but really a head taller, a long slender thing, bright-eyed and bright-cheeked that day when Milly got back from her honeymoon, and found her on the steps in Mandeville Park Road to welcome her. She had looked like a vivid flower, in spite of the mourning she was dressed in for their father. Milly had put her arms round the electric young body and hugged it to her heart, whispering, with kisses, that she was going to take such care of her. And so she had taken care of her, till the day three months later when, without a word of warning, Agatha eloped in the middle of the night, appalling Milly, who hadn't then realized that people sometimes do do things like that, even when they are one's own sister.

If she had had ten pounds in her purse, instead of not much over four, she would have gone straight to Agatha, without waiting to see the solicitor about her money, which could be sent on afterwards; but Agatha lived in an almost inaccessible region, and Milly was sure that it took more than she had to get to her. Perhaps, though, it was just as well she couldn't go that day, she said to herself, as she sat drooping in the corner of the taxi, for she was very tired now, and much exhausted by her long hurried walk to Tulse Hill. She would have liked to have slept properly before she saw Aggie and told her about everything; she felt she could bear no more emotions or exertions till she had slept. If she could get into some quiet room and go to sleep, begin with sleep, and then, when she had slept and slept, have some food, she might be able to see more clearly and think better. While as it was, thought Milly, staring out of the window with dim eyes, she wasn't able to think properly at all. Just confusion in her head, and confusion in her heart, and both so heavy, and aching, and afraid. . . .

§

She stopped the taxi at the corner of Russell Square. From there she would walk, and into the first house that had rooms to let she would go and take one, if it was cheap enough, and lock herself into it, and sleep.

Russell Square didn't appear to desire lodgers; at least, she saw no signs of such a wish, and she went on into Woburn Place, and stood a minute staring at the church she had been married in. From there she drifted into the square where her father had lived—one of the humbler ones, for, though intelligent, he was poor, and

the thought came into her mind that if she could find a
room in that square she would sleep more profoundly
and healingly than in another.

Her old home was right away in the farthermost
corner, and before beginning to make inquiries, in spite
of being tired and foot-sore, she felt she must go and
look up at its windows; and as she got nearer she saw
there was a notice board on its railings.

Her heart gave a thump. She hurried her steps.
Probably it was only the announcement of a school or
some institution. Catching hold of her bag and suit-case
with one hand, she impatiently lifted her veil with the
other so as to see better, and as the letters of the first
line on the board were big and gilt and shone in the sun,
in another yard or two she was able to read:

THE HOME FROM HOME

APARTMENTS TO LET

and in yet another yard or two the smaller letters of the
succeeding lines, which were arranged like this:

EVERY COMFORT

LADIES ONLY

NO GENTLEMEN OR DOGS

INDIVIDUAL STUDY

Milly stood gazing. How wonderful. How providential. Wouldn't this bring her peace, to go back into
the very house of her happy youth? Wouldn't this be
the place of all others to hide in, to rest in, to grow calm
in, and perhaps to pray in? For it was really remarkable,
she thought, considering her long neglect of her prayers,
how much not being able to say any worried her.

The door stood open, it being the moment of the day

when air was admitted, and she went up the familiar steps. Positively the last time she had been on those steps was going down them on her wedding day as Ernest's bride. Her father died suddenly while she was on her honeymoon, and Agatha, telegraphed to, had moved herself and her belongings to Titford by the time Milly got home, so that she had never entered the house since—no, nor even been to look at it since Arthur came into her life, and quieted her. Before that she had made occasional wistful pilgrimages to the scene of her youth, but for more than ten years now she hadn't been that way, and the last time she saw it the house was still a private house.

Now, just in time for her, it had thrown open its doors. Was she, after all, being guided? And there was that other strange coincidence—the widowing of Agatha three months before her own, both their husbands, who had seemed so permanent, disappearing almost simultaneously, and so making room for her reunion with her sister, for their taking up life together again at the point where it had so cruelly been broken off. Did there not, in these things, appear to be a hand?

She put out her own right one to ring the bell; but the manageress—the owner of the boarding-house called herself the manageress, suggesting behind her a grave company of elderly men, to whom she could refer when she needed support—who had been observing Milly from the dark background where she was superintending a servant whose habit it was to sit down directly she wasn't superintended, darted forward, and in accordance with her practice of making every lodger or possible lodger feel she was her special friend, clasped her hands and exclaimed sympathetically, as her eyes flicked over mourning figure, "You poor, poor *dear!*"

"Can I—have a room?" asked Milly timidly, for she

had again forgotten for a moment what she looked like, and was again taken aback.

"A room? I should *think* so. *Fifty* if you like," said the manageress enthusiastically. "Why, I wouldn't turn a *dog* away if it had lately lost its——"

She broke off, and taking Milly's suit-case from her drew her quickly into the dining-room, for her new guest struck the manageress, who prided herself on the rapidity with which she sized up lodgers, as the sort of person who had to have her mind made up for her, and until she was safely in the dining-room, and the door shut, she might go away again; and competition was severe, and opulent widows scarce, and one had to be quick and snatch, if only to save ladies from all one's rapacious neighbours.

"It would be for quite a short time," faltered Milly, shrinking under the effect the well-known old dining-room, combined with the hungry-eyed new authority in it, produced.

"*Any* time, short *or* long," said the manageress, pushing up an easy chair and somehow getting Milly into it, and then, with swift sweeping movements, clearing up a litter on the table which looked like the remains of someone's supper. "But I wouldn't mind making a bet, if I ever did such a thing, which of course I don't, that it'll be *long*, Mrs.——"

"Bott," said Milly.

"Bott," said the manageress. "My friends—I always look upon the ladies here as my friends, and no gentlemen or dogs admitted as you saw on the board outside, for they only lead to trouble—ah, yes, and *don't* they," she added, stopping to gaze with warm compassion at Milly. "I mean the gentlemen of course, though dogs are a great nuisance too. Well, we won't speak of that now," she went on, carrying what she had cleared up off the

table to the sideboard, "will we? Later on you'll tell me
all about it, won't you, Mrs. Bott. And meanwhile we
won't be morbid, we mustn't give way, *must* we? We owe
it to our dear ones, *don't* we, not to do that. What *you*
want now, I can plainly see, is breakfast. Isn't it? For
you can't have had any yet, and it does make such a
difference whether one has had something to eat or not.
Yes—as I was saying, my friends, my ladies here, never
want to leave. It's *home* you see, Mrs. Bott. Real *home*.
Comforts. Individual study——"

Ah no, thought Milly, not this place; she couldn't
bear this place. "I expect your charges——" she began
timidly. "I can't afford——"

Charges? Afford? The spirit implied by these words
seemed to the manageress unworthy of the scale of
expenditure which had obviously been applied to her
new client's clothes.

She ignored them.

"You're not to think of *anything*, you poor dear," she
said, smiling down at her with such determined encouragement that Milly's heart sank, "except that you've
come home. We'll talk business, if you want to, when
you've had some breakfast. I was a V. A. D. in the War,
and know that breakfast comes quite *first*."

And she hurried out of the room calling to the servant,
and, getting no answer, because she had withdrawn into
the basement, where she was sitting down, went along
the passage to the head of the back stairs.

How well Milly knew that passage, and the back
stairs hidden round a bend at the end of it. She got up
quickly, very red and ashamed, and stole to the door,
picking up her suit-case on the way. She must get
away from this. She couldn't stay here. What silly
sentimental idea of finding comfort in the past had made
her come in? As though past happiness could ever com-

fort, as though it could ever do anything but stab one! Escape, escape, she thought, as she had thought during the night in her bedroom; escape while there was still time. . . .

And she stole out on tiptoe—it struck her, humiliatingly, that she was becoming practised in stealing out of places on tiptoe—and finding the front door still open, for the house's habit was to air itself for half an hour, was about to go through it and make with what dignity she could for the nearest corner, when the manageress in the basement, warned by some instinct that all was not well above her in the hall, suddenly reappeared.

"Why—Mrs. *Bott!*" she exclaimed.

Absurd situation. Ridiculous to mind what this strange woman thought. Yet Milly felt as much ashamed as if she had been a naughty child caught doing wrong. Why couldn't she say, why hadn't she been able to say at once in the dining-room, that she didn't think the house would suit her, and simply go? Why should she always be silent, faced by determined people, and give the quite wrong impression that they could do what they liked with her, and then have to get out of her difficulties by deceit?

Very red and foolish, she came back a little way into the hall. "I'm afraid——" she began.

The manageress was full of suspicions. Was this merely the latest form of thief, and were spoons at that moment in those crape pockets? Or was she another of the shilly-shallying vulgarians who didn't know either when they were well off or what was due to a lady running a house, and walked out without so much as a good-morning? Vast had been the manageress's experience of the seamy sides of lodgers, and she had learned much firmness in dealing with them; indeed, one either had to be firm in her profession or go under and starve. Whatever this one was, thief or vulgarian, she couldn't be allowed to leave in such a manner, but nothing ever being lost by diplomacy, the manageress knew, she said, very nearly as warmly and sympathetically as before in spite of her black suspicions, "Afraid? Poor Mrs. Bott. Poor, *dear* Mrs. Bott. Nothing to be afraid of here, you know. And I've just been ordering you some nice hot coffee, and a poached egg on toast."

"I was thinking——" began Milly again.

"I know, I *know*," interrupted the manageress, taking the suit-case firmly out of her hand. "But you mustn't, you really must *not*. No good thinking and brooding—it only makes it all so much worse."

"I was thinking," said Milly, making an effort, "of leaving."

"Leaving!" echoed the manageress, in a voice of astonishment. "Leaving what?"

"Here," said Milly.

"But you've only just come."

"Yes, but——"

"You poor dear," said the manageress soothingly, "you're in such a state of mind that you don't really know what you want. But I know—it's breakfast. Gladys!" she called down the passage, "be quick, now. We want that breakfast up *at* once. And when you've had it," she said, turning to Milly and taking her arm, "you shall go on your way rejoicing. Only I wouldn't mind betting, if I were the sort of person who does bet, which of course I'm not, that you don't. Not rejoicing. Nobody has ever left me yet rejoicing. They want to stay here. They hate having to go. It's *home*, you see, Mrs. Bott. Suppose," she suggested brightly, "while we're waiting for that breakfast, we go upstairs and take our bonnet off, and bathe our eyes in some nice cool water? Yes, I know what—I'll have the breakfast sent

up to your room, and then you can rest quietly, and
perhaps get right into bed and have a good sleep."

A remarkable woman, thought Milly; and really
seeming to understand what one needed most at the
moment. If only she herself had a tenth part of such
single-minded determination.

She gave up. Breakfast and sleep. After that, after
having had those, and been restored by them to clearness and courage, she could still go away. Nobody could
force her to stay there, and meanwhile it wasn't worth
while arguing.

She found herself being led up the familiar stairs,
covered now with neat linoleum instead of the shabby
old carpet of her youth, up past the drawing-room on
the first floor, up to the next landing, where her bedroom used to be, and Agatha's.

"No, not in there," whispered the manageress drawing her away, for she had paused instinctively before the
shut door that had once been hers. "It's engaged. A
lady arrived late last night—in fact in the small hours,
but I never turn trouble away. A widow too, I'm
afraid. Ah, dear. Sad world, isn't it. I hope she's still
asleep, poor dear. Out of breath? They *are* rather steep.
Just one more teeny, weeny little flight—the rooms on
this floor are gone, but upstairs—it's lucky, for I'm
usually full right up. Well, sit down a moment, then.
Yes, yes—I can see you're out of condition, poor Mrs.
Bott. Sh-sh we mustn't *talk*—my poor new friend in
there——"

Milly, sympathetically assisted by the manageress,
did sink down on a chair that stood on the little landing,
out of breath after climbing stairs she used to fly up two
steps at a time, generally chased by Agatha, whose aim
was to pinch her legs. Outside what used to be her bedroom door stood a pair of black boots, trodden down at

heel and so much wrinkled that they seemed to be frowning, and on the mat, awaiting the pleasure of the lodger within, was a small and battered brown tin can of hot water.

The manageress, her finger on her lip in case Milly, who up to then had hardly spoken a whole sentence and was evidently without breath to spare, should begin to talk, and perhaps be so much unlike her clothes as to ask what her room was to cost before she had been got safely into it and used it, placed herself in front of the boots and hot-water can, neither of which, she felt, did her establishment credit; and while she was standing like that, and Milly on the chair was panting, and both were silent, the bedroom door opened, and the lodger, in search of her hot water, appeared.

The manageress sprang aside, and the lodger, surprised to find two people where she had expected emptiness, because of the silence which had succeeded the talking that had been annoying her for the last ten minutes, stood a moment, staring.

Milly stared back, her lips apart. They stared at each other.

She was a tall, bony woman, with thin grizzling hair scraped together on the top of her head preparatory to washing her face, which was much lined and strong featured—a discoloured face, battered by exposure, apparently, to hard winds and hard water. And round her shoulders she held together a petticoat thrown over her nightgown, and her nightgown was of flannel.

"Oh, dear——" exclaimed the manageress, but not with nearly so much emphasis as she used to Milly, because of the boots. Really those boots. In the dim light of the late arrival the night before she hadn't noticed them. "I'm sorry. We've wakened you, and I meant you to have a good rest."

The lodger said nothing, because she was staring at Milly, who was staring at her. Then she stooped, and without a word picked up the can and shut her door.

Milly shifted uneasily on the hard chair. Her eyes were fixed on the shut door. What a grim woman. And staring as if one were a ghost. . . .

"Rested?" inquired the manageress, brightly smiling, because even if this lodger were an impostor, and were trying to get away with the spoons—she would go and count them the minute she was free—she did look exactly like the kind one is proud of, in her beautiful expensive mourning, and brand-new patent leather shoes. "Feel like going on up?" she asked cheerily.

Milly looked at her a little bewildered, collecting her thoughts. She had forgotten the manageress. Yes— she supposed she did feel like going on up, she said in rather a dazed way—"If you ask *me*," the manageress said to herself, "I should say she wasn't quite all there."

And, helped by the firm hand on her elbow, she did so; and neither she nor Agatha knew that, after twenty-five years, they had just met again.

*❊(*IV*)❊*

THE reason Agatha lived in Switzerland was because she had married a Swiss.

The Botts' view of her, for many years past not discussed any more, but none the less perfectly clear in their minds, was that she had brought scandal on the family, shame on Milly, and ruin on herself by eloping under particularly shocking circumstances. It is true that by the time Ernest died she had done it a very long while ago, but that made no difference to the Botts, who absolutely drew the line at any public scandal; for this scandal, which had been very public—even the local papers were full of it—had neither been forgotten nor forgiven. Gross immorality combined with gross ingratitude, and getting into the local papers—who is going to forgive that? Even if one manages to forgive it one can't forget it, the Botts felt. And they didn't; and they hadn't.

Received into Ernest's house on her father's death as an orphaned and penniless sister-in-law, received with kindness and hospitality, and not a word of reproach, in spite of it being no joke for a man to wake up from his honeymoon and find he has got to keep two women instead of one, after only three months of it Milly's sister revealed the sort of deplorable stuff she was made of by getting out of a window in the middle of the night, and running away with a Swiss. A *Swiss*, mind you, said the outraged Botts to each other, who, if ever they had thought of Swiss persons at all, which was practi-

66

cally never, had thought of them solely in connection with clocks, alps, and waiters.

This was bad enough, surely, by itself; quite bad enough, without having anything more added to it. There was, however, more added to it, for it presently transpired—and this, though it didn't get into the local papers, was whispered in the local drawing-rooms —that the pair had lived together at first without being married. Milly, they understood, tried to explain to Ernest, who very properly declined to discuss it and desired her to rule her sister out of her life once and for all, that it wasn't Agatha's fault, but was owing to some unexpected delay because of the different nationalities. As if that could excuse immorality! And what was delay for, except to wait in? It was only after three weeks of shame, so the Botts learned, and also the whole of Titford, that the position had been legalized, and the girl proceeded with him who had been her paramour—the Botts shrank from the word, but pronounced it—and was now indeed, it seemed, her husband, to Switzerland, where he kept, the Botts receiving their last straw in shocked silence were given to understand, an hotel.

They couldn't get over it. They never had got over it. Kind and affectionate as they were to Milly, devoted to her as most of the brothers afterwards became, they yet deep down in their hearts remembered what her sister had done. Useless for them to try to wipe Agatha out of their minds; they only succeeded in wiping her out of their conversation. An hotel-keeper as Ernest's brother-in-law. A person who bowed to one on a doorstep, and rubbed his hands. A person who presented bills on departure, which one paid. What a nice thing to have become mixed up with! No such connection, nothing approaching such a connection, had ever yet got into their

family. Alps became sore points with them. The word
hotel made them start. When they went to Italy they
went by the Mont Cenis and Modane. When Le Bon—
his name, they considered, should certainly have been
Le Mauvais—a cordial man, who wanted to be friends
and wore a glossy black coat and a white tie even at
breakfast, invited them, as he did to begin with, to come
and stay at his hotel as long as they liked free of charge,
it was regarded as the deadliest insult and ignored.
When his wife wrote, as she did to begin with, letters of
apology, and even of affection, to Ernest, for Agatha at
the time of her disgrace was only nineteen and an
optimist, not only did he take no notice of them but
forbade Milly to do so, either then or at any time during
the rest of her life. And when at last Le Bon died, which
he did in his wife's arms, a place he had rarely been out
of and was not displeased, after twenty-five years of it,
to have an opportunity of leaving, for *la bonne Agathe*, as
he called her, was so energetic—*d'une énergie formidable*,
he thought sometimes with a sigh, he having latterly
become very tired of the hardness of life, and realizing,
on the verge of leaving it, how little real pleasure it had
given him—when at last he died, the Botts were unaware that the creature, as they referred to him in their
thoughts, had ceased to exist.

Milly didn't tell them. To tell them would have exposed her own steady disobedience and deceit. Besides,
he was unmentionable. Milly didn't care to imagine
what Ernest's face would look like if she suddenly began
mentioning Le Bon. She did tell Arthur of his death;
and he said, very kindly, and completely uninterested,
"Poor fellow," and after that, except in Agatha's letters,
Le Bon seemed to drop finally out of life.

But in Agatha's letters, with how strange a splendour
did he now begin to glow. From the first they had been

written in a strain of almost exaggerated satisfaction with her marriage, so that Milly well knew Aggie had loved her Swiss and been happy with him, but she hadn't realized how great that love and happiness had been till she read the letters written after his death. What pale things her condolences and sympathies seemed, offered to that flaming sorrow. Agatha's letters, during the whole twenty-five years, had been on the romantic side, and apt to be rather taken up with Swiss meadows and mountains and moons, and the sorts of things one felt in their presence when love walked beside one; but they now became drenched in poetry. She seemed to have read a great deal of it, and had it apparently at her ready disposal in her mind. Arthur and Milly had read a great deal of it too together, during those quiet afternoons of sin, but it had never got into Milly's letters,—not to quote, that is, not to put in verse after verse. Agatha's letters, after her husband's death, were so full of it that it was difficult to find the places where it left off and she began. She hardly said anything about herself any more. The things became passionate applications of the great thoughts of poets to Le Bon. Shelley, Tennyson, Matthew Arnold—all were grist to Agatha's elegiac mill, and all of them, according to her, must have had Le Bon prophetically in their minds. They *described* him, she wrote.

Milly marvelled. She was stirred by the *post-mortem* letters to her depths. This was love. This was the real, blazing thing. The very envelopes, mourning-edged, seemed to scorch her fingers with black fire. Fancy all that having been inspired by a Swiss! Milly couldn't get over it. Except at the beginning with Arthur, she had never felt what Agatha appeared to feel every day as a matter of course; compared to the rich, warm blood Agatha was full of, Milly realized that she herself was mere milk. "It's wonderful how fond Aggie was of her husband," she said to Arthur one afternoon, coming to their meeting fresh from another letter. And Arthur again said, very kindly, and completely uninterested, "Poor fellow."

At no time had there been nearly as many letters from Agatha to Milly as from Milly to Agatha, but they made up for their infrequency by being extremely long—as long as they possibly could be, without having to have another stamp. After Le Bon's death they became even more infrequent, and once or twice hadn't a stamp on them at all, so that Milly knew how deeply distracted poor Aggie must be. Yet how splendid she was through all her distraction, going on with the hotel in spite of the weight of her sorrow, carrying on as Gaston, she wrote, would have wished, even launching out into new developments and opening it, for what remained of the winter, as a ski-ing resort. Such grit deserved success; and success and happiness, Milly reflected proudly, but also wistfully, had attended Aggie's footsteps from the moment she had taken her own life into her hands and fled from Ernest's house—the success and happiness which await those who dare, who defy, who go straight for what they want, and don't sit at home smiling anxiously at husbands.

Still, at this time, some weeks before Ernest's death, and entirely unconscious that he had found her out, Milly wasn't really wistful; she was quite content, really, with things as they were, enjoying her popularity in Titford, and the affection of the Botts, and, unknown to a soul, as she supposed, the devotion of Arthur.

Or was it, she sometimes wondered, her devotion to him that she enjoyed?

Well, perhaps. It didn't matter. So long as there was devotion, thought Milly, her good and sweet eyes—they

had remained good and sweet, in spite of her life of
sin—maternally watching Arthur, as he sipped his tea
and warmed his lean hands round the cup—so long as
there was devotion, after ten years of intimacy what did
it matter whose it was?

And indeed she was right about Agatha's grit. Agatha
was all grit. Such was the amount of it in her character
that, for a whole quarter of a century, she was able to
suppress any word in her letters which didn't breathe
pure contentment and happiness. Because, from the
first, she had set her teeth and had made up her mind
that neither Milly, her well-off, comfortable sister, nor
the hostile and unjust Botts to whom she belonged,
should ever know she was being punished.

§

Yes; she was being punished all right, the Botts, who
believed in justice, would have been glad to hear, though
it was also true her marriage was a success. It was a
success, that is, in every way except one; but that one
way was so important that its absence sent Le Bon at
last from sheer underfeeding and anxiety to his grave,
and ground Agatha to the bone. For there has to be
money; there has to be some money somewhere if a man
is to be placid, and his wife not become just bone. Le
Bon, kind and incompetent, whose nature it was to be
happiest in tranquillity—*la tranquillité avant tout*, he
used to say to himself in the early days of his marriage,
before he was so hungry, when Agatha had reproachfully
been reaffirming her belief in *l'amour avant tout*, a belief
which really surprised Le Bon, who never would have
eloped with Agatha if she hadn't eloped with him, not
being by nature an eloper, and who felt that much
amour, indeed any, once the honeymoon was over, was
incompatible with marriage and the increasingly sordid

absorptions of their life, and Agatha herself was later to replace the word *amour* by *le manger*—Le Bon had less and less money with every year that passed.

Every year his hotel was a little emptier than the year before, and accordingly also his pockets, and also, disastrously, his stomach; every year new and bigger hotels in more convenient and quite as beautiful spots sprang up, and they had central heating and modern sanitation, and his hadn't. His was a small wooden house by itself, far from railways and three miles from the nearest hamlet, tucked away in a dimple on the face of the mountains,—a very lovely dimple once one was in it, but difficult to reach except for hardy persons who didn't mind mules. In the early days, the relatively prosperous days, when Agatha was young and full of determination to make the thing an enormous success, and show Milly and Ernest and all those other base Botts that they had been wrong about her marriage and she gloriously right, active English clergymen, including several of the wirier bishops, used with their wives, who also were wiry, to spend their Augusts there. Madame Le Bon being English made it, they declared, so comfortable and home-like—who was she by the by? Oh, nobody particular; suburbs. She knew about thin bread and butter, and real English tea. She knew that water, unless it is cold, must be hot. And if she couldn't let one have proper baths in a bathroom because of there not being a bath-room, she at least understood about sending up tubs. The wives talked friendlily to Madame Le Bon—a nice young creature, quite a lady, they said; the bishops were most kind, never failing to give her a cheery word as they passed in and out, even courteously asking her to sit down when they called her to the *salon* to consult her about a mountain excursion; and everybody punc-tiliously paid their bills.

Great days; compared, that is, to what came after them. But even in them there were money troubles. The season was so short; the English—scarcely anyone who wasn't English was fond enough of exercise combined with frugal living to come up that steep bridle-path to the simple little hotel at the top—only had holidays in August and September, and by the middle of September the sun went off the dimple early, and it became so excessively cold that however hardy the visitors might be they needs must go down to warmer places; and then the shutters were shut, and the desolation that was to last ten months began, and no more money for another year was to be expected.

Winged by pride and youth, and determination that those Botts should never be able to say, "I told you so," Agatha did all, and more than all, mortal woman can do to help her Gaston through the empty months. She scoured, and cooked, and baked; she diligently collected fir cones and wood for the fire he liked to dream by; she dragged the bedding out of doors with her strong young arms, to air it on the frozen snow in the hot mid-day sun of winter; she industriously mended and patched the thin, torn sheets—clergymen seemed to kick a good deal in bed, she thought; she anxiously cherished the important goats, and hung maternally over the important chickens; and, having settled Gaston comfortably in his chair by the fire after tea, and given him the pipe that was to persuade him he had eaten his fill, each day she walked forth alone in the tremendous twilights, when evening filled the distant valley as if it were a bowl, creeping slowly higher and higher, putting out the red reflection of the sunset as it crept, till at last only the solemn circle of the highest mountain-tops stood above it in a ring of light, and with her face turned upwards to the freezing purity of those lonely slopes of snow, solitary in the utter silence, she replenished her courage and renewed her faith; for, at the end of a long day's work, both of these things, Agatha found, were apt to flicker.

They shouldn't flicker, she vowed. She wouldn't let them. It was so beautiful there, she thought while she was still young. She lived in the very heart of beauty. She lived too in the very heart of affection. Outside, that marvellous winter purity, that honeyed loveliness of June, inside, waiting for her, her kind Gaston. She had only to go out for a minute at the end of the day to be calmed and rested. Why should she let herself be cast down because they had no money? Things were going to be better. She would *make* them be better. Those Botts should never——

At this time Agatha was in her early twenties, and very strong. Ten years later she was still doing these same things, and still going out every evening to the stars; but only now so as to get a breath of fresh air, and not thinking very much about anything in particular as she blinked at them with tired eyes. She was tired. She had had, by then, fifteen years of it. Each of these years had been harder than the one before, and her body, with no such thing as a roundness or a softness left anywhere about it, had become very bony.

Still—those Botts. They shouldn't know, thought Agatha, laying back her ears; not one of them should know. If she wrote to Milly of her distresses she would help her, no doubt, but sooner or later, being a Bott, and to judge from her recent letters a settled-down and contented Bott, she would leak, and that vindictive Ernest get to know of her plight, and rejoice. Besides, how rich she was really in her Gaston. As far as *he* went, his disposition, his unfailing gentleness and courtesy, how happy she was. He was exactly like his surname.

She often wrote this to Milly, how exactly like his surname Gaston was. And he couldn't manage for a single
minute without her, he entirely relied on her. Agatha
loved to be relied on. She had no children, but she
didn't miss them, with Gaston relying on her. He was
her child; more to her, indeed, than any child could
have been, and needing her every bit as much. It was
always she who, in the constant crises of their economi-
cal life, comforted him and held him up. She was the
stronger. She loved being the stronger, loved having
her energetic finger in even the smallest of Gaston's
little pies. For instance, without her he couldn't so
much as decide which tie he was to wear. She loved that.

And she dared say those Botts were imagining her
regretting what she had done. Regretting? Never, said
Agatha, still said Agatha even fifteen years after she
had done it, such was her pride and such her indomitable
determination. And she blinked with tired but defiant
eyes at the icy bright stars above the glittering, empty,
silent slopes of snow. Such a lot of snow. Pity one
couldn't eat it, she thought.

Ten years later nobody would have known Agatha.
By that time she was forty-four, but she looked, as the
other working-women in those high parts looked at the
same age, the infrequent mud-coloured peasants, not to
be distinguished at a distance from the soil they worked
on, well over sixty. Her skin, stretched tight over the
bones of her face, had a curious varnished appearance,—
that was because of the fierce sun, and the fierce snow-
light, and the great biting winds that brought the win-
ters, and the water that cut one, when one washed, like a
knife; and her body was a dry, taut rope. These years
had included the war years. The war finished the hotel.
Nobody came. It stood quite empty, with its shutters

shut. She and Le Bon lived entirely on the milk and cheese they got from the goats, and the bread they made from a patch of rye they cultivated in the summer. Le Bon relied on her more than ever, but he no longer asked her which tie he was to wear, because there were no ties left. This, however, didn't matter, for as he didn't shave any more his beard grew, and it presently hid the place where there wasn't now a tie, and he looked as neat as ever. His beard, though, was very white, and Agatha finally saw what she hadn't so much noticed before, because he had been a tidy, bald man for a long while, with hardly any hair to show what time was doing to him, that her husband was old. Very old. A small patriarch he looked, once his snowy beard really began to flow, and she sometimes caught herself staring at him in surprise, so unlike the man she had eloped with was he. He too, for his part, sometimes let his pale glance rest on Agatha in anemic wonder. This knotted, battered, gaunt woman—was it possible? Le Bon sighed, and closed his eyes.

In the twenty-fifth year of their marriage he began to die; not from any specific disease the doctor, reluctantly ascending the mule-track, could discover, but from inability, apparently, to go on living. Also he didn't want to go on living. He had had enough. It was so cold alive, and his stomach was so empty, and his bed so thin and hard. His poor Agathe also was thin and hard. Enough, enough. *"C'est assez,"* were his last articulate words, caught by Agatha as she bent over him in despair; and even in his choice of last words Le Bon continued kind, for what he really wanted to murmur was, *"C'est trop."* But that would have hurt his poor faithful *amie.* Gentle and polite to the last, Le Bon died; and the hotel was sold at once for almost nothing to the proprietor of the big hotel down in the valley, who had had his eye on it for a long time past, for he wished to acquire a small *dépendance* high up, as an object for the excursions of his more active clients.

Agatha was kept on as book-keeper. The post was offered her partly out of kindness, partly because she knew the conditions so thoroughly, and partly because she would be cheap. She took it in spite of the tiny salary, for where was she to go? She had to live somehow; and less than ever, now that Gaston was dead, was she going to say a word to Milly about being poor, and so confess his incompetence, less than ever, after so long holding up her head as the wife of the successful and flourishing, was she going to throw herself, penniless and beaten, on the Bott compassion. Besides, what was the use? The inexorable Ernest still cut her off from Milly, who still, she wrote, had to hide their letters. So that even if she humbled herself enough to go as a suppliant, she would probably be spurned. A suppliant? Gaston's widow a suppliant? She would *starve* first, muttered Agatha, laying back her ears.

So she stayed on as book-keeper, and grimly watched what just a little capital and just a little competence could do in turning Gaston's failure into quite a promising concern.

It was at this point that she took to the poets. Compared to the huge labours of her former days she had hardly anything to do, and was also being fed properly for the first time for years. So she began reading poetry —little volumes grateful clergymen, not quite liking to tip her, presented to her on leaving the hotel. They were Golden Treasuries, and Oxford Books of Verse; and as she studied *Thyrsis*, and *Adonais*, and *In Memoriam* it seemed to her uncanny how they all might have been written of and for Gaston. She couldn't send many letters to Milly because she couldn't afford the stamps, her salary going in paying off the bills for her mourning, which she had been forced to buy on the instalment system, but, when she did, her reading filled them with the strange threnodial passion which made Milly marvel. Up in her room under the roof she copied the splendid stuff into her letters with clumsy, determined fingers, for her hard work out of doors and in had stiffened and coarsened them; but no difficulty ever stopped Agatha from doing what she felt was right, and surely it was right, it was her sacred duty, to let Milly, and perhaps through some dropped word of hers also those vindictive Botts, know the kind of man Gaston had really been. Noble and misjudged; gone to his grave noble, and patient, and misjudged. Agatha wept to think of it, tears of scalding pity for Gaston, tears of scalding indignation at the long-drawn-out implacability of the Botts. Milly, her little sister, who alone in the world, now that Gaston was dead, represented love for Agatha—there she was, surrounded and hedged in by the inimical family, and out of reach of anything except letters. On Milly's behalf, Agatha said to herself, wandering alone, as she had so often wandered in the icy dusk along the snowy track that led up the mountain, she would unhesitatingly and gladly have laid down her life. But Milly didn't need her life. Nobody needed anything that she could give, who could give so much, so lavishly, of devotion.

Agatha wept. Then one day at the end of March, when the snow was beginning to be patchy, and gentians seemed suddenly to have been poured out over the grass as from the gigantic bucket of a god, and the last of the ski-guests were preparing to leave, Agatha saw in the *Continental Daily Mail*, which was the English newspaper provided for his *clientèle* by the proprietor because it was cheap, that Ernest was dead.

She was much shocked. She walked over to the window, and stared out without seeing anything. Ernest dead, with all his unkindness still upon him. And little Milly a widow now, going through what she herself was suffering—the loneliness, the gnawing loneliness.

She knew no details. Ernest's death came under the heading *London Traffic Alarming Increase in Accidents*, and was lumped together with several others. But the name and address caught her eye at once; and at once, before she turned away from the window, she had made up her mind.

No obstacles separated her from Milly now. They were both, alas, free. She knew where her place was: it was at Milly's side. And however painful it would be to meet the rest of the Bott family again, she would bear more than that, oh, far, far more than that, she who by this time was so much used to bearing, so as to be with Milly in her sorrow. Ernest had been a stern man, and —she must say it, in spite of his being dead—a cruel man as far as she was concerned, but not, she understood from Milly's letters, otherwise. Milly had seemed content and happy, especially during all these later years, and certainly had had everything that money could buy. And Agatha was so tired of being poor, so much afraid of the dreadful future, when she wouldn't be wanted even as a book-keeper. With Milly, she would get into harbour at last, into a safe, quiet harbour, even if a sad one; though indeed Milly's wealth was not why she so instantly decided to go to her—it merely made it possible.

Determined as ever where someone she loved was concerned, she at once threw up her post, scraped together all her worldly goods, which were so few that the same small bag she had run away from Titford with was emptier than it had been twenty-five years before, and going down the bridle-path she would never probably tread again, she went to the mother-hotel in the valley, and told the proprietor so firmly that he must lend her money for her fare to London that, hypnotized, he did it at once. Her sister would pay back, said Agatha, her gaunt head held high with pride. Her sister was rich. . . .

The proprietor, who had been about to give this poor Madame Le Bon, this excellent woman who had so much suffered and whose hotel he really had picked up very cheap, the fare as a parting gift, hereupon gave it to her as a loan. Foolish, he thought, if the sister were rich not to allow her to pay; and the poor creature, even for the loan, was all gratitude.

And when she arrived in London close on midnight, and tried to go to Titford so as to fold Milly to her heart at once, fold her even as she herself had been folded by Milly that long-gone day of homecoming, and promise to take care of her and tenderly love her, even as Milly had promised—Agatha remembered each word; she never forgot words—to love and take care of her, when she tried to go to Titford she found she couldn't, for the last train had left. So, taking her bag in her firm grip, for these exertions were child's play to Agatha, taut and sinewy with labour, she set out in the London night to find a cheap lodging, walking—it was nothing to her, a walk like that—all the way to Bloomsbury; for she too recollected, as Milly next morning was going to recollect, that in Bloomsbury there used to be many lodgings, and she too thought it would be consoling to spend the night in the place where she used to be young. And though she lost her way, and found herself in Picca- dilly Circus when she was aiming at where she remem- bered Trafalgar Square used to be, she was treated with respect, and in no way interfered with; and when she did finally reach the squares that had clustered round her childhood, she was unable to resist, in spite of its being so late, going first, before she searched for a room, into the very one she and Milly had lived in—just for a moment, just to look at the house a moment after all these years, and all that had happened in them, and because her heart was brimming. And she too then saw what Milly was going to see next morning, that there was a notice board up.

The light from the nearest lamp enabled her to read its legend.

She stood gazing at it.

How strange. How providential.

And going up the steps, although it was by now past one and the house was shrouded in sleep and silence, she rang the bell.

The board said *Apartments to Let.* It said nothing about their not being to let at night, Agatha remarked to herself on getting no answer; therefore she would go on ringing till somebody came.

She did; and the first person who came was a policeman. He walked slowly along the square, looked at her, and then walked away.

The next person who came was the lady next door, who put her head out of an upstair window, and said it was no good ringing because they were deaf in there, but, if it was rooms she wanted, she herself——

Then came the manageress; hurriedly, in a dressing-gown; instinctively, through her slumbers, feeling all was not well down on her door-step. And quickly un-bolting the door, she was just in the nick of time to prevent that harpy in the next house, that vulture, that low-down non-player of the game, that snatcher-away of other people's ladies, from carrying off her lodger.

"You poor, poor *dear!*" she cried when she saw the tall mourning figure, remembering even at that hour to welcome sympathetically.

"I want a room, please," said Agatha briefly coming in and firmly putting down her bag on the hall table.

"Why, that's just what I *want* you to have," the manageress assured her, who hadn't yet seen her boots.

This was how Agatha came to be in their old home next morning when Milly arrived, and they didn't recognize each other.

⁘(V)⁘

THERE is no forgetting a voice, however.

That evening, after having slept the whole day the sleep of complete exhaustion, hardly stirring from the position she had dropped down in on the bed directly after her breakfast, Milly woke up to find the room dark, and the day manifestly over.

She sat up, instinctively tidying her hair, and by the light of a lit window in the house opposite saw that the breakfast-tray was gone, so that someone must have been in the room since she fell asleep. And she hadn't heard a sound; not all day had she heard a sound.

O blessed sleep ! O comfortable bird ! quoted Milly—for by now, having had so much poetry read aloud to her by Arthur, she knew quite a lot of it inaccurately; and she apostrophized sleep in this manner because she felt quite different, restored, by those few hours of withdrawal into unconsciousness from the pressure of life, to clearness of mind, her head no longer aching, and not even remembering for several minutes that she was a fugitive and a penitent.

When she did, it came as a shock, for she felt so good and peaceful. Was she really wicked? Of course she was. The Botts knew all about it by this time. It was their knowing that made her wicked; it was Ernest's having found out. If nobody had ever known. . . .

She turned her mind resolutely away from a line of thought manifestly discreditable in one who repents.

Here she was hankering after the comforts of secrecy again, the shelter of deception. She would get up, and go out into the square for a little, if it weren't too late, while her room was being tidied for the night, and try to think more rightly. Just having had a good sleep mustn't be allowed to blind her to the facts of her situation; conscience couldn't be a thing at the beck and call of one's physical condition.

And as she was feeling her way across the room to where her bonnet was, for there seemed to be no matches or candle or electric light, and the blind of the window on the other side of the square had been pulled down, something suddenly smote her motionless.

A voice.

She stood listening, stiffened into an intense attention. Whose?

She held her breath, pushing the hair back from her ears. Was this house really haunted?

Downstairs it was. But whose? Whose voice? Oh —but *whose?*

Trembling, she felt her way to the door, and opened it a crack.

The voice went on. Down in the hall, it seemed to be. And another voice mixed up with it—that manageress woman's, apparently.

Years seemed to roll back from Milly as she listened, staring into the dark, spell-bound.

"No, no—it is much too late, thank you," she heard the voice say distinctly, "much too late for dinner, thank you. Yes, I was aware it was at half-past seven, but I have been delayed. Is there no letter for me? I was expecting one. No doubt I shall be receiving it by the first post to-morrow, then. And after that I shall be leaving——"

"Leaving?" It was the manageress's voice which here became distinct. "You can't."

"How—I cannot?" inquired the other voice.

"Not without a week's notice. This isn't a hotel."

"And after that," repeated the voice with a kind of melancholy firmness, "I shall be leaving. I am only waiting to hear from my sister. She lives at Titford. I wrote to her this morning, and her reply should certainly be here by——"

Milly waited to hear no more. She pulled open the door, flung herself through it, groped wildly till she found the banisters, for no light was on up there and only a very dim one was burning far below in the hall, and hanging on to them, obliged to feel for every step because it was so dark, she got down the stairs somehow, catching her feet in her long skirt, kicking them free again, stumbling, clutching, and making queer little noises as she went.

"Aggie! It's me—it's Milly—I'm here too—Aggie, Aggie!" she called out, frantic lest the voice should go away before she got to it, lest something should happen and they miss each other, lose each other again, disappear again into more endless, heart-breaking years. "Wait! I'm coming! Aggie! Oh—*Aggie!*"

And there was a tall enveloped figure, bonneted and cloaked, dark even in the darkness, running up towards her, reaching up the stairs towards her, exclaiming, calling out too, and Milly's last words were sobs in Agatha's arms.

§

"*Well*," thought the manageress.

She stood unnoticed at the foot of the stairs, an astonished witness, in the dimness, of the rush together of her two latest lodgers. Fancy the quiet-spoken Mrs. Bott making such a noise. And the other one, the hatchet-faced one, as soft and sobby now as you please. Such a hullabaloo she hadn't heard since that Miss Scrymgeour left, and wanted not to pay most of her bill.

She stood hesitating a moment, wondering whether this perhaps was one of the rare occasions on which the bright front-door light oughtn't to be turned on, the light reserved for arrivals, but decided that it wasn't. No good wasting. She would be, however, tactful. Evidently an unexpected reunion. She would show that she knew when not to intrude. So she withdrew into the dining-room; but in order to avoid possible unpleasantness, for emotional ladies were apt to wander out of the house when they were having their attacks, and forget all about things like bills, as a precaution she softly locked the hall-door, and put the key in her pocket.

§

At that time of evening the ladies of the *Home from Home* were supposed to be either in the drawing-room, which had what was needful though not excessive in the way of lights, or in their bedrooms, which were furnished each with a candle. No provision was made for conversations on staircases. The staircases and the passages were left in darkness. Ladies, the manageress had discovered, were patient about lights, content to grope their way to bed; therefore, naturally, she didn't give them any. One had to save where one could. Life was hard, and bankruptcy at all times just round the corner.

So that it was in the dark that Milly and Agatha met again, and knew each other only by their voices. Mere shadowy blotches locked together on the stairs, they swayed to and fro in the closeness of their embrace, while the manageress, withdrawn into the dining-room because she was tactful, kept the door ajar because she was interested.

They could see nothing, they could only hear and feel; and what they heard, for a long time, was just sobs, and what they felt for a space they didn't notice, because their minds were empty of everything except the blessed, blessed comfort of there being two of them. Two. In a desolate, frightening world, what magic in just that!

"Oh, nobody should *ever* be only one!" sobbed Milly clinging, her face buried in Agatha's crape, overwhelmed by the pure joy, the exquisite relief, of having as by a miracle reached protection and love already. Bliss flooded her heart. It was like coming home after long, distressed wandering; it was like being safe after deadly fear.

"Why, my Milly? What, my bereaved one?" wept Agatha, clasping her tight, and washed by such deep emotion that the feel of Milly's figure, definitely substantial and different, in fact not the least like Milly, caused her no surprise, didn't even get through into her consciousness.

"My Aggie—oh, my *Aggie !*" sobbed Milly in reply.

"My Milly—oh, my *Milly !*" wept Agatha, clasping her even closer.

And the manageress, just inside the dining-room door, thought, "*Well.*"

It was one of those rare moments of love surprised, of complete surrender to emotion. No questions came into their heads, because for those few seconds they had no heads, only hearts. They didn't think; they felt. Sweet, and warm, and incredibly comforting was it to be close to one's sister again, touching her, holding her to one's heart for the first time for such long years. Milly forgot everything that had happened since she last saw

Agatha; she forgot there had ever been any Botts, and a man called Le Bon; Ernest was wiped out as completely as if he had been the merest temporary mess; Arthur wasn't given a thought. Blood was all that mattered,—blood, and the binding memories of childhood. Only one's sister had the same memories, only one's sister could love one without wanting anything back, with no after-thought, with just sheer, single-minded love.

"Do you remember how we used to laugh?" sobbed Milly into Agatha's crape.

"Alas," was Agatha's reply, also a sob.

Twenty-five years—"Oh, think of it, *think* of it, Aggie,—it's twenty-five years!"—since last they had heard each other's voices, twenty-five years since that casual good-night on the final evening in Mandeville Park Road, the usual casual good-night, Milly really casual, nodding at the door of her bedroom, Agatha feverishly determined to be casual, as she went into hers only to get out of it again almost immediately through the window. How vividly Milly remembered Agatha as she had seen her last, standing with her hand on the knob of her bedroom door, reed-like in her tall grace, a mass of dark hair bundled together low on her little white neck, her head turned towards her, and the light from the gas-burner shining down on her flushed, bright young face. And Agatha, holding Milly tight and subconsciously feeling her so substantial, had an equally vivid vision of the small, slim thing calling out carelessly, "Good-night, old Agg," across the passage—her bird-like little sister, a year older than herself and already married, but so untouched, so free from the tremors and complications which collect the minute one has told a man to wait for one beneath one's window.

"Milly—my little Milly——"

"Aggie—darling sister——"

And the manageress, just inside the dining-room door, her ears stretched, thought, "Sisters. *Well.*"

§

It was a great moment. It couldn't possibly go on. It ended when Agatha loosened her hold to take out her handkerchief, and wipe her streaming eyes. Then Milly, whose face had been buried in Agatha's crape, which had an odd smell, she was subconsciously aware, neither quite like ink nor quite like glue, but very like what both would be like if they got together, drew her head back a little so as to breathe; and the minute she could breathe she began to talk, and the minute she began to talk Agatha began to talk too, and the minute they both began to talk, instead of just sobbing and exclaiming, the spell was broken, they left off being only hearts with no heads, and the pure unquestioning joy, the pure unquestioning thankfulness, was over.

"But how—but why?" asked Milly, having hastily wiped her eyes, peering up into the shadowy face surrounded by the folds of thrown-back veil.

"Is it not strange," said Agatha, her voice vibrating and her *r*'s much more in evidence than they used to be making her sound almost as if she were a foreigner, which of course she wasn't, Milly said to herself, except perhaps technically, "that we should meet again like this, and here."

"Oh, Aggie—*isn't* it," said Milly, awe-struck by these coincidences, and oblivious to the fact that she and Agatha were on a staircase, and that probably everybody in the house could hear. "Both widows."

"Both widows," repeated Agatha vibrantly. "Old widows, my Milly."

"Not very old," said Milly. "It's only three months

since you—— And poor Ernest—it only happened last week."

"Alas, in that sense we are both tragically young," said Agatha. "I was thinking of our ages."

"Our ages?" echoed Milly, who hadn't been used to thinking of her age, what with Arthur, and her admiring brothers-in-law, and she always having been so much younger than Ernest, and one thing and another. "Why, I'm not so very old, and you're a year less, Aggie darling."

"I am old," insisted Agatha in her deep voice, "old, and broken."

"I never heard of such a thing," cried Milly—almost laughed Milly, still lit up with the joyful confidence the miraculous reunion with Agatha gave her. That wasn't how they were going to begin life together again, by being old and broken. However old they might be, and of course they weren't young, they were *new*, Milly said to herself—from that day on she, anyhow, was going to be brand-new. It was the only way to make up, to wipe out, to start fresh.

"How can you be old and broken, Aggie darling, if I'm not?" she inquired.

Whereupon Agatha put her away from her, holding her at arm's length as though to search her face, which she couldn't do because of the dark and said, "Do not tell me, my Milly, that you are one of those women who refuse to accept age?"—and a faint surprise, very faint, hardly surprise at all, fell like a tiny shadow across Milly's brightness.

"Let's go to your room or mine," she suggested, suddenly realizing from a little sound in the hall below that they weren't perhaps quite as much alone as being in the dark made them feel they were. "There's so much to say. We can't talk here——"

"Indeed and indeed there is much to say," agreed Agatha; and as they began slowly ascending the narrow stairs, their progress made difficult by their clothes, and also because Agatha encircled Milly with her arm, which felt like a hoop of iron round the soft, abundant flesh, Milly went on, "We shall have to sit up all night talking. How did you know, Aggie? How is it you are here—in this house, of all houses?"

"How is it *you* are here, my little one, away from your home so soon after——"

"But how did you know about Ernest? I hadn't time to write. It was all so sudden, so dreadful——"

"Hush, hush," Agatha interrupted, tightening her hold as if to protect from sad thoughts; and the stairs being steep, and their skirts long, and their bodies of different sizes, it was very difficult to get up like that at all. "Do not dwell on that side of it—not on the shocking outward circumstances. You must only think of him as happy now, my Milly, and at rest."

"But how did you *know?*" persisted Milly, unable after her experiences in that haunted bedroom to believe Ernest was at rest, but unwilling to say so to Agatha,—not yet, not at that moment, not on the stairs. Presently she was going to tell her everything, from the beginning. Her confession was to be complete. There shouldn't be the shadow of a secret between them, there shouldn't be the shred of a veil of pretence. What one had done, thought Milly, aware of many things she hadn't realized before she was found out, could never be as bad as pretending to someone one loves that one hadn't done it; it was that which rotted one's soul. Besides, why pretend? Aggie was her sister, who loved her. Love always understood and forgave. It didn't judge. It never condemned. There had only to be enough of it for it not to be able to help understanding, and therefore forgiving. Aggie's

love and hers for each other was great enough to get
over fifty Arthurs. And in that high moment of reunion
Milly felt that she would with perfect confidence have
told her much worse things than Arthur, if she had had
any to tell.

"How did I know?" repeated Agatha, her voice
vibrating. It seemed to have grown much deeper and
bigger. It pulsed. It reverberated through one, and
made one feel as if one were full of bees. Perhaps it was
like that because she lived among great mountains, and
her voice grew to match them—her voice, her heart, her
whole outlook. Witness her letters. So wonderful, so
full of—well, outlook, finished Milly, unable to express
it any better.

"There seems," Agatha went on, as they slowly continued to ascend, "to be a fate which decrees we shall
always know quickly enough of sad things. I chanced to
take up a paper at which I usually do not look—the
Continental Daily Mail—and there it was. Such a shock,
my Milly—take care, don't stumble—such a shock to
read of it suddenly in cold print. His name caught my
eye immediately. He was with other accidents. Poor,
poor man. Harsh in his judgments, perhaps. Perhaps,
too, narrow in his views. And I have sometimes
thought obstinate in the persistence with which he held
them——"

"Ernest," thought the manageress, straining her ears
now in the hall, into which she had crept from the dining-room because the voices, receding, were becoming
indistinct, "must be the late Mr. Bott."

"Aggie," thought Milly, "talks differently from the
way she used to. Or is it my imagination?"

"But that," continued Agatha, "is all over now. His
death filled me with nothing but pity—I assure you,
Milly, with nothing whatever but purest pity and for-

giveness. I owe him no grudge now, gone like that, in
a moment. Poor Ernest." She sighed. "I came at once."

"But suppose we had missed each other?" said Milly,
stopping a moment to get her breath, for not only did the
stairs make her pant but she was struck by the extreme
unpleasantness for everybody if she had arrived on
Aggie's mountain to find her gone, and Aggie had jour-
neyed to Titford to fall into a nest of violently hostile
Botts. "Wouldn't that have been too awful——"

"How could we have?" vibrated Agatha, stopping too
but still keeping hold of Milly. "I would have waited
for you in Titford till you returned. I wrote you there
by the first post this morning."

"But I wasn't going to return. I was on my way to
Switzerland."

"To Switzerland?"

"To you. My one thought since yester—ever since
it happened, has been to get to you."

"But——" began Agatha, struck in her turn.

She was silent, staring at the dim face before her.
Really the way Providence was intervening was little
short of miraculous. She too had made up her mind
there should be no more pretences between herself and
Milly; she was going to tell her everything at last—
lay aside the pride she had wrapped herself in since
the day of her elopement, and explain at last the whole
distress and struggle of her life. Painful, most painful,
after the things she had written; but infinitely more
painful if Milly had gone to the hotel and heard the
story from other lips, heard just the sordid facts without
the excuse, indeed, the justification, of the motive—
a motive which surely, Agatha said to herself, was not
ignoble? To love the husband of one's choice, and
protect that choice from the attacks of vindictive rela-
tives, all waiting for a chance to let loose their intolerable

"I told you so's"—was that ignoble? But she would rather tell Milly about it herself; much rather. After all, she had consistently and for years given wrong impressions—her enemies might even say that she had been untruthful,—and to confess this was going to be difficult indeed, with Milly no doubt remembering the tone of her letters, the constant praises she had sung, and meant, of the good, the beautiful, and the true. Best of all would be, of course, if it were only possible, to continue to conceal, thought Agatha, shrinking from what she had to do; but being with a person constantly, as she was now going to be with Milly, was very different from merely writing to that person. It would be impossible, she was afraid, in daily conversation to keep up that which had been easy in letters.

"Had you done that," she said, her voice deeper than ever with the profound dislike for the necessity of so soon having to lay herself bare, "you would not have found what you expected."

"No," said Milly, reaching up and kissing her. "I wouldn't have found *you*, darling."

"That is not quite what I meant," said Agatha; and added, after a pause of struggle, "I have a confession to make, Milly."

"A confession?" repeated Milly. "You, Aggie?"

"A confession?" repeated the manageress under her breath, creeping up a few stairs, anxious to hear to the last.

"Perhaps I should say an explanation," said Agatha, her pride kicking even on the way to its death-bed.

"I'd rather it were a confession," said Milly with a nervous, small laugh. If Aggie too had something to confess, how much easier it would make everything. The idea, however, was ludicrous—what could Aggie, alone up on her mountain, possibly have done? One

had to be helped when it came to sinning. Besides,
there was Le Bon, and there were her wonderful letters.

Milly laughed nervously. She oughtn't to want Aggie
to have done wrong, but she did. It would halve her
own difficulties. In the same boat, they would feel quite
warm and reassured and able to be repentant together.
On whatever level, thought Milly, of saints or of sinners,
communion was a comfortable thing.

Her laugh, small though it was, sounded very strange
to Agatha, and still more strange when she considered
the remark that had accompanied it.

"Laughing, my Milly?" she questioned, surprised
and jarred. Or was it hysteria? Probably. Agatha
tightened her hold. Poor, worn-out little sister. . . .

And pressing Milly's cheek firmly against her crape-
clad chest, the crape being of a very rough kind, and not
the sort to soothe anybody, though Agatha didn't think
of that, she observed, "You are unstrung."

"Not quite all there, if you ask *me*," thought the
manageress on the stairs below them.

"I have been," said Milly, shocked herself at what
she had been thinking, and at having laughed, however
uneasily, with the funeral only a day old and her own
disgrace so heavy on her heart, "but I'm not going to be
any more. It'll be so different with you with me, Aggie
darling. I shall be able to say things now. I've never
been able to say things—not really, not as one can to
one's sister. Even with Arthur I——"

"Ernest," corrected Agatha gently.

"No—Arthur. Even with him——"

"Milly dearest, your husband's name was Ernest,"
said Agatha very gently, beginning to draw her onwards
up the stairs again, to somewhere where there was a bed.
For she must lie down. Quite evidently she was in a
state of hysteria, poor little thing, and unfit to bear any

more at present. Better defer her own explanation till next day. She must have a night's rest before hearing it.

And Milly was just wondering what had made her suddenly bring out Arthur before his time, unprepared for and on a staircase, when, arrived at the second floor landing, she found herself being led by Agatha towards the bedroom from which in the morning she had seen the staring, grim woman come out to fetch her can of hot water.

She drew back quickly. "No, no," she whispered. "Not in there. It's let. Come up to mine."

"Let?" repeated Agatha, astonished.

"Let?" marvelled the manageress, now only a few stairs below them.

"Yes. There's someone in it," whispered Milly. "I saw her."

"Someone in it?" repeated Agatha, astonished.

"Someone in it?" marvelled the manageress.

"Sh-sh. She'll hear us," whispered Milly. "Come up to my room."

"But——" began Agatha.

"Sh-*sh*," said Milly.

The last thing the manageress, left marvelling, could distinguish as the voices receded to the floor above and she, rooted in astonishment, remained where she was, was the word amazing, uttered with emphasis by the hatchet-faced one.

"I should *think* so," agreed the manageress: amazing indeed. And the instant the door of the bedroom on the third floor was shut she hurried into the bedroom on the second floor, to see for herself who had dared——

But the room was empty.

"*Well*," she said to herself, staring; and decided that these two black birds of passage were not only highly undesirable inmates of her establishment, what with their being connected with death in shocking circumstances, and having confessions to make, and wanting to leave almost as soon as they arrived, and wearing boots, one of them, that were a disgrace to a doormat and bound to lower the house's credit, but that they also weren't quite all there, pretending rooms were sub-let without her knowledge—"If you ask *me*," she thought, staring round and seeing nothing but the same instruments of a meagre toilet which she had already examined and appraised earlier in the day, and, under the bed, the same pair of slippers which had been there before— slippers worse even, if one were at all particular, than the boots.

✲(VI)✲

In the room above, Milly was feeling about for matches, hampered in her movements by Agatha, who came too, holding her with loving solicitude by the arm.

"I want to see you, Aggie darling," said Milly, clumsily groping. "I *long* to see you."

"What I at this moment long for, my worn-out little sister," said Agatha, "is to see you resting. And then," she added with sudden sternness, "I will go down and ask that woman what she means by——"

"I've been resting all day," said Milly, proceeding, accompanied by Agatha, round the room and fumbling with her free hand. "Sound asleep for hours."

"Are you able to sleep?" asked Agatha, surprised, for she remembered how after Gaston's death she had not closed her eyes for many, many nights. But she added, after a brief pause, that she was glad indeed it should be so.

"They don't seem to go in much for light here, do they," interrupted Milly, fumbling.

"And yet," said Agatha, experienced in these practices but resenting them when applied to herself, "it will no doubt be charged us heavily in the bill. I suppose," she continued, moving about the room with Milly, holding her arm, "you now have electricity—it used to be gas, I recollect—installed in your home, even in the servants' quarters, and never need mind even if it should be left burning all night."

"Ernest minded," said Milly, absorbed in her search,

and knocking over what was evidently a candlestick; something anyhow fell on the boards with a tinny sound, and didn't break.

"Poor man," sighed Agatha. "He minds nothing now."

"I wonder," said Milly, stooping to grope on the floor, and upheld by Agatha's hold on her arm.

She found the candlestick, but it hadn't any candle in it. Once it had had one, for little beards of grease stuck about its rim, and broke off in her fingers.

"My little Milly," said Agatha, very lovingly, "you must have no doubts. You must think of Ernest as quite free now, with nothing more to worry him, poor man. "'Climbing,'" she quoted, though Milly didn't know it, "'other heights with other friends.'"

"I don't think he'd climb," said Milly, intent now on finding matches; perhaps there was a candle somewhere in the room if she could only see. "Ernest hated anything one has to go up. Last year he had a lift put in. Just to take him from downstairs to bed."

"*So* rich?" said Agatha, who knew what lifts cost to put in, because when, at the beginning, she and Gaston thought they were going to have a successful future, with more stories built on to their hotel and lifts added, they had spent their evenings consulting catalogues.

For the life of her she wasn't able to feel a twinge at this. A lift costing hundreds of pounds, thousands of francs, just to take a healthy man to bed—for accidents, she reasoned, are not like illnesses, and do not make one unhealthy beforehand,—while she in her mountain did not know where to turn for a daily dinner for her delicate husband.

"Yes, he was rich," said Milly, rubbing her hand along the top of the chest of drawers, and getting it very dusty.

Agatha struggled with and overcame her twinge; after all she too was now, however belatedly, going to benefit by Ernest's wealth. "How glad I am for you, my Milly," she said, "placed for the rest of your life beyond the reach of care and anxiety."

"Well," said Milly, her fumbling hand encountering a vase and catching it just in time as it was going to fall on the floor, "it isn't quite like that. Oh, Aggie," she broke off, "I've got so much to tell you!" And laying her cheek a moment against Agatha's shoulder, and finding it very bony, she added, "How *thin* you are."

"Naturally I am thin," said Agatha. "Sorrow whittles away."

"Does it?" said Milly a little uneasily, and continuing her groping—for what about herself? She, certainly, wasn't whittled. Still, nobody, she argued, could expect a figure that had been accumulating for years to disappear in a single week. Aggie's had had three months. Surely the most acute distress couldn't in a week ——?

"Indeed it does," said Agatha. "It prepares us."

"What for?" asked Milly, moving along, followed by Agatha.

Milly, thought Agatha, under the shock of bereavement said strange things.

"What for, my bereaved one, except reunion?" she said gravely, "Is not that now our only hope, all that is left to us? That, and the comfort of knowing our dear ones are happy and at peace. You must think of poor Ernest now like that, Milly—as happy and at peace."

"Do you think he is?" said Milly. "I've been feeling—" she shivered a little—"that he was somewhere near—quite close to me—not really *gone* at all."

"Nor is he really gone, my Milly," Agatha assured her. "He is indeed close, watching over you."

"Not over, but just watching," said Milly, shivering again as she remembered the night in her bedroom at home.

"Watching *over* you, Milly," Agatha gravely insisted. "Watching over you in love. What did you say?" she added, as Milly, knocking against another ornament, made a noise which drowned her answer.

"I said I didn't think he was," said Milly.

Agatha stood still, and forced her to stand still too.

"My little sister," she said very gravely, "do not tell me that the shock you have had has destroyed your faith?"

"No," said Milly; and indeed it hadn't, for that sort of faith, the faith with which Agatha's letters lately had been filled, she had never had, so it couldn't have been destroyed. Gaston might or might not be doing and feeling the things that Agatha declared he was doing and feeling—he was a Swiss, and perhaps they were different; but that Ernest should be watching over her in love she simply didn't believe. Why should he? He hadn't loved her when he was alive; had hated her, indeed, so much that his one thought had been how best to prepare an elaborate punishment for her. She, by her wicked behaviour, had brought this hatred into his heart, this mean and cowardly—surely it was mean and cowardly?—plotting, and that he, in return for her having filled his heart with evil, should love her, was rather too much to expect. Hers was the double guilt. She was responsible for Ernest's meanness and coward-ice. And for Arthur's departure from virtue she was responsible as well. Her sins were thick upon her. She must tell Aggie—not let her go on a minute longer under false impressions—bother the candle—she would tell her at once——

And she was just going to give up the search for light
and then and there pour out everything into Agatha's
ears, when her hand brushed against a box of matches.

"Here they are," she exclaimed. "I've got them——"
and freeing herself gently from Agatha's loving hold,
she opened the box and struck a match.

Exactly in front of her, under her very nose, was
another candlestick, this one with a candle in it, and
sheltering the flame of the match in her hollowed hand
from the draught coming through the open window, she
turned away from Agatha to light the candle.

"I have so much—oh, so *much* to tell you, Aggie
darling," she said, her voice trembling a little now that
the moment of the confession had really come.

Holding the match in the loop of the bent-in wick to
melt off the grease it was stuck in and get it free, she
went on, "You'll have to be patient, patient"—her
hand, and the match in it, shook—"and love me, love
me. . . . Will you always love me, Aggie?" she asked.
Whatever I have d—— whatever has happened?"

"My Milly," said Agatha, to whom this sounded
once more like overstrain, but also oddly like what she
herself was presently going to require of her sister,
"have I not come all the way from Switzerland just
for that—to love you always, and in turn be always
loved by you?"

"I can't think," said Milly, with a sigh of comfort at
this, and succeeding in freeing the wick and lighting the
candle, "how I've managed to exist all this time without——"

She was going to say, "my own darling sister," but
turning round at that moment, the lighted candle in her
hand, her answer broke off. It froze and stopped dead.
Silence engulfed it. Silence for ever swallowed it up.

They stared at each other.

And Agatha said, after what seemed to be a long while, in a voice of deep amazement, "Milly?"

And Milly said falteringly, as though her mind were groping for a way out, any way that shouldn't be this way, "It was *you*, then this morning . . ."

§

A great politeness overcame them. The room seemed to go stiff with it. And Milly's eyelids fluttered down, as the eyelids of those flutter who remember it is rude to stare at a stranger.

Turning away, she put the terrible candle carefully down on the chest of drawers—very carefully, because her hands were so unsteady.

Aggie. Where was she? Who was this she was shut up alone with? Her sister—what had become of her? This gaunt, stern woman, with the great eyes full of—yes, astonished hostility (why hostility?), this woman wasn't Aggie, couldn't be Aggie, she was only somebody who had stolen her voice. *My sister—oh, my sister!* rang like a frightened cry through Milly's heart, grown suddenly empty of what had filled and warmed it all her life.

She hid in politeness. So did Agatha, profoundly shocked and surprised by Milly's appearance. Indeed she wouldn't have known her again, thought Agatha, covered up in all that fat. Only her eyes and voice were left, and the rest of that which had once been Milly had disappeared into what seemed to Agatha, accustomed to the bones of life, to the highest thinking and the lowest living, to be the undoubted outward characteristics of long-continued, steady self-indulgence.

The word bloated came into her mind. She was deeply estranged. She stood in silence, staring at Milly's abundant and expensively clothed back. She had come to comfort her suffering sister, and where was her suffering sister? Real wretchedness, she said to herself, is never fat.

"I'm afraid," said Milly politely, still turned away, forcing herself to say something, and speaking in a voice so different from the one she had been talking in before that she noticed it herself, "you are very tired."

"Not at all tired, thank you," said Agatha, equally politely. "Merely older."

There was a silence. Milly, bent over the candle, busied herself adjusting the wick, which was inclined to smoke.

My sister—oh, my sister . . .

One could not, of course, Agatha knew, in a single week grow thin and grey-haired, though even that had been done by the great sufferers of history—indeed, some of them had only needed a single night, at least for the grey hairs,—but one could show traces of what one had been through. Milly showed none. Not a sign of any serious reaction to her recent experiences, or to any experiences. She looked like a doll; a plump doll. Pink and white, too; pink and white at forty-five. Could there be much real feeling, much real depth, in a woman who still, after a quarter of a century of further life, which, however prosperous, must have had at least ups and downs in it, looked like a pink and white doll? How, Agatha asked herself, was one seriously to comfort and help a doll?

The silence continued, and Milly, so as to do something to break it, for it was becoming unbearable, fetched the one chair, and brought it over to where Agatha was standing.

"Won't you sit down?" she said, not looking at her.

"Thank you," said Agatha, not looking at her either. But they saw each other; they saw everything.

The chair was rickety, and too low for Agatha, who sat on it cautiously, her long lean knees sideways. The last few days alone, she thought, her eyes fixed sternly on the chest of drawers, the awful last few days, each hour of which must have been packed with anguish for any woman who could feel well, were enough to drag furrows down the smoothest face. Not a furrow on Milly's face could Agatha see, not a wrinkle. There was a slight swelling and redness, certainly, about the eyes, but she hadn't come all the way from Switzerland to comfort a slight swelling and redness about the eyes. Meals, meals, she thought, her thwarted, unneeded protecting love and sympathy curdling within her as she remembered all the meals she and her poor Gaston had had to do without. Even in this last week, the week since the tragedy, Milly must have gone on having regular and abundant meals, or she couldn't possibly . . .

Agatha was deeply estranged. For a long while after Gaston's death she herself had only been able to touch an occasional cup of tea, and a little piece of bread. The first thing real love does, bereft of its beloved, is, she was certain, not to eat. What was there in common, what could there be in common, between herself and such only too evident shallowness?

Milly sat down too, on the edge of the bed at right angles to her, while the flame of the candle, flickering in the draught of the open window, threw a gigantic bonneted head on the wall high up near the ceiling, an unquiet shadow that waved grotesquely. Agatha's profile was turned to Milly, for it pained her too much to look at what Milly had become, and the profile wasn't as completely strange as the full face, because profiles last longer than full faces; in its general scheme it did seem faintly familiar to Milly, as if some elderly aunt with a family likeness to Agatha, one of those like-

nesses which chill intending husbands, had come to pay
a call. But nothing to do with *Aggie*, thought Milly, a
sense of loss, tragic and profound, bleakly crawling
round her emptied heart—nothing to do with her own
sister, the one who used till five minutes ago so
brightly, so warmly, to fill her heart.

She smoothed her dress over her knees, and clasped
her fingers together on her lap, eyeing them carefully, as
though to see that they were behaving properly. But
though she eyed them she didn't see them. She saw
Agatha; she saw with perfect distinctness this stranger
with the voice of Agatha.

My sister—oh, my sister!

"When did you leave Switzerland?" she asked, paralyzed by politeness, nervously saying the first thing
that came into her head so as to avoid another silence. The stranger on the chair didn't seem to mind
silences. She anyhow did nothing whatever to break
them.

"At dawn the day before yesterday," Agatha replied,
staring at the chest of drawers.

"But you must be worn out," said Milly, apparently
addressing her fingers.

"Not at all," said Agatha, apparently addressing the
chest of drawers.

The shadow on the wall gave a violent lunge, and
leapt across the ceiling. Milly got up and shut the
window.

"I'm afraid you feel a draught," she said solicitously,
relieved to be doing something, and struggling with the
catch, which didn't fit.

"I never mind draughts," said Agatha, motionless
on her chair.

"I suppose there are lots in Switzerland," said Milly,
struggling. "All those mountains."

"Of what do you suppose there are lots?" inquired Agatha with bleak patience.

"Draughts," said Milly.

"Possibly," said Agatha.

Ah, but wasn't this nonsense, thought Milly—wasn't this the ghastliest nonsense, talking about draughts, she and her sister, after a lifetime's separation, being polite, being stiff, behaving as though they had never set eyes on each other before, when each was all the other had—all, now, of love and comfort in the world?

But she would, she *would* be natural, Milly thought, she would force herself. . . .

"You've changed, of course," she said, her arms still stretching up trying to fasten the window, for either the catch didn't fit or her hands weren't steady enough to get it to, and anyhow it was an excuse to turn her back. "But it doesn't matter, Aggie"—astonishing how difficult it was to call the stranger on the chair Aggie— "bodies don't matter. Outsides are really nothing."

"They are apt to be symbols," said Agatha, from the chair.

"I don't believe it," said Milly.

"I beg your pardon?" said Agatha, who indeed hadn't heard this, because of the noise Milly was making with the catch.

"No, no, *no!*" cried Milly, turning round quickly, and facing the motionless figure. "Don't talk like that— don't say, 'I beg your pardon' to me—to *me*, just as if —just as if——"

The words died away. She couldn't go on. Acute loneliness overwhelmed her. This frozen stranger, who wouldn't look at her, the mean little room, icy with alienation, tragic with loss. . . .

My sister—oh, my sister! Lost, lost, gone for ever, that dear one the thought of whom, loving and understanding—yes, always loving, always understanding, whatever one did or didn't do, had been like a lit lamp shining along the years. . . .

"Just as if?" Agatha coldly encouraged, as Milly paused.

She made a great effort. All this was idiotic. They simply *must* free themselves from this paralysis of hiding, and if they didn't like each other's bodies they must get past the silly things, through them, round them, to their naked spirits, and to what surely was in both their hearts—the old, dear, warm, simple sister-love.

"Aggie," she began, forcing herself to say the word.

"Yes, Milly?"

"Have I changed so much? Can't you even look at me?"

"You have grown stouter," said Agatha evasively, her eyes on the chest of drawers.

"Yes, yes—I know. One is bound to grow something in twenty-five years."

"Indeed that is true," said Agatha.

"But it doesn't matter. What does it matter? After all, it's natural, I suppose, to fill out. What is *really* important is——"

"Have I?" interrupted Agatha.

"Have you what?"

"Filled out, as you put it."

No; certainly Agatha hadn't filled out. She had done the precise contrary, and entirely lost whatever there had been of her original filling. But was that a reason for congratulation? Again in her voice there seemed to be hostility. Why hostility?

"If," said Agatha, as Milly said nothing, and still keeping her eyes fixed on the chest of drawers, "I seem

a sad woman to you, you must forgive me, and try to
remember that I *am* a sad woman."

"But aren't I too?" said Milly. "Aren't I a sad
woman too? I mean——"

She stopped; for was she a sad woman in the sense
in which Agatha, really mourning, was? Was not what
she was a guilty woman, who was miserable only because she had been found out?

"I know," said Agatha in a level voice, "that you
must be very sad, and I have come all the way from
Switzerland to comfort you. But——"

She too stopped; and the room seemed to re-echo
with the melancholy of her voice. Even the word comfort, beautiful word of warmth and good tidings,
sounded, laden with that odd suggestion of reproachful
hostility, like a knell.

Milly crossed over to her, and sat down on the bed
again. "It was dear of you—very dear," she said, resolutely taking Agatha's hand. If it had been dark she
would have kissed her. That was the right thing to do,
she was sure; but with the candle alight she found she
couldn't. Kissing was much easier in the dark. Everything was much easier in the dark, she reflected desperately, her eyes wavering away from Agatha's stern
profile. But even so, dark or no dark, kisses are things
which have to leave off sooner or later, and there you
are again. And though the dark was extremely helpful
in many cases, if it hadn't been for that candle she
would by now have been telling Agatha all about
Arthur.

She shuddered. Very awful, thought Milly; very,
very awful, to have told the dreadful story to somebody one believed to be one's sister, and then have lit
the candle and found a stranger sitting listening. The

candle had saved her. Yes—but only for a moment. She had got to tell Agatha ultimately. She couldn't go with her to Switzerland and eat her bread unless everything was clear between them. Besides, some explanation would anyhow have to be given of the manifest fact that she had hardly any money, and it should be the true one. No more lies, said Milly to herself.

But first she must get over what Agatha now looked like—get used to her in her new disguise, learn to see through it, to find the love behind this strange surface—

My sister—oh, my sister . . .

Stoutly Milly, sitting on the edge of the bed, turned a deaf ear to the cry that kept on tearing through her heart. Presently the strangeness would wear off; presently Agatha wouldn't mind Milly so much. It was evident she was much shocked at Milly's changed appearance, and Milly felt that perhaps she could bear Agatha's own alterations better if Agatha weren't having such obvious difficulty in bearing Milly's. They would get used to each other. They would——

Milly's eyes, wavering away from Agatha's profile, chanced to fall on the hand she was holding, and remained riveted. What she was thinking came to a sudden end. Her lips dropped open. She stared a moment in silence.

"Aggie——" she presently breathed, staring, for the hand Milly was looking at for the first time was a ruined hand; not merely deformed and spread with work, and discoloured and scarred by exposure but——

She hung over it.

"Aggie——?" she breathed again, pointing to the other one, unable to get more words out; for weren't the hands—could it be that they were the hands of someone who for a long time hadn't had enough of anything, not even—*My sister, oh, my sister!*—enough to eat?

And Agatha, her eyes following Milly's pointing finger and looking down at them and at the face bending over them, at the complete contrast of the smooth, plump, unlined face and the shamefully ugly, spoilt hands, was seized by a sudden desire not only at once to make the confession she had been shrinking from, but to make it, so some strange impulse drove her, as exact and as painful as possible. Curiously, she no longer wished to make the best of it, she wished to make the worst of it.

"Work," she said briefly. Adding after a pause, her eyes on Milly's sleekness, almost as if considering into which soft bit of her she would plunge the knife, "And hunger."

§

The candle lit up two motionless figures looking into each other's eyes. Milly's were full of puzzled horror.

"Hunger," she repeated in a whisper. And then, again, "Hunger——?"

"Are you not acquainted with the word?" inquired Agatha, herself surprised at the surge of bitterness that was flooding her, as if the great volumes of it which had been accumulating for years secretly in her heart, kept under and carefully not recognized while she walked, as she had often insisted to herself, her head high with pride, her eyes full of angry tears, on her mountain-side hand in hand with God, were now all being let loose on Milly.

Was it because up there, where the few scattered inhabitants also struggled and were poor, there had been no one to compare her own misery with? Was it because, though she had always known Milly was prosperous, not seeing her she hadn't realized how blatant that prosperity really was? The very crumbs from Milly's overloaded table would have saved Gaston and herself from those pinches of poverty, those pangs of the inadequately nourished, which had so deeply distressed their later years. True she had had sufficient food during the last few weeks, but it would take more than a few weeks to remove the traces of privation from her body, and never would they be removed, she felt, from her seared heart.

But Milly didn't seem to hear her bitter question, and continued to look at her with eyes of horror. If that were so, her mind was slowly grasping, then Aggie had been—was—desperately poor; and if that were so, and she had come to live with her as her last hope, what was to become of them both?

"Tell me," she whispered. "Tell me everything, Aggie——"

§

Agatha told her. She told her thoroughly, sparing neither of them.

After the first few sentences Milly left off staring at her with those horror-stricken eyes, and slid down to the floor at her feet, her arm round the lean knees and her cheek against the knuckly hands.

It was just and right, thought Agatha unrolling her tale, that this comfortable, cotton-woolled sister should be made to understand for once what life was really like, and what it can force one to do. Evidently she hadn't an idea. Her comfort, both spiritual and physical, was complete.

She couldn't see Milly's face, who sat quite still and silent, her head against Agatha's hands, and very soon, at the memory of all she had gone through with and for Gaston, while everyone else was having an easy time— people like the Botts, and their friends, and relations and hangers-on, even people like the Botts' servants, pampered, and of course over-fed—very soon tears were flowing freely down her thin face.

It really seemed, she said, as if all that was needed for a successful and happy life, happy, that is, on the lower levels, was to be without a capacity for feeling. The moment one felt—fine things, beautiful things, the things, in fact that are immortal,—one became marked down by misfortune, dogged by it. She and Gaston had been dogged; she and Gaston, who cared so much for ideals, who felt so keenly. The most extraordinary things, which happened to no one else, happened to them—she would give a few examples—they seemed almost trivial against the great background of suffering and death, but they all had helped in the weaving of that background: clients, for instance, who had engaged the best rooms ahead, and obviously were indifferent to what they paid, either fell ill or had accidents at the last moment, and never came. One client died in the hotel at the beginning of a promising season, and because he did so immediately after dinner the others were afraid, and left in a body, creating an impression which was hard indeed to remove, and was not lived down for several seasons, that something was wrong with the water or the drains. Once there was a fire; confined, it is true, to two rooms only, but those two rooms were completely gutted, and as they were not insured, owing to lack of money for the premiums, the loss was serious. Misfortune of these kinds went on all the time. Pipes burst; the weight of the snow crushed in the roof; the hens contracted diseases from which other hens were free; the goats failed to breed, and continually perished; the potatoes were preyed upon by blight; great rains came at harvest time, and beat down the rye they had tended with such care; and when the feet of clients tore holes in the sheets, they declared it was the fault of the sheet. Then, finally, there was the war, and with that real hunger began. She herself had been so strong that she was able to bear what Gaston couldn't, and so had mercifully been in a position to do without food better than he, and to nurse him in his illness. She had, indeed, been able to bear everything, thanks to God who had endowed her with as strong a spirit as a body, except one thing—and that one thing was the jeers which would have been flung like mud against her loved husband, the triumphant jeers of that cruel Ern—— that cruel family, the Botts, had they known of her sufferings.

They should have helped her, said Agatha, drawing one hand out from under Milly's cheek to stem the flow of her tears, instead of jeering. Too much worldly prosperity, however, deadens people's souls. If Gaston had had a little capital, quite a little, if he had merely had an occasional temporary helping hand, he would frequently have been saved from his predicaments, none of which were of his own producing. At his death a little help would have spared her the bitterness of having to sell the hotel. As it was, it had been sold for a song, and she had had to accept the post of book-keeper in what had been her own house. Probably what the Botts spent on feeding unnecessary servants would have been ample to put Gaston on his feet and keep him on them.   He wouldn't have grown old and ill with work then; he would have been alive at that moment. She was not speaking of Ernest, for he was dead, but of the Botts as a family. Ernest had done what he no doubt thought was right in separating her from Milly, and she was not criticizing him, for he was dead; but his action had made an outcast of her, and had implied that her husband, than whom no one nobler had ever

trodden God's earth, was a scoundrel. Any woman with
a grain of pride, and she had many such grains she was
glad to say, would have done what she did and concealed the real state of affairs from Milly, who, though
she was her sister, and as such entitled to know the
truth, was also the loyal loving wife of the man who
was keeping them apart, and as such was in the enemy
camp. Not that she wished to speak of Ernest as an
enemy, for how could he be when he was dead? There
existed people, however, who thought of success only in
terms of money, and were incapable of comprehending
the successes of the spirit, which were all in terms of
love. Her marriage had been as successful and prosperous as Milly's, but on a plane which Ernest would never
have understood—the plane where there was nothing
but love.

This was in no sense a criticism, for how could she
criticize one who was dead? But she couldn't help re-
garding the whole of her bitter misfortunes, and the
wrong-doing she had undoubtedly been guilty of in
writing things to Milly which had not been really true,
(except in a spiritual sense, which would be difficult,
perhaps, to explain) as due to one cause only—the unjust, narrow, and cruel attitude towards her marriage
taken up by—well, by the Botts.

"But I am no longer concerned," she continued, laying the hand with which she had been wiping her eyes on
Milly's shoulder, but withdrawing it quickly because
the shoulder felt so very like a well-stuffed pillow, and
she was forced to ask herself once again whether acute
grief, the kind her own was, and the kind that every
woman's was who loses a loved husband, especially if
she loses him, as Milly had, suddenly and violently,
could ever be encased in such resilient plumpness, "I
am no longer concerned with other people's injustices.

I have passed beyond that, and am prepared to overlook the grievous harm this family has done me, and live—withdrawn from them, perhaps, as much as is polite, yet amiably, in their midst. I came here to help you, Milly—to help and comfort you, and I shall not allow the Botts to prevent my doing so. My duty and my love, now that the barrier separating us is no more, brought me to you instantly in your hour of——"

She was going to say, and wished to say, need; but was there any real need except her own? Alas, that cushiony shoulder, that sleek, smooth portion of cheek she could see, half hidden by hair without a sign of grey in it, on her lap! Emotion and hysteria there had been in plenty on the stairs, but since the lighting of the candle what evidence had she seen of need? A plump, smug, expensive-looking woman, who shrank away from her gaze and said foolish things entirely unsuited to the tragic, the solemn occasion—that is what she had seen and heard, and the fact that she was her sister mustn't blind her to the truth. So she substituted the word widowhood for need, this at least being accurate. "In your hour of widowhood," finished Agatha; and paused.

Milly, on the floor at her feet, said nothing. Her face, except that glimpse of hair and cheek, was hidden, and Agatha, sitting stiffly above her, wiping her eyes with her free hand, struggled within herself as to whether she should leave her motives for so quickly coming to England at the two she had mentioned, and continue to conceal that further motive, the baser, material one.

So she paused, struggling. Why did not Milly say something? Why did she sit there as if she were inhumanly asleep? She was not asleep, Agatha knew, for she could feel the movement of her eyelashes on the hand her cheek held imprisoned beneath it. Why, then, did she say nothing?

"Besides," went on Agatha, winning her struggle and bowing her head, for this bit of truth cost her a very great effort, "I am weary of poverty—weary, weary." Her voice sounded hollow, and incredibly tired.

"See how I confess my weaknesses to you," she said, after another pause. "I will withhold nothing. It is not, I believe and hope, that I am materially minded. I dislike and condemn luxury. All I ask is safety, security. I have a great longing"—she stopped to steady her voice, which she was ashamed to hear shaking—"for freedom from sordid care. I wish to be free from fear. Life is very difficult when one is afraid—afraid of the future, afraid of not being able to save enough to keep one's old age secure from cold and hunger. Under such circumstances it is indeed difficult to retain the freedom of one's spirit, for it becomes absorbed in the most wretched preoccupations. My salary as book-keeper was one hundred francs a month—less than fifty pounds a year in your English money. The new proprietor advanced me the fare of my journey to you. I told him you would repay it. How long should I have kept my post had I stayed there? Have I not told you I am old and broken? How long could I expect the proprietor to have patience and pity? Day and night the question of how long haunted me. Then this happened—this sad death of Ernest, and sad and terrible as it must be for you, if you loved him as I loved my dear husband, it has saved me. I will be absolutely truthful. Love did bring me here—great, great love for my sister in her sorrow, and also duty, the sacred duty of helping and comforting her. But I came, too, to a refuge, to a harbour. I came to what I know is the end, at last, of bitter and hopeless poverty."

There was a silence. Agatha had said her say. She had exposed herself quite naked for the first time in her life.

And Milly, who during the whole of her recital had sat without moving or speaking, presently said, very softly, almost as if she were talking to herself, "You know, this is so dreadful that I can hardly bear it."

"I beg your pardon?" said Agatha, supposing she hadn't heard aright; for that Milly should declare herself hardly able to bear the mere description of that which Agatha during twenty-five years had actually borne, seemed too much of flabbiness and selfishness to be credible.

"Such punishment," murmured Milly, again as if talking to herself.

"I beg your pardon?" Agatha said a second time, sitting up straighter and stiffer than ever. "You mean," she said, "that you regard what Gaston and I went through as punishment? Might I inquire what for? No—do not tell me," she instantly added, holding up her free hand. "I can guess your thoughts, and they are unworthy. How can you, my sister, after all these years bring up that one small, strictly temporary, and in the circumstances inevitable, divergence from rigid convention?"

But Milly didn't answer. She sat without moving. And Agatha felt something wet slowly trickling along her land.

⁂(VII)⁂

TEARS.

"Now what," thought Agatha, looking down at the silent figure, and feeling extraordinarily hardened because of that word punishment, "has Milly got to cry about? It was I who suffered, not she."

In fact, Milly's behaviour was entirely unaccountable. Tears—of sympathy with herself, apparently, that her tender ears should have to listen to such a tale—and then that heartless, unjust word.

But Agatha forgot the tears, forgot the word, when Milly, sitting up after a moment and drying her eyes, told her that Ernest had left her, Agatha, a thousand pounds in his Will.

"I beg your pardon?" said Agatha, staring.

Milly was sitting up now, with her back to her, dabbing at her face with a very much crushed handkerchief.

"Yes," she said, her voice muffled by the handkerchief. "I think—he wanted to make amends."

"A thousand *pounds?*" said Agatha. "You do not mean"—she leaned forward and touched Milly's shoulder—"you do not mean francs?"

"No—pounds," said Milly, busy with her handkerchief. "Will it help you at all, Aggie?"

"Help?"

Agatha drew in her breath.

"Help!" she said again.

Why, a thousand pounds was twenty-five thousand Swiss francs. She counted it up quickly. Why, if she

119

had had only half of that two months ago, she could have gone into partnership with the man who bought the hotel. He had offered to take her in if she could find twelve to fifteen thousand francs—out of courtesy, of course, well knowing she couldn't find such sums; but suppose she had been able to, and had said yes? To be independent, to share in a successful enterprise, to raise up on the very spot of Gaston's failure a monument to his memory, to make his hopes at last come true—compared to that, what could existence in Milly's house at Titford, eating the bread of idleness in an atmosphere thick with Botts, offer her?

A thousand pounds. Agatha sat awestruck. So much money in her whole life had not come her way. Ernest leaving her a thousand pounds, recognizing the wrong he had done her, magnificently making good. . . .

But it had come too late. The hotel was gone. She was pledged to the comforting of Milly. Fate even in its gifts—and this was the first she had ever had, except her youth, which was hardly a gift because it got taken away again, and her Gaston, who got taken away too —continued hostile. Still, how wonderful, how very wonderful, to have a thousand pounds. What a background, solid, golden to her life; what an alteration in her position; what a difference at once in her relations with the Botts.

"See," she could say, when they were rude to her or cold, "your own son, your own brother, recognized he had done me a grave injury, and set it publicly on record that he had in his Will——" and the family, confounded, would be forced to behave.

Very solemnly she raised her hands, as if in posthumous blessing. "I have misjudged Ernest," she said, overcome. "He was at heart a just man."

"Yes," said Milly.

"He repented," said Agatha, "and he made good."

"Yes," said Milly.

"This action of his will entirely rehabilitate me with the Botts," said Agatha.

"Yes," said Milly. "Except," she added after a slight pause, still busy with her handkerchief, "that there won't *be* any Botts."

"How, no Botts?" inquired Agatha.

"I've left them. I'm not going back."

"Left the Botts? Left Titford?" exclaimed Agatha. "Were you then—was it your idea, Milly, to come permanently to me in Switzerland?" And a vision suddenly flashed into her mind of herself and Milly going together now to her mountains, and Milly's money buying back the hotel—not merely a share in it but the whole thing—and a new life opening for them both, full of prosperity, and peace, and capital, and competence, she competently, and to the benefit of them both, manipulating Milly's capital.

"Milly," she said, laying her hand on her shoulder, and this time leaving it there, "was that your idea?"

And Milly said, after a little gulp, as if she were swallowing something difficult to get down, that it wasn't. "I was only going to take you the money, Aggie," she said in a choked voice. "And—and just see you again, because I did so long to see you again, and then—well, then—I was coming back."

"But coming back to what, now that you have left the Botts? No, no, my Milly"—Agatha pressed the shoulder—"no, no, my little sister. Your place is with me. Our futures lie together. Together we will go to those better, purer, simpler surroundings, far away from everything that has distressed you. Hand in hand we will begin afresh——"

"We can't," said Milly, shaking her head. "We can't

do anything hand in hand, Aggie. I've got no money.
Ernest didn't leave me anything. Except for your
thousand pounds, he left everything he had to charity."

§

Sitting listening in silence to Agatha's story, such
acute distress had twisted Milly's heart, such almost
physical pain, that it had been hardly possible to bear.
Be sure your sin will find you out—yes, she knew all about
that by now; but why should it find Aggie out as well,
who had done nothing but be good? Pressing her cold
hands together in her lap, she sent up little darts of
prayers—hardly prayers so much as agonized inquiries:
"What am I to do? How can I hurt her least? Isn't
it very wrong to punish her because of what *I* did?"

But prayers, she remembered, don't get answered;
hers didn't. And, leaving go of them, Milly, who had
made such recent vows to relinquish it for ever, fell back
once more into lying.

How avoid it? By lying, Agatha could be given the
thousand pounds and think it was hers. At least she
should have that. It was the one thing Milly could do for
her. If only it had been ten, twenty times as much!
Apart from this, however, she wouldn't lie. There should
be no lying about Arthur, though she was not any longer
sure Aggie was going to understand about Arthur. How
gladly, how very gladly would she have suppressed him
altogether. But she couldn't suppress somebody who
was likely now at any moment to become Agatha's
brother-in-law; for plain was it to Milly that, penniless,
she must marry Arthur, and as she must do so with what
in an ordinary widow would be indecent haste, nothing
but the truth could explain it. How difficult, though, it
was going to be. Icy doubts slid down her spine as to the
way Agatha might take it. Suppose she was horribly

scandalized? There was that about her appearance and behaviour which suggested rigidity of principle. Grown into rigidity she had—for the impassioned, vivid creature of Milly's youth had been like quicksilver.

Milly pressed her cold hands together. No wonder people didn't tell the truth very often, if only out of loving kindness, out of courtesy, out of a desire to avoid shocking and hurting. Or was it out of fear? Was she once again, as so lamentably often, just simply a coward?

That was it, she was afraid, for at the mere thought of explaining Arthur she found she was in a perspiration. She sighed, and put up her hand to hold Agatha's on her shoulder, because, on hearing of Ernest's gift to charity, it was making movements of withdrawal.

"Does that mean," Agatha was saying, in a voice both appalled and incredulous, "that you are poor, Milly? *You?*"

"Penniless," said Milly. And repeated, in a kind of astonishment at the word, "Yes,—penniless."

"You are left entirely without resources?" asked Agatha, her voice gone cold to match the cold flooding into her heart; for here was Fate, at it again, striking her down at the very moment when she was beginning to raise her head. Milly poor? She herself, by a turn of fortune's wheel, the one of the two with money, and the legacy perhaps having to do for them both? Ah, but impossible. Ernest could not have entirely—— And why should he? Why should he do anything so un-natural?

"It seems queer, doesn't it," said Milly, "after the way I've wallowed for years." And she added, gripping Agatha's hand very tight, "Didn't I tell you, Aggie, that you would have to be patient with me, and—and love me very much?"

"Naturally, Milly, I love you," said Agatha, trying

again to draw her hand away. "It would be strange
indeed if sisters did not love each other. But I know
from bitter experience that love is difficult where there
is real poverty."

"But you said you and Gaston——"

"I said, I said," interrupted Agatha with something
which sounded very like exasperation. "I tell you it is
difficult, and I fear my thousand pounds will hardly——"

She paused.

"Be enough for us to love on," Milly finished for her
softly.

"Be enough for us to *live* on," corrected Agatha.
"Surely it is plain that one must first be alive, in order
to love."

"No—one must first love, in order to be alive," corrected Milly in her turn. "Which is why"—she seized,
tremblingly, the opportunity—"which is why—which
is really what—in fact, just that is the explanation of
Arthur."

Arthur.

There was a silence. Agatha sat looking down at
the back of the sleek head, and the more than sleek
shoulders, leaning against her knees.

Arthur. Was not that the name Milly had said on
the stairs? Who and what was he? And why should he
keep on entering the conversation?

She fumbled in her memory. Perhaps he was one of
the innumerable Bott brothers-in-law. But if so, what
had he to do with the nonsense Milly had just said
about loving in order to be alive?

"Is that a Bott?" she asked.

"No," said Milly. "The exact opposite."

"The exact——?"

And Milly, leaping into the icy waters of truth, and
in her agitation letting go of all her grammar, said

with a gasp. "He's the man Ernest left his money to a charity because of." And while Agatha was endeavouring to unravel the meaning of this remark, she elucidated further, her voice suddenly quite clear and steady now that the moment had really come and there was no help for it, "He's the man I'm going to marry."

§

It was just on ten o'clock when Milly said this, but not till after two did Agatha leave her, and go down to her own room for what was left of the night.

"I have no more to say," were her last words, as in the dark, the candle having long burnt out, she went away.

And Milly, by this time half lying across her tumbled bed, her arms flung out, her face buried in the pillow, was too much exhausted to do anything but murmur, "I should think not——" which, fortunately, Agatha didn't hear.

"So that's the end of *that*," thought Milly dully, as the door shut behind her she had dreamed of as her sister. "One has to——" the words passed idly through her battered brain—"face facts. Yes, facts are—what one must face—no good pretending things aren't—what they are—simply silly—doing that——"

And slowly sitting up she began, her eyes shut, her head nodding, to drag off her clothes, for she couldn't spend a second night without undressing, and then, creeping under the ruffled blankets of the bed, she dropped like a stone into sleep.

On the floor below her Agatha neither slept nor undressed. To do so, to do these things of routine and a quiet mind, would have seemed to her a betrayal of every right feeling on the night of the discovery that she had been loving and believing in somebody whose life had been a treachery, and all her words lies. That she, of all women, should have a fallen sister, and one who was publicly branded as fallen by the terms of her husband's Will, struck Agatha, apart from its shame and horror, as fantastic. Never, she felt, would she forget the hours she had just passed through. Surely they were the worst of any of the many miserable ones Fate had plied her with? For in the others there had yet been dignity, there had yet been the hope that is at the root of defiance, and the pride of seeing how high one can keep one's head beneath blows. There was no dignity and no pride and nothing to defy in the wretched tale of sordid sinning the person who once was Milly had so cynically unfolded. Yes, cynically; for at one point she had dared compare her behaviour—years and years of adultery—with Agatha's behaviour; she had dared say, when she had listened for some time to Agatha's expressions of horror, words to the effect that after all she, Agatha, had done the same thing with Gaston.

"But he was my husband," Agatha indignantly had pointed out.

"Not to begin with," Milly had actually replied— once more throwing, once more having the effrontery to throw, in her face that brief and unexpectedly inevitable departure from convention which had preceded the sacred marriage of a lifetime. And when Agatha, almost speechless but trying to be patient, pointed out that no one ever is a husband to begin with, Milly, with incredible and indecent flippancy, replied, "Oh—do you really think as badly of women as that?"

What was one to say to such a speech? Poor, unhappy Ernest. Good, wronged man. His patience had been a marvel. His conduct in saying no word, in continuing to extend the protection of his roof and name to the woman he knew was betraying him, was that of a saint. And even this patience, this conduct, Milly, until Agatha sternly silenced her, had been inclined to criticize. The fallen woman criticizing the upright man. What next? Agatha asked herself, at whose feet a pit of unimagined wickedness yawned.

On her mountains such sinning was simply unknown. Like the deciduous trees, it did not flourish above five thousand feet. No one committed adultery up there. There was no one, thank God, to commit it with. A few scattered husbands dwelt there, practically snow-bound, each with his lean, hard-working wife, their one concern the business of keeping alive. They did not even drink where she lived, though down in the valley among the vineyards drunkenness, she knew, was prevalent. Down in the valley, among the vineyards, drunkenness; and down in the cities, among the idle and overfed, adultery. Prevalent. It must be. For actually in her own tiny family of two, one of the two had committed it.

Ah, she would take the money Ernest had left her, and shake the dust of these dreadful places for ever from her feet. Back she would go to purity, and leave Milly to her second, her disgraceful, husband. Marry the man she must, of course, for there was no other way of expiating what she had done; but it did seem terrible that God's holy ordinance should be used as a kind of cloth to mop up sin.

From this, however, there seemed no escape. In no other way could the two atone for their sin. Merciful indeed, and yet another proof of poor Ernest's foresight and care, that Milly should be without means, for if she had had any, Agatha believed from several things she had let fall, she would not have married the man, and then no atonement could have taken place. But suppose Milly, having married him, were to be happy?

What would then become of atonement? Agatha
could only shake her head at the topsy-turviness of
life.

She sat at the window, looking out at the stars
twinkling through the branches of the trees in the
square, and tried to hope in all things for the best. One
must cling to one's ideals; never, however hard circumstances pulled at one, must one let them go. And then
she remembered that it was at this very window—in the
old days it was Milly's room—they used to sit together
when they were young, before going to bed, and build
bright castles in the air. How sad life was. How differently it turned out from what, young, one expected.
In those days they were sure it was going to be magnificent. There wasn't anything fine and noble they weren't
going to achieve. And one night Milly—she could see
the small figure in its nightgown now—had flung up
her arms towards the light-strewn sky, and cried that
she was going to reach right up to heaven before she
had done, and catch hold of the very stars.

Alas. Just was her punishment; fitting that it should
fall upon her. But—alas, poor Milly. And alas, too, to
compare the thoughts with which she, Agatha, had
travelled over from Switzerland to the thoughts with
which she would travel back again. And most alas of
all—yes, tragically alas—to know that she would never
now see Milly, the Milly she had supposed existed, again.
Finished, that was; and an immense, the longest, chapter of both their lives closed. Henceforth she would be
completely alone. The person Milly had developed into
was going with her to the solicitor in the morning to
fetch the legacy, and it would be their last walk together. After that they would go their several ways;
they would say good-bye, and it would be for ever.

She stared at the stars, sitting without moving. The affection of a lifetime, the belief of a lifetime. . . .

The stars became a little blurred.

Perhaps, as there was no question of sleep for either of them, they should spend the few remaining hours together, even if they said nothing, but just sat near to each other. The person Milly had developed into still had good in her. She had been quite ungrudging about the legacy, evidently glad that Agatha should have it. Yes; there was good in her still. Agatha, softened, thought she would go up to her once more, and say, "Milly, this is in all probability our last night on earth together—" and if Milly were again to say, as she had certainly said several times during the recital of her terrible tale, only Agatha, in her surprise and horror, had waved it sternly aside, that she was sorry for what she had done, Agatha thought she would perhaps kiss her. Yes; she would kiss her. Poor, sinful Milly, lying tossing in the room above—she should have one last kiss from her sister, before they parted and saw each other no more.

And lighting the candle, and holding it high above her head, she did go up to Milly's room, opening the door softly so as not to rouse anyone in the house, and crossing over to the bed began, "Milly——"

But there lay Milly, deaf and indifferent to tenderness, deeply, and comfortably, and cynically asleep.

§

Hopeless; quite hopeless she was, thought Agatha, sternly descending to her room again, her softened heart once more frozen hard. Imagine sleeping soundly immediately after a scene so painful, so terrible that it made her sister feel as if she would never be able to close her eyes again! And Agatha, blowing out the candle and stiffly resuming her vigil at the window, felt full of that curious itch of exasperation which follows a thwarted benevolent impulse. She had gone upstairs ready to bestow valedictory love, and it had not been required. She had gone actually prepared to suggest, though not expecting it would be possible for the suggestion to be accepted, that Milly should try to get a little sleep; and there she was, getting a great deal. Hopeless, hopeless,— or, rather, the person she had developed into was hopeless.

Agatha thought her even more hopeless when next morning, having duly bathed her burning eyes in cold water, she came down to breakfast—she had no desire for food, but knew she would have to pay for breakfast, eaten or not—and was met by the manageress with a message from Milly that she had gone out, and wouldn't be back, probably, till twelve o'clock.

What can be done, Agatha, staring outraged at the manageress, asked herself, with such wriggling duplicity? What can be done with a person who says she will accompany you immediately after breakfast on a most important mission, and then slinks away, entirely unaccountably, before that meal, merely leaving word she will not be back till noon? Noon? Half the day gone, the important busy day on which Agatha was to receive her legacy and depart with it for Switzerland; for go back to Switzerland she certainly would, and by the very first train, once she had got her money. Milly did not know in so many words that she was going that day, but surely she would take it for granted that she would get away by the first possible train from the place where she had lost her beliefs, and become acquainted with shame? The first possible train, since the morning trains would be missed while she was at the solicitor's,

would be the two P. M. *via* Laon and Berne. She needed
no time-table. She knew all the trains by heart, having
learned them in those days when there were still people
in England wishing to come and stay in Gaston's hotel,
and who had to be met at the station in the valley by
mules. She had never forgotten them. Life changed,
but trains went on. At nine, at eleven, at two, and at
four, people weary of London and its dirt and sins left
it, and twenty-four hours later stepped out into the clear,
cool calm which was Switzerland. The two o'clock was
the train she had decided in the watches of the night
she would go by, leaving the morning free for the visit to
the solicitor. Now, owing to Milly's inexplicable conduct,
the two o'clock would be missed. Perhaps even the four
o'clock would be missed. Really such behaviour. . . .

Her great eyes, weary from want of sleep, blazed at
the manageress.

"Well, that's what she *said*," said the manageress
petulantly, turning away into the dining-room, where
her one other lodger was waiting to be fed. "*I* can't help
it, can I, Mrs. Le Bon?—Le Bone if you ask *me*," she
added to herself, measuring out Agatha's portion of
porridge with swift practised movements—"figure and
nature and all."

And as she dabbed the plate down in front of the
chair placed ready for her gaunt guest, she thought that
the sooner she took her figure and her nature somewhere
else the better pleased she would be. Except that she
would take her sister with her. That was the snag of
her going. After all the sob-stuff on the stairs the night
before it wasn't likely, she was afraid, that they would
separate; and the manageress not only approved of
Milly, her face, her clothes, her soft voice, and the
gentle manner which made her so easy, she was sure, to
do what one liked with, but locked up at that moment

in the bureau of her private room was Milly's handbag, with four one-pound notes in it, given to her to take care of on her leaving the house an hour before.

The manageress liked being given handbags with pound notes in them to be taken care of. It made her feel safe, and relaxed the necessity of having to watch the front door. How such a real lady as Mrs. Bott came to have a sister like this Le Bone she couldn't imagine. And she decided, her decisions being always rapid and frequently rash, that Le Bone must be a bastard.

"That's it," she thought, a bright and hostile eye on Agatha, who was putting more sugar on her porridge than was either necessary or lady-like. "Not much holy wedlock about *her*."

§

Meanwhile Milly was wandering about London.

It seemed an odd thing to be doing on a day which was going to be too short for all there was to settle in it, but it was forced upon her by circumstances. Agatha, who of course didn't know the solicitor's name and address, had instructed her the night before, in an interval between one set of horrified reproaches and the next, that she was to show her the way to his office directly after breakfast. Obviously, then, Milly had to be well away before breakfast; obviously she must be out of the house before Agatha could join her. For if she joined her and came too, she would find out that the legacy was but another lie, and suffer a very cruel shock and disappointment.

Agatha had had enough shocks and disappointments in the last twelve hours, thought Milly, shaking her head. She needed that thousand pounds far more than Milly needed it, who had Arthur; in fact her need was desperate. And she might refuse to take it because of her principles—though perhaps, on the other hand, she mightn't, reflected Milly, clear-sighted now, and without illusions. So she crept with peculiar caution past Agatha's shut door, and thought that it would be nice when the need for all this creeping was over. She seemed to have been doing it now for so long that it was surprising to remember it had only begun about twenty-four hours before. Anyhow it was a miserable way of getting about, she said to herself, and she would be glad when she could bang a door again.

Fortunately breakfast wasn't till nine o'clock at the *Home from Home*, the manageress having long discovered that ladies in bed were less trouble than ladies vigorously roaming about the house, so that Milly had plenty of time before Agatha would start on her hotwater can; and the front door being open, for it was once more the hour of airing, she was proceeding to slip through it—nice when the necessity for all this slipping was over—when the manageress, seeming to surge up from nowhere, waylaid her.

"Why—Mrs. *Bott!*" she exclaimed, much as she had exclaimed the morning before, on catching her doing the same thing.

But this time Milly was equal to her. "Sh-sh," she whispered, pausing a moment and glancing up the stairs. "We mustn't disturb the others——"

And before the manageress could say anything, and she had much to say, for the disturbing or non-disturbing of the others was exclusively her own affair, Milly opened her bag, took out some loose silver, showed her there were four one-pound notes still in it, thrust it into her hands, begged her to take care of it till she got back, asked her to tell her sister she mightn't be in till twelve, and was down the steps and round the corner into the next square like, the manageress said to herself, amazed

by these rapid and purposeful movements in one who
the day before had seemed such a mass of inertness, a
streak of ink.

Once round the corner she walked more slowly. There
was no hurry. The solicitor wouldn't be at his office
before ten at the earliest, and it was then only half-
past eight. Her mind was very clear, and she idled along,
arranging her plans, in a kind of dead calm after the
deep sleep that separated her from yesterday. That
sleep seemed to have washed her clear of illusions and
sentimentality about Agatha. It was as though she had
been plunged, drunk, into icy water, and come up sober.
She knew exactly what she was going to do—all the
small details of the next two hours, the sending of a
telegram to Arthur, who must have got back to Oxford
from his holiday the evening before, for he had said he
would and he was a man who kept his word, then breakfast at an A. B. C. shop which used to be near the
British Museum and probably still was, then a walk
down to the Embankment, where she could sit and
watch the river till ten o'clock, which was the earliest
moment, she judged, familiar with the habits of business men, she could expect to find the solicitor at his
office.

These were the things she would do next. After them,
there would be the handing over of the money to
Agatha, the seeing of her off, for she would be sure to
want to leave by the very first train—no, she wouldn't
see her off, because it was Victoria she would have to
start from, and that was the station for Titford, and she
might meet Botts—the saying good-bye to her, then, at
the boarding-house, and after that an omnibus to Chelsea, and the meeting with Arthur at his flat.

Those were the next things.

And after them—well, the best thing to do, and certainly the cheapest, would be to stay in the flat till she was married, Arthur—for there should be no more sinning till they were married—going back to Oxford as usual. And when the woman who occasionally cleaned came in and found her there, she would explain, and say: "Mr. Oswestry has lent me his rooms. We are going to be married." And the woman, who of course would be surprised by her widow's mourning, so fresh, so evidently only just begun to be worn, would probably say, her mouth opening, "Married?" And Milly would say composedly, "Yes—married."

She walked very slowly through the sunlit squares, killing time, detached and observant, noticing the roofs of the houses glittering against the blue sky, and the rush of a flight of pigeons, their wings glittering too, and the light on a girl's hair as she scrubbed a door-step, and the whistling of a boy with a milk-cart, and the smell of the coffee and bacon all Bloomsbury, apparently, was going to have for its breakfast, and the whole untiring zest with which the world each morning lays hold of its new day. Life had strangely straightened itself out. Aggie had disappeared, and Agatha had taken her place. Arthur as a sin had disappeared, and Arthur as a husband was going to take his place. Just as well, she said to herself, thinking of Agatha with acquiescence; nothing like seeing things as they are. And, considering Agatha, she saw that the lies one tells oneself are even more numerous than those one tells other people. One lives and fattens on the lies one tells oneself. For years she had been nourished by the lies she told herself about Agatha. And was it Agatha's fault? Foolish, surely, to blame her. How could she help what she, Milly, was determined to believe about her? It came to this, thought Milly, that what one wanted beyond everything else in the world was love, and one would do anything to get it, and if it wasn't there one invented it. The least little word, the smallest encouragement, set one off inventing love. Agatha being of the same blood had started it; and what could be more silly than to suppose that love had anything to do with blood? On the contrary—what naturally proceeded from the same blood wasn't love, but claims to it; which, she thought, avoiding a banana skin as she crossed the square to go to a post-office she had caught sight of down a side street, was nothing but upsetting.

Upsetting. A mild word. But she felt so mild—cleared out, empty of feeling, numb. Mere eyes she seemed to be this bright morning, quiet eyes looking straight and recognizing. And among other things she recognized was that however much she had believed she would be turning her back on her sin by going to Agatha in Switzerland and leading a new life, the plain fact was that expiation lay in marrying Arthur. Agatha had been quite right about that, though she needn't have said it in such terrible words. After all, it was what decent people in her and Arthur's position invariably did; it was certainly what he would want to do; and though being turned into an instrument of expiation struck her as an unexpected end for Arthur, who had started off so flamingly as a wonder and a secret joy, yet it was an end that had the restfulness of the finish of a struggle, of a correct solution, and also the great comfort, the real solid comfort, of propriety.

Love must either begin or end in propriety if there is to be any peace, thought Milly, pushing open the door of the post-office. It must, that is, either begin or end in a husband. Happy are those women, she thought, searching for a pen or pencil that would write, happy and blest are those women who start with both. Theirs, surely, is the kingdom of heaven. If she and Arthur had been able to marry when they first loved, it would indeed have been wonderful. Now, having loved, they were able to. *Having* loved. . . .

Well anyhow, she said to herself, borrowing a pencil from the young lady behind the wire-netting, who had never been known to lend a pencil before, but whose rocky heart melted at the sight of Milly's pale face in its shroud of crape, it was the right thing to do, and only in doing the right thing lay peace. Peace was what one wanted after a certain age. Hers was the certain age. She would seek peace and ensue it. Besides, married to Arthur he could tell her at once, instead of having to wait till they met, about his colds.

She smiled faintly as she wrote her telegram. Was that cynical about the colds? She didn't feel cynical; she only felt empty, and as if nothing was really much worth bothering about—gone numb, perhaps, from the reproaches Agatha had piled on her in the night. Wicked as she knew she had been, she hadn't really known how wicked until Agatha, as it were, took the matter up, thought Milly, faintly smiling again at the phrase, so inadequate to the situation. According to Agatha, she was past praying for. Being past praying for, however, seemed to have its points—it did bring relief with it, it did clear the atmosphere. Look how clear and calm the atmosphere now seemed. Also it was comfortable; one gave up, one let go, one rested. Rest was comfortable, and the atmosphere she was now in was certainly restful, for she was delivered from the convulsions and confusions of doubts, and knew that she had to marry Arthur. Another curious and unexpected end for Arthur: he had become the alternative to starvation.

So she wrote her telegram, asking him to meet her at the Chelsea flat that afternoon at three, instead of the afternoon in the next week, which was the one they had arranged to meet on before he left England; and after a moment's thought she added the word *Urgent*, though much disliking using such a flurrying word to Arthur. But then supposing he didn't come? He would be busy, she knew, resettling himself in his rooms after his four weeks' absence, and wouldn't see, unless she put in something like that, why the plan they made last time they met—they never wrote letters—couldn't be kept to. It was to the last degree unlikely that he should have heard of Ernest's death. He didn't read newspapers on his holidays. Besides, if by some chance he did know, he would at once have written to her, the necessity for not writing, which was Ernest, having been removed.

No; he didn't know. But he would when he opened the door, and saw her in her widow's dress. And in answer to his astonished eyes she would nod; and he would then draw her inside, and fold her in his arms, and be so kind and sympathetic, because he knew that death, even when it didn't mean loss, was a tremendous thing, and that no one could be near it without being brushed by tragedy; and then presently he would say, "Well, now we must be married"; and then, habit being strong, and he accustomed to tell her everything, he would talk about his holiday and all he had seen, as they sat on the divan side by side, her head on his shoulder, his arm round her, and how easily and often one caught colds travelling abroad.

And wasn't that a good thing? Wasn't it really right and sane to pass on to something else, to the next thing, and not linger stirring the same emotions round and round? Women, thought Milly leaving the post-office and going in search of breakfast, like to emphasize and perpetuate a situation. They like to put it into capital

letters, envelop it in exclamation marks, and keep it
for ever just where it originally was. It is fortunate for
them that men don't and won't, or life would become an
unending series of violent explosions on the same spot.
After all, one has to get on with one's living—or is it
one's dying? The sore throat of to-day is of more interest
than the passion of ten years back. What one is doing
is important, not what one has done. And—"Aren't
I thinking platitudes!" she said to herself; and concluded that that was probably what one did, when one's
whole emotional content could be expressed by a shrug
of the shoulder.

The A. B. C. shop was still where it used to be, and
still with apparently the same cakes in the window. In
it she breakfasted, taking as long over it as possible, and
the waitress was assiduous and kind. So assiduous and
kind was she that Milly, looking up into her pleasant
young face as she hovered above her, was moved at last
to say gratefully, talking simply out of a heart entirely
simple and empty, "I think people are so wonderful to
each other when they are strangers, and don't know
what they are really like."

But there was no response from the girl; she only
stared at her, her pleasant face gone stupid with alarmed
surprise.

"That wasn't very clever of me," thought Milly,
picking up the bill and giving the girl half of what it
came to. "I suppose one doesn't talk to strangers about
anything except the weather, though they are really the
only people in the world one could talk to with complete
truthfulness."

And she smiled at the waitress as she went away, who
pretended, much embarrassed, to be wiping coffee which
hadn't been spilt off the marble top of the table.

She walked to the Strand, and down to the Embankment, and sat down on a seat near Cleopatra's Needle to wait till it should be time to go to the solicitor.

He was a Mr. Jenkyns, of the firm of Jenkyns and Rowe, whose office was somewhere near there in a street called Essex Street. She knew the address well, having often seen it on letters Ernest had written, and Jenkyns and Rowe were names familiar to her on his lips ever since her marriage. At the wedding Rowe was present, and at the funeral Jenkyns. Rowe had died some years before, and the firm had become only Jenkyns, though still calling itself Jenkyns and Rowe. Rowe she remembered as a kindly, smiling man, but perhaps that was because he was at a wedding. Jenkyns she had never seen. She was sure he would be hostile, and twenty-four hours earlier she would have shrunk from having to face him. Now she didn't care. It was a thing that had to be done, and what did it matter what Jenkyns thought of her? Whatever he thought it couldn't possibly be as bad as what Agatha, her sister, the person who said she loved her, thought. As one of many and much more unpleasant things it sank into insignificance. At least, then, she reflected, watching the shining gulls, there is some advantage in having lots of misfortunes.

And a man, passing at the moment between her and the gulls, paused to look at his watch and blotted them out, and Milly, her eyes necessarily on this obstruction, gazed at it unaware that here, actually, was Jenkyns.

§

It was Mr. Jenkyns's practice, on sanitary grounds, and not because he liked it, to walk every morning to his office in Essex Street from his house in Kensington, and in the evening to walk back again. The result was that he arrived at each end a little cross, for it is a long way,

and the pavements are hard. But he persisted, and was
of opinion that it was owing to this practice that he kept
young. He said so to his wife when, disappointed by
their evenings, she suggested his taking a taxi at least
one way, and on her asking with real surprise, "But
have you?" he, being offended, was silent.

His daily walk led him along the Embankment, and
when he got to Cleopatra's Needle he would take out
his watch to see if he were late, in which case he would
hurry, or early, in which case he would linger, because
he as much disliked the unpunctuality which arrives too
soon as the unpunctuality which doesn't arrive soon
enough.

On the morning Milly was on the Embankment he
found he had two minutes and a half in hand; and feeling for some reason, probably the sudden descent on
England of Spring, a little more tired than usual, he
thought he would sit down. He would not have sat
down if the person he saw on the seat had suggested, as
so many persons on seats do suggest, insects, but the
well-dressed widow in brand-new black, looking like
somebody's ideal client, which she no doubt was, for
widows need solicitors almost as much as solicitors need
widows, inspired him with confidence that near her all
would be clean; so, slightly raising his hat and preparing
to sit, he said politely, "You allow me?" and Milly,
equally politely, replying, "Do," they sat side by side,
and together silently watched the gulls.

It seemed to make a bond between them, watching
the same gulls. At least Mr. Jenkyns felt it did, whose
daily exercise had anyhow kept him young enough to
know an attractive little woman when he saw one. This
was an attractive little woman. And he thought,
glancing down at her heavily craped knees, "Poor
thing." And he added, glancing sideways at her pale

profile with its delicate nose and long dark eyelashes, "Poor young thing." Not a girl, of course—which was fortunate, for Mr. Jenkyns didn't get on with girls—and plumped out, perhaps, rather more than was necessary; yet quite sufficiently young to be arresting and pathetic as so very recent a widow. Thirty, Mr. Jenkyns decided, who used to be thirty himself, and knew that it was one of the pleasantest of one's many ages; and, clearing his throat, he asked her with the equivalent in a lawyer of that which in a doctor is a good bedside manner, with, that is, sympathetic yet controlled *empressement* combined with a suggestion of limitless reserves of discretion, whether she didn't think it a fine morning.

Milly said abstractedly that she thought it a very fine morning; and then looking at him, and perceiving him respectable, with his gloves and attaché case and all, she asked if it were far to Essex Street.

"Essex Street? I'm going there," said Mr. Jenkyns, struck by this coincidence.

"Is it far?" repeated Milly, for this didn't seem an answer to her question.

"That," said Mr. Jenkyns with the prudence of his profession, "would depend on the pace at which one walks to it. It may be done, and has been done, in ten minutes, but I would not advise it. Personally I allow eleven. A lady, perhaps, might require, say, twelve."

"I want to be there at ten o'clock," said Milly.

"Indeed," said Mr. Jenkyns, struck by this second coincidence. And added after a slight pause, during which he considered the claims of caution and decided that in this case it had none, "So do I."

He took out his watch and stared at it, frowning.

"It is now," he said, "twelve minutes—no, pardon me—twelve and a half to the hour. From here, as I said,

it takes eleven minutes. But a lady would need twelve.
If you will allow me," he continued, "I will show you
the way."

"It would be very kind," said Milly.

He got up. So did she. And they proceeded together
along the Embankment.

Pleasantly conversing, taking pains to please, pointing out objects of interest—"That," he said, "is the
dome of St. Paul's,"—Mr. Jenkyns suited his pace to
hers. He would be a few minutes late that morning, he
realized, but it was of no consequence. It kept one young,
this sort of thing, this walking with and talking to a
strange lady. For a long while now he had wished that
he might have some sort of little adventure, just as an
assurance that he was not yet old. Almost anything
would do which fulfilled the requirements of caution.
The lady—naturally there would be a lady—must be
beyond reproach morally and socially, for he had a profound aversion from anything approaching shady, and
also she must be attractive. His profession had brought
him into sad contacts, and taught him that the combination is rare. Along the paths of adventure it would be
almost impossible to find. Indeed, he found it difficult
to imagine the form a respectable adventure could
possibly take. And here he had found it, on a seat on the
Embankment.

Gratified, and faintly excited, he walked beside Milly,
chatting and feeling ten, no, twenty years younger, for
he had got to the age when being ten years younger
wouldn't have done him any good at all. He asked so
little. At his age it was no use, he knew, asking much,
and as a family lawyer of the highest standing it was
risky asking anything at all. But this lady, should anyone see him with her, could only do him credit as a
companion, and no one would ever guess that he didn't

even know her name. Indeed he asked very little. He only wanted some nice and pretty woman, who wasn't married to him, to show interest in him, to be aware that he was a man, to listen, to smile. This one listened and smiled very sweetly, occasionally looking up at him when she answered with particularly good and charming deep blue eyes—eyes still liquid, Mr. Jenkyns, observing them sympathetically, opined, with the tears of bereavement.

"You will pardon me," he said, while they were waiting to cross the road, "for speaking of it, but I fear from your dress you are—that you have—no, not yet," he broke off quickly, catching her by the arm as she was about to step off the kerb into what would have been certain death. His wife did that sort of thing, and it exasperated him. It didn't exasperate him in Milly, for she wasn't a wife but an adventure. Also it gave him the opportunity, having saved her, of holding her by the arm, and presently piloting her across into the security of the other side.

"May a stranger," he resumed, his hand still on her elbow in case she started off again, "offer you his condolences?"

"Thank you," murmured Milly, bowing her head.

"A dove," thought Mr. Jenkyns. "A dove." And he let go her arm, when holding it was no longer necessary, with reluctance.

What then was his surprise and dismay to discover, on approaching his office and inquiring of Milly which number in Essex Street she wished to go to, that she wished to go to his number and that she was none other than the disgraced and disgraceful Mrs. Ernest Bott. In answer to his sudden question, light having flashed like an extremely unpleasant sword through his brain, she said she was. Of course. Fool that he had been to be taken in. When she asked, this new-made widow, if it were far to Essex Street, he ought to have guessed at once who she was. Why, he actually had been expecting her. Mr. Herbert Bott had been in to see him the previous day in a state of much anxiety, inquiring if he had seen her or if she had communicated with him, and saying that she would be sure to call soon because she had no money; and he had asked him to hand her over a thousand pounds, the amount to which her legacy entitled her, when she did call. He had arrived with the notes all ready in his pocket-book, and said he wished her to have them at once, and that she would repay him when the necessary formalities for the release of her legacy had been fulfilled, and that meanwhile she must not be allowed to starve.

Mr. Jenkyns considered, and felt it his duty to suggest, that the thousand pounds would probably never be repaid, but his suggestion had been repudiated with heat.

Mr. Herbert Bott had then asked, as a personal favour, that the loan should not be mentioned to the lady as a loan, but that she should be allowed to suppose it was her legacy. He would tell her himself later, he said; and, as he joined to this request a further request that no reference to his visit should be made to his brothers should they call, Mr. Jenkyns was left with the strong impression that here, if this poor client Ernest Bott had chosen to bring a divorce suit, was the co-respondent.

Ernest Bott, then, had been more magnanimous even than his friend and solicitor had imagined. Declaring, "I don't know the man's name and don't want to," he had been shielding his own brother. Natural indeed was it that a man thus wronged should have been unable altogether to resist some slight revenge, and the codicil,

in Mr. Jenkyns's eyes, had been the very mildest form of
it which a betrayed husband could well take.

He therefore looked at Milly, who had but so recently
been charming to him, with real aversion. How profoundly he detested these women who prey and betray.
No man was safe from them. They come along with their
long eyelashes and little round busts, he thought, eyeing
her with deep dislike, and before a man knows where he
is he has been flayed of his honour and his happiness.

"A wolf in widow's clothing," he sternly said to
himself, looking at her with eyes gone steely.

"I suppose you are Mr. Jenkyns," faltered Milly,
aware of the instant and humiliating change in his
manner.

The finger of scorn—that was what she was up against
for the first time in her life; and she didn't like it. Thus,
then, did good men look at bad women; men, that is,
who felt they were good, at women they were sure were
bad. Now she knew. In spite of her humiliation she was
interested, the rôle of bad woman being so new to her.
Was this the sort of thing she must expect? But after
all, she had been prepared for hostility from Jenkyns.
Why did she mind it so much? Perhaps because he had
been so very pleasant and kind a few moments before,
and so manifestly admiring. She felt whipped.

Icily polite, freezingly stately, the long, lean Mr.
Jenkyns held the swing door of the building his office
was in open for her, and followed her up the worn stone
stairs. Leading her straight into his room, through the
room his confidential clerk sat typing in, he said, indi-
cating a chair, "You have come for your legacy?" and
without further speech unlocked his safe, and took out
the envelope Bertie Bott had left with him the day before.

"I think you will find these correct," he said, handing

them to her and not looking at her. "Perhaps you will
be so good as to count them."

And while she counted them with fumbling fingers,
for she wanted to cry—absurd, absurd to want to cry
because of Jenkyns, she angrily told herself—her head
bent over the notes, her veil fortunately falling over
her face, Mr. Jenkyns, sitting at his table, took up the
telephone and engaged in a long and technical conversation with somebody, just as if she had ceased to exist.

So she had, except unpleasantly, for him. Added to
his temperamental dislike of such women, was the
annoyance of having been attracted and taken in. Also
there was an unaccountable feeling of frustration, as if
his drink had been snatched from him. True the drink
had not been anything more heady than, say, a cup of
tea, but such refreshment as can be got out of a cup of
tea had been rudely dashed from his expectant lips.

When she had finished counting, Milly sat quiet. She
couldn't very well get up and go while he was still telephoning, nor could she interrupt him to say that the
notes were correct; and she sat feeling every instant
more like some evil and castigated kitchenmaid. Mr.
Jenkyns had much to discuss with the person at the
other end of the telephone, and did so leisurely and at
length. When at last he hung up the receiver, after an
urbane leave-taking which seemed to Milly to last at
least another five minutes, he pressed a button on his
table, and, as she was opening her mouth to speak, the
clerk she had seen typing in the other room swiftly and
silently appeared.

She shut her mouth again, and waited. "I don't
care," she thought, trying to give herself courage.
"What do I care for Jenkyns?"

But she did care.

"Write out a receipt for one thousand pounds," said

Mr. Jenkyns to the clerk, who went swiftly and silently away to do it.

"This," he said to Milly, but not looking at her, and sitting quite still, his elbows on the arms of his revolving chair, his finger-tips joined, and his eyes looking down his nose, "is highly irregular."

"What is?" she asked, her voice a little uncertain, for she was afraid he was going to say something personal and dreadful.

"Handing over this money to you."

"Why?" she asked, recovering her breath.

"Because I have no proofs of your identity."

"Oh," said Milly, considering this. Neither, if it came to that, had she. She had been told she was Milly, and had early accepted it, but how could one prove it?

"You mean—" she hesitated—"you can't be sure I'm Mrs. Bott."

"Mrs. *Ernest* Bott," he amended severely.

"Mrs. *Ernest* Bott," repeated Milly; and reflected.

The result of her reflections was that after a minute she said, "Well, I am."

Mr. Jenkyns was silent. He sat motionless, gazing down his nose.

Then, remembering that her name and Ernest's were engraved inside her wedding ring, Milly hastily pulled off, or rather wrenched off, her left glove, which was tight and resisted.

"Look," she said, offering the ring to him across the table. "There's my name engraved inside it, and Ernnest's, and the date of our marriage."

Mr. Jenkyns didn't look; he merely made a gesture of aversion.

"Quite; quite. No doubt; no doubt," he said, much shocked by the tactlessness which could adduce the very symbol of the vows she had broken in evidence

that she was indeed his poor client's wife, the very ring
which had been placed, full of trust and affection, on the
hand that was to betray him. "In a court of law, however, that would be no proof at all."

"But we're not in a court of law," said Milly.

Mr. Jenkyns's mouth seemed to become even thinner
and smaller. That was the way his wife reasoned. They
were all alike in brains, if, fortunately, differing in
morals.

The swift and silent clerk reappeared, laid the receipt
on the table, and vanished.

"Please sign here," said Mr. Jenkyns, dipping a pen
into ink and handing it to her.

He held it with severe patience while she pulled off
her right glove. The glove was tight and resisted. It
was tighter, and resisted more, than the left-hand one.
New, and of kid, they were a size too small, but had been
ordered by the family along with the rest of the mourning, and the family, seeing her small, had supposed her
hands matched the rest of her. So they did, but they
were plump as well as small, and the plumpness that is
comfortable in six and a half goes with difficulty into
six and a quarter; also it comes out again with difficulty.

Milly's plumpness wouldn't come out. Mr. Jenkyns,
pen extended, his eyes carefully averted, was patient.
Milly, struggling, was hot. The glove stuck. Stupid
glove—oh, stupid, stupid *fool* glove, she thought, agitated. And while she tugged, flushed and nervous, the
notes on her lap fell off on the carpet, and Mr. Jenkyns,
forced by convention, was afraid he would have to pick
them up.

He found he couldn't bring himself to. No; he couldn't
stoop and grovel on the floor at such a woman's feet. So
he rang for the clerk.

"Oh, thank you," said Milly, confused and warm, and

trying to get her glove off and take the notes from the clerk at the same moment. She smiled a little from habit as she looked up at him and said thank you, and her smile was kind and sweet.

How good she looked. Mr. Jenkyns disliked her more than ever. That she should look good when she wasn't was an outrage.

"A serpent," he said to himself, his mouth very tight and thin. "A serpent masquerading as a dove."

*⁂(*VIII*)⁂*

SHE was back in Bloomsbury before eleven, the thousand pounds, in nine notes of a hundred each and twenty of five, for Bertie Bott had thought of everything and knew she would need small notes to go on with, in an envelope inside the front of her dress. Mr. Jenkyns had not detained her. He watched her stuffing the notes into what he reluctantly thought of as her bosom, with sternness. He made no inquiry as to her address, for in his opinion it was much better that nobody should know it. Let her disappear. Let the family be quit of her. Mr. Herbert Bott had asked him to telephone to him at his office directly she called, alleging it was important that he should get into touch with her; but Mr. Jenkyns had no intention of doing any such thing. Why should he? It was not his way, and never had been, to encourage co-respondents. Get into touch with her! No doubt. An appropriate phrase. But that he should ask him to help him to do so seemed to Mr. Jenkyns rather as if he took him for a fool. And when Bertie rang up just before lunch, and inquired, his voice as anxious as ever, whether his sister-in-law had made any signs, he received the brief reply that she had been and gone; and when he prefaced whatever he was going to say next with a voilent explosion, which sounded at first like a fit of coughing, but which resolved itself into oaths, Mr. Jenkyns sedately hung up the receiver.

Milly walked back to the boarding-house turning her thoughts away from Mr. Jenkyns. He was, as an incident in her life, over, and it was foolish to mind him. Considering how many other things she had to mind, it seemed to her rather odd how much he rankled. But no man had ever been rude to her before, except of course Ernest, and her skin tingled as if she had been slapped. What could be more rude than the sudden change from urbanity, and an obvious desire to please, to that icy, that annihilating politeness? Ernest must indeed have told him terrible things about her to produce it. Well, she wouldn't think of it. Shake him off; shake off Jenkyns, she said to herself, instinctively making a movement with her shoulders as though she were doing it, and finding the same sort of comfort in calling him Jenkyns without Mr. that a small boy finds in putting out his tongue at an unconscious back. But though she held her head high, her eyes were full of humiliated tears. Ah, if she ever met a sinner, how kind she would be, how uncritical! And then she reflected that perhaps she was always meeting sinners, only they had been cleverer than she had, and hadn't been found out.

She got back to the *Home from Home* more than an hour earlier than she had said she would. She was sorry about this, and walked as slowly as possible, being reluctant to arrive; but her interview with Mr. Jenkyns had been short, and here she was, back before eleven.

As usual, from nowhere, the manageress hurried forward to meet her, giving her her bag with many assurances that she would find its contents intact; also, she said, she would find Mrs. Le Bon waiting for her in her bedroom, who would be glad, the manageress was sure, to see her, having seemed a little put out by the message Mrs. Bott had left—"If you ask *me*," said the manageress.

"Have you ever sinned?" Milly was wondering, her eyes on the manageress's face as she mechanically took her bag. "I mean, major sins—the ten commandments —not just being cross. Have you ever done any of them?"

She looked at her in silent speculation, trying to reconstruct her twenty years earlier, which would probably, judged Milly, be about her time for falling out with the commandments.

No; she was sure she had not. But then the manageress would be equally sure that she, Milly, hadn't sinned either, and how much mistaken she would be. Nobody could ever be sure. Perhaps even Jenkyns . . .

Going slowly and thoughtfully upstairs she rejected Jenkyns as a sinner, however, on the ground that if he were one he surely would be less steely. Did sin, then, make one soft? Did it make one generous? Did having sinned incline one to pitifulness, to understanding? If so——

Milly broke off. It was all very difficult. And after a pause of reluctance at Agatha's door, she knocked and went in.

§

Agatha was very angry.

"I was afraid you would be," said Milly contritely, fumbling at the fastenings of her dress so as to get out the notes.

"That you should disappear in this manner when we have such a vital appointment to keep!" cried Agatha, towering over her like a black pillar of indignation.

"I kept it," said Milly.

"You kept it?"

"Yes. And got the money. Here it is," said Milly, extricating the packet. "The thousand pounds," she explained, as Agatha made no movement to take what was being offered.

Agatha stared uncomprehendingly.

"What?" she said. "My legacy?"

"Yes. Here it is."

"My thousand pounds? They were handed to you?"

"Yes. Won't you take them?"

Then Agatha did take the packet, and having got it held it tight in both hands, staring at Milly as though she were frightened, as though she had had a narrow escape from unthinkable disaster. For there, merely tucked into the front of Milly's dress, and carried in that way through the streets of London, a place notorious for its accidents and its thieves, had been her rehabilitation, her honour, her happiness, her life.

"Did you *walk?*" she asked in a low voice.

"Yes," said Milly.

"Milly—you carried this enormous sum openly through the streets?"

"Not openly. I was buttoned up."

"Why," said Agatha, staring and clutching the envelope to her breast, "you might have been run over."

"Well, I wasn't," said Milly.

She went to the window, and sat down dejectedly. She was tired; she was hot; she wished she were safe with Arthur, and the next few hours over. Agatha would now begin to cross-question her as to how she got possession of money not belonging to her, and why the solicitor should, without authority, so incredibly have given it to her; and Milly would be forced to make up some story, and no story that she could make up would be much good. There simply wasn't a story, thought Milly wearily, searching about in her imagination for something plausible. And then if Agatha guessed the truth, who knew but what her pride wouldn't make her refuse such a gift from what she might regard as a tainted source? Milly felt that Agatha would certainly now think of her as a tainted source, and if she did what would happen? The only other alternative to her being cast adrift penniless would, in that case, be help from Arthur, and he too, of course, as a source was tainted.

But she needn't have been troubled, because Agatha forgot everything when she opened the envelope and looked inside. A queer little shiver shook her bonnet—she was dressed ready to go out the instant Milly returned—when first she actually beheld riches. To her a thousand pounds were riches. With the contents of this envelope, she was certain she could conquer the world.

She stood a moment holding her breath as she looked, and then walked over to the bed as solemnly as if she were walking to an altar, bearing in her hands the chalice that was to give her life; and kneeling down, and taking out the crackling notes, clumsily because of her excitement, she spread them side by side on the coverlet with what seemed to Milly reverential awe, and became absorbed and lost in counting them.

Milly sat watching her. She left off wiping her hot face, and leaned forward in the chair, her eyes on the figure by the bed. Even more than Agatha's ruined hands and body did this ecstatic worship reveal what the depth of her poverty must have been. Oh, poor Aggie—poor, poor Aggie, thought Milly, pity and tenderness washing into her heart again. Heart-breaking what poverty, real extreme poverty, could do in grinding away the graces and charities, thought Milly. And grace and charity had been there, Milly knew, well remembering the young, generous body and mind which used to be Aggie's. Too generous she had been, too believing. Excess of faith and hope, excess of the very virtues we are asked to cultivate, had sent her swinging off to the heights with her lover, and excess of pride had kept her defiantly declaring she was still on them when she had long sunk down miserably into depths. But it was magnificent to have stuck to her sinking ship like that, a splendid piece of courage; and she herself, Milly, the comfortable coward, the dealer in daily treacheries, had let her vision of Agatha's qualities, qualities gone curdled only by misfortune, be blotted out because she was not very pleasant. Not very pleasant! What, in her shoes, would Milly herself have been like? Something worse than not very pleasant, she was only too sure. Certainly nothing approaching magnificent. Probably a great groaner, with no pride anywhere about her..

And watching Agatha's blissful absorption, Milly couldn't help reflecting on the strangeness of the fact that it was her own sinning which was the ultimate cause of it. Arthur's adultery with her and Ernest's punishment of her had both ended by making joy possible for Agatha. It was exceedingly queer. It made one feel giddy. It was altogether more than her brain could deal with. Best not to think too much, she thought, realizing that she had rescued Agatha far more effectually than by the kind of rescue living with her in the comforts of Mandeville Park Road, surrounded by indignant Botts unable to forgive the elopement and the hotel, would have offered, if Ernest had never found out about Arthur and she had come into all his money. Agatha would have hated being dependent; Milly would have writhed in her perpetually resentful company. Indeed Ernest had done better than he knew, when he left her only that thousand pounds. So could she bless Agatha, and let her go.

"Are they all right?" she asked, when the counting seemed to have come to an end.

"Yes," said Agatha without turning her head, beginning carefully to put the notes together.

She collected the small ones first, the five-pound ones, and spread them out neatly one on top of the other. Twenty of them. Twenty notes, each worth a hundred and twenty-five Swiss francs. And each of the bigger notes was positively the same as two thousand five hundred francs—two thousand five hundred!—and there were nine of them.

She knelt before them, worshipping. On these crisp bits of paper she was going to be wafted back to where she heart and soul belonged, and buy herself into the management of the hotel. Bought in, the proprietor, before he knew where he was, would be bought out; she wouldn't rest till she had turned over enough for that. Then she would reign supreme. She could do it all—she could, she could. There was nothing she couldn't do, given a chance, given capital. *Madame la Patrone* . . .

It was as though, thought Milly watching her, she were praying, kneeling there, her hands clasped in front of her, gazing at the little pile of notes. Then, folding them and reverentially putting them back into their envelope, she came out of her golden dream, and said, turning to Milly with knitted brows, "But I still cannot understand what your reasons were for evading me this morning, and fetching my money without any authority from me. Also," she went on after a pause, as Milly said nothing, "I consider it extremely wrong, and probably criminal, of the solicitor to have given it to you. In Switzerland he could and would be sued."

"Anyhow you've *got* it," said Milly, turning her head and looking out of the window, away from Agatha's eyes.

"But how was it possible?" she insisted. "And why did you evade me?"

"Oh, Aggie—" sighed Milly, "what does it matter as long as you've got it? I just was up rather earlier than usual, and so I—I thought I'd go for a walk. And then, as I happened to be out, I thought I might as well go and fetch the money, and save time."

A poor story, thought Milly; a thin, poor story. . . .

For a moment Agatha, who was buttoning the envelope into the front of her dress, said nothing. Then she remarked, "I should like to know your real reasons for acting in this manner."

"Oh, Aggie—bother," said Milly, drooping on her chair. "I couldn't explain them if I tried."

"All reasons can be explained," said Agatha, rising from her position on the floor, her distrust becoming deeper every moment—for suppose Ernest had left her more than a thousand pounds? How was she to know that he had not? She was in ignorance, except of what Milly had chosen to tell her. "Unless," she finished, "they are discreditable."

And Milly, silent, wondered whether it mightn't after all be the good who needed to be dealt with uncritically and patiently, rather than the sinners.

§

Fortunately at that moment the manageress knocked at the door. She wished to tell the ladies, she explained on coming in, that lunch was at half-past one.

"I am leaving," said Agatha, much annoyed at the interruption and turning on her with lofty displeasure, "I shall not require lunch."

"Sorry, Mrs. Le Bon," said the manageress crisply, "but if you leave without notice you'll have to pay for the week. I told you last night this house isn't a hotel. It's a private boarding establishment. And the rule is a week's notice or a week's pay."

"I shall pay for what I have had," said Agatha, still more lofty, "and I shall pay no more."

"The rule is——" repeated the manageress, her eyes beginning to emit sparks.

"Your rule is not my rule," Agatha interrupted. "Let me have my bill."

And there followed an altercation which could only be described as unseemly.

Milly from the window looked on, an extremely unwilling spectator, but the other two were between her and the door, against which the manageress stood, so that no one should get through it till she chose. Milly therefore had to stay where she was, and listen. They said rude things to each other—at least, the manageress said rude things, and Agatha, with infuriating iciness, swept them aside and stuck to her guns. Milly, herself so evasive, such an anxious compromiser at the mere scenting of a scene, such a quick giver-up in the face of demands, marvelled at the unflinching determination of Agatha not to be done. She herself would so much rather be done than do. It seemed an outrage on something very delicate and brittle tucked away deep inside one, something that would get hurt much more by winning than by giving way, to fight. But perhaps that was a poor, abject way of looking at things. Several times she tried to pour the oil of her gentleness on these furious waters, but the manageress's voice was too shrill and persistent, and Agatha's too big and booming, for Milly's soft piping to get through. Difficult, thought Milly, reluctantly listening, to live with Agatha. One hadn't to live with the manageress, so she didn't matter, but she had longed to live with Agatha a few hours earlier—how much she had longed! It would have been difficult, she now knew. So much and such ready courage, such excessive quantities of grit. . . . Grit was good, and she admired it, but not such quantities of it. Le Bon—how had he managed? He hadn't managed; he had died.

Yes, but not for a long while—for twenty-five years he had lived with all that grit. What sort of a man could he possibly have been? Wouldn't he and she have been rather good friends? Wouldn't they, after a bit, have been inclined to comfort each other?

Ah, but this was getting worse, the things they were saying—Agatha telling the manageress with scorn that she cared neither jot nor tittle for English laws or police, because she was a free and independent Swiss, and the manageress retorting that she ought to be ashamed of herself for being a thing like that, and actually in her excitement proceeding to add something unintelligible to Milly, but manifestly insulting, about Agatha's parents.

Agatha's, and therefore, her own, parents?

This time Milly intervened more energetically. She got up from the chair she had been sitting on, and went to the manageress and laid her hand, with all the firmness she had, on her arm.

"Don't," she begged. "Please——" and kept on saying it till the manageress heard her.

"Please don't," begged Milly earnestly, having got her attention. "My sister——"

"She your sister?" cried the manageress, glaring with distended nostrils at the unflinching Agatha. "I don't believe it, Mrs. Bott—not for a single instant. You may *think* she is, and I dare say she is in a way, but not a way any of us would much like to mention, if you ask *me*. I should say your father——"

And the manageress, got completely out of control, was on the verge of openly bringing out her theory as to Mrs. Le Bon's birth, when Milly, feeling something awful was coming, stopped her by interjecting that she was paying the bills herself for both of them, flinging her words quickly in front of whatever the manageress had been going to say.

"My sister is going to Switzerland," Milly went on breathlessly, "and has to catch a train that leaves at two o'clock. She couldn't possibly lunch. I'll settle everything with you. Shan't we go downstairs and do it now?"

"Why, you're not leaving me too, Mrs. Bott?" exclaimed the manageress turning to her, softened by this speech, and remembering the four one-pound notes in Milly's handbag.

"I'm afraid so," said Milly, her quick smile, a little anxious now, but inevitably sweet, at once producing an answering glimmer on the manageress's heated face. "I'm so sorry——" Her voice became very gentle, almost caressing; anything, anything to calm people. "I would have liked so much to have stayed. You've been so kind. I shall hope to come back——"

But Agatha sternly put a stop to this scandalous and completely uncalled-for insincerity. Lying, terrible to have to recognize, seemed to be the unhappy Milly's speciality; but why she should stoop to it in order to please and flatter a harpy was past comprehending. "Untruths," she interrupted, with a great sweep of her arm, "nothing but untruths. My sister is not sorry. She would not have liked, either much or at all, to have stayed any longer with you. You were not kind. And she will never come back."

And once again Milly thought, looking at her in flushed and startled embarrassment, that it wasn't the sinners who needed understanding and patience and uncriticalness so much as the good.

§

An hour later Mr. Jenkyns, having just bowed out an important client, was told by his clerk that a Mrs. Le Bon wished to speak to him; and on inquiring if she had an appointment, and being told that she hadn't, he refused to see her.

But the clerk came back, and said she was so urgent in her desire to see Mr. Jenkyns that he couldn't get rid of her. "A widow, sir," said the clerk. "Been waiting half an hour. Says she won't keep you more than a couple of minutes."

A widow. Mr. Jenkyns reflected. He rather specialized in widows, who, when newly made and in the first confusion of disaster, were easy clients, both grateful and guidable; and though he was a man with as big a practice as any in London, yet a new client who was also a widow should not, perhaps, lightly be turned away.

"Does she—er—look——?"

He wished to say opulent, poor widows being worse than none, but said respectable instead.

"Oh quite, sir," the clerk assured him. "Very. Couldn't be more."

Mr. Jenkyns sighed, and fingered the pencil lying by his pad.

"Five minutes, then," he said. "Come in at the end of them, and call me away."

But at the end of three he was ringing for his clerk. "Show this lady out," he said, his thin face much flushed; for Agatha, who prized direct methods more highly than tact, and was also full of distrust, had started the interview unfortunately, severely inquiring of the surprised man, in a room in which severity had till then been his monopoly, by what right and by whose authority he had handed over the legacy Ernest Bott had left her to a third person.

Mr. Jenkyns was so much astonished that for half a minute of the three the interview lasted he gazed at her over his spectacles, speechless. Then anger, thick and hot, surged within him, for the incredible creature was actually threatening him with the law—threatening him, a lawyer, with, as it were, his own law.

When he recovered he made short work of Agatha, who in her turn was rendered speechless by what he told her. No mention at all of her in the Will? The money not her own by right at all, but a present from Milly? "And a very handsome present too," said Mr. Jenkyns sternly, pressing the bell on his table. "If I may make a suggestion, madam, I would bear the saying in mind as to the undesirability of examining a gift too closely."

"Then my sister," said Agatha for the third time, her eyes bigger than ever as she stared at Mr. Jenkyns every bit as inimically as he was staring at her, "fabricated the entire story?"

"To what end I am incompetent to judge," said Mr. Jenkyns, putting some papers together with exasperated movements. "Show this lady out," he added, on the clerk's appearing.

Agatha got up slowly. Deep were her suspicions. How did she know that what this man alleged was true? He might well be nothing but a rascal. Was not the expression "rascally lawyer" proverbial? Had she not frequently enough in her reading come across it? Besides, how unlikely, how incomprehensible, that Milly should divest herself of such a sum, and make her a present of it. People didn't make presents of fortunes. And she remembered her words when she told her of the legacy, and how she had said, and it had seemed most right and natural, Agatha thought, that Ernest in this way wished to make amends for the wrong he had done her.

There was, undoubtedly, something strange and suspect about this lawyer.

"Be so good," she said, towering tall and black on the other side of the table from which Mr. Jenkyns, in the act of slightly bowing, had half risen, "as to produce that Will. I desire to see it for myself."

At this Mr. Jenkyns rose completely. He straightened himself out till he was as tall as she was, and looked at her in silence, with eyes that were two points of bright steel.

"Remove her," he then said, briefly, to the clerk.

§

It was now nearly one o'clock. At two the train for Switzerland left. Agatha stood uncertain on the pavement in Essex Street, a kind of black Cenotaph, on either side of which washed the indifferent flow of passers-by. There wasn't much time to decide in. If what that man said was true, and there was something about his wrath at the end which convinced her it was, pride demanded that she should return to the boarding-house, fling the packet of notes at Milly's feet, for ever relinquish all idea of happiness, and go forth penniless to struggle for what still might be left to her of existence. After all, she was used to suffering. Oh, yes, she hoped she knew how to suffer as well as anybody, she thought, with an upward jerk of her chin. Or she might take out one of the small notes for her fare—Milly was careless, she was sure, and not the kind of person who counted notes—and go back to Switzerland and throw herself on the mercy of the hotel proprietor, and get reinstated in her miserable post. Base? To take the note and not tell? No, because it was merely a temporary taking—ultimately, from her painful earnings, to be repaid.

She stood in a tumult of indecision. Traffic washed round the island she made. Her hand, held tightly against her chest, pressed the packet of notes. How could she bear to let them go, and with them every hope? Ah, how—how?

She walked a few steps up the street, and stopped again, and again pressed the notes against her chest, and again the passers-by divided on either side of her and streamed along, the ceaseless flow of absorbed, indifferent, busy people.

Mr. Jenkyns himself, on his way to lunch, was one of them, but he wasn't indifferent, for on catching sight of the motionless figure he immediately crossed to the other side, and there held on his way indignantly. "Pah," said Mr. Jenkyns to himself—a man not at all given to exclamations of the kind; but the expression seemed to describe his state of mind. He had a desire, unusual at that hour, to have a bath. After the encounters of the morning, first with that woman who had all but made a fool of him, that scandalous widow of poor Ernest Bott's, and then with her outrageous sister, he felt he needed a bath. There should be some soap invented, he thought as he hurried along, which washed off irritation; some Cuticura of the mind . . .

And Agatha continuing up the street, mechanically grasping the front of her dress, felt that not since Gaston's death had such desolation been hers. If she had only refrained from insisting that Milly should tell her the solicitor's address! Milly had tried not to tell her, and the more she tried the more Agatha had insisted— naturally, for such reluctance, such distressed reluctance, merely confirmed her suspicions that something was being hidden from her. And so something had been; and now she knew what it was; and it was the precise contrary of what she had been suspecting; and it destroyed her.

For how could she keep this money? Quite apart from what it represented—the contemptuous gesture, a kick almost, a parting kick from the outraged husband to the unfaithful wife, her principles would never allow her to take money from anyone fallen. Impossible. She could not even imagaine such a thing. A Magdalen's money. Better crusts in gutters than prosperity and honour at such a price. The wages of someone else's sin—how could she touch them? And Milly had known she couldn't and wouldn't, and therefore had invented the story of the legacy.

Kind of Milly? Kind to wish her to have the money? Yes, she supposed it was kind. Yes; it did seem quite kind. But if Milly had been virtuous, if she had remained a chaste wife, there would have been no need for all this complicated and lie-entangled kindness. The wages of someone else's sin—she couldn't touch them; but the punishment for someone else's sin appeared to be hers alone. Milly could go to the partner of her guilt, and they would marry, and perhaps even be happy, and anyhow cease to feel guilty. She would be comfortably provided for, and for the rest of her life, as in the past, not have a care; while her sister, who had never done anything but strive to live nobly——

Two tears slowly forced themselves from Agatha's eyes, and trickled down her face. She had had too much to bear. She was most weary of bearing. Now it was all to be begun again. . . .

And the passers-by—for she was in the Strand now, being jostled and noticing nothing—stared, seeing this weeping woman; and some were sorry, and thought fleetingly, "Poor old thing."

§

All the way to Bloomsbury Agatha wrestled with herself, tears on her face, and at her side walked her two bleak angels of Pride and Principle. By the time she had reached the boarding-house she had won her battle, and made up her mind. What was right had once more, she thanked God, got the upper hand with her, and she would acknowledge Milly's good intentions and give her back the packet, merely asking for a loan of one of the five-pound notes, so that she might at once travel back to Switzerland. There should be no secret taking of any note, and there should be few words. Indeed, there was time for nothing but the utmost brevity if she was to catch that train—and catch it she must, thus as quickly as possible closing this tragic chapter in her tragic life, this ill-fated attempt to bring love and comfort to a sister who for the past ten years had existed only in her imagination.

Neither to the right nor to the left would she look; neither at the hopes with which she had come, nor at the desolation in which she would go back. That way lay despair. Head up, mouth firm, thoughts nailed to the actual moment—this was how she was going through the rest of her life. "I refuse to be beaten—I *refuse* to be beaten," she kept on repeating to herself, her hand pressed against her bosom, where lay, warmed now by her warmth, the little bundle which held the possibility of the fulfilment of all her dreams—"Like a child," she suddenly thought, pressing it closer; and immediately was ashamed of such extreme absurdity.

Proudly, for she had won her battle, she turned the corner into the square, and up to the very last moment, when she was in the hall of the *Home from Home*, she was repeating, her head high as she walked past the servant at the door, "I refuse to be beaten——"Then, at the actual instant when she opened her mouth to make her brief speech of thanks to Milly, who came out of the dining-room hesitatingly, as if afraid to meet her, at the actual instant when her hand was preparing to draw out the packet of notes and give them up, she was beaten.

Her hand wavered. The words she had prepared refused to be spoken. Instead of drawing out the notes, she pressed them fiercely and hard against her chest. And looking at Milly, and drawing a long breath, her great eyes very wide open, her face defiant, she said, "I did not go to the solicitor after all. I feared—I came to the conclusion it might make me miss my train."

§

At the station, at the last moment, when porters were shutting doors and late passengers were scurrying about in confusion, Agatha, sitting straight and rock-like in the corner of her second-class compartment, and until then of the fewest possible words and a stony impassivity, suddenly gripped the window-sill with her cotton-gloved hand, and said in a queer voice, "Milly."

Milly was standing outside the door, vaguely looking along the platform, so as to not look at Agatha. She had come to see her off after all, no longer caring whether anybody from Titford saw her or not. Agatha had lied: speciously, recklessly, with the splendid and defiant despair of a God-fearing child driven into a corner, and Milly's heart was full of love. Poor, poor Aggie—what desperate fear and misery lay under her lying! But on no account must she notice any tenderness, or she would suspect that Milly knew, and be crushed by humiliation. All Milly had said, on receiving the lie square in her face, —and she had to say something after recovering her breath,—was that she was very glad Aggie hadn't gone that long way and tired herself out before her journey; and then, averting her eyes, she had pretended to be busy fastening her cloak and pulling on her gloves.

"I'm coming with you to the station," she said.

"Pray do not," said Agatha, very stiff and grim.

In the taxi—they were obliged to take a taxi, the time being short—they hardly spoke, each looking out of her own window. At the station there was a rush to get the ticket, and no talk was possible. Now, Agatha established safely in her corner, and Milly on the platform at the door, and the minutes of the rest of their time together this side of eternity rushing along till at last they were only seconds, they still said nothing, they still averted their eyes.

Once Milly remarked, watching with apparent interest the activities at the farther end of the platform, that she thought the crossing would be good, because there was so little wind; but Agatha didn't even answer.

Then, just as she was thinking, "But this is dreadful —another moment and she'll be gone for ever——" she heard that voice behind her saying, "Milly."

She turned quickly. Agatha was looking at her, her face working strangely.

"Milly——" she began.

"Yes, Aggie?" said Milly.

"I wish to say—I would like to say——"

She gulped, and looked speechlessly at the face in the window-frame.

Then she did get it out. "Bless you," she finished suddenly, her face all twisted.

In an instant Milly was on the step of the carriage, her arms round Agatha's neck.

"Bless *you*?" she whispered, drawing her close.

Then Agatha suddenly began kissing her wildly. "Milly, Milly——" she gasped, wildly kissing.

"Stand away there, please," shouted the guard.

⚹(IX)⚹

IT WAS the established custom that Arthur, on the afternoons of their meetings in Chelsea, should be at the flat
a little before Milly, watch from behind the window-
curtain for her appearance at the corner of the street,
and open the door for her the instant she was on the top
step. This had been arranged at the beginning, when
they were both terrified lest she should be seen, and it
had become a fixed habit. Automatically Arthur took
up his position, and automatically the door opened,
with him behind it, not showing himself till she was inside. Then, at the beginning, what a falling into each
other's arms, what an enraptured silence and close
clinging! Not now, of course. Years pass and holds
loosen. Naturally, Milly told herself, reasonable and
sweet, when first Arthur's hold became definitely looser.
Ecstasy can't be kept up for ever; something much better takes its place—infinitely better, she assured herself;
and then sat and wondered what it was.

When he began to loosen, Milly, instantly aware of it
and delicately taking her cue from him, loosened to
match; but for all her apparent equal loosening the
second stage in loving had nevertheless been entered
into, the stage in which it is the woman who is the fonder. She was very fond; so, fortunately, was he, but not
as fond. He loved Milly dearly, but she loved him
more; and it was she, now, who brought and arranged
the flowers. Then, as the years passed, the third stage
was reached, when nobody brought flowers, and they

had quite settled down into comfortable, secure, equal
affection, without fuss or bother of any kind. The door
still opened as if by magic, but that was just habit, and
there was no magic waiting behind it. Composedly, unhurriedly, it was shut when she was inside, and composedly, unhurriedly, pleasantly, they smiled at each
other. Anybody might have seen them; anybody might
have heard them.

"Well, dear?"

"Well, Arthur?"

"I all but missed my train to-day. It actually started
a minute before its time."

"Really? I hope you didn't get hot hurrying? How
is your cold, darling?"

That was the sort of thing. Naturally, thought Milly;
for sin too settles down, and becomes indistinguishable
at last from virtue. Everything settles down. Naturally,
she thought.

On this occasion—the very last, she realized, of the
many occasions on which the journey had been made—
Milly, who usually went to King's Road from Victoria
in a taxi, walked. And she walked for two reasons: first,
because it was early, and Arthur's train, the one he
always came by, with a restaurant car enabling him to
lunch comfortably on the way, didn't get to Paddington
till three, and then because, on paying for the taxi from
Bloomsbury she had been reminded by the emptiness of
her bag that the manageress, refusing to be satisfied
with less, had got her four one-pound notes. After paying the taxi there was very little left in the bag—two
shillings to be exact, a threepenny bit, and five pennies.

Therefore she walked. And it occurred to her with
some surprise, for she hadn't thought of it till then, that
Arthur would have to begin at once paying for her needs,
and feeding and lodging her—yes, and clothing her too;

for even a registrar's office, a place accustomed to the absence of sentiment, might think it tactless if she were to be married in fresh widow's weeds. Arthur's first present to her as his betrothed would have to be a complete new suit of clothes.

Not that he would mind; nor would she mind asking, for being used to having money, being ready herself to give, she was also simple and unconcerned in taking. And he wouldn't mind either her having been left with only a thousand pounds. He cared nothing for money, and would merely applaud the gift of it to her sister. Besides, he had recently become Senior Tutor of his College, with a house and garden attached to the position roomy enough for a large family, and he was well able to support a wife. She had pointed this out smilingly to him—sometimes she was less sensible, and tried to make him say things—when at her request, she went down to be shown his new possession and have tea in it, and he had answered, "Indeed, yes," and hadn't said, as he always was saying at the beginning, "Ah, if we could only be married!" Naturally, thought Milly, one ends by putting impossibilities out of one's thoughts; and this impossibility had now so long been out of Arthur's that he failed to notice the obvious opportunity of referring to it. Instead, he began to tell her of a fragment recently discovered at Naples, which appeared to belong to an inscription in honour of C. Duilius, the victor over the Carthaginian fleet in 260 B.C. Naturally, thought Milly, who knew he was just then much interested in Duilius.

Into this house she was now after all going; and walking by roundabout ways, for she had time to fill up, to Chelsea, the first stage of that going, her thoughts, a little sleepy in the relaxation succeeding the tension of Agatha's departure, idly wandering, she remembered

that the garden had an apple-tree in the middle of its
grass plot, and she saw herself sitting through many
placid May days beneath this tree, dreaming as sweetly
as the dreaming spires themselves, while Arthur, in his
languidly charming voice, read to her of what he was
at the moment interested in. And, as her mind dwelt on
this vision of peace, she couldn't help wondering where,
then, what with Aggie gone away blessing her, and
Arthur, all kindness, taking her into his life legitimately,
expiation came in.

It didn't seem to come in anywhere, thought Milly,
her face still burning from that last desperate kissing,
her heart, released now because of it from unkindness,
comforted and quiet. Aggie had blessed her. Their bitterness and disappointment with each other was wiped
out. Still there was love between them in their thoughts.
And what a debt she owed her very severity! For it
was because of her shocked conviction that the only
amends Milly could make for her sin was to marry
Arthur, that her path at that moment was so straight
and clear. Aggie had sobered her. Those frenzied ideas
that Arthur must be fled from, that if she married him
Ernest would for ever be rising up accusingly between
them, were so many twisted cobwebs she had swept
from Milly's brain. Arthur to be fled from? Milly, relaxed, wondered at herself for having thought so. Why,
he was all she had now in the world, her one link with
some sort of love, some sort of warmth. Also he was the
only person she really kissed; and every woman had to
have someone in her life she really kissed, else she
starved. That was what was the matter with Aggie,
over and above her poverty—that she had nobody really
to kiss. And as for the frightened nonsense about
Ernest's memory worrying Arthur and herself, if at any
time it were to cross their minds it would be greeted,

she knew, by Arthur, who had never felt any hostility towards Ernest, and who would be sure to be genuinely sympathetic over the manner of his death, with the kindliest, "Poor fellow"; and no ghost, however obstinately set on haunting, could stand up against that gentle welcome.

Really, she didn't see quite where expiation came in. Life with Arthur, far beyond sight and sound of the Botts, would be nothing but restful. In Oxford no one would dream she was a person with a past, for the Botts were not in touch with Oxford, having all been educated, as Ernest put it, privately, and it would be impossible just from her appearance to guess she had got such a thing. How was it, wondered Milly, considering her case, and slowly advancing westwards through the sunny streets like a slightly torpid beetle—she was suddenly immensely tired—how was it she was being let off so lightly? Why, lightly wasn't the word; entirely was the word. For there was no punishment anywhere, and her plans for expiation were all confounded. Peace, security, affection were going to be hers. Coals of fire were being heaped on the heads of two sinners. Justice was staying its hand. Mercy was having its way unhindered. And again, her eyes half shut, and swaying a little as she walked, she saw herself under that apple-tree, being read aloud to through the summers of the future, or, in the winter, as in the Chelsea studio, being read aloud to by the fire. It used to be Keats and Shelley they read together, she remembered, dreaming of the past as she walked, hardly seeing the streets she was going through, or the polite, kind people making way for her; Keats and Shelley it used to be, in the first fervours. Ah, the wonderful time, that beginning time! She hadn't realized how wonderful till it was over. He was like a boy, shaken and torn out of the groove of

middle age by love, and she was so glad to be dragged
back with him by his passion to youth. Ah, sweet,
absurd time. . . .

Well, never mind; they were still so fond of each
other, and everybody was bound to grow older. They
had begun to grow older when, after Keats and Shelley,
came Milton and Blake, and were definitely older when
he tried to teach her Italian, and make her read Dante.
Gradually all the poets were left behind, and the excava-
tion period set in. History was what was studied in this
period, and great books were lent to Milly to read, for he
liked her to share his interests—books she took home
with her, and had to hide as carefully as if they were
some kind of enormous love-letter. For seven years now
the reading aloud had been of excavations, and she
didn't suppose he would emerge from them again.
Nothing except ancient Greece and Rome seemed really
to rouse him any more, to bring him back to life; and
just as she had inaccurately picked up poetry because
he had loved it, and inaccurately picked up Italian
because he had wanted her to learn it, so had she picked
up what was needed of facts connected with excavations
to be able to give him the comfort of believing he was
being intelligently listened to. Even—she smiled a little
to think of it—even she reacted satisfactorily when he
wished to talk to her of telamones and heroons; taking
him in, of course, but after all one had to be one's man's
companion as well as lover, and if one were ignorant
one must manage somehow to pretend one wasn't. Yes—
and one had to be his mother too, soothing headaches
away, pillowing him on one's bosom when he was tired
and needed a bosom—fortunately in whatever state her
brains might be, every woman had a bosom—brewing
him hot drinks to stave off his oncoming colds, being
sorry for him, petting him. Perhaps only in this relation-

ship had she had no need at all to pretend, she reflected; it came very natural to her to be a mother. If Ernest and she had had children, she probably wouldn't have wanted to get away that day of dissatisfaction and rush up to London, and then she never would have known there was such a person as Arthur.

But wouldn't that, honestly, have been a pity?

Ah, yes, yes—to have missed love, not to have known love. . . .

"What? She really thought that? She really thought it would have been a pity not to have committed adultery?

Milly was startled. Of course she didn't mean that. Of course she——

Well, she couldn't go into it now, she said to herself, pushing these questions on one side; for here she was—here was the corner of the street off King's Road, and there, halfway down on the left, she could see the familiar door.

Her heart began to beat a little faster as she turned the corner. This was no ordinary meeting. Great events had happened since the last one. The occasion was solemn with death, serious with the close of an epoch, hopeful with the beginning of a fresh one. At least, she thought with a feeling of gratitude and rest, there would be no surprises for her in the man she was going to marry; she knew him so well, so completely, that she could tell beforehand almost the very words he would use, and what he would do, and how he would look. Now, for instance, to-day, in another minute, when he opened the door and saw her in her widow's dress, she knew exactly what his face would look like, all sorry and all—she was going to say glad, but put the word pleased instead, as perhaps more accurately descriptive of Arthur's mild reactions these days. And she said to herself, with a feeling of having got safe into harbour, into calm water, how, after ten years of love, there are few things a woman doesn't know about her man; in fact, she amended with a small smile as she went up the steps, there are none.

But for the first time during the ten years of love, Milly was mistaken.

§

To begin with, the door didn't open; she actually had to knock.

Such a thing had never happened before.

She knocked, and waited, and knocked again. The street became interested, but no one came.

Then she remembered that he, watching from behind the curtain, couldn't possibly guess that the shrouded figure on the door-step, the strange widow, was Milly. Stupid of her to arrive with her thick veil over her face.

She put it up, and knocked again; and the street became still more interested, and still no one came.

Inside she could visualize Arthur, astonished at this visit from a stranger, turning away annoyed and perplexed from the window, determined not to show himself, to lie *perdu*, till the creature on the steps, the impudent widow, had gone, hoping to goodness she would go before Milly arrived, and putting her down as some charity collector, or someone frankly begging.

Well, she must bring him to the window again, so that, her veil now thrown back and her face turned towards him, he would see who it was; and once more she knocked, loudly, persistently; and the street became absorbed.

He did come at last—not to the window but straight to the door, outraged that anyone should dare go on making such a moise. She heard the irregular, limping footsteps, and immediately afterwards the door was flung open, and Arthur, indignant, appeared.

"Milly!" he exclaimed, his brown eyes wide with amazement. Then, "*Milly*——" he repeated, his voice dropping, a strange expression taking the place of amazement, an expression she found she didn't know—she who had been so sure she knew them all.

He forgot to shut the door. He stood gazing at her clothes. "Are you—is it possible——?" he said in a low voice; for Arthur, though short-sighted and generally unobservant, did know a widow when he saw one,—besides which Milly, as a widow, was impossible to miss. Of her class she was, perhaps, owing to the Botts' tradition, the most perfect specimen.

He looked at her in dismay. The expression on his face, which she had never seen before and couldn't place, was simple, stark dismay. She, however, passed quickly from wondering about it to wondering, in her turn, at his appearance. What was the matter with Arthur? Bronzed from his holiday as he had never been after any holiday, he not only looked amazingly well, but he produced an unusual effect of cleanness, though he had always been clean, and of awakenness, though he had never been sleepy. Curiously on the spot too, he seemed; come back to the present. And even his voice, naturally languid, was in some odd way brisked up. Also, incredibly—her lips dropped apart when she saw them—he was wearing spats.

She stared. She was so much surprised that she forgot all about her own appearance.

"How *well* you look, darling," she said, a little hesitatingly, her eyes rising from the spats to his face. The strange expression was still on it. It didn't go at all with the rest of him, especially not with those optimistic

spats. What was it? she wondered. In anyone else,
she would have said it was——

Her thought stopped short. He was motioning her
inside. Of course; they were still standing on the steps,
in full view of the street.

She went in, and he shut the door. In the little space
partitioned off from the studio by a curtain, he said,
laying a finger for an instant on her sleeve, "Milly——
Why? What has——?"

"Ernest," she said, nodding slowly, brought back at
once to the seriousness of the occasion; and, her eyes on
his face, she waited to be taken in his arms.

But Arthur's behaviour was as strange and unusual
as the rest of him. He didn't take her in his arms; he
stood looking at her in silence, the expression she
couldn't place more marked than ever; and all he said,
after an appreciable pause, though he said it with
evident feeling, was, "God."

This outburst too was entirely unlike him, and surprised her afresh. God? She couldn't remember his ever
having said such a thing before.

"I knew, darling," she said softly, "that you would be
much shocked——" and as he said nothing at all to this,
but in silence was holding the dividing curtain aside for
her to pass through into the studio, she passed through
it.

He followed. Still no sign of any of the things she had
been so certain he would say and do, and always that
expression on his face which in anyone else she would
have said was—— But of course it wasn't; it couldn't
be.

"Darling——" she began, taking off her heavy bonnet and laying it aside.

He interrupted her. "When, Milly?" he asked
abruptly.

"Friday," she answered.

"Friday? This last Friday? Less than a week ago? But—why? Why should he——?"

"An accident," she whispered; and again Arthur, after staring at her a moment in silence, burst out strangely and abruptly, and said, "God."

Milly leaned against the table. For some reason her legs were shaking. The long walk, perhaps, she said to herself, from Victoria, on top of the long walk that morning to Essex Street and back. But why didn't Arthur kiss her? He always did kiss her—affectionately and kindly, when she arrived. Why didn't he to-day, of all days? He must know she couldn't have been anything but deeply wretched; he must realize that what had happened meant their marriage.

She put up her hands with a nervous movement to smoothe her hair, ruffled from the wearing of the bonnet, and discovered it wasn't only her legs which were shaking, but her hands too.

This surprised her. Her hands had nothing to do with walking. Why should they shake? Here she was with Arthur, safe with Arthur. . . .

But was she safe with Arthur?

Suddenly it seemed as if a door in her heart blew open, and an icy wind rushed through it. Quickly she shut it, banged it to again, leaning against it with all her might. Oh, nonsense . . . oh, nonsense. . . .

He was standing in front of the empty fireplace, his elbow on the mantelpiece, looking at her; and his brown eyes, so kind always, were full of—what? Distress; extreme distress, decided Milly. Evidently he was more shocked by Ernest's death than she had supposed possible. She had expected some shock, but not this. Perhaps he was one of the people whom death, any death close enough to be realized, appalled. She hadn't known

this side of him, because there had been no death within
measurable distance of him during their intimacy, and
the subject had hardly been mentioned in their talks,
except generally. If so, if this was it, and he was simply
horrified, and his horror was increased a thousandfold
by the sight of her dreadful clothes, naturally he shrank
from her, naturally he couldn't bear to take her in his
arms.

Rapidly Milly gave herself explanations, but even
while she gave them she was aware that they didn't hold
water. There was something else the matter with
Arthur. At least she knew him well enough to know
that. And again she leaned with all her might against
the door in her heart, which the freezing wind of desolation was trying to burst open.

"Darling," she said at last, her voice trembling—but
why? Wasn't he Arthur? Wasn't she Milly?—"it has
all been sad and horrible, but it isn't *going* to be. Some
day"—she tried to smile at him, and her mouth merely
twitched—"some day there'll be—we'll be———"

Her words petered out. She stood looking at him.
Then she said, suddenly, desperately, quickly going over
to where he stood, "Arthur, why don't you kiss me?"

He stared down at her. He was so tall, in spite of his
stooping shoulders, and she was so short, in spite of her
high heels, that when she was close to him she had to
crick her neck almost so as to look up into his face.
She did so now, holding on to his coat with both hands
to steady herself, for he made no attempt to put his arms
round her; but there was such distress in his eyes, such
evident trouble, that it was she who put her arms round
him, letting go his coat, holding him to her breast.

"Don't, Milly—don't, dear," said Arthur in a low
voice, gently loosening her arms; and the door in Milly's
heart blew right open, and swift, icy fear tore through it.

She stood away from him looking at him, her arms hanging by her side. Fumblingly she said, as though she were trying to find him in the dark and were faintly calling after him, "Arthur——?"

"Listen, Milly," said Arthur, trying to be very matter of fact, and failing, "I have a good deal to say to you."

He took her hand, but there was no heart in the way he held it, all loose.

"A really extraordinary thing has happened," he went on. "A thing, I suppose, that doesn't happen once in a hundred years——"

And another expression came into his eyes, blotting out the first one, an expression she knew she had seen before in them, but a long time ago, such a long time ago that it must have been when——

"What—thing?" she faltered, as he paused, suddenly flushed, she could see, beneath his sunburn.

He looked down at her, loosely holding her hand; she looked up at him, and the expression on her face brought dismay back to his.

"Perhaps," he said helplessly, dropping her hand and turning away, "we had better sit down——" and his glance wandered vaguely round the room, in search of a suitable spot.

There was no suitable spot; none, that is, suitable now in his eyes. The room had a divan in it, and a table, and a gas-ring for making tea, and a sink with a tap. They had never needed more furniture. On the divan they had loved, and then, as years passed, merely sat peacefully among its cushions; and sometimes, while he was reading aloud, she would slide on to the floor and sit at his feet, leaning her head against his knee. But Arthur had no knee now for Milly's head, and nothing would have induced him to go with her on to the divan, because that had happened to him which, in his ignorance, he thought never did happen, or only once in a thousand years, and he had been fallen in love with by a girl. He, fifty-five; he, amply old enough to be her father.

The girl had had great trouble in getting him to believe it. It was only with the help of her mother, who at last had had to take him aside and point things out, that he had been brought to see what was so evident to every-body else. Then, in his turn, he had fallen in love—deeply, helplessly, with the irresistible heavy falling, the stone-like swift drop, of the elderly when faced by radiant, worshipping, willing youth; and to her, to the girl he was going to marry, the slim wonder with the mouth like some lovely fruit and the lithe movements of a boy, he owed it that he should keep off divans. Besides, the bare idea revolted him. Strange to say—and it did cross his mind as strange, remembering how habitual the caressing of Milly among cushions had so long been, and how even more habitual the being caressed among them by her,—the thought of the divan, and its cushions and its caresses, now revolted him.

He didn't want to touch her, or be touched. A moment ago, when she put her arms round him, it had made him feel most uncomfortable, and curiously ashamed as well as sorry; yet last time they met, five weeks before, they had stood on that very same hearthrug, saying good-bye in almost identically the position, and with no feeling at all on his part except that it was natural.

"Well, I can't help it," he thought—irritably, because he was so much worried, so much taken aback by Milly's unexpected widowhood, and so genuinely sorry that he was going to have to hurt her. "*Conceive* Ernest's dying at such a moment!" he said to himself, distressed and exasperated, and still looking about the room for some-thing satisfactory for them to sit on.

"But Arthur—" said Milly, "tell me—what thing?"

"There's nothing to sit on," he said impatiently, as if he couldn't tell her anything unless he sat.

"Why not the divan?" she asked.

"No, no," he said quickly; and then her last uncertainty, the little shred she was still holding on to, disappeared; and she knew.

§

Coming up in the train that day, and indeed whenever since his engagement Milly crossed his mind, Arthur had told himself that, being reasonable, she would understand. Obviously she couldn't marry him herself, Ernest being alive, and surely, then, it was natural that in the fullness of time, and after long years of devotion to her, he should marry and settle down. She might even be relieved, he thought; glad not to have to make any more journeys to Chelsea, now that she was older, and presumably more easily tired.

But Ernest had done, poor fellow, what no one would ever have dreamed he would do, and Arthur was much afraid that Milly would expect to marry him. Naturally she would expect it, seeing she didn't know what had happened to him in Rome; and equally naturally she was going to be terribly hurt by what he had to tell her.

Not, mind you, he said to himself, still looking about for chairs which weren't there, all these thoughts passing through his mind in a kind of extremely disagreeable flash—not, mind you, for the only reason which could justify marriage, passionate love on both sides, the love which was transfiguring his own life and so marvellously restoring him to youth, but because she would think it the right thing.

In her case, of course, there could be no love as Arthur at that moment understood it. She was forty-five; a middle-aged woman. And middle-aged women, Arthur said to himself, who was ignorant, have finished with that sort of thing. He hadn't thought of her as middle-aged before, time having slid along for them both unnoticed on the smooth wheels of use and wont, but he remembered that she was the first time he had emerged sufficiently from the intoxication he fell into, on discovering he was loved by youth, to be able to remember anything. Then he remembered Milly, and her age, and everything about her, with extreme clearness; and it seemed to him natural, in his desire to believe it was natural, that a woman so old as that would be glad not to be bothered with even the mildest, most shadowy of lovers.

Surely for years now he had been a most mild lover; surely it would be the easiest thing in the world for them to proceed from the pretence of being lovers to the reality of being friends? Friends were what one-time lovers should be when both were middle-aged, and he and Milly would always be the best of friends, and never would he forget how much he owed her, at a lonely period of his life, of comfort and peace.

He was very fond of Milly; very fond of her indeed. She had made an immense difference to his life. But he was now fond of her only as a friend. She must know that, though undoubtedly there had been a season of love, even of passionate love, between them, for a long while past it had been mere affection; and mere affection wasn't enough to marry on. Imagine, thought Arthur, used to his regular life alone, imagine taking a woman into one's house, letting her loose among one's habits, living with her all round the clock in the closest intimacy, on a basis of mere affection! One only married, surely, because one couldn't help oneself, because one had fallen in love, because if one didn't, if one didn't seize this strange, intoxicating opportunity of becoming young again at the touch of youth, of being magically made alive, of being restored to poetry, to beauty, to eagerness and excitement, to all the things one used to feel and for such melancholy ages had felt no longer, one would just crumple up slowly into what one had already begun to be,—a limp, boneless, indifferent old man.

Incredibly but genuinely, this girl he had met in Rome loved him. How refuse such a gift? It would be like turning one's back on life itself. Of course he was old for her, ridiculously old; but since she didn't think so, and only laughed when he talked about it, why should he mind? It was most extraordinary, a girl like that loving someone old enough to be her father, thought Arthur, who was ignorant; and just as extraordinary was it that he, of the age of the riper fathers, should have fallen as utterly in love as if he were twenty, he thought, continuing ignorant.

He couldn't help being rather proud of this—of knowing that he still was able to fall in love, and that he had; while as for his pride in her, it overwhelmed him. To be seen in streets and picture-galleries and tea-shops with this girl manifestly concentrated on him, drinking in all he said, and so pretty, so adorable, that everyone looked at her, made him glow with a kind of hot pride. No one had ever looked at Milly when he and she walked along King's Road in search of a taxi. Hers was the kind of charm—and he hadn't forgotten that she had been of much charm—which only becomes apparent on closer acquaintance. She had never been a woman to attract notice in a street. But a man, he discovered with much surprise, likes to be able to be proud of the woman he is walking with and taking care of, likes to know it isn't only himself who thinks his companion desirable, likes to see other men's eyes become interested as she passes, even though he may wish, in return, to fell them to the ground.

Foolish? Probably. But to have such feelings showed one was alive, and better to be foolish and alive than wise, indifferent and semi-dead. He had been wise, indifferent and semi-dead so long now, he recognized; resigned to dullness, petrifyingly comfortable. And this enchanting child had flashed into the gathering shadows, this shining thing of untouched innocence and eager worship—she thought him distinguished, bless her, she thought him brilliant—calling him forth, like some bright angel of the Resurrection, to renewed life, and youth, and love.

Refuse it? Refuse to listen to that clarion call from heaven? Who would?

No one, of course; no man in the world, he said to himself.

But then—what about Milly?

"That's it," thought Arthur, leaving off looking about the room for what wasn't in it, and turning a rueful and distressed gaze on Milly. "That's the difficulty."

§

She was standing quite still, her eyes on his face.

"Poor little thing," he thought, very sorry, asking himself what one did on these occasions, what one could do to avoid hurting. "It's awful if she's going to mind. I wish to God——"

But what he wished to God he couldn't have said; certainly not that this hadn't happened to him, this miracle of new life.

And to give himself courage he asked himself why, after all, should Milly want to keep him—supposing, that is, that she did? Illumined by his recent experiences, he saw now how poor and dull a lover he must have been for years past, what a habit he had got into, started perhaps by her ready sympathy and soothing ways, of talking about himself and his ailments—never about her and her ailments, and she must occasionally have had some and not felt well,—taking for granted that the things which interested him, his work, what he was reading, were also the only things which interested her, and if they hadn't been the only things, if she in her turn had begun to talk of interests of her own, he wouldn't have listened, he couldn't have listened, he would simply have been bored. Why should she want to be bothered any more with someone so unsatisfactory? Still, Ernest being dead, he was much afraid she——

He looked at her very ruefully; and she, looking at him, was thinking, "So this is it. This is what Fate has been keeping up its sleeve to hit me with."

§

As if it had been a dream, Milly remembered her walk from Victoria and how she had thought she was being let off lightly, and how she had wondered where expiation, or any opportunity for its practice, came in. Lots of opportunity now . . . lots of opportunity now . . . sing-songed in her head, swung through it backwards and forwards, idiotically.

It struck her that she must be making a silly sort of face; she could see by the expression on his that something had happened to hers, and she made a great effort to pull herself together. It would be indecent, she told herself, to wince, to let him see her wincing. And of what earthly use was it making them both wretched? One wretched person was enough. And he looked so unhappy, standing there in his poor, happy spats; he looked like—she gulped down a strange, gasping laugh—

some poor baby who has got into trouble with—yes, its mother.

"I think," she began, trying to smile—why won't one's mouth do anything but wrench itself into a ghastly grin just when one wants to look most natural? She was sure it must be a very ghastly grin; what else could it be with that ice in her heart?—"I think, Arthur," she nodded slowly, trying to smile naturally, "that you've fallen in love."

He was so much astonished that he could only stare.

"And that," she went on, "you want to get married."

He stared, his mouth open beneath his rather ragged moustache. Milly smiling? Looking quite pleased? Was it going to be all right after all?

"Isn't that what you've got to tell me?' she asked. "Arthur"— she laid her hand on his sleeve, but withdrew it quickly because of the way it was shaking— "isn't that the extraordinary thing? But why extraordinary?" And anxious only to wipe the troubled look from his face, she added softly, "Darling."

His thin face flushed. That word—it was all right, then. At the bottom of his heart he had been sure of it. Ernest or no Ernest, Milly wouldn't fail him, wouldn't ever do anything or want anything that wasn't sensible and kind.

"My dear!" he exclaimed, his face lit with relief and gratitude. "My dear, dearest friend—you don't mind?"

"Mind?" repeated Milly, insisting to her mouth that it must go on smiling, dragging it by force of will up at its corners. "Mind?" she said again, to hide the sob she was strangling.

She turned on herself ferociously, menacing the soft thing inside her which was trying to disgrace her.

"You've got to *behave*," she furiously cried out to it. "You're not to start whimpering. What's the good of you, anyhow, if you can't when you're in a tight corner *behave?*" And she held out her hands to him, smiling very hard, and said, "Why, it's *wonderful* news!"

Arthur drew a deep breath. Flushed up to his forehead, his face all gladness, he gripped the hands she was holding out, and said with profound conviction, "From the first you've been the best friend a man ever had."

"Have I?" said Milly. "I'm glad I've been something."

And then to cover it up—for it had slipped out, and certainly she had no intention of being bitter—she was going quickly to say something else, anything else, when he interrupted, holding her hands very tight, beaming down on her—Arthur, who hadn't done anything approaching beaming for years.

"How did you know?" he asked. "How on earth could you guess, Milly?"

"What—that you've fallen in love?"

She drew her hands out of his. "Oh, well—really, Arthur," she said; and achieving another smile, and bending her head while she blinked back the tears from her eyelashes, she pointed to his spats.

("I've cried enough," she said sternly to herself, blinking the tears back. "I've done nothing but cry lately. I won't any more. I will *not*." While as for that soft part of her which wanted to say useless, regrettable things, she wasn't going to let it; she simply was not going to let it. Oh, she knew the sorts of things it would say if she gave it a chance—the squashy, fool things with tears in them. Tears? She had had enough of tears. Or perhaps, even, betrayed by the ridiculous desperation of her situation, appeal. Appeal? Good God, no; for ever *no*.)

"Really, Arthur—" she said, her head bent, pointing, "your beautiful spats."

"Yes,"he said,looking down at them and smiling too,
an ashamed, boyish smile. "Yes. I hardly know why
I——"

He looked up from them to her, grateful, happy,
letting himself go to his relief, foolish, proud of being
foolish—in fact, fatuous. His young love admired these
spats. She had said, and it much diverted him, that she
always considered spats the mark of a gentleman. He
would like to tell Milly that; it would amuse her.
Couldn't he tell Milly that? Presently, perhaps——

And Milly thought, in bleak wonder: Arthur fatuous.
Her scholar, her serious, absorbed man.

With an absurd stab she remembered that he had
never worn spats for her. "He wasn't so old, though,
then," she said to herself in a flash of insight; adding, lit
by another flash, "nor was I as young as—as I expect
this one is."

"I suppose," said Arthur, rather sheepish and apologetic, but feeling very safe and comfortable now with
Milly, "the idea at the back of my mind must have been
to improve myself."

"I suppose," she said, able to smile again, "it was.
Though I don't admit you need any improving."

"Ah, Milly, you were always a flatterer," he said;
and he thought with gratitude how simple it was being
after all, and how perfectly naturally everything was
panning out, as Sylvy—his young love's name was
Sylvia—was so fond of saying. He even wouldn't now
mind sitting on the divan with Milly, just as two old
friends, and nothing in it, while he told her all about
what had happened—well, not quite all, perhaps, but
the main features. And Milly was astonished at the ease
with which she was able to take him in, how he saw
nothing, how completely satisfied he was at once, without the least further search or doubt that all was well

and he free to be happy. But at this moment he was only wanting to be taken in; if he were not able to believe, if she could not do him this last service of lies, how miserable he would be—and no good done to anybody. Also, he was in love; no good shrinking away from the words; and a person in love, as she well knew, doesn't look very attentively at other people.

"But, Milly," he said, after all not quite so blind, so satisfied, as she had just been thinking, and insisting on taking her hands again, "why do you look so pale? I've never seen you so pale, dear."

"Oh, that's because of Ernest. And—and everything," she reassured him quickly.

"My God, yes—of course," exclaimed Arthur, remembering Ernest. For the last few minutes he had quite overlooked him. Poor fellow. At that moment Arthur was truly sorry for anyone who was dead. Rough luck indeed to be out of a world brimming with the most gorgeous miracles.

"It must have been terrible, dear," he said, subduing his voice to the proper concern. "What a time you must have had, you poor little thing. You must tell me about it—" for decency demanded that before he told her his own happy story she should tell him her sad one.

Yet not sad really, he thought, except for Ernest; not sad for Milly, once she had got over the first inevitable shock of death. Because Ernest, poor fellow—and probably because he couldn't help it, Arthur thought, indulgent in his happiness to the whole world—had been a trying husband, and now Milly would be free, besides having all his money to do what she liked with. A desirable position. She would see how desirable presently. But meanwhile he must certainly comfort her. . . .

"Tell me about it, dear," he said, carefully damping

the happiness out of his voice; and again she was what
he knew she was, to be relied on utterly for understanding and common sense, and, guessing how difficult it
would be for him that day to tune himself down to
commiseration, she wouldn't let him, but declared she
had had enough of sadness, and wanted now to talk of
happy things.

"I'll make tea," said Milly, to whom a way of at least
relaxing for a few minutes while she had her back to
him over there in the corner, of not having, for a moment, to smile, had occurred—"I'll make tea while you
tell me. I haven't had any lunch, and I——"

"No lunch, Milly?" exclaimed Arthur, almost as
much shocked at this as he had been by her widow's
dress—no, that is an exaggeration; but he was shocked.
"How came you to have no lunch?"

"I think I forgot," she said, preparing to withdraw to
the corner where the kettle was.

Arthur, however, limped off to it himself. "You sit
down," he said, waving her towards the divan. "I'll
make it. You shall have it at once. At once. No wonder
you look like a ghost. So wrong of you, dear," he went
on, busily filling the kettle, dusting the cups with his
handkerchief, shaking biscuits out of an ancient tin,
amazingly active for one who had long been torpid,
"so very wrong of you, at a time when you need all your
strength. Now where have those matches got to?
Where on *earth* have those matches got to?"

He was just what he had been ten years ago, she
thought, dropping on to the divan, alive, eager, making
tea for her, excited and happy, returned, as he had then
returned, for even ten years ago he had been middle-
aged, to youth, to boyishness. And watching him, she
said to herself, "Only love does this for a man. Last
time it was love for me. Now——"

She shut her eyes, her head leaning back on the cushions, her mouth relaxed. Darkness was in her heart; dreadful questions crept about her mind—what next? where? how? And her body seemed nothing but deadly, leaden fatigue.

"Milly," said Arthur, hunting, "there were matches here last time, weren't there? Didn't we have tea?"

"I expect they're on the shelf," she said without moving, her hands limp by her side, her eyes shut. "Why don't you let me do that?"

"Why should you?" Arthur answered, lighting the spirit lamp, measuring out tea—ready to do everything for her, she thought, except love her. Love her? How could he love her if he didn't?

"You know," said Arthur, busy and making a great clattering, "I always made our tea"—and this was so remote from the truth that Milly smiled almost naturally.

"Not always," she said.

"Well, very often," insisted Arthur.

§

The tea was made, and they both sat on the divan— Milly at one end, propped against cushions, Arthur at the other, rather awkward on the low edge, for divans are uncomfortable things unless one gives oneself up to them. Between them, like Siegfried's sword, was the plate of biscuits.

Now, he thought, he would begin and tell her all about it. But he didn't like to, somehow, unless she helped him to start. So he waited, restraining his eagerness, while she drank her tea.

"You're to eat every one of these," he said, pointing to the biscuits.

"I couldn't," said Milly, shaking her head. Even the

tea made her feel as if she might be sick, while as for
those biscuits——

"They do look rather nasty," said Arthur, peering at
them. "Mouldy, aren't they?"

"I think they've been here for years," said Milly.
"Like us," she added, smiling at him.

"Yes—it has been a long time, hasn't it?" said
Arthur, clasping his thin hands round his even thinner
knees, and dying to begin his story. "But it was nice,
dear, wasn't it? You're not sorry?"

"I think it was very nice," said Milly pleasantly.

"And after all," said Arthur, "life has to go on. If old
things didn't come to an end new ones couldn't begin."

"I hope, Arthur dear," said Milly, smiling across the
biscuits at him, "it's not me you're describing as an
old thing?"

"You, Milly? My dear, I was thinking of epochs,"
he said; but, looking at her as she sat against the cushions, taking up a good deal of the divan—she sloped it
down, and the plate of biscuits kept on sliding towards
her—he thought that compared to some people she
certainly wasn't young, poor Milly. Still, why should
she be young, and why should he call her poor Milly?
She hadn't, he was sure, the least wish to be young
again, or anything but what she was—a dear, good
woman, a staunch friend to whom one could always turn
in moments of need. While as for being poor, her
situation, with Ernest removed, was about as agreeable
as he could think of. Rich and free and a great dear,
bound to be surrounded by people devoted to her—what
could be more satisfactory, more generally enviable?
Yet—poor Milly. Perhaps it was all that black stuff she
was wrapped up in. Such a heap of black she looked
piled up on the divan, and on top of it a little round,
white, puffy face. . . .

And suddenly she was blotted out by a vision shooting up before his eyes like a spray of light—Sylvy, his young love, in a blue frock as he last saw her, with the sunshine on her bright hair, so slender that she would almost, he had told her, be able to be pulled through her own wedding-ring.

He stared at Milly without seeing her. On his face was the same expression that she had seen a few minutes before, when he told her something had happened to him that doesn't happen once in a life-time pride, wonder, extreme tenderness; and Milly recognizing it, and remembering how it had once been there for her, thought, "Why should I stay here and be tortured? I won't. I'll go. I'll get away—anywhere——"

But the only result of her sudden movement to get off the very low divan was that she broke her cup. It shook off its saucer, and fell on the bare boards, and broke, and made a pool of tea.

"There," said Arthur, picking up the bits and wiping away the pool with his handkerchief, "now we've only got one left."

"I'm so sorry. But we don't want them any more, do we?" said Milly, sitting still again, caught, obliged to stop where she was and listen. And wasn't it the only thing to do, to listen, to hear him out, if she were not to betray what she was determined never to betray, and show herself to him as one needing pity? Pity! Poor Arthur. How miserable he would be, and she herself how shameful—clinging, and calling out.

She set her teeth, and sat quiet. In these cases, she was dead sure, all that was left to be done by the one who minded was to pretend that she—surely most often a she—didn't mind; and to pretend so well that she was entirely believed.

"That's true," said Arthur. "Shall I break the other one, so that no one else will ever be able to drink out of it?"

"How romantic," smiled Milly.

"Well, I feel romantic," said Arthur. "We've been happy here, after all."

"Very," said Milly.

"Though I do think," he went on, remembering how for years he had held her down among the ruins of Greece and Rome—to Sylvia he hadn't so much as mentioned them; with her he was reading Keats and Shelley—"I do think I must have bored you terribly."

"Only sometimes," she smiled.

"The fact is, I get so much wrapped up in what interests me," he said apologetically, "and I'm afraid when I get hold of a hobby I ride the wretched thing to death."

"With me on the pillion," she said. "But I liked it," she added quickly, smiling. "And it was very educational."

"Educational! I don't know that——"

He broke off and got up, carrying the fragments of the cup to the sink.

"Shall I really break the other one?" he asked, over his shoulder.

"The other what?"

"Cup."

"No. Take it to Oxford with you as a memento. A Present from Chelsea for a Good Boy." And Milly, now that he wasn't looking, leaned her head back on the cushions again, and whispered to herself, "Oh, I'm tired, tired—oh, I want to go home—oh, why can't I go home. . . ."

"Milly," said Arthur, his back to her, his long thin

fingers piling the broken bits of cup one on top of each
other in the sink, "tell me frankly—do you think me a
fool?"

"Why, dear?" she asked, her eyes shut. "For wanting to break the other cup?"

"No. For marrying."

"Dear Arthur—why should you not?"

With a movement of his hand he scattered the little
pile he had made, and came back and stood before her.

"She's only nineteen," he said, a sort of ashamedness
struggling with pride and wonder on his face; and Milly
looking up at him thought, "What can possibly be
younger than the not young, when for any reason they
return to being young?"

She felt very old, and dismally, wretchedly lonely.
"That's just the right age for you," she said gently,
holding out her hand.

"You don't think so really, of course."

She sighed. These efforts . . . oh, it was more than . . .

"But I do, Arthur," she said. "Won't you sit down
and—tell me about it?"

"It seems so——" he touched her crape sleeve, and
hesitated. "It does seem rather—with this just having
happened to you——"

"Oh, but please," said Milly.

"You know, if I had had an idea——"

"But you hadn't. Sit down and tell me."

"If I had had an idea," he persisted, his hand on her
sleeve, wanting to say the right thing, the kind, decent
thing.

But he couldn't. He found he couldn't pretend that
Ernest's death would have made a difference if he had
known it, because he knew it wouldn't have—not once
he had met Sylvia.

"Please——" begged Milly. "Won't you sit down?"

§

Now Arthur was a humane man, and would not willingly have hurt anybody, least of all Milly, his one really close friend, his one comfort during otherwise lonely years; and therefore, beginning his story, he picked his way carefully among words. But pick as he might, small ecstasies burst through, and little jabs of happiness. He did his best to present Sylvy—

"Sylvy?"

"Yes. Her name is Sylvia, but I—her mother calls her Sylvy."

"Oh."

—he did his best to present Sylvy in a sober light, as a good, intelligent girl, with a most sensible mother,who would make an excellent wife, he thought, being intelligent and brought up carefully by a most sensible mother—he dwelt with insistence on the sensible mother, obscurely feeling that her sensibleness made the whole thing sensible—besides becoming less young, of course, every day, and also she would be a good mistress, he believed, for his house, which really was, as Milly had seen for herself, a good deal more than he could manage alone; yet, try as he would to be thus sober—and he tried so hard that he perspired—Sylvy danced and laughed and sparkled through his words like the thing of light she indeed was, and Milly saw her dancing, heard her laughing, and suffered.

"Absurd I am—*absurd* I am," she told herself, doing her best not to suffer. "I, at my age, still wanting to stick. Is it possible? Is it credible? Why can't I give him up nicely—really nicely, not just pretending? I've had him for ten years, and I've often and often been disappointed in him, and secretly impatient, and not liked his having all those colds. But then——"

She stared at the thought an instant, before turning her mind away from it. It was, *He's all I've got.*

Faintly she said, noticing that he had stopped, "Go on, Arthur——"

"Aren't you well, dear?" he asked, struck by her whiteness.

"Yes, I'm quite well," said Milly. "Go on. She sounds—" she managed to smile naturally enough to satisfy him—"your little girl sounds so—so nice."

Nice. He liked that adjective. It exactly described the impression he wished to produce of a good girl, who would make a good wife, and no nonsense about the marriage, just reason and sense.

He held out his hand across the plate of biscuits. She put hers into it, still smiling.

"You know," he said, for after all it was true, "for years I wanted to marry *you.*"

"I know," she answered, giving his hand a friendly little squeeze before drawing away her own. "And we weren't able to. Go on."

Arthur went on; and inevitably, as he proceeded, his words grew warmer, grew less able to hide his pride and amazement that this should have happened to him. He did try. He thought he was succeeding, really doing it very well, keeping as much to facts as possible; but the facts themselves were so marvellous, glowing so hotly that his face was flushed as red by them as if he were toasting it at some great fire. Sylvy—that child—loving him, bringing him back to life. . . . He, modest man, couldn't get over it. If Milly only knew how wonderful she was! But of course he didn't say this; he was most careful, most tactful; eliminating, so he thought, every trace of excitement.

Leaning forward on his elbow closer to the barrier of biscuits, he kept to the safer facts, such as his stock blindness, and how her mother positively had at last to take him in hand and make him see what everybody else in the pension had long ago seen, and how Sylvy herself had told him afterwards that she had been quite ashamed of—well, of liking someone who never even looked at her. But how natural that was. Didn't Milly think it natural that he should never have dreamed——?

"Very natural," agreed Milly; and asked herself whether, when men were older, they often became like this. Or was it only Arthur, bewitched, caught in a spell, caught perhaps—who knew?—by the mother?

"Is there a father?" she asked.

Her father, Arthur explained, was dead; and her mother, left a widow with a young family on her hands and the eldest only nineteen, was of remarkable courage and resource. She was determined, she had told him, to do her very best for them whatever it might cost her of self-denial, giving them every possible advantage, however much she herself had to do without things; and one of the advantages she considered indispensable was educational travel in foreign countries—which was how she came to be in Rome with her eldest daughter, and, miraculously, in the same pension as himself.

He made friends with her before he even saw her daughter, though for a whole week the child had actually been sitting opposite him at every meal. Didn't Milly think that most extraordinary?

"But you saw her mother, for you said you made friends with her."

No, Arthur explained, he hadn't seen her mother either, till she came up and spoke to him. Then he saw her, of course. He wasn't much good at seeing, as Milly knew, if he happened to be thinking of other things. She, kindly soul, noticing that he was always alone at meals, made friends with him. She had read in some paper of his appointment as Senior Tutor of Zebedee, and asked him if he were the same Arthur Oswestry, and was much interested, because one of her nephews was there.

They soon were friends. She told him she was having a pretty stiff struggle to keep things going, and it was a great comfort and relief to her, she frankly confessed after it had all happened, to know that her eldest child, at any rate, was safely provided for.

"I gather, then," said Milly, "that they are poor."

"They are. Completely so," said Arthur.

"Do you mean really completely? Have they only got two and eightpence in their bag?"

"I don't know about two and eightpence," said Arthur with a slight impatience, for the question seemed irrelevant, and as if Milly were not listening to him with real seriousness, "but they haven't much. I expect it would seem nothing at all to you. Even to me—Mrs. Finch-Dawson told me, of course, how they stood—yes, that's their name, Finch-Dawson—it seems very little. How the poor soul has managed at all is a mystery. And that child always so prettily dressed——"

He broke off, he saw it, he gazed at it, the enchanting figure, the dear, delicious blue-frocked figure, with the sun shining on its bright hair. . . .

Milly made a small movement, and then sat still again.

"When do you suppose——" she said, "when do you think of being——"

"Married?" said Arthur.

She nodded.

"Well——"

He cleared his throat, and became carefully matter of fact, while before his eyes quivered bliss.

"Well,—as the house is all ready, and badly needs

someone to look after it, we thought, her mother and myself—and Sylvy thought too—that it ought to be—well, rather soon, perhaps."

There was no hurry, of course, he went on, but that was what they rather thought. He was only just back, as Milly knew, so that no actual decision had as yet been taken. They had all travelled home together, and to-morrow her mother—and Sylvy too—were coming to Oxford to spend the day with him and have a thorough look round. Fortunately—they were much pleased with what he had told them of the house, and Sylvy was especially pleased about the garden and the apple-tree, and said—he turned his face away, because he felt it was betraying too great a happiness—she would do all her sewing there, she being, he was glad to say, a properly brought up young woman, and good at that sort of thing. It was nice to think, he continued, of all those rooms going to be filled, and the place soon cheerful with children's voices——

"Children?" echoed Milly, faintly.

"She has dozens of small brothers and sisters," said Arthur, reddening, turning to her rebukingly, shocked by what she was evidently supposing, and that she should think him capable of such execrable taste; and he hurried on, with a slight feeling of estrangement from her, of disappointment, to praise the behaviour of these children, so well brought up, those he had seen, and so very good-looking. Their looks, indeed, were unusual—the mother's too; while as for Sylvy——

He stopped. He wished he could tell Milly. He wished he could let himself go to the one person he was accustomed to talk freely to, and who always understood and sympathized, about the sweet beauty of his young love.

Couldn't he? Damn tact, thought Arthur, glancing

at Milly to see if there were any encouragement in her face for him to go on. But on looking at her he was seized with compunction. "I'm tiring you," he said, struck a second time by her extreme whiteness, her drooping attitude of evident fatigue.

She sat up quickly, and began smoothing her hair. "Oh, no," she said. "But I do think perhaps——" she looked round vaguely—"I'm afraid I ought to be going."

"It's only half-past five, dear," he said, jerking up his wrist watch, "and we never leave before six. But of course if you——"

"I really think I ought to go, Arthur," said Milly, who could bear no more. Why should she stay there being tortured? He was absolutely happy, completely secure and satisfied that she was pleased about it all. Helped by his readiness to believe, she had done her part very well. But she had done it. It was finished. Let her go.

She made definite movements towards the edge of the divan. But here was a difficulty: it was so low that she never could get up off it unless he helped her, and it was his habit to take her by both hands, and, with a great pull, pull her on to her feet.

The impetus invariably sent her straight into his arms, and for some reason the sudden jerk to his breast had always amused them. It was so sudden that she arrived each time with an effect of surprise; and then they laughed, and, laughing, kissed.

The laughter, it is true, had long become a smile, and the kissing absent-minded on his part, or as often as not just an affectionate pat; but, as she couldn't get off the divan unless he pulled her, pull her he still did, and the pull, which had to be a hard one, inevitably landed her against his breast.

She glanced at him. Had he forgotten she couldn't move unless he helped?

He was staring straight in front of him, his elbow on his knee, his fingers absently tugging at the ends of his straggly moustache. In spite of his sunburn and his new tie and his spats, he looked to her after all what he was; a delicate elderly man, thin of cheek, stooping of shoulder; and his sudden return to youth and its excitement only made him seem more brittle, more frail.

"Oh, I hope she will always love him, always be kind to him," thought Milly, who had loved him so much.

He was staring, Milly knew, at Sylvy, and she herself had vanished, and the room and the present moment had vanished, in dreams of happiness. If she could have got up off that divan alone and crept away he wouldn't notice, she thought, he would go on sitting there, lost in dreams; but she couldn't move, not decently, without his help. It would be possible, she supposed, by rolling off on to the floor, though she had never tried it, and scrambling to her knees, somehow to get up, but what a spectacle! And he, jarred out of his dreaming by these strange convulsions, looking on in astonishment. . . .

Milly shuddered away from the picture. "I'm afraid, Arthur," she said—at her voice he came to actuality with a start—"you'll have to—do you mind helping me off this wretched thing?"

He got up at once. Some crumbs of biscuit, he saw, were on his trousers, and he briskly brushed them off before holding out his hands.

"Not too quickly," she said, at all costs wishing to avoid that sudden fling against his breast.

Arthur, however, was quite awake again now, and he remembered perfectly what had been the invariable finish to the pulling up. He hadn't thought of it when he told Milly to sit on the divan while he made tea; he had forgotten the peculiar difficulties of that seat for a person of her weight and figure and present age, and he was as anxious as she was to get her off it decorously, and keep her, at the end, at arm's length.

Slowly, therefore, and with caution, he drew her to her feet. It was much more difficult to draw her up slowly than to do it with a heave and a rush, and the veins stood out on his forehead. Milly really was extraordinarily heavy, he thought, for somebody so short; at one moment her weight very nearly pulled him off his balance, and he was within an ace of toppling forward on to the divan in a supremely undignified and awkward mix-up. But he just managed not to; and very red, and breathing rather hard, he got her safely on to her feet.

For an instant they stood looking at each other, he panting, she very pale. Then she thanked him with a polite smile, and went to fetch her bonnet from the table where she had laid it. The monstrous thing, when he had finished wiping his forehead and turned and saw it eclipsing her, her hair disappeared inside it and nothing but a bald white face and two heavy eyes to be seen, brought home to him once again what he had kept on losing sight of in the absorption of his own affairs—the fact that Milly was in trouble.

"My dear," he said, his eyes suddenly worried, "I hate to think of all you must have been through while I was so unaware and happy."

"Dear Arthur—you mustn't," said Milly.

"But I do. And I'm afraid, till you get straight and all the unavoidable business part of it settled, you've a dreary time ahead of you. But you *will* get straight, dear. It will come right. And they've always been very kind to you, haven't they, those Botts?"

"Very kind," said Milly.

"I wish I could help you through it," he said, looking

down at her with kind, troubled eyes. "But I'm afraid"
—he smiled—"our past rather disqualifies me from
appearing among the Botts. Milly——" he stopped
short, struck by a sudden thought, and took her hand.

"What, Arthur? Tell me quick, because really I
can't stay any longer."

"Yes, of course—you must have so many things to
see to, poor little thing. But, dear, you don't mind——"

"Oh, I've *told* you I don't mind!" she interrupted,
trying to pull her hand away. "And that I'm pleased,
I'm glad. Let me go, Arthur——"

"I'm not thinking of the present," he said. "What
has occurred to me is that perhaps you mind our past."

"Mind our past?" she repeated.

"And may have thought it needs—rectifying."

She could only repeat, "Rectifying?"

"I don't know," said Arthur, his face much troubled,
"because I never thought of it as wrong. But I'm not
so sure that you didn't. At the beginning I know you
did. You don't still think so, do you, Milly? You see,
don't you, that we only didn't marry because we
couldn't? You're not worried about it, dear, are you?"

She assured him with earnestness that she wasn't.
"I long ago got over all my prejudices, dear Arthur,"
she assured him. "And one of us, at any rate, is going
to marry and settle down respectably," she added,
smiling.

But he still stared down at her, his forehead puckered.
Was that true, he wondered?

"Anyhow, you're well off," he said, "and won't have
to bother about money. Really, dear, it's a great comfort to know that—the very greatest comfort. Good
God, how anxious and distressed I should be about you
if it weren't so!"

"Darling Arthur, you needn't be," said Milly; and

instinctively she put up her free hand to smooth away
the puckers from his forehead. She had always done this
when he had been worried about anything; she couldn't
bear to see him troubled.

But Sylvy flashed between them, and Arthur drew
back.

So did Milly. "Oh, I'm sorry——" she said quickly,
her hand dropping at her side.

"It's only——" began Arthur, feeling a fool; but
really he couldn't endure anything approaching a caress
from anybody just then, except his betrothed. A fero-
cious chastity had come upon him. He was Sylvy's.
Such as he was she wanted him, and such as he was he
was altogether hers.

"I must go," said Milly, terribly ashamed, desperately wounded, looking round for her bag.

She picked it up from the table, and went towards
the door.

"I'm coming with you to the station," said Arthur,
following her. "I'll see you off. We needn't mind being
seen together, now that poor Ernest——"

"Oh, but now there's—Sylvia," said Milly, pausing a
moment, before getting the name out.

So there was. Arthur paused too, his hat and stick
in his hand, his eyes troubled again as he stared at her.
It hadn't occurred to him that Milly would be someone
he couldn't well explain to Sylvy. To her mother, perhaps, no, even to her mother he couldn't explain
Milly—not well, that is. Sylvy, dear innocent, wouldn't
understand, but her mother would perfectly understand; and suppose, she, being one of these unworldly
women, suppose she said that he was not, then, a fit
husband for her daughter? Why, if she said that,
thought Arthur, he was sure he would give up, immediately grow old, and die.

"Yes," he said, staring at Milly, and seeing her in a new light, the light Sylvia's mother would probably see her in, "that's true. I'm sorry, Milly."

Perhaps after all then she wouldn't, as he had hoped, be able later on to become Sylvia's friend; perhaps after all it would be too difficult. He hadn't thought the thing out properly. It might mean having to pretend to Sylvy. And most clear in his mind was it that he would never, please God, pretend to Sylvy.

He stared at Milly, very sorry. It was a pity. They ought to have gone on being dear friends, the other thing forgotten—as indeed he had forgotten it, hardly able now to believe it had ever existed, so completely was it gone. Civilized people, thought Arthur, should not make such a fuss over these things. Civilized people, he was sure, didn't. But there was that about Mrs. Finch-Dawson which convinced him he would find her, on subjects such as these, incompletely civilized. Perhaps naturally so, with a large young family depending on her for safety, and five of them girls. Naturally, however, or not, it was the one aspect of that sensible woman which Arthur found less excellent. Women—older women—were frequently, he feared, retarders of civilization. Why should not people be present friends, even if they had been—surely the more that they had been—past lovers? He didn't know many women, it was true, but he did know Mrs. Finch-Dawson; and she, in her certain attitude towards Milly, if Milly were explained to her, was undoubtedly a retarder.

All this passed through his mind, as in silence he stared at Milly. Was he not going to see her again, then? Was she departing, poor little black thing, to her bothers, and he not know any more what was happening to her?

"You'll write, dear, won't you, if you want anything —if I can be of the least——"

"We never did write."

"Because of Ernest. But now———"

"Now we can't because of—Sylvia."

"Do you mean to say," cried Arthur, addressing the universe generally, "that because a man was fond once of a woman he must never———"

"Oh, Arthur!" gasped Milly, wincing at the dreadful word "once."

Tremblingly she pulled her veil down to hide her face. "What's the good of talking?" she said. "What's the *use?* I must go. Good-bye. No, don't bother—I can open it———"

And she pushed the curtain aside, opened the street door, and with a shaky, "Bless you," was gone.

He stood a moment without moving, his shoulders drooping, his hat and stick in his hand, looking at the curtain still swaying from the pull Milly had given it.

It was a devil of a business after all, this breaking off, this finishing. And no sense in it.

⁘(X)⁘

HURRYING away from the studio for ever, Milly turned into King's Road and waited at the nearest stopping-place for the omnibus which went to Victoria. She was going back to Titford, to face the Botts.

Before she got to the corner of the street she knew it, lashed into clarity of vision, illuminated by it into the farthermost recesses of her consciousness. Gone now definitely out of Arthur's life, separated from him as completely, and far more dreadfully, than if he had been dead, her exhausted emotions, unable to react any more, dropped into numbness, and her mind was whipped free of that foolish, long-drawn-out dream of being loved, and of trusting, and of supposing she mattered.

She didn't matter. Accept it, accept it, she said to herself. She was of no consequence whatever to anybody; there was no one now in the whole world who would care if she were happy or unhappy, ill or not ill, alive or dead. If she were run over at that moment and killed, as Ernest had been killed, who would mind? The Botts would be relieved; and Arthur, after saying, and meaning, "Poor Milly," would proceed with his happiness. Perhaps Aggie—but Aggie was so far away. Besides, why pretend? Aggie might well be relieved too—probably would be, set free from having to be grateful because of the money, rid for good of an immoral sister.

Well, it was a detached condition. She sat in the corner of the omnibus, being swayed and heaved towards

Victoria, bleakly considering it, this condition swept clear of love—also swept clear of love's illusions, the most persistent and comforting of which for ten years had been the conviction that there was someone thinking often of her, missing her, counting the hours till he saw her again. And, passed beyond feeling, become merely a brain perceiving, Milly realized without emotion that Arthur hadn't done any of these things, not after the first weeks,—neither thought of her often, nor missed her, nor counted hours.

Incurable romantics, women were, she reflected dispassionately, forced to see clearly by the sheer pressure of her desolation; incurable romantics, eternally yapping after love, and more love, and yet more love. But only after love as they considered it ought to be, and were sure that somewhere, if they could but hit on it, it was. Naturally they never did hit on it. The man wasn't born who could go on satisfying them for ever. Just at first he outdid them, because in everything, if he were sufficiently moved, he could always outdo a woman equally moved; but it couldn't be kept up, not at that pitch. And the trouble with women, she thought, relentlessly pursuing her frigid dissections, was that they insisted it should be kept up, and exactly at that pitch, and, when it wasn't, they stuffed out what was left of it with their own illusions, and then, some day, there they were—"Like me," she thought; though it didn't seem to concern her.

Nothing seemed to concern her. She regarded her being, as she put it, there, impartially. One had to be somewhere. If women chose to go in for love-making outside marriage, as she had chosen, sooner or later they would be where she was then—going away from nothing, going towards nothing, being carried along in some sort of dreary vehicle like this omnibus, shut up with

strangers who all had left their lovers for the last time,
or were going to leave them on some future day, shrug-
ging their disillusioned shoulders, their brains full of
icy light.

"Rather horrible," she reflected, critically. But she
didn't mind its being horrible; she wasn't touched; it
didn't seem to concern her.

Clearly the crowning cowardice of her life had been
that shameful flight from the Botts. Whatever they
had thought of her, and said to her, and done to her, she
ought to have stayed and submitted. Dignity, and
repentance for her sin, both demanded it. And so did
ordinary humanity; for to run away like that, leaving
her humiliated relations to find out from servants that
she had gone, stabbing the family, as she well knew, in
its most sensitive spot, was plainly a cruelly cowardly
thing to have done. It took from the Botts their last
doubt, supposing they had had one, of her guilt and of
the justice of Ernest's Will; it definitely branded her.
Well, she was going to undo as much of that as she
could. It was true that she was driven to go back to
them, with only two and eightpence in her bag, but if
she had had her thousand pounds she still now would
have gone, and said, "Here I am. I've been wicked and
disgraced you, and I'm sorry. Tell me what you wish
me to do, what is the best thing for you that I should do,
and I'll do it." And whatever music the Botts should see
fit to make she would face it, however furiously it
crashed about her ears she wouldn't shrink away.

At least she would take her punishment standing up
—only, strangely, it seemed no longer to need courage,
the facing of the Botts, the taking of her punishment;
this too didn't seem to concern her. She would be there,
her body would be, and they would pour out their
indignation and contempt, and she wouldn't feel it. It

was her mind which recognized the need for making
good, for decency and an end of lies; her heart, stunned
unconscious, was indifferent. What did it matter? In
Titford with the Botts, working out her punishment, or
away from Titford and the Botts, somewhere alone and
forgotten, there would be the same dead routine of life
to be gone through each day, the waking up, the dressing, the feeding, the sitting, the walking, the undressing,
the sleeping—over and over again, buttoning only to
unbutton, tying only to untie, putting in hairpins only
to pull them out, and everywhere, wherever she was,
she would be there, the ageing fool. "And," thought
Milly, the corners of her mouth for the first time in her
life cynical——

"Didn't you say Victoria, mum? 'Ere we are," interrupted the conductor.

"Oh, thank you."

She got out.

"—and," she continued, when she was out, "all this
is evidently the sort of thing a woman thinks when her
man has thrown her over. She should, of course, be
ashamed of herself, and she isn't. She should give herself
a shake and start afresh, and she can't. One single man,
one Arthur, blotting out hope—really amazing, really
quite contemptible," thought Milly. Could idiocy go
farther? An Arthur, as against the whole of life. Yet it
was what happened to women, to all that immense long
category of fools who let themselves become absorbed
in some particular person, betrayed by their maternal
instincts, those instincts which dressed themselves up
in so many tender and lively names, while all the time
they were ruthlessly intent on being nothing less to the
object they had fastened on than God Almighty—dis-
pensers, that is, of happiness, insisters on dependence,
absorbers of freedom.

She crossed the street.

Deep in thought, she was all but run over. What she was thinking, her mind turning away from Arthur and everything to do with him, was that at least she wouldn't be a burden on the Botts, because in the house in Mandeville Park Road there were jewels, as well as fur and laces, legitimately hers, either given her by Ernest, or bought by her out of her ample allowance, before Arthur was ever heard of; and these she would sell, and on the proceeds, after she had stayed in Titford long enough to stop its tongues, and when and if the Botts were willing to let her go, she would withdraw and live frugally somewhere till she had found something to do. Surely there was something in the world that she could do? If she took lessons? If she learned? "It's a pity," thought Milly bleakly, arrived at the opposite pavement and unaware how narrowly she had missed extinction, "that one doesn't die in time."

She went into the station.

The omnibus fare had been twopence, and the first-class ticket to Titford would, she knew, be one and threepence—she couldn't, returning, travel third class as she had done escaping, for now she had once more to consider the Botts,—so she would have enough left out of her two and eightpence to take a taxi from the station to Mandeville Park Road. Not yet was she composed enough to meet people she knew in the streets of Titford, and she was, besides, so tired that she felt she would never get there at all unless she drove. Silence; darkness; to be alone;—these were what she would best like to find waiting for her. But whatever the day still held she wouldn't try to avoid it, and should she find the house full of Botts she would meet them calmly, and should she find it empty of servants, they having either left or gone off for the evening enjoying themselves, it wouldn't trouble her. Her latch-key was still in her bag, and she would let herself in and put herself to bed in the bedroom she had been so much frightened of, and which was, after all, only a bedroom like any other —a place to rest in, and forget the yesterdays, and not think of the to-morrows.

She took her ticket.

In the chill light of the common sense which had replaced every other emotion, it was with contempt that she remembered how she had imagined that bedroom haunted by Ernest's malevolent eyes. Panic does queer things to one's brain, she thought, coldly wondering at her own folly. Ernest had no further power. He had vanished, and was nothing now but a rather—not very, "Don't let's pretend," thought Milly—pitiful memory, a memory of lost opportunities, of all the missed occasions on which she might, by keeping straight, have avoided goading him into baseness. She would sleep in that room as well as in another. It would make no difference to her. Sleep. How blessed. Oh, how profoundly blessed. If only it were time, already, to sleep. . . .

She emerged from the booking-office; and, proceeding in the direction of the platform the Titford train started from, immediately ran into George Bott.

§

"Ran into" is hardly the right expression, for both were walking so slowly that it might be said they sauntered into each other. Both knew there was no hurry, the train not starting till six thirty-five, and both were reluctant to go on to the platform before they need, because neither wished to meet, unnecessarily, any of those numerous business men and their wives who lived in Titford, might return by this train, and were accustomed to think highly of the Botts. Milly, if asked, would have said that she preferred never to see anyone who had ever thought highly of her again; while as for George, he and his family were just then particularly desirous of keeping themselves to themselves.

"Good God!" ejaculated George, when he saw who it was that he had all but walked into, stopping dead, and staring at her through his horn-rimmed spectacles.

For two and a half days now, he and the rest of his family had been concentrating on presenting a united front to the world. It was a front of almost unnatural composure; and behind it, since the reading of Ernest's Will, and, more fiercely, since the discovery of Milly's flight, raged a particular desire to keep themselves to themselves. At first Titford, sympathetically considering the bereaved family, took it for granted that it should be serious, that it should avoid contacts, that it should be of few words when it was met in railway carriages, during the first days, almost the first hours, after the burial of a brother. Except when proceeding on their lawful occasions, no Botts were anywhere to be seen; and this, too, Titford sympathetically took for granted. But, it presently having become known through the usual channels—tradespeople calling for orders which couldn't be given—that Mrs. Ernest, the newly-made widow, had disappeared, and disappeared without either having been seen disappearing or any word left as to her return, Titford, in spite of the statuesque composure of the Botts, began to ask itself what could have happened; and they, waiting in a condition of raw suspense for this inevitable moment, were at once made aware, by unmistakable small signs, that it was upon them.

In anxious conclave the unhappy family had considered measures for staving it off. Meeting together on each of the painful evenings, they had done their best

to think out steps which might yet be taken to shield
Milly, and therefore themselves, from scandal and disgrace. During Wednesday, the day of her disappearance,
they did succeed in persuading the bewildered and half-
rebellious staff at Mandeville Park Road that their
mistress had gone up to town on business, and would
be back to dinner—and they succeeded because there
were Botts, that day, who themselves believed it. It
was not to be expected, Fred Bott told the crowding
servants,—he was the first to recover his presence of
mind when he and Alec and Bertie called that morning
to inform Milly of the plans they had made for her welfare, and were faced by a house in upheaval—it was not
to be expected, he said, that a lady in the first grief of
so sudden a widowhood should remember to give
orders or leave messages; and the maids, calmed by the
authoritativeness of him who was the wealthiest of the
brothers, besides having discovered for themselves that
their mistress had taken no luggage with her, were
ready, though still puzzled, to believe these words of Mr.
Fred's, and settled down to their usual duties, and tidied
the house, and made preparations for the evening's
dinner.

To that dinner Milly never came; and Alec Bott,
telephoning at nine o'clock—the family had decided
that he, as the eldest, should do the telephoning, it
being desirable to avoid indiscriminate and agitated
calls,—received the news that she had never come with
such evident consternation, with such an entire inability to conceal his amazement and alarm, that the
maid at the other end hastened to inform her fellow-
servants of the way the old boy—thus she spoke of
him—had got the wind up. And the next day, when
Alec's wife went round with her suit-case directly after
breakfast, prepared, according to the latest hasty

decision of the shattered family, to stay in the house till something more definite could be arranged, they met her in a body, demanding a month's wages and their immediate departure.

Fred had had to be telephoned for. It had needed all his authority and conciliatoriness to induce them to stay. Lightly he touched on the legal aspect of their leaving like this—but very lightly, because he saw they were in no mood to be cowed. Insolence trembled visibly on the cook's lips. He felt that they had somehow scented the approach of scandal, and it revolted him, it simply revolted Fred, to know that one of his family, a Bott by name if not by blood, and certainly always treated kindly and affectionately, had put herself in a position, and accordingly the family as well, in which servants could sniff.

Sniffing servants. A nice thing to be exposed to. They had been listening at the door, he presumed, and they had heard that confounded Will read, and no doubt the ensuing family argument. And he cursed Milly in his heart as he stood there facing a heated cook, a pale parlourmaid, and a lesser fry of capless and apronless rebels, all intent on getting out of a house they quite evidently believed to be of little credit to them, when he ought long ago to have been in his office.

Somehow he persuaded them to stay; at least till they had cleaned up thoroughly, and set the house in proper order. He appealed to their sense of fair play, he flatteringly alluded to their years of excellent service, he hinted that wages would be increased during this time of extra hard work, and he assured them that their mistress, detained in London on business, would very shortly be back.

How much he hated himself and them for this having to cajole; what a job for an important business man.

"Look here, Cook," he said, detaining her when the others, still rather disposed to murmur, had straggled out of the room, "you're a sensible woman, and one of the best cooks I ever came across, bar none—just see that they all get busy, like good girls, so that Mrs. Ernest will find everything ship-shape when she gets home. We don't want to add to her troubles, do we?" And he pressed a note into her hand.

It was only a one-pound note. He would have liked to have made it a fiver, he thought, but was afraid she might imagine he was afraid. And he took his sister-in-law aside, Alec's pious wife Ruth, who had stood by trembling, for the sole purpose before he went to his office of relieving his mind by cursing Milly.

"Indeed it's all very unpleasant—very unpleasant indeed," said Ruth, trembling away from the words he used. She was sixty-five, and much shattered by this her first approach to rebellion in the lower classes, and, in her own, to what she feared she must call actual vice.

Alec, too, was shattered; Bertie was in what his wife, watching him, called a state; the whole family was shaken to its foundations; and George, the most phlegmatic of them all, was shattered in his quiet way as much as any of them. On each of those anxious mornings, Wednesday and Thursday, they went up to their offices with stony faces and troubled hearts, and on each of those anxious evenings, Wednesday and Thursday, they returned to their agitated homes more troubled than they had left them—except George, whose trouble took on a different colouring the second of the two evenings, when, heavy with gloomy thoughts after long hours of work badly done, preparing to return to a home he knew he would find seething more than ever with questions to which the only answers possible were unpleasant, there, at Victoria Station, he barged into the cause of the whole beastly business—Milly. No wonder then, that stopping dead and staring at her through his horn-rimmed glasses, his ears—he was a pasty man, and showed such rare emotion as overtook him only in his ears—gone crimson, he ejaculated, "Good God!"

This was unlike George. He didn't often say things like that, but he was shaken out of his customary phlegm.

It was Milly who seemed to have any phlegm there was about. Stodgy, she looked, thought George, staring; stodgy, and—yes, sleepy. Mooning along, she was, when he came upon her, and when he stood still and exclaimed she didn't seem at first to see him,—not very clearly, that is, and said tentatively after a moment, with an effect, somehow, of shading her eyes, "George?"

"That's right," said George, wishing with all his heart it wasn't. Why couldn't it have been one of the others who had barged into her—Fred, or Bertie? They would have made a better job of it than he possibly could. What on earth ought one to say to her? And ought one to say anything at all to her? Hadn't she——? Wasn't she——? Oh damn, thought George, again shaken out of his phlegm.

"You going down by the six thirty-five?" he plunged. Here she was, anyhow; it was Milly, all right—or rather all wrong, and he couldn't not speak to her. But he did wish he knew what one said on such a confounded unpleasant occasion.

She concentrated her mind on his question, her brows drawn together. George, she was thinking; George. The first notes of the music she had come back to face. The, as it were, prelude.

Bowing her head, she accepted him. "Yes," she said, "I'm going home."

And George thought, "Home. That's good. Home, indeed!"

He went on staring at her, searching for something to say. The situation was beyond him. Why he should have been picked out for this job, a quiet, unworldly chap like himself, he failed to understand. The only thing he could think of to do at the moment was to buy her an evening paper; so he beckoned to a passing news-boy, and did.

"Thank you," said Milly, as he put it into her passive hand.

"Something to read in the train," explained George.

"Yes," said Milly.

Again he stared at her in silence. What on earth Providence was up to, fixing on him like this, when any one of the others would have been a thousand times——

"Shall I carry that thing for you?" he asked, noticing she had a handbag, and seeing it as something to tack a remark on to.

Milly looked down, and noticed too that she had a handbag. She gazed at it, faintly puzzled. Usedn't there to be a suit-case there as well? When she went away that time—hadn't she been carrying a suit-case? And going up the steps in Chelsea, she seemed to remember. . . . Then, where——? Tiresome if, finding it in the studio, Arthur took it into his head to send it back. Ridiculous as well as tiresome if the last word of their loving was to be a returned suit-case. That curtain was rung down now. It would force her to laugh horribly if it had to be hauled up again, and lo, in the middle of the empty, dark stage, a suit-case.

"No, thank you," she said. "It's quite light."

Again he was silent. Then, continuing to stare at her, not wanting to, but fascinated, he emerged sud-denly once more from his phlegm, for he too, like his

brothers, had been fond of her, and burst out, "Hang it
all, Milly——"

And, as he paused, she asked, her eyes wide open and
fixed on a point just below his spectacles and not looking
as if she really saw him, "Why?"

Oh, well—if she was going to brazen it out. . . .

Scrutinizing her, however, more closely through her
veil, he thought he saw that she didn't look very
brazen; she looked pale and puffy, and extremely un-
wholesome, but not brazen. Then, if she weren't, why
did she behave callously like that? Callous did seem the
word to George; it wasn't right, he was sure, just to be
stodgy and apathetic on such an occasion, and say
"Why?" like that.

Once more he wished that it were Fred or Bertie
tackling her, instead of himself. He was no good at all
at making out what women were after, or what they
were feeling, or what, if anything, they intended to
convey, nor had he a notion of the proper line to take
with a returning prodigal. He hadn't met a prodigal
before. In his orderly life there had been no such person. This one had certainly given his family more
anxiety, and caused it more unhappiness, during the
last two days than a decent family should be called upon
to bear. Yet, knowing that it was a great thing, whatever she had done, to get her back, and his part having
been cast by an inscrutable Providence as first welcomer,
he much wished to say and do the right thing. Scandal,
as to his brothers and sisters, was loathsome to George.
Beneath his stolid exterior he was as anxious as any of
them to hush up all that might yet be hushed. With
Milly fled, there was no possible means of hushing up
anything; with Milly actually in their midst, able to
be produced, and looked at, and talked to, some way
ought to be found even now, and would be found if they

laid their heads together, of making things seem, at least, to be all right. Yes, it was a great thing to get her back; no doubt about that. And he would give a good deal to be able to hit on the right thing to say to the woman.

What he really wanted to know—waiving the question of guilt, as to which the Botts, after having hesitated, some of them, the day before, were now of one mind—what he would very much like to know was, seeing that she had come back, why had she ever gone? Obviously it was a flight, it wasn't an ordinary going. Then why, having taken all that trouble to disappear, placing the family in a devil of a fix, doing the very thing of all others bound to expose her and hold up her relations to public shame, why was she here now, ticket and all, waiting to come down by the six thirty-five?

George was deeply perplexed. To a plain man such conduct was inexplicable. And as though she knew the very words of his thoughts Milly said, her puffy face expressionless, her voice monotonous, her eyes fixed on a point just below his spectacles, "I expect you were all surprised I left so early that day."

"Yesterday," amended George.

"Yesterday?" repeated Milly; and added after a moment, accepting it, accepting the incredible fact that it was indeed only yesterday. "Yes—yesterday."

"We were very much surprised," said George shortly. Surprised. A good word that, he thought.

Then sudden, acute alarm seized him, for what would he do, what on earth would he do, if she started confessing to him, here, in the middle of Victoria Station? He knew what she had done, and he didn't want to be told its wretched details; it would put him in the most confoundedly awkward fix if she began. Women should shut up, or tell other women, or priests or somebody, but not him.

"Nice day, hasn't it been," he said, desperately stemming what he feared was going to be the tide.

But Milly didn't seem to hear that; she appeared to be thinking of something else, her eyes fixed on that point below his spectacles. "I went to get the money," she said, after a moment.

"What money?" asked George.

"My legacy."

"Your legacy?"

"Yes—the thousand pounds Ernest left me. I went to the solicitor."

"Well, *we* could have told you that was no good," said George, relieved more than he could have supposed possible by what seemed to him the naturalness of this explanation.

He filled out his chest with relief. Not a confession. Perhaps he'd get her home after all without that happening to him. Idiotic, of course, to rush off like that, making things look blacker than ever for herself, but then she was a woman, and women did do idiotic things —great Scott, yes, and didn't they! Besides, her nerves were probably in a poor condition—must have been, what with Ernest's accident and the being cut off in his Will, and her conscience all rotten. In any case, thank goodness it was a natural explanation, and one the family would be able to understand.

"You should have asked us, Milly," he said, so much relieved that his voice was quite kind, "then you wouldn't have had the journey for nothing. These things take time. There are formalities——"

But, just as he was feeling able to be kind, he remembered that she had been away two days and a night. For a moment he had forgotten that. A journey from Titford to London to see a solicitor doesn't take two days and a night. The explanation wasn't, after all, likely to soothe the family, and didn't, after all, relieve him.

He stared at her, on the verge of asking how she had managed to be so long about it, but refrained. It might be true that she had tried to get the money, but she must also have been with her—well, he hardly liked to say her what. It wasn't his business, nor had he any wish, to stir up the mud of Milly's secrets. Disliking that particular kind of mud very much, George was of opinion that it really was peculiarly shocking of Milly to have gone rushing off to her what d'you call him with poor old Ernest hardly in his grave. No doubt was in his mind that part, if not all, of this absence had been spent with the fellow. He hoped that at least they had only talked. True, she didn't look as if the visit had been much of a success; but, on the other hand, neither did she look, nor had she ever looked, like a woman who went in for that sort of thing.

Angry and upset again, he said, "Why didn't you ask one of us? It would have saved you a useless journey, and saved—well, a good deal besides."

"But it wasn't useless," said Milly. "I got it."

"Got what?"

"The thousand pounds."

"You got it? How?"

"From Ernest's solicitor. Mr. Jenkyns. It was there ready for me."

George could only stare. It seemed inexplicable. That thin-lipped, tight-jawed Jenkyns, who had so evidently disapproved of the lot of them, who had behaved, in fact, as though they were all tarred with Milly's own wretched brush, must have advanced her the money. Yet he didn't look like a chap who advances money.

Still, a woman must know whether she has got a thousand pounds or not.

He stared; and the fantastic idea shot through his mind, the one fantastic idea of his life, that perhaps it was Jenkyns himself who was Milly's what d'you call him.

"I hope," said Milly, her voice very small and tired, "no one worried too much because I went off like that."

"That's putting it mildly," said George.

"I'm very sorry," said Milly, sighing; and, as she spoke, she made an odd, sideways movement, as if she weren't quite firm on her feet.

He caught hold of her arm. "What's up?" he asked quickly, a vision of Milly fainting, and his having to do something about it, rising before his troubled eyes.

He gripped her arm tightly. He was no good at that sort of thing, he told himself, much upset; he hadn't a notion how to cope with a collapsing woman in a railway station. "What's up, Milly? Not got the staggers, have you?" he asked anxiously.

She reassured him. "I only lost my balance," she said, drawing away from his grip. "I think my heels are rather high."

"They would be," thought George. Aloud he said, severely, because he had been frightened, "You're tired—that's what it is."

"Yes. I'm tired. I think I'll go and sit in the train. I expect it's in by now——" and she began moving slowly towards the platform the six thirty-five started from.

George went with her. He hesitated a moment as to whether he oughtn't to offer her his arm. Did one offer one's arm to a—to somebody who had——? But though he was in doubt about his arm, he wasn't in any doubt that it wouldn't do for them to be seen separate, not travelling in the same compartment when they were going down by the same train; so he walked by her side, keeping his eye on her, ready to catch hold of her if she started tottering again. She looked very white; as if she might do anything in unreason—be sick publicly, or something awful like that.

To his relief she didn't do anything, nor did she speak again; and walking along the platform with her, in spite of his eyes being carefully lowered, he somehow managed to see how many people there were on it whom they both knew, and, aware of a hush of interest as they approached, was thankful indeed to have got Milly in tow, to be taking her home. Silently they walked, both looking at the ground, while everybody on the crowded platform made room for them, those who didn't know them, impressed by their deep mourning, as respectfully as those who did. Silently they presently sat facing each other in two corners of the railway carriage, George pretending to read his evening paper, of which he didn't see a word, and Milly not pretending anything, but simply sitting. Silently they got out at Titford, George gravely inclining his head to those acquaintances who, pushed in at the last moment, had unwillingly shared their carriage and had spent the journey being unobtrusive; and silently they walked up the stairs together, and into the station yard.

A melancholy pair they looked—like two unhappy but rather grand crows, George's clothing, in its way, being as handsomely sombre as Milly's. Those who saw them were much pleased, so well did they fill their rôles; and there was, besides, a genuine feeling of gladness at seeing Mrs. Ernest reappear, and by her reappearance putting a stop to the ugly whispers that were going round. How miserable she looked, too, poor thing. The onlookers couldn't help feeling gratified to see her so utterly crushed by her bereavement, for it gave them the assurance that the world's heart must still be in its right place if its widows felt their losses like that. Nobody, of course, greeted the sable pair; tact was shown in every possible way; and the place might have been deserted for any obstacles George and Milly encountered in their progress up the stairs.

Outside the station George said, "My car is here. Perhaps you had better let it take you ho—— to Mandeville Park Road."

Milly acquiesced. "Thank you," she said.

But George wasn't going with her; not he. He regarded his job of first welcomer as finished, and badly wanted to be rid of her. So, after handing her in with suitable solemnity and care, conscious that they were being watched, he said, standing at the door, that he would go straight home himself in a taxi, because he had promised his brothers to meet them at his house at seven o'clock.

Milly acquiesced. "Thank you," she said again; and as she was driven away, and George dropped out of sight, she fell to pondering over the question, as one ponders over a question laboriously in a dream, whether it would be possible to offer the chauffeur a tip of one shilling,—which, with three pennies, was all that she had at that moment in the world.

§

In the end she didn't remember to give him anything.

The parlourmaid, capless, came running to open the door when she heard the car, and Ernest's Pomeranian was there too, yapping.

This was the dog, Milly remembered, which had yapped at her that morning long ago when she thought she was going to escape. Odd things one thinks one is going to do. Escape? Nobody ever escapes. Absently she stooped to pat him. He backed away growling, and the parlourmaid rebuked him.

"We weren't expecting you, m'm," said the parlour-maid, apologizing for everything—the dog's growls, her caplessness, Milly's own behaviour in going away without saying a word.

"I ought to have let you know," said Milly vaguely, her eyes on the contents of the hall—the suits of armour, the grandfather clock, the terra-cotta baskets of ferns, all there, each in its same place, after the æons of time since she saw them last. Faintly the smell of Ernest, his coats and mackintoshes and cigars, floated round her nostrils. She put out her hand, and steadied herself by holding on to the hat-rack. She had got what George had called the staggers again.

"Yes, m'm. We was quite worried about you, m'm. And Mrs. Alec——"

"I want to go to bed," said Milly, holding on to the hat-rack.

"Yes, m'm. Early, m'm?"

"Now, please."

"Yes, m'm——"

"And I don't want any——"

But who was this, coming slowly and reluctantly out of Ernest's study, a red spot high up on each cheek? Wasn't it Ruth?

Yes; it was poor Ruth, to whom this unexpected appearance of Milly was the last dreadful straw to a miserable day. Why, she asked herself trembling, when through the window she saw who it was sitting in the car, should she be the one of the family selected to cope with so distressing an encounter? She couldn't cope with it. She was too old. It was unfair. But, after a brief struggle forcing herself to carry out what appeared to be her duty, she went into the hall, and advanced, stiff and dignified outside while inside she was mere jelly, her hands clasped tightly together in front of her, and said, "Good evening."

Milly looked at her, collecting her scattered thoughts.

Ruth. The second part of that prelude whose opening bars had been George.

Very well. She accepted her. Not hers to choose the order of the music she had come back to face. But it did seem as if there were rather a lot of Botts about; it did seem a pity not to be able to go straight to bed. And an absurd jingle began lilting through her head as she looked at Ruth—*She shall have music wherever she goes.* Yes—and the first line, the one before that—wasn't it, *With Botts on her fingers and Botts on her toes?* No, it didn't go like that, of course; it couldn't have been Botts. One had nails on one's fingers and toes, and sometimes chilblains, but not Botts. "How do you do, Ruth," she said politely. "What an enormous family we are, aren't we——" and fainted.

*⁂(XI)⁂

THE meeting of the brothers at George's house was not till nine o'clock that night, but he had told Milly it was at seven so as to have an excuse for getting away from her. Chaste women were what George liked; and the fact that he had been believing in and admiring one who wasn't, upset him a good deal. Apart from the family disgrace, it upset him.

He didn't go home in a taxi as he said he would, because he wanted to have time to think before plunging into the society of his wife, who was so extremely healthy and lively that he never rejoined her, after his daily absence in the City, without this feeling of plunging, this slight preliminary reluctance, as of one who stands on a brink.

Sometimes he thought he would have preferred a quieter wife, but it was no good thinking of that now. Milly used to seem to be rather what a man wanted to come home to—which showed, in George's present view, how you never can tell. His wife, with her one child at school, hadn't enough to do, and therefore by the evening of her long day of idleness, when George got home tired out, was alarmingly fresh and ready for anything. George, who was ready for nothing except dinner and a quiet smoke and bed, found this trying. He never said so, because no Bott ever complained of his wife, either to her or behind her; and now that he realized what poor old Ernest had had to put up with in the way of a wife, he was pleased enough these days with

his own. Nora might be noisy and super-healthy, but
she was straight. It cut the bottom out of a man's life,
George said to himself walking home and slowly turning
over in his mind all that had happened, if his wife wasn't
straight.

The other brothers were also having a kind of second
wind of appreciation of their wives—except perhaps
Bertie, who never had liked his very much,—and Fred
that very day had bought Mabel a new pendant, and
Alec was thinking of getting Ruth something—perhaps
a new garage, which he badly needed, the one they had
being inconveniently small; while those men who were
the husbands of the five Bott sisters were glad enough
to have steady women at their backs, and not to have
to bother wondering what they might be up to.

"It does a woman no good to be too attractive," one
of these men, commenting on the situation, remarked to
his wife—unguardedly, and as he might have spoken
to a brother; and it was things like that, remarks of
that sort, which the women of the family, now that
Milly had become what the Bible called a hissing and a
reproach, found themselves unable to stand. Attractive,
attractive; what was attractive? The husband who had
used the word—unguardedly, and as he might have
spoken to a brother—said that he didn't know; nor, he
said, now that he came to think of it, did he know why
the word had occurred to him. They were busy men, the
five who had married Botts, and couldn't be bothered
with the discomfort of quarrels at home. At all times
they were ready to placate their wives.

George, walking home to his, decided he would have
dinner before he told her the news; but Nora, her hair
blowing up in the wind, ran out to meet him, having
been watching for him from the dining-room window,
and told it him herself. They all knew it. In the brief

period of his walk from the station not only had the
parlourmaid at Mandeville Park Road telephoned, but
directly after that Ruth had telephoned, and since then
everybody had been telephoning to everybody else, all
asking each other if they had heard.

"Such a relief!" cried Nora, warmly embracing him.
"Porge"—for some reason she insisted on calling him
Porge, and it was no use asking her not to, because she
still did—"isn't it exciting!"

"You talk as if it were a sort of picnic," grumbled
George, whose coat was being helped off him; and it
wasn't any use asking her to let him take it off by himself, because she could no more stop being active than
a squib, once lit, can stop crackling round. Lit into
energy by excessive health, Nora couldn't let George
alone when he was within reach. Sometimes he thought
he would prefer a wife who was—well, not ill, but occasionally a little less well, though he knew this wasn't
a nice thought to have.

"And isn't it?" cried Nora. "Isn't it what we've
all been praying for for two mortal days? You're not
going to be glum *to-night*, Porge?"

"Look out," said George; for they were in the hall,
and servants were probably listening.

Nora, however, couldn't look out—not if all the
servants in Titford were listening could she at that
moment restrain herself. Seizing him by the shoulders,
and twisting him round so that he faced her, she again
exhorted him on that night of all nights not to be glum;
and George, facing her, was unable to resist saying, for
now that it was over he somehow felt proud, "I brought
her back."

"You?" cried Nora. "You did it?"

She stared close into his eyes in her astonishment.

George nodded. "I sent her to Ernest's in the car.
I walked," he said, looking modest.

Nora was so much lost in astonished admiration that
for a moment she was dumb and immobile, her hands
on George's shoulders, staring close into his eyes. *Her*
man getting a move on; *her* man being the one of the
family to net Milly and bring her safely back, while
these others, the smart ones, Fred and Bertie, who
talked such a lot and made themselves out so important, did nothing at all.

"She was coming in any case," George, being honourable, found himself forced to admit. "Just by chance I
met her at Victoria."

"But it was *you* who persuaded her to come back—
I know it was!" cried his wife, flinging her arms round
him. Sometimes he thought he would have preferred a
wife who hadn't any arms; and there was a bit in the
Bible they read out in church about everlasting arms
which made him glad he didn't believe in heaven.

"Let go, Nora," he said, trying to disentangle himself,
"I want to go up and wash."

"But I must hear everything—*everything*," she cried,
kissing him.

George didn't like being kissed. He liked women who
received, rather than who gave: women who waited.
But there it was—Nora was a frequent kisser, and one
had to put up with it.

"After dinner," he said, succeeding in getting loose,
and going upstairs.

She followed him, talking all the way, holding on to
his coat, pulling herself up by it two steps at a time.
George sometimes thought it was a pity he had married
someone so much younger than himself. He was sixty,
and she was forty. Forty, it is true, sounded as if it

were a quiet age, but it was nothing of the sort, he had discovered.

"Ruth's coming to dinner," Nora informed him breathlessly—not breathlessly because of the stairs, for she was as active as a lizard, but because of all the words that were wanting to come out at once. "She rang up to ask. She says there's no need for her to stay with Milly now she's come. She says Milly has gone to bed. I couldn't get anything else out of her. And the others are coming round after dinner with Fred and Bertie— Mabel and Edith are. So are Joan and Mary. Maud rang up to say she may be late—that *telephone!* It's been going without stopping. I never heard anything like it. Maud said she may be late because of Edward's knee, but she'll turn up as soon as she can. Everybody's coming. Maggie can't, because Bee's worse this afternoon, and we didn't ring up Katie because she's stuck at Denmark Hill, and it would only make her miserable to know about it all and not be able to leave mother. And anyhow it's no good stirring up mother—she'd want to pounce on Milly, and carry her off before anybody's even seen her. What a *mercy* our house happens to be in the middle, and easiest for them to meet at! Porge, isn't it exciting—fancy Milly turning up again! And fancy *you* being the one to—— Did she say anything? Did she tell you who the man is?"

But George, having reached the landing and got into his dressing-room, turned with his hand on the doorknob, remarked, freeing his coat, "One moment, Nora ——" and shut her out.

§

During dinner not much could be said because of the servants. Even Nora, once the servants were in the room, moving about before her eyes, realized that and

watched her words, while Alec's wife Ruth, still shaken
by her unexpected encounter with Milly and the shock
of her fainting—the servants had got her up to bed, and
she had come to after a while, so that there was no sense
in staying—could hardly be got to talk at all. She
hadn't thought it necessary to mention the fainting.
She had desired the parlourmaid not to alarm the
family by reporting it. It was over, so no use fussing.
Besides, Milly had brought it on herself, and one
couldn't feel much sympathy with people who brought
things on themselves. Nervously she crumbled her
bread, and when she tried to drink she spilt her wine.
She was sixty-five, she reminded herself, and ought not
to be called upon to mix with unpleasantness. There
seemed to Ruth little use in being an old lady, in having
struggled up to the age of sixty-five, if one were still
going to be dragged into unpleasantness.

George, at the head of the table, felt there were remarks which ought to be made for the benefit of the
servants if only one could think of them; remarks
about Milly—casual, easy references to her, giving the
servants the proper cue for their own opinion. He was
sure Fred and Bertie were saying the right things at
that moment for the benefit of theirs; he felt that not to
mention her was a mistake, as the servants knew Ruth
had just come from seeing her; but he wasn't used to
this sort of thing, he could only find his way about, as
befits a decent man, in straightforward transactions.
Milly was a great deal more bother and worry than any
living woman was worth, he resentfully thought. Still,
he had a feeling she ought to be mentioned.

"How do you think she's looking?" he suddenly
burst out, addressing Ruth; and Ruth, who was at that
moment being offered pudding, started so much that
she dropped the spoon into it.

The room seemed to hold its breath. Was it George's fancy, or did the servants really slow down in what they were doing, and become almost immobile?

"Who?" asked Ruth nervously. Really George was most annoying. Why couldn't he let the subject alone while servants were present?

"Milly," said George, determined to say it so naturally and casually that it came out with a roar.

"Oh, yes. Very well, I think. No—tired I mean," said Ruth, bending her head over her plate, and wondering how old a woman had to be, then, before she was allowed to stand aside and keep out of unpleasantness.

"Poor old Milly," said Nora eagerly. She longed to talk about her, to hear what Ruth thought, what Milly had said, what she looked like; and here she was obliged to sit quiet and wait interminably, because of the servants. "If only *dogs* could be trained to do things!" she thought passionately.

"She'll be all right in a day or two," George said with vague heartiness, drumming a tune on the table with his fingers; and then he remembered that a widow is supposed to take more than a day or two before becoming all right.

A flush appeared on Ruth's delicate elderly cheek as she tried to eat her pudding. It had been so very painful, meeting Milly like that all by herself, without Alec or anyone to help her, and then having to see her flop down on the floor. It didn't seem right that she, of the whole big family, should be picked out to fill such a part. All her life she had shrunk from anything not nice, all her life she had turned her eyes away from ugly things, and had carefully brought up her children to do the same. She had long now been a grandmother, and she couldn't help feeling that touching pitch wasn't a game for grandmothers. In obedience to the family's wishes she had gone to poor Ernest's so that the servants might have some authority over them, willing, as always, to fulfil her obligations as the wife of the eldest son, anxious to do what Alec and the others thought right, though it had been sad enough being all day in poor Ernest's deserted house; but she shouldn't have been left there to bear the brunt of Milly's return and fainting unaided, she should never have been put in such a position. George knew she was there; why, when he sent Milly round in his car, did he not come too? She was very sorry for Milly—very sorry indeed, as she was sorry, she hoped, for all women who went astray, but she didn't wish to be with her. Not yet, in any case. Not till something definite had been decided as to what they were going to do about it all. And certainly she didn't wish to be with her by herself, and have to see her dropping down at her feet in a heap.

Afterwards in the drawing-room, when the servants had brought coffee and at last been got rid of, she told George she thought she ought not to have been left in the lurch like that, without an idea of what to say,— still not mentioning the fainting, so as to avoid useless fussing.

"That's how I felt at Victoria," said George, filling his pipe; an inadequate reply to her just complaint, Ruth felt, but George had always been irritating.

"I wish to goodness I'd been at Ernest's when Milly got back!" exclaimed Nora.

"What would you have done?" Ruth asked with a slight shiver; for Nora's vitality invariably made her feel extra frail and old, as if she were sitting in a draught —and not any ordinary draught, but her last earthly draught of all.

"I'd have kissed her," said Nora.

"Kissed her?" echoed George, turning to stare.

"Really, Nora," shivered Ruth, drawing her fur closer about her.

§

Yet this, later on, when the brothers had assembled in George's drawing-room, and their wives were all there, and three of the five married sisters were there too, was roughly the attitude they ended by deciding should be adopted. Not actual kissing; that wasn't necessary. But the kindliness which in happier circumstances would find its culmination in a kiss was from every point of view desirable.

Ruth, frail and old, and still after close on' fifty years of marriage believing husbands knew best, was willing to follow any line she was instructed to, once it was made clear to her that it was in Alec's view right. She saw what they all meant, she quite understood that private feelings must be pocketed in the interests of the family's good reputation, and she also remembered that Christ had forgiven women like Milly. Therefore she submitted, and sat quiet by the fire holding her fur close round her chilly shoulders, saying little, resigned to obedience; and gradually there emerged from the tangle of voices the authoritative voice of Fred, who took hold of the meeting and firmly outlined what the family had got to do, and what it perfectly well knew in its heart it had got to do.

Open kindness was the proper, the only attitude, he said; and Bertie heartily agreed, and so, after a moment, did Alec and George. Escaped, through Milly's unexpected and unhoped-for reappearance, from the disaster of an unhidable disgrace, they were going to take no risks—and stand no nonsense of opposition from the women, Fred went on, looking round; and Bertie nodded agreement, and so, after a moment, did Alec and George.

The one thing to be done with Milly, he declared, was what Walter Walker had suggested the other day— take her into their homes, and be kind to her. As kind, said Fred, eyeing the women, as if they were really fond of her; as kind as if they couldn't be happy without her. Anyhow for some months they must do this, till suspicion had lulled. Then, when things had blown over, perhaps she could go to Denmark Hill and look after the old lady for the rest of her days, as their mother had suggested. But not now; not at first. After this last straw of her running away she must be in their actual midst, apparent to everybody, gradually, as the period of mourning lightened, being drawn into ordinary life, being seen in church, being seen by callers, being seen taking exercise, being seen—this was the crux—with *them*, and not only with them, but cherished by them.

Visibly cherished Milly was to be, however great a strain it might put upon them. Their children were to see it, their servants were to be forced to notice it. And as for expense, it was absurd to fuss about that, he said, looking severely at the women. What did a guest cost? Milly, after all, was only going to be a guest, and before she had begun to cost anything she would be moving on to the next host, he added with a grin. Besides, she had her thousand pounds.

Fred and Bertie, supported by Alec and George, who were both glad to be given a lead, looked round the room at the seven women, as who should say, "You dare make difficulties!" But not one of the wives and sisters, now that this was really upon them, so much as murmured. Since that first shock of the reading of the Will they had been through a great deal, and were ready to adapt themselves to necessity. Like Ruth, they were willing to submit to what their husbands and brothers decided, and even Bertie's wife Edith was thinking, as she listened to Fred, that nothing should be shrunk from which could stop people's tongues. Hateful to be questioned by her daughters, one of whom was being courted by the senior curate of St. Timothy's, who would certainly shy off marrying into scandal, as to what Aunt Milly had really done; revolting to have her sons, cynical enough as it was, becoming aware from hints and looks that aunts, too, weren't always what they seemed. Besides, she, with the others, was intensely relieved that Milly had come back, and in her relief, like the others, ready to do much which in a calmer moment would have seemed impossible.

So that the resolution to take Milly into their homes, each in turn, and make much of her, was no longer opposed, and only when it came to discussing details was there any further argument—details, for instance, such as how long the visits were to last, who should be the first host, whether it should go by age, whether the four brothers should begin one after the other, or whether the married sisters should be intercalated.

The married sisters protested at this suggestion. They didn't wish to be intercalated. They considered the men of the family should all come first, regardless of age. And anyhow they would have to ask their husbands.

"Why aren't they here?" Fred inquired.

Well, really Milly couldn't be said to be anything to do with the husbands of the sisters of her deceased husband, Maud, the eldest of the sisters, declared.

There was a silence. They all looked at Alec. He, aware that they were looking at him, pulled at his beard and said nothing.

"What about it, Alec?" asked Fred, seeing that he remained silent. Alec seemed to be showing signs of not wishing to be the one to begin taking Milly. Yet he was the eldest; clearly it was his duty.

"What about it?" Fred asked a second time.

Then Alec, clearing his throat, explained that he knew he was the eldest, but that he couldn't help it, and that Ruth had lately been feeling her age. Also, he explained, Ruth was, he was glad to say, and as they all had long been aware—he looked at her affectionately, and she smiled at him—a particularly religious woman, and perhaps a religious woman—not that the others were not religious, but Ruth made rather a point of it—well, he meant to say that perhaps a particularly religious woman oughtn't to have to be the first to have a—well, Milly in her house.

He stopped, an undefined idea possessing his mind that Milly might be purer after having passed through the sieve of other visits, and more fit to stay with his wife; but he couldn't get it clear enough to put into words, and he sat with his long fingers buried in his beard and his thin shanks crossed, wishing to goodness the wretched woman had never been born.

Ruth, by the fire, looked gratefully at him, and drew her fur still closer round her throat, coughing a little as an involuntary testimony to her frailness these days of being sixty-five. Besides, having already encountered Milly and gone through that fainting scene, and without being prepared for it either, which made it so much worse, she felt she had done her share for a while, and should be put at the bottom of the list. She too obscurely thought that by the time Milly had been on a few of the visits she would somehow be more purged.

"You're not feel ingcold, dear?" asked Alec solicitously, prizing his wife; and Fred too, prizing his, turned to Mabel at once when she made some inaudible observation, with an affectionate, "What's that, old girl?"

and George, prizing his, but not given to easy words, showed his appreciation of virtue by stooping and picking up a liqueur chocolate she had dropped on the carpet, and cleansing it of fluff with his handkerchief before handing it back to her.

Only Bertie remained untouched by the general warm-up of affection. He didn't like Edith very much at any time, and he saw no reason why he should like her any better because poor little Milly had gone off the rails. On the contrary, it made him like her less, her thin-lipped, superior virtue annoying him. Also he was apt to be unfaithful, and resented having to feel that he wronged her. Flushed, and full of the port he had drunk after dinner to assuage his worries, he sat away from her and close to his brothers. He was extremely worried about Milly, and had been immensely shocked by the discovery that she hadn't kept straight. Milly not straight? It seemed unbelievable. Yet no other construction could be put upon her action in bolting,—she bolted because she couldn't face the family, and she couldn't face the family because she was as guilty as Ernest had insinuated in his beastly Will.

Bertie was unable to make up his mind whether he condemned her, or whether he wasn't glad that the poor little soul had had some happiness in her dreary life with that sneak Ernest. But what had happened to her in London? What unexpected catastrophe had forced her to come back? That tale she had told George and Ruth about going up to fetch her legacy, that was just eyewash. Well, she got the money all right from Jenkyns, he was glad to know, and George and the others might beat their brains till they were blue as to how it came to be given to her—they'd never find out. That chap Jenkyns was a scoundrel, but a close one. A mean scoundrel too, not ringing him up as he had promised, when Milly called. If he had been able to have a word or two with her then, he might have helped her a good deal, he might even have saved her from this ghastly being whitewashed by the family and clasped to its heart.

Unfortunate little Milly, he thought; it seemed to be her fate to have to deal with mean men. The chap who let her down—why was she back again if he hadn't?—he must be a pretty mean brute too; and Bertie was so much worried about her that he had had to drink more wine than usual at dinner, and looked more flushed even than he actually was, sitting between the silvery Alec and the sallow Fred.

He was the only one of the family who wasn't thankful that Milly had come back. Far rather would he have had her stay away, for then at least he could have presumed that the fellow she had carried on with was doing the right thing by her. Bertie couldn't understand how anyone should not do the right thing by Milly—a little soft thing like that, and so kind always. How could any man behave so rottenly? He had himself always been good to the women he had had anything to do with—in that way, he meant. Perhaps he hadn't been very good to Edith, but then she—— What was that? What was George saying?

George was saying that Milly was already in possession of her legacy. "She told me she went to Jenkyns, and he gave it to her," George said.

"That's odd," remarked Fred.

"Very odd," said Alec, drawing his fingers slowly through his beard.

"I wonder how she managed that," said Fred, thoughtfully.

George stared at the carpet. "Well, I think he must have advanced it," he said. "Jenkyns must have."

There was a silence. The women were silent, because they didn't see why Milly shouldn't be able to get her money as soon as she liked; but Alec and Fred were thinking that she must have got round Jenkyns, for no man advances a thousand pounds to a woman who has no claims on him and perhaps won't pay it back, unless he has been got round; and if Milly could get round that grim-mouthed solicitor, was there any limit to her wiles?

Unpleasant thought. The last thing they wished for their own peace was to have wiles practised on themselves. Let loose in their homes, what mightn't Milly do if she gave her mind to it? And though of course they personally would remain adamant, their wives might imagine that they hadn't, and then——

"I think I'll ring up Jenkyns," said Fred.

"I wouldn't do that if I were you," said Bertie quickly.

"Why not?"

"Best let things be," said Bertie, pouring himself out a glass of whiskey and soda. "No good beginning to stir round in Milly's past actions. If you take my advice, our line ought to be to make a clean sweep of her entire past, especially her immediate past, and start fair on a basis of—well, to put it rather like a parson, of hopeful confidence."

"Perhaps you'd better be the one to begin with her, then," suggested Fred sarcastically.

"Oh, no——" Bertie's wife intervened. "Why, we're the youngest of all. Bertie is, I mean. We couldn't possibly come out of our turn."

"And by the way," Bertie went on, distracting their attention from Jenkyns and the legacy, "I made inquiries to-day, and my solicitor thinks those words in Ernest's Will—you know, 'My wife will know why'—those words are defamatory, and he's going to apply to have them omitted from the order of probate. He says it's pretty certain the judge in the Probate Division will regard them as inserted to air a grievance, and will rule they're not to be published."

"I thought Wills were sacred," said Nora, who had been thrilled by this sentence in Ernest's, and didn't want it suppressed.

"Not any parts of them that the judge rules are unjustified or injurious," explained Fred, greatly relieved by Bertie's news.

"But this wasn't unjustified," said Edith.

"And therefore can hardly be called injurious,' said Maud.

"Well, it's going to be left out anyway," said Bertie shortly. "And we can all bless our stars that Ernest's craving for post-mortem punishment has been frustrated."

"Yes—I think we must all be glad of this," said Fred, looking round. "It makes it much easier to save Milly from scandal." And, since Alec agreed, and said, "Indeed we must," and George nodded, the wives and sisters were obliged to appear satisfied too.

But they didn't like the way, the wives and sisters didn't, Bertie talked of poor Ernest, and never would. On the day of the funeral it had been disgraceful the way he spoke of him, and now listen to him using such ugly words. Edith ought to make him behave better; Edith oughtn't to let him get out of hand like this. And Edith, watching Bertie with narrowed eyes, was suddenly invaded by a dreadful suspicion. "I wonder," she thought—and it must be said she struggled hard against thinking it—"whether Ernest's reason for not divorcing Milly was because he knew the man was——"

But she couldn't go on. She mustn't, she simply mustn't let an idea like that, so horrible, so completely destructive of her peace, get a footing in her mind. "Out with it," she said to herself, pushing it away with might and main; and asked Nora, for she felt ill, if the window could be opened.

There was an interlude, in which they fanned Edith and opened the window.

Directly they opened the window, Ruth, by the fire, began to cough.

"You see?" nodded Alec, when she had stopped sufficiently for them to hear what he was saying. "I must get her away. To Brighton, or somewhere. I've been thinking of it for a long time." And he added, tapping his own, "Chest."

"You're shirking, old man," said Fred. "You only don't want to fill your proper place as eldest of the family, and be the one to start in on Milly."

Upon which Ruth interrupted again with a worse fit, a fit that shook her thin body, and was really distressing to listen to.

"She's had this cough all the winter," explained Alec when she left off for a moment, taking no notice of Fred's words, "and I think, considering her age——"

"Well, then, Maud—what about you?" Fred asked, looking at his eldest sister. "There's no reason why one of you girls shouldn't be the first. After all, it's much more of a woman's job than a man's. Suppose we begin with the eldest sister, as the eldest brother won't?"

"My dear fellow, it's not a question of *won't*," began Alec, backed up by more coughing from Ruth.

"You're joking, Fred," said Maud severely, when Ruth stopped. She was frowning at Ruth as much as at Fred, for coughing is an irritating noise. "Edward would never allow it. What has he got to do with Milly and her miserable affairs?"

"Yes—and we're not even called Bott now," Joan, another sister, pointed out.

"We ought to be last of all," said Mary, the third one. "After all of you have had your turns."

Nora leaned forward eagerly. "Why not George and me begin?" she asked. "I'd *love* to have Milly."

The others stared at her shocked, except Bertie, who would have liked too to be the one to welcome Milly.

"Really, Nora," Bertie's wife recovered enough to say; and Ruth too, feebly because of that last fit of coughing, said, "Really, Nora."

"My dear, we can't have her out of our turn," said George, frowning at his wife. "If Alec won't——"

"Can't," corrected Alec.

"—there's Fred comes before us."

"Yes. I think that as I shall be taking Ruth away at once," chimed in Alec, "you and Mabel must step into my shoes, Fred."

"Gracious," murmured Mabel, faintly.

Fred looked round at them from beneath his thick black eyebrows. Mean of Alec to get out of it. He might have taken Milly with them to Brighton—indeed, that would have looked rather particularly natural and well.

But he knew when Alec had made up his mind not to do a thing no power on earth would move him; and feeling that it was up to him to set an example, he decided that he would shoulder his burden with at least an appearance of alacrity and goodwill, and show them all how the thing ought to be done.

"Right," he said, bringing his fist down on the table next him, the one with glasses and whiskey on it, and making them jingle, "I'm game. Aren't you, Mabel? We'll begin, then. How long are the visits to last, did we say? Three months?"

"Gracious," murmured Mabel again, faintly.

"Well, say two months. What? Not so long? Oh, nonsense. Six weeks, then. What—not even that? All right—a month, then. But not a day less than a month each. We'd hardly get into our strides under a month."

So it was decided that each of Milly's visits should last a month, and that the first one, to Fred, should begin the next day.

"Gracious," was Mabel's helpless comment, as they led her home.

§

That evening, at half-past eleven, the telephone rang outside the drawing-room door of the house on Denmark Hill, where old Mrs. Bott, who needed little sleep and stayed up till twelve every night, was playing patience.

Her youngest daughter Katie Noakes, who was staying with her for a few days, ran out to answer it, while the old lady, going on with her game, waited placidly to hear the news.

News of some sort it was bound to be, these agitated days since poor Milly had taken to her heels—and there, upstairs, was the best spare room all ready for her, and the bed made, and no Milly to sleep in it. Such a pity. Why not stretch her poor tired little body out in those nice cool sheets, and know that nothing was going to hurt her, instead of rushing about thinking she had to try and get away from something or other? A spell seemed to be laid on these misguided children, preventing their seeing and understanding how simple things really were. They only had to kiss each other and be friends. But some of them had got an idea into their heads that they were going to be scolded, and the rest of them had got an idea into theirs that it was their duty to scold. Well, she could tell them, only they wouldn't listen, that no good ever yet came from scolding. Just cobwebs, these ideas were; unhappy cobwebs; the stuff that dreams are made on, thought old Mrs. Bott, putting down a card, who knew her Shakespeare even better than her Bible, and in her heart preferred it, because she didn't care about foreigners.

"Well, Katie?" she said, not looking up, her hand hovering over the cards, as her daughter reappeared.

"Milly's back," said Katie breathlessly.

"What—here?" she asked placidly, her eyes on her game.

"No—she's at Ernest's. Nora rang up. She's to go to Fred's to-morrow."

"She isn't coming here, then?"

"No—they want to have her with them in Titford."

"Ah," said the old lady, putting down another card. Then she added, "You've all been wrong about poor Milly, you see."

"Yes—that's the idea," said Katie, much flushed, and beginning at once to adopt the attitude prescribed to her by Nora in the name of the others.

"I hope you'll try to make it up to her," said the old lady, finishing her game.

"Yes—that's the idea," repeated Katie, comforted by the fact that she, as the youngest sister, was at the very bottom of the list.

⁎(XII)*⁎*

THE Fred Botts lived in the most expensive part of Titford, where all the houses were big and all the gardens
were grounds. They had a billiard-room, a suite of
reception-rooms, an oak lounge hall with a galleried
staircase, and a Winter Garden. Also they had a butler,
and dressed for dinner. No other Botts had a butler,
though several dressed for dinner, but the Winter Garden had somehow led up to him, and when Fred first
embarked on giant ferns it was only a question of time
before he proceeded to a butler.

Mabel, wispy and insignificant, and at all times of a
faint heart, was crushed by the butler. Her lunches
alone, with him waiting on her, were nightmares. It
seemed so awful, she thought, to be watched by a man
from behind. One's back was so helpless. It had no
eyes in it. And he disapproved of her, she was sure,
and offered her the food as though it were reproaches.
Awful to lunch, most of her days, alone with the butler.
In the silence of the room, while he, behind her chair,
waited to remove her plate the instant she laid down her
knife and fork, she could hear him breathing, for he was
one of those butlers who breathe. He did it down her
neck, too, when he bent over her with dishes, and made
the straggles of her hair, which never would keep pinned
back out of the way, wave about unpleasantly. She
suffered. Also, having been for years in the service of a
bishop, he had somehow forced family prayers on her,

to which Fred and the boys wouldn't come; and how her voice shook and trembled when she read out bits of Bible and whole collects before the semicircle of stony servants, headed by the butler looking down his big nose.

Mabel feared him. He was a man of the highest principles for his employers. She knew in her bones that his god was respectability, and his standard bishops. How was she going to break to this virtuous man that he was to wait at table for a whole month on poor, shady Milly? She had no doubt whatever that he knew all about Milly; she was certain, from many unmistakable signs, that the Will, the flight, and the reasons for both, had been thoroughly discussed and judged in the servants' hall.

Dejectedly, Mabel walked home from George's, Fred's arm supporting her, and with a sunk heart and a distracted mind listened to his instructions. If only somebody else were going to be the first to have Milly! Horrid of Alec, whose duty it was to begin, to shuffle out of it. It did seem hard that it should fall to her, the one of the family who had the high-principled butler. And it wasn't only the butler: Rosemary, her severe daughter, would be home before the end of Milly's month, a girl of austere piety who was spending her Easter in Jerusalem, and wanted to become an Anglican nun. What about her? Wouldn't she ask questions? Wouldn't she want to know why Aunt Milly suddenly was poor, and had to stay with them? Whatever else the family could hide it couldn't hide the fact that Milly was poor. Her clothes would gradually grow shabby; her tips would certainly be small. Perhaps she and Fred, thought Mabel, her forehead corrugated with anxious thought, had better do the tipping for her, in case she should disgrace them by its meagreness. She could say, after Milly had left, "Mrs. Ernest asked me to give you this. . . ."

And then there were the boys. One was married, but two still lived at home, and were back from business every evening to dinner. What about them? They had heard the whispered anxieties of the last two days; they had—she had noticed it—pricked up their ears, though saying nothing. Were they going to be persuaded, fine, intelligent young fellows that they were, that all had been well between their Uncle Ernest and Aunt Milly, and that it had been pure philanthropy impelling him to leave his money to charity? Oh, she hoped, she did so much hope, they wouldn't ever know which charity it was! There oughtn't to be such charities, not with young men about in the world. Why should wicked women be rescued? And to have one of them coming to stay with her as an honoured guest, a guest, Fred was commanding as they walked—she did wish Fred wouldn't command quite so much, and then leave her to do the obeying as best she could—who had to be petted, threw her mind into complete confusion. And Fred was so determined, so sure it could and should be done. Manlike, he would fetch Milly next day, drop her on his door-step, and then go off to his peaceful office, leaving the burden on his wife's shoulders.

She walked homewards with dragging footsteps. What did he know about that burden really? What did he know, for instance, about the butler? He only saw him in the mornings and evenings, whereas Mabel had him all day, and all day was under his voiceless disciplines. Being rich was nice, of course, but not if it led to butlers, thought Mabel, faced by the necessity of having to inform this particular one of Milly's arrival. She hadn't minded the other stages in her progressive splendour; had rather liked them, in fact, once she got

used to them; but the butler she couldn't get used to,—
not to this particular one, who looked at her down his
big nose as if she were only about three feet high. And
it was never the least use trying to tell Fred her troubles,
for he wouldn't listen; directly she began he went deaf,
and stayed deaf till she stopped. Yet often there were
things, real things, as now, which. . . .

"You'd better give your orders to-night," said Fred,
cutting across her whimpering thoughts as he opened the
door with his latch-key. "I shall fetch her round directly after breakfast to-morrow."

"But suppose," faltered Mabel, with a last dim hope,
"she won't come?"

"Come? She's got to come. She'll *come* all right,"
said Fred.

"Oh, Fred——" began Mabel, faintly.

"Now then, old girl, buck up," he briskly encouraged,
who himself wasn't feeling much bucked. He hadn't
bargained for having to be the one to begin; he had
taken it for granted Alec would be the first host, and
wasn't as ready for the part as he would have been if he
had had more time to think. Mabel would have to work
out the details, he decided, and get things going on the
right lines next day while he was in the City. Pity she
didn't take to the idea more enthusiastically. After all,
it was a woman's job tackling Milly, not a man's. He
only hoped Milly wouldn't start any tackling game herself though, he thought uneasily as he hung up his hat,
remembering how she must have tackled Jenkyns the
solicitor, getting that advance out of him. Suppose,
instead of supporting the family's efforts to whitewash
her by behaving herself, she began to exercise her tackling powers on himself and his sons? There was no
limit, he understood, to what a woman, once fallen,
wouldn't do. Being a nephew or a brother-in-law wasn't

a protection; and to have a soft little thing sidling up to a man, after dinner, say, after a good dinner, when one's wife happened not to be in the room. . . .

"Run along, old girl," he said to Mabel, giving her an unusually affectionate good-night kiss, quite clinging to her, in fact, a minute. "I'll go and tell the boys their aunt's coming."

And he went into the library, where he knew he would find his sons, who being, like himself, more absorbed in money-making than pleasures, spent most of their evenings at home.

"Your aunt," he said, going over to the fire and standing looking down at them, "is coming to stay with us to-morrow."

"Which aunt?" asked Percy, the eldest boy, without raising his eyes from *The Financial Times*, and also without enthusiasm, for he had eight of them.

"Your Aunt Milly."

"Oh, well—it might be worse," he mumbled, going on reading.

"I thought new-made widows stayed at home," said Dick, the younger boy.

Then Fred explained the philanthropic zeal of their Uncle Ernest, and how his desire to benefit charities had caused his widow to be without a home to stay in. He explained in outline rather than in detail, adding some general observations on the impossibility of ever knowing the secret places of any man's heart, and how one's own brother sometimes turned out, as in this case, to have had ideals and enthusiasms nobody would ever have suspected.

"Rough luck on poor old Aunt Milly," remarked Dick, when his father had finished.

"Yes—that's what *I* think, not being a philanthropist myself," said Fred. "We must make it up to her,"

"Do you mean financially?" inquired Percy, his eyes still on his paper.

"Kindness," said Fred.

"Kindness! Well, that's cheap, anyhow," said Dick.

"And easy," said Percy, turning the pages. "I always liked Aunt Milly."

"Yes. She's not a bad old thing," agreed Dick.

"But why did Uncle Ernest——" began Percy, looking up.

"I told you. I've been telling you for the last ten minutes. When philanthropy gets hold of a man——"

Fred broke off and took out his watch. "I'm going to bed," he finished abruptly. "I've had a heavy day, and I'm tired."

§

Milly arrived next morning about twelve. Fred, who went for her at nine, had to wait all that time while she packed, sacrificing his valuable morning from fear that if he didn't actually stay in the house till she was ready and take her to Mabel with his own hands, she might once more slip through the family's fingers.

But Milly offered no resistance. She came like a lamb. She was in bed when he arrived—the parlour-maid had some yarn, to which he didn't listen, that she hadn't been very well the night before,—but got up at once on hearing he was there wishing to speak to her. At first she seemed taken aback when he told her they wanted her to stay with them in turn, and didn't appear quite to get the hang of it, Fred thought; but presently, after looking rather stupid for a while, she grasped it all right, and said the proper things about kindness. They didn't look at each other while he explained, and she thanked; they looked, he out of the window, and she at the fire. But it was he who insisted that she should pack every single thing that was hers personally, and not just take away some of her jewels, as she suggested —"The more you have," said Fred, looking out of the window, "the less you'll want."

"Yes. I understand," said Milly, looking at the fire.

"My God, how slow she is over that packing," thought Fred while he waited, every few minutes taking out his watch; had she no idea of the value of a man's time at that hour of the day? Long after he had settled with the cook, and through her with the rest of the household, which was to receive a generous indemnity and clear off that same day, Milly was still up in her bedroom, packing. It really was too bad of her, he said to himself, to keep him hanging about like that. And what annoyed him even more was that for the first time in his life she made him feel shy. Why, when she came into the room, he hadn't been able to meet her eyes. Most annoying; and so cramping. If she had looked more like what they now knew she was, if she had been bold and defiant, or crawling and hang-dog, an obviously unchaste woman caught out, he would have known what to do, and been perfectly capable of dealing with her. But she looked so infernally good, thought Fred, much put out; she looked just as modest as ever, and was exactly the same little quiet dove-woman he had always had quite a fancy for, with the added claim on his heart strings of a white face and heavy eyes. It wasn't what he had expected, and it threw him out of his stride. Also, he couldn't help thinking, suppose their suspicions, or rather their certainties, were baseless? Suppose they, and Ernest before them, had done the poor thing an outrageous wrong?

The bare thought afflicted Fred, and set his mind off into a kind of stutter. He recovered, however, on remembering how she had taken to her heels, and stayed hidden two days and a night. If she were innocent, she wouldn't have done that.

Yes—but she had come back. . . .

Oh, hang it all, Fred exclaimed, frowning; and in any case, guilty or not guilty, she was a fool, who had all but wrecked the family honour, and still might do it if they didn't look out.

But when she came down at last, ready to go with him, black and shrouded and acquiescent, and again said something polite about his and Mabel's kindness, he found himself feeling shy again, and touched, and uncertain, for heaven knew there wasn't very much kindness in this business.

This would never do, he thought, pulling himself together. It was what had happened to Jenkyns. He too must have felt touched and uncertain, and it had ended in his parting with a thousand pounds. Fred, as a rich man, knew the exact value of a thousand pounds, and didn't at all like the idea that in his turn he might be so sorry for Milly that presently he began to part, perhaps, with money. True she looked like the last person in the world to try to get anything out of anybody; but see how she had taken them all in already. They would have to be extremely cautious with her this time, and take good care that——

It was an immense relief to him when he at last could hand her over to Mabel, his Mabel, the woman he knew all about and who was exactly what she seemed to be. She was waiting for them, according to his instructions, on the door-step, and directly he saw her his shyness vanished, and he felt able to play his part of cordial host.

"Well, here we are," he called heartily over his

shoulder to Mabel, as he helped Milly out of the car; and Mabel said, coming down the steps, very red and nervous and holding out a limp hand, "Oh—Milly. Yes. How nice. How are you? I—I'm so pleased." And, catching Fred's eye, she hastily bent forward, and pecked at the crape veil.

Fred's heartiness increased. Escorting Milly into the house he told her, the butler hearing it, that she was to treat the place and everything in it exactly as if it were hers. "We only want you to feel at home," he said— so heartily that the oak rafters rang. "Mabel and I just want you to rest here and get fit again, and do what you please. Liberty Hall, you know—eh, Mabel?"

And then he actually patted Milly's shoulder, for the benefit of the butler, and looking at his watch remarked hastily, "Well, so long, ladies," and hurried out to the waiting car, leaving Mabel to her fate.

"Fred!" she called after him, running down the steps, "Oh—*Fred!* You'll be back to dinner? You won't be late?"

But Fred, having done his part, opened his *Times* and became absorbed in other things.

That was the last Mabel saw of him through the window of the departing car, absorbed in his *Times;* and she slowly went up the steps again, and there in the hall, patient, waiting to obey, was Milly, and there too, waiting to shut the door and looking down his big nose, was the butler.

What a pair to be left alone with—what a *pair,* thought Mabel in much agitation, her knees seeming to have water in them instead of bones. "Please, Smith," she faltered, meek as always when speaking to the butler, "will you see that the luggage is taken up to the mahogany room?" And, after a hesitating look at Milly, according to her instructions she began to try to pet, and forced herself to go so far as to take her sinning sister-in-law gingerly by the arm.

"Shall we go upstairs?" said Mabel. "You'll like to take off your things after your——"

That was what one said to visitors arriving—"After your journey," but she stopped, because she remembered Milly hadn't had a journey.

"It was very kind of Fred to fetcn me," murmured Milly. "And it's very good of you both to take me in."

Mabel's hold on her arm became slightly less loose, and she drew her quickly towards the stairs. Take her in? Of course it was what they were doing, but it sounded as if she were in need of a refuge; and Fred had impressed on her, during the better part of the wakeful night she had just passed, that the servants were at all costs to be made to understand that the visit was voluntary. As though they would believe that. As though they weren't perfectly aware of the true meaning of it. Still, Fred wouldn't listen when she told him so, but she did hope that at least Milly would be careful what she said before them, and especially what she said before the butler. At luncheon, for instance—Mabel had read a book on etiquette which laid down as imperative that one must always say luncheon when what one wants to say is lunch—they would be in his presence and hearing for half an hour, and it would be ghastly if Milly talked as though he weren't there; too ghastly if she said anything that was true. She must ask her to be careful. She must remind her that——

But ought Milly to need reminding of the dreadful cloud she was under? Wasn't she the last person in the world who should ever, for a moment, forget it? And Fred said it was on no account to be mentioned, the cloud wasn't; it was to be ignored, blotted out. How could that be done if Milly herself alluded to it? Not directly alluded to it, but sideways—like this she had just said about being taken in? Taken in! With the butler standing there listening. . . .

"We *love* having you," said Mabel desperately, her small black eyes, staring anxiously out of her flushed face, making her look like a worried shrimp.

She drew her pale guest up the stairs; and the butler, watching grimly from below, said to himself that it was a pretty state of things, this being required to see after the luggage and attend to the wants of somebody dressed as an afflicted widow and yet no better than she should be. White sheets were what *she* ought to be in, thought the butler,—white sheets, and excommunicated from the church. His lordship would have made short work of such as her.

The butler—his name happened to be Butler, and he much objected to having been re-christened Smith by his new employers, for the bishop had called him by his own name without making the least difficulty, merely replying to the not infrequent query of strangers as to why he called his butler Butler, "Because he *is* a Butler," —the butler indignantly went to do as he had been told. But when at lunch-time Mrs. Ernest, as he supposed he must still describe her, reappeared without her bonnet and veil, and one could really get a good look at her, her hair so neat that it was a lesson to his own so-called lady's untidy poll, her face grave and quiet just as it should be, and her brow pure and open enough in his opinion to belong to a blameless Christian, he began to hesitate; and breathing over her as he handed food, and noting how waxen her cheeks were beneath the dark sweep of eyelashes—just what sad cheeks should be, in his opinion, after the death of a husband—he hesitated even more, for upon his word, thought the butler, she could have been transplanted then and there, and not a thing altered, straight to the luncheon-table at the bishop's palace, and been nothing but a credit to it.

Mabel too, furtively watching her, couldn't help thinking that she looked very good. How deceitful of her, thought Mabel; however had she the face to? It was better, of course, for everybody that she should, but how ever had she the face to? They knew all about her, and she knew they knew all about her. She knew they knew she was a firebrand, and it was sheer shamelessness to behave like one's idea of a damp squib. Exposed as a serpent, really it was horribly deceitful to seem to be a dove—of all animals, thought Mabel, in her agitation not sure whether doves were mammals or not. What mixture could be more dreadful than an adulterous dove? Mabel asked herself; and immediately was much shocked by her own expression.

Adulterous dove. What a sentence. Where had it come from? From what unexplored and ugly part of her mind? Words like that had never entered her head before. Were they, perhaps, an emanation from the figure quietly eating mutton? Goodness, what an upsetting idea; how horrid if Milly were one of those carrier people, and even if she were good herself—which she wasn't, interpolated Mabel, determined not to be fooled ever again—managed to put bad thoughts into blameless brains. Nice, very nice, with her innocent boys within daily range for a whole month, and even Fred—she could imagine nothing more hateful than having to look on while Fred was gradually being polluted.

Much worried, Mabel furtively watched Milly. She oughtn't, she thought, to be eating mutton. It didn't seem right, somehow, to Mabel—obscurely unsuitable, she felt, though she couldn't have said why. True she was eating it half-heartedly; but still,—mutton. Toast for widows, Mabel felt vaguely; dry toast for widows, and certainly dry toast for found-out sinners. Besides, if Milly had refused the mutton she could have said, "You are eating nothing," and Milly could have answered, "I'm not very hungry," and Mabel could have said, "You really ought to *try*, you know"—which would not only have been hospitable, but conversation.

As it was, what did one talk about to Milly? Sitting all anyhow on her chair, too nervous to bother, as she usually bothered when the butler was present, about deportment, Mabel tried vainly to think of things to say which wouldn't be tactless. Everything seemed tactless, and dangerous as well. Ordinary subjects, such as weather, sounded heartless when one was talking to a woman with a husband only three days in his grave. Gossip as to the family's doings was impossible, not only because gossip sounded heartless too, but because the family's doings lately had consisted entirely of horrified discussions of Milly herself. Ernest couldn't be mentioned; even if they were alone, without the butler, he couldn't be mentioned, now that he was a wronged husband as well as being dead—one couldn't, that is, comfort Milly any more about him. The Will was taboo. So were clothes, because there she was in weeds. So, even, were things like gardens, because they naturally led to flowers, and flowers—well, wreaths were made of flowers, and there you were, at once landed in cemeteries. Oh, it was difficult. And all the time, all through each long silence, one could hear the butler breathing.

Mabel, damp and flushed, thought with dismay of having to have a solid month of these sorts of luncheons —or nearly a month, till Rosemary came home, and then they would only be worse. Useless, too, to invite any of the relations to join her and help her out, for they would say they were going to have quite enough of Milly when their turn came round, and would refuse. If only one knew *really* what she had done, thought Mabel—who she had done it with, she meant, for they knew only too well which commandment she had broken,—it would be such a help. One would know better where one was, then. Ruth, the evening before, had whispered that Milly had arrived home in George's car; she didn't want to suggest anything, Ruth whispered, but the fact remained that it *was* George's car. Probably there was nothing in that, thought Mabel; but it just showed how awkward it was for everybody to be in the dark, and how easily it made one think things. George? Her own brother-in-law? Oh, no—too shocking. Besides, George always wore enormous spectacles, and Mabel did think it must be impossible to commit—well, what Milly had committed, with somebody who wore enormous spectacles. Of course, hesitated Mabel towards the end of the meal, if poor Milly hadn't done anything, and they were all, beginning with Ernest, accusing her wrongfully, she must say it would have been rather a shame. . . .

§

When, after what seemed centuries of time, the butler, performing his final rites, had breathed his last, and they could get away from the dining-room, she asked her waxen guest if she didn't think she ought to rest up in her room till tea, while one of the maids unpacked for her and put her things away. It would be such a good thing, thought Mabel, for everybody, if Milly rested quite a lot; safe in her bedroom; out of the way.

"Do you want me to?" asked Milly, turning her heavy eyes to her.

Now if that wasn't tactless, thought Mabel, reddening.

"No—of course I don't *want* you to," she said, vexed.
"I was thinking of you."

Milly went and rested; and Mabel, having given
orders tea was to be sent up to her at five o'clock,
escaped in the car, going for a long drive away from
everybody, right into the depths of Kent, and not coming back till it was time to dress for dinner, so as to shake
herself down inside a little, and recover, before having
to face the evening. And pausing a moment outside
Milly's door on her way upstairs when she got back,
she heard a man's voice talking, and it was Percy's.

Percy. In there.

Well, why shouldn't he be? How natural to go in
on getting home from his office, and greet his aunt.
Funny that it should stab her. Percy knew nothing—
could know nothing, for everyone had been most careful
to keep that sentence in the Will, and their aunt's disappearance, from the younger generation; yet stabbed
she was. She didn't want him to be in there, talking
to Milly—not alone, she discovered; violently she didn't
want him to. It had come so suddenly upon her, this
having to have Milly in her home, that she hadn't got
the details at all clear of what it would be really like
with the boys about, and all made so extra difficult
because of her being their aunt. *They* didn't know she
was an adulterous aunt—and, "Oh, dear," thought
Mabel, "there I am thinking awful words again!" But
now she saw the bigness of the sacrifice Fred was asking
of her. Rot about the family, she said to herself indignantly; who cared for its silly old honour, and not
being touched by scandal and all that stuff, when it
came to the protection of one's own children?

"I'm sure it's time to dress, Percy," she said, opening
the door and speaking in an unusually sharp voice.

There he was, sitting on the rug in front of the fire,

and Milly was lying on the sofa, and it all looked so pretty and cosy, what with the flowers and things Mabel herself had put in.

"Is it, mother?" said Percy, not moving. "But I am dressed. I got back earlier, so as to see Aunt Milly."

"Oh," said Mabel; and shut the door again, and went on to her own bedroom, and stood in front of her looking-glass passionately sticking more hairpins into a head already full of them, which was what she called doing her hair, and asked herself whether the sanctity of the home wasn't to be considered, then, and if it wasn't more important by long chalks—Mabel's thoughts, when she was really roused, easily clothed themselves in expressions which were not refined—than whitewashing Milly. Why should she help to whitewash Milly? Because the Botts would say—oh, she was fed up with the Botts!—that only by doing so scandal could be kept at bay. That was the answer, she knew, and she didn't care a fig for it—not a *fig*, she told herself, indignantly.

§

But at dinner, with Fred and Dick there too, as well as Percy, and Milly so quiet and passive and looking as if she were half asleep, she was ashamed of her sudden flare-up of suspiciousness. It really was rather ugly of her; very ugly, to be quite honest. Repentant, she renewed her attentions to her guest, eagerly backing Fred up in his hospitable speeches, pressing food and drink on her, doing her utmost.

Fred rewarded her with an approving glance, and she redoubled her efforts. It wasn't anyhow half as difficult as lunch had been, she felt, with her three men to support her, and Percy no different to his aunt than he had always been. They really got through dinner very well, thought Mabel thankfully, and Fred helped nobly, talking about business every now and then to the boys, and thus easing the strain of general conversation.

But what she had felt outside Milly's door was the sort of thing she was going to feel, she was sure, on the slightest occasion. Unfair and unfounded or not, she was bound to feel it. It was an impossible position Fred had put her in. Sooner or later——

Afterwards they sat in the Winter Garden for coffee, with the fountain turned on so as to show the butler that Milly was a particularly honoured guest, because only for the best guests did they turn the fountain on; and then they went into the billiard-room while the boys played billiards, taking Milly with them, and sitting watching the game on the raised dais through a cloud of cigar smoke; and when they had done that for some time, not having to talk because of watching, they took her back to the principal drawing-room—it made the time go more quickly, changing rooms—and had some gramophone music on their super-gramophone, their so to speak eight-cylinder sixty horse-power gramophone, being careful, Mabel was, anxious to play her part as well as possible till the moment when it left off being possible, that Dick only put on sacred records like *Oh for the Wings of a Dove*, and not having to talk, because of listening.

Such a blessing, not having to talk, Mabel felt. As long as they could avoid doing that, things might jog along. It was talking which upset everybody. No wonder royalties and restaurants had bands.

The evening wound up with soda-water. There was whiskey as well, but soda-water was what Fred gave, a glass each, to Mabel and Milly. At ten o'clock punctually it appeared, and at five minutes past ten Milly was being said good-night to, and taken up to bed.

Mabel went with her, turning on the lights in the mahogany spare room, feeling for the hot-water bottle between the sheets, plumping up the pillows, being solicitous.

At last came the moment when she was forced to leave off fussing, and turn round. Would there have to be kissing? Yes; no getting out of that, she was afraid.

"Well—good-night, Milly."

"Good-night, Mabel."

"I wonder if you've got everything?"

"I'm sure I have."

"Well, then——"

Bracing herself, Mabel advanced to kiss. It was slightly less of a peck than the kiss on the door-step, though still of a darting, beaky nature.

Milly received it passively.

"I believe she's asleep," said Mabel to Fred, when, thankfully, she rejoined him.

"Already?" asked Fred, surprised, looking at his watch.

"Oh, I don't mean *really*," hesitated Mabel, trying to catch what she did mean into words.

§

Left alone, Milly stood in the luxurious room without moving, her eyes fixed on the door through which Mabel had departed with such evident relief.

So this was it, she thought; this was what it was going to be. The music she had braced herself to face was to be all sweet. She was to be taken to the Botts' bosom, and however much it hurt them, clasped close. Coals of fire were to be heaped on her head. Fatted calves slaughtered. And, sure she was guilty, they had made up their minds to behave as though they were sure she wasn't.

Titford . . . family honour. . . .

Slowly she began drawing the hairpins out of her hair; mechanically dropping them from her fingers one by one on the carpet, not aware of what she was doing, only knowing that her head felt heavy and she must lighten it. Strange and unexpected development, she thought, staring at nothing; but she had no doubt at all that here at last she was in the very arms of expiation,— and none the less expiation that it came to her so disconcertingly, with a smile on its face.

That smile. It paralyzed her. She knew she mustn't pick and choose among punishments, but how much rather would she have had to meet abuse. At least abuse would have been genuine, and though terrifying at the moment presently over, and she allowed to go her way. This embarrassed kindness, this pretence of affection, wouldn't ever be over: it would go on. Having started on these lines, unless she did something more that was wicked, the Botts wouldn't be able to leave off again. She and they, for the rest of their lives as far as she could see, would be stuck together in their own terrible honey.

A round of visits. She had entered on a round of visits. It seemed incredible. Slowly, having dropped all her hairpins on the floor, she began plaiting her hair in its customary bedtime plaits. At the end of the visits, would she be let go? Or was it to be a round and round of them, and when she had worked through the whole family would she have to begin again at Fred's, and so on, over and over, till death released everybody? Unhappy Botts. They too, then, were expiating. And unhappy Mabel, with her flushed, worried face, forcing herself to kiss, to be hospitable, heroically trying to carry out what had evidently been strict instructions —wasn't it hard that she too, without ever having set eyes on him, should have to suffer because of Arthur?

It was very hard; and Milly, mechanically plaiting her hair, could see no way out of it. What could she do except pretend, except play up to the family, except make it easier for them by behaving as if she were really as innocent as they apparently were going desperately to insist? And what, in that case, became of her resolve to have done with lying?

"I can't—I *can't*," she suddenly said out loud, her hands dropping at her sides; but even as she said it she knew she must and would. Hadn't she sworn to herself to make amends to the Botts, to do in all things what they wished? And if this were what they had decided was the best way for them out of the situation she had put them in, then mustn't she help in whatever way she could? But what a punishment, she whispered under her breath; for everybody, what a punishment. Ah, if it had been real, the welcome, the kindness, in spite of what she had done—why, then, with what flooding gratitude, with what quick response of love, she would have applied herself for the rest of her days to goodness. . . .

That, however, was nonsense. She resumed the plaiting of her hair. How could it be real? What right had she to real affection from the family she had disgraced? The Botts weren't saints; and only saints didn't mind sinners. Also—she, at least, would face the truth—if she had been going to marry Arthur, if that had been settled and happy, would she have minded much about the Botts?

"Oh, I'm contemptible," said Milly, again aloud, her hands dropping once more at her sides, staring wide-eyed at nothing.

⁂(XIII)⁂

THE next day was Saturday, and when the gong went for breakfast no Milly appeared.

Mabel, always the first in the dining-room because of prayers, fidgeted about nervously among the coffee-cups, glancing frequently at the door; but minutes passed, and first Percy, and then Fred, and then Dick, came down one after the other, and ate their porridge and proceeded to their sausages, and still there was no sign of Milly.

Late; she was going to be late. Slowly relief began creeping round the table. "She's late," Mabel half whispered once, and the heads bent more assiduously over their plates in a kind of hush of suspense, lest this remark should be overheard by Fate, and immediately produce her.

But more minutes passed, and nothing happened. The relief increased. No one wanted Milly at breakfast, not even the boys, who felt that their white-faced, black-garbed aunt wouldn't mix at all well, somehow, with sausages; and Fred, as he ate his, found they tasted better and better the longer she delayed, and Mabel became gradually almost sprightly.

Mabel, indeed, all through prayers had kept an anxious eye on the door, in case Milly should come in before they were over. She was, Mabel had already discovered, a painstaking guest, and on her first day had been where she ought to be each time not merely on the tick but a minute or two ahead of it; so that Mabel had greatly feared she might, on the first morning, in the excess of her zeal to give no trouble in small things because she was giving so much in big ones, be over-punctual at breakfast, and thus tumble into the middle of prayers.

Passionately Mabel didn't want Milly at prayers. She positively raced through them, and only dared breathe again when the Bible was going out and the porridge coming in. How could she have prayed with Milly present? It was bad enough doing it with the butler present, but he at least was known for a moral man. Milly's presence, among the stonily hostile serv-ants, would have dried up the collects on Mabel's very lips. She had tried to get her to stay in bed for breakfast, asking her the night before, when she accompanied her upstairs, whether she wouldn't like it in her room, but she seemed to have lost her tact as well as her virtue —that famous tact they used to hear so much about— and said she would rather come down. Some idea, Mabel supposed, of not giving trouble; as though the worst trouble of all wasn't having her wandering round in contact with the boys, and everybody having to pre-tend!

Bed, of course, was the best place for Milly, Mabel thought as she poured out coffee, one ear cocked, listen-ing for footsteps approaching across the hall; anyhow for a bit. A slight illness was really what she ought to develop, Mabel felt—naturally nothing much, but enough to keep her upstairs during the next week or so. It was almost her duty, in the first stage of a widowhood caused by violence, to have some sort of breakdown. People would expect it; everybody would think it natural; and if it could be spread over the whole month of her stay, then Mabel, instead of being the worst off of the family for having to be the first to welcome her, would think herself the luckiest of the lot. What could be an easier way of getting through the visit—*any* visit, thought Mabel, at all times an awkward and reluctant hostess—than for the guest to stay in bed? In this way no one would see her except the maids and Mabel herself, Percy would be preserved from harmful contact, Fred would be spared irksome efforts to talk, and the butler wouldn't have to wait on sin.

And, as though in answer to these unspoken wishes, the butler, who at breakfast only hovered occasionally and didn't stick, came in with a message the head housemaid had just given him from Mrs. Ernest, saying she was very sorry but she had rather a headache, and might she be excused from coming down.

Might she? Oh, hallelujah! sang Mabel to herself.

Fred was all heartiness. "Certainly, certainly," he cried, reaching across the dishes in front of him and spiking a pat of butter on his knife. "No place like bed when one is—when one isn't—Send word, Smith, we're all deligh—we're all very gl— I mean, we're sorry to hear it. No—hold on a minute. You go, Mabel, and see if she's got everything. Tuck her up, and tell her to take care of herself. That's all right, Smith," he nodded dismissal to the butler. "And you might ask her," he continued to Mabel, whose hallelujah had already died down at the prospect of having to go and tuck up Milly, "where she has put that thousand pounds."

"What thousand pounds?" instantly asked Percy, jerking his head up from his plate.

"Your aunt's legacy," said Fred shortly, regretting he had mentioned it before the boys. One thing leads to another, and in what concerned Milly all the things were damned unpleasant.

"I thought there wasn't a legacy. You said last night——"

"Pass the marmalade," commanded his father.

"How did she manage to get hold of it so soon?" persisted Percy. "I thought——"

"Daresay you did," interrupted his father; and waving him aside with a gesture of the marmalade spoon, he continued his address to Mabel, who was reluctantly preparing to obey him and had pulled the cloth askew, and spilled some coffee, in the process. "It's somewhere up in her room," he said. "It mustn't lie about loose, tell her, over the week-end. I'm going to invest it for her on Monday, and meanwhile it mustn't lie about loose. Ask her to let me have it to put in my safe."

"But, Fred—do you think I ought to? If she's got a headache?" hesitated Mabel. It was Fred's job, surely, she thought, to do any talking to Milly which approached business; she had more than her share of her as it was. "I don't see how I can bother her if she isn't well," she said, doubtfully.

"Then go and have a look round the room, and see for yourself where it is."

"Oh, Fred——" Mabel feebly protested.

"It's not fair to the servants to have a sum like that lying in a woman's bedroom," said Fred. "It's putting temptation in their way. Besides, they'll talk, and we shall be burgled sure as Fate."

"Good gracious!" exclaimed Mabel at that, who lived in dread of burglars; and she went away rather quickly to the mahogany bedroom.

But when she got there, and after knocking and getting no answer opened the door, she found Milly was asleep—or seemed to be. Her eyes were shut, anyhow, and stayed shut in spite of the noise the door made.

"Milly——" began Mabel, tentatively.

No answer.

"Asleep," she decided; and stood hesitating, wondering whether she had better go in and wait till she woke up, or go down and finish her breakfast. She decided to finish her breakfast, and she shut the door softly and went back to the dining-room.

"She's asleep," she said.

"Then go and wake her," said Fred. "I've got to catch the 10.15, and must lock up that money before I go."

"But how can I wake her if she's got a headache?" Mabel again protested; and the boys too seemed to think it rather a shame.

Fred, however, had made up his mind, and was adamant. Looking round the table he requested his family to allow him to be the judge of what was the proper course to pursue; he wasn't going to risk the loss in his house of a thousand pounds merely because a woman was having forty winks and they thought it a shame to disturb her; also he had to catch his train. Mabel must go up again at once, he ordered. And Mabel, bound to obey when Fred spoke in that voice, went.

But when, on opening the door a second time, she found the same picture on the bed of closed eyes and apparent sleep, opposition, away from Fred's eye and voice, became more active, and instead of waking Milly according to orders, or even looking round among her helpless things according to orders, she softly tiptoed across the room to a chair by the fire, and sat down and waited.

It was quiet there, and safe—the one place in the house Fred couldn't come into without permission. Plenty of time, thought Mabel, noiselessly sitting down, to find out about the money when he came back to lunch—to luncheon, she corrected herself. Being Saturday, he would be back almost as soon as he had started, and Milly would be awake by then, and perhaps up and dressed, and he could talk to her himself. There wasn't any hurry. Burglars wouldn't come before dark; maids wouldn't be tempted while there was someone in the room. Ridiculous of Fred suddenly to fuss, thought Mabel, becoming more courageous every minute in that safe place. He hadn't said a word about the wretched money the day before—all night long it had been lying somewhere in Milly's room, and he hadn't even mentioned it. He had just simply forgotten it yesterday; and if he could forget it, it couldn't be so terribly dangerous and risky for it to remain wherever it was a little longer.

Mabel settled herself more comfortably in the chair. She would stay where she was till after Fred's train had gone. There wasn't another door in the house she could shut against him, but she could shut this door, and it was so much easier not to obey him when she knew he couldn't get at her. Afterwards, if he was very angry, she could say she had had to do things for Milly.

Poor Milly. Let her sleep. There could be little fun for her, these days, in being awake, thought Mabel, so much obliged to her for being in bed that she felt quite softened. Whether she had done whatever she had done or hadn't done it, she must know they all thought she had, which must be horrible for her. Why had she come back? Mabel in her place would never, she was sure, have had the face to come back, especially not if she had a thousand pounds in her pocket. She ought to have gone to that sister of hers. Birds of a feather. . . .

But were they birds of a feather? Watching her from her chair by the fire, Mabel thought she might quite well at that moment be taken for a good school-girl, her figure hidden under the bedclothes, and her fair hair in two thick plaits down each side of her smooth face. Mabel's own face was all crumpled up into creases,

though she was only two years older than Milly—but
how much better to be creased than wicked, she thought.
Perhaps creases had something to do with virtue, and
one either had both or neither, she said to herself, gazing
at Milly, ready to turn away quickly at the first quiver
of those quiet eyelashes. Since Ernest's accident she
hadn't had such an opportunity of studying her, and
really and truly, Mabel said to herself, almost as if she
were reasoning aloud with Milly, she had no right to
look good like that if she wasn't. It made it so difficult
to be *sure;* and it was so worrying not to be *sure.* Because, suppose——?

Well, they couldn't all be wrong, the whole family,
and Ernest at the head of them, she told herself. Still
—again she hesitated—suppose they were?

And then she started, for Milly, unexpectedly opening her eyes, caught her, after all, staring at her.

"Oh—you're awake," said Mabel, embarrassed, getting up and going over to the bed.

Milly put out a languid hand. "Do you mind my not
coming down?" she murmured, raising her heavy eyes
to the face above her.

Mabel took the hand. What can one do but take a
hand put out?

"No, of course not," she said. "We like it. I mean,"
she hastily corrected, "we like you to do what you like
to do."

"You're so kind," said Milly in a low voice. "So
terribly, terribly kind——" and added, her eyelids
drooping as if too heavy to stay open, and her hand sliding from Mabel's loose grasp back on to the quilt, "I've
got such a headache."

"I'm *sure* you have," said Mabel fervently, almost
as one who congratulates on a propriety. "I mean," she
went on in some confusion, herself noticing this tone,

"it's natural you should have one, isn't it, after—after all."

To this Milly said nothing, but lay, lax and motionless, her eyes shut, her mouth slightly open, overcome by a hopeless fatigue.

Mabel stood staring at her. Was she going to be really ill? Ought one to send for her doctor? It would look well, of course, for Milly to need a doctor, but suppose she developed a temperature, and talked before him, as people with temperatures do sometimes talk, and let out what was, what must be, so heavy on her conscience? That would be awful. No, she mustn't be allowed to be as ill as all that. She must just lie there quietly and rest, and Mabel would look after her herself—indeed, Mabel felt she would nurse Milly with real enthusiasm if only she would stay in bed quietly, out of everyone's way, and not get worse, and not get better, but just simmer along till it was time to get up and go on her next visit.

"You'll be all right if you stay in bed," she said, trying not to sound too eager.

"May I?" asked Milly, without opening her eyes. Her headache was so enormous—as big, it seemed, as the whole world.

"Of course. It's *much* the best place for you," said Mabel, with such conviction in her voice that Milly opened her eyes and looked at her languidly a moment.

Then she shut them again, and turned her face to the wall, muttering something Mabel couldn't catch.

"What did you say?" asked Mabel, bending over her.

But Milly seemed to have once more dropped off to sleep; and after waiting a minute, Mabel, knowing that by now Fred must have gone to catch his train, tiptoed away to give orders for an immediate and lavish preparation of beef tea, jelly, and barley-water.

§

For ten days Milly was really ill; but, fortunately, so reliably ill—by which Mabel meant she was comatose rather than excited, and didn't wander in her head and let out secrets—that a doctor could safely be sent for. Not a nurse. This, Mabel felt sure, would be dangerous, because one becomes so familiar with one's nurse, and easily tells her things. Mabel remembered how she herself, in her confinements, had told her nurse all sorts of intimate and not at all proper things about Fred, which still made her hot to think of. No; Mabel would do the nursing, and was very glad to, for Milly wasn't in the least alarming in her apathetic, drowsy state, and it relieved Mabel of all anxiety about Fred and the boys to know her safely in bed and nobody, except the doctor and Mabel herself, able to get at her.

The doctor was most sympathetic. He said it was what he had been afraid of, but expected, after such a shock, and prescribed quiet and tonics. Really it was all exactly what Mabel would have wished. She went about full of thankfulness; and Fred was so nice and kind, and several times called her old girl, which was his highest form of praise, though he did rather worry about not being able to get hold of the thousand pounds.

"You must wait," Mabel told him—quite important these days, a real somebody, she felt, at last; and since it seems to be difficult to wash and feed people for any length of time without becoming fond of them, by the end of a week of plying the unresisting Milly with beef-tea she began to soften towards her, to believe she had been wronged, and found herself developing a tendency to allude to Fred's deceased brother as "that Ernest."

Once she spoke of him in this way, before she knew what she was saying—which was indeed her usual method of conversation—in the presence of her sisters-in-law Edith and Maud, who, with the rest of the female portion of the family, now that they were sure they wouldn't meet Milly, frequently dropped in to hear how things were going. It slipped out, somehow, as the things in Mabel's head did slip out, and they stared at her in shocked surprise.

"Mabel, I can't let you speak in such a way of my poor brother," said Maud, *née* Bott, after a scandalized pause.

"Milly's getting round you," declared Edith, her thin lips drawn down at the corners.

Getting round her? Mabel felt all the customary indignation at the suggestion, but could think of nothing to say back, she being of those who can't when most they need to, except, "I like that."

Yet Edith turned out to have been right. Mabel, at the end of another week, had bitter occasion to admit it. How *could* Milly, Mabel asked herself, after the way she had nursed her, the really devoted way—she had seemed like a baby, a grateful baby, in Mabel's hands—oh, never, never again would Mabel believe in man, woman or child—and as for poor Ernest. . . .

What happened was that, at the end of a fortnight, Milly had so much benefited by the quiet and the beef-tea—in fact, by Mabel's kindness, Mabel reminded herself—and was, though apathetic, so evidently better, that the doctor said she might get up and lie on the sofa for a few hours every day so as to begin to get her strength up; and directly he heard this, Fred insisted on paying her a visit. Mabel's instinct warned her, she afterwards remembered, that it was funny of Fred not to be able to wait till Milly came downstairs, but he was so positive it was most important he should see her and have a business talk, that Mabel gave way. Business!

How many wives, thought Mabel afterwards, must have heard that word applied to the sort of conduct she caught Fred indulging in? And she remembered afterwards, too, how restless he had been, how more and more fidgety every day, always asking when Milly would be up again, always pretending he wanted to see her on business. Business! Mabel felt she would never believe him again, when he talked to her of business.

"You can't," she said at first, when he wanted to go up, still feeling authoritative and important after being in sole command of Milly so long. "What an idea."

"Why not? She's dressed, isn't she?"

"You can't go into Milly's bedroom, Fred. It wouldn't be proper."

"Not proper? What, when she's dressed and up, and I'm her brother-in-law? Don't be silly, Mabel."

Then Mabel began to falter, in spite of her instinct. Perhaps he was right, and she was silly. After all, sofas weren't beds, and Milly had all her clothes on, except her crape and hairpins. She couldn't really object to Fred's going up, any more than that first night she had been able really to object to Percy's visit to his aunt's room. Still, she didn't like it. Fred knew Milly was different from an ordinary sister-in-law, or believed he knew she was. Mabel herself no longer believed it, because she had been nursing her, but she was conscious this wasn't a good reason and that the family would make short work of it. Fred, though, did believe it, and accordingly oughtn't to wish to go into such a room.

"Why do you want to?" she asked, uncertainly; for though her word had been law with Milly for a fortnight it hadn't been law with Fred, who was just as masterly and headstrong as ever.

"I want to talk business," he said. "You know I do.

You know I've been worrying about that money. I want to talk over investments. I want to find out where it is."

"Can't I find out just as well as you?"

"You wouldn't before, when I wanted you to, so now I'm going to myself. I'm responsible to the family for its safety. You don't seem to understand the value of money. Tell her I'm coming up after tea."

"Oh, Fred—you can't after tea. She goes back to bed then."

"Well, to-morrow. First thing after breakfast."

"Oh, but you can't after breakfast, Fred—she isn't up then."

Mabel, however, had now over-reached herself, for after staring at her a moment from under his heavy eyebrows, Fred said, "Then I'll go now."

And he went.

§

It was Saturday again—the day fortnight from Milly's first being ill. Fred had arranged to play a round of golf with George on the West Titford links after lunch, but George would have to wait, he said to himself, for he was damned if he'd be put off any longer by Mabel and her Oh but you can'ts. During this fortnight he had seen a good deal of his brothers and brothers-in-law, who all thought it very risky that Milly's money should be somewhere in a bedroom for so long, and told Fred so, and seemed to think it strange that he hadn't placed it in safety the very first day Milly arrived at his house —which added to his own uneasiness and annoyance with himself. Still, he couldn't very well raid a sick woman's bedroom, could he? he asked them. And they admitted he couldn't; especially not this particular bedroom.

"You may take it from me," Fred assured them, "that I'll seize the first opportunity"; and this was the first opportunity, and he seized it.

Mabel had been a brick and all that, he knew—indeed, she had rather overdone the brick business, he had been thinking lately—but he wasn't going to let her come between him and his duty to that thousand pounds. Latterly he had hardly been able to sleep, knowing such a sum was lying about in his house just because he had so unaccountably forgotten to ask for it the first day. It had been worrying him more and more; and Milly's being confined to her bed, which otherwise would have been a reason for congratulation, became, as the days passed, an increasing exasperation. Besides, if anything happened to the money while under his roof the family would probably regard him as responsible, and expect him to make the loss good, and he saw no fun at all in that.

The thought made him go upstairs two steps at a time and knock very loudly on Milly's door, and when he didn't get an immediate answer he opened it a slit, and said, automatically becoming hearty, "Any admittance?"

There was a pause inside the room of evident surprise. Then Milly's voice, small and slow after all the days of being in bed, said, hesitatingly, "Is it you, Fred? Oh, yes—come in."

She was on a sofa drawn up to the fire, and the room was bright with flowers and early afternoon sunshine. The windows were open, and it smelt sweet. Books, barley-water, grapes, violets—all the accompaniments of well cared-for convalescence, were on a little table by her side. Clean and attentively nursed she looked in her rose-coloured wrapper, her hair plaited in two long plaits. Mabel certainly had done her duty by her. But the

minute he saw her Fred felt as much embarrassed as he
did the last time he was alone with her, when he fetched
her from Mandeville Park Road—more embarrassed, in
fact. Perhaps Mabel was right, and he oughtn't to have
come up. He hadn't seen Milly in plaits before, and they
somehow produced an atmosphere of intimacy which
was the last thing he wanted. So he began to be boister-
ous, trying to appear genial and at his ease.

"Hello, Milly," he said, striding across to the sofa and
speaking very loud, "how are you? Feeling pretty fit
again? Sorry you've been seedy, but you'll be all right
now. Keeping your pecker up, eh?" he added, noticing
a tray with food on it. "That's right. Splendid."

And checking a desire to rub his hands, so as to give
himself countenance, he drew up the chair Mabel
usually sat in, and settled himself in it for, he informed
her, a talk.

The quick flush of the weak flew into Milly's face,
and as quickly flew out again.

"I've been worrying ever since you've been ill," he
said, settling himself in the chair; and there was such
unmistakable sincerity in his voice that Milly looked at
him, startled and touched.

"You needn't have," she murmured, flushing again.
"Mabel has been an angel to me."

"I've been worrying," Fred, doggedly stalking his
subject, persisted, "about that money."

"Which money?" asked Milly, who for the moment
had quite forgotten it. There had been so many things
to think of, a whole existence to rearrange, while she
lay in bed slowly coming back to life, and the thousand
pounds, belonging to the wretched past and gone anyhow, had drifted during her illness out of her mind.

"Which money?" repeated Fred, pulling a grape off
the bunch on a plate beside her, and putting it in his

mouth so as to give himself something to do, for he couldn't very well smoke in a sick room. "Have you got any more, then?"

"Oh, you mean——"

She made an effort to concentrate, and little beads came out on her upper lip because of her having been in bed so long, and this being her first day up. "You mean what Ernest left me. No, I haven't got any more."

She hesitated.

"Not yet, that is," she went on in her slow, weak voice. "Not till I've sold my jewellery. I hope—perhaps I'll be able—to do that soon."

"A good idea," approved Fred, nodding. "But George told me you got your legacy, and you'd better let me have it to invest for you. I think I can get you a safe five per cent. I wouldn't advise more, though of course I could——" he turned over in his mind, his mouth, with the grape in it, screwed up, a few of the slightly less sound and slightly more profitable investments he knew of, and dismissed them. "No," he said, shaking his head, "I wouldn't advise it. Best be on the safe side. Of course I ought to have asked for the money at once, directly you arrived, and not wasted a fortnight's interest."

"But," said Milly, confused, "I haven't got it."

"Haven't you?" said Fred, so much surprised at this that he found himself looking straight at her. "Why, George told us you'd been to Jenkyns, and he——"

"Yes," said Milly as he paused, "but——"

The flush was fixed now on her face. It hadn't occurred to her that her not having the thousand pounds would surprise the Botts unpleasantly. She hadn't thought about it at all from their point of view, not foreseeing, not dreaming, that she was to be on their hands as their permanent guest. During those three

days before she collapsed into bed, what time had she
to think? Engaged as she had been in perpetual flight
from one dreadful situation to another, what time had
she had to do anything but feel? Now, however, it
occurred to her; very clearly it occurred to her. And
her eyes, fixed on Fred, were startled.

"But—I did," she faltered.

"Did what?" Fred asked.

"I did get it."

He stared. 'Then where——" he began, his mouth
working because of the grape in it, which was big.

Before saying any more he had to swallow it. Having
done so, he began again: "Then where is it? Excuse my
asking, won't you. But as I explained the day I brought
you here, we're taking you on now, the family is—a
pleasure, I'm sure—and we must get the financial side
straight."

"I thought," said Milly, the beads on her upper lip
spreading to her temples, "it was mine"—a remark
which sounded ominous to Fred.

"Certainly it is yours," he said; but he didn't go on
because he had an unpleasant feeling that he was getting
near something very objectionable, something which
might land him, if he questioned further, right up
against—well, the wretched fellow Milly had obviously
been in London with. *He* had got the money, Fred suddenly felt terribly sure. Bad enough that, in all conscience; but worse if he questioned Milly till she admitted it, for then good-bye to ignoring him, good-bye
to ignoring her adultery, good-bye to saving the family's
good name.

Frowning, he pulled off another grape, with movements so significant of mental disturbance that Milly's
eyes became more startled and afraid than ever.

"Of course," he went on, not looking at her as he ate

it, "it isn't really my or anyone else's business. If you haven't got it you haven't got it. But if you've deposited it in a bank"—his voice lightened at the possibility—"you might just tell me. It'll help, you know—the interest will."

"It isn't in a bank," said Milly.

There was a tiny pause, and Fred gulped down his grape.

"I've—given it away," she said.

"Ah," said Fred.

So that was it. The fellow had got it. Just as he suspected. Perfectly revolting. And now was she going to make it worse, make the whole position impossible for everybody, by telling him who she had given it to? It looked like it. She was beginning to speak——

"For God's sake, Milly," he said sharply, suddenly glaring across at her from under his shaggy eyebrows, "let's leave it at that. I don't wish to——"

"But, Fred—I want to tell you. I gave it to my sister."

"To your sister?"

He stared at her. "What," he said, "the one who——?"

"I've only got one," said Milly.

"But—doesn't she live in Switzerland? I seem to remember she——"

"Yes. But when she saw Ernest's death in the paper—" Milly stopped a moment to wipe the beads off her upper lip—"she came over to—to see me."

"And did you see her?"

"Yes, I saw her in London. I gave her the money."

Fred was silent, staring at her. Then he said, on a sudden impulse, his voice quite different, "I beg your pardon, Milly."

"Oh, Fred—what for?" she asked; adding, before he could say anything, for she didn't want an answer to that ill-advised question, "I couldn't not have given it

to her. Anybody would have, in my place——" and
speaking slowly, pausing and going on again, the hair
round her ears quite wet now with effort, she told him
of Agatha's situation, of how desperate it had been for
years, and of how she had come over to live, as she
thought, with Milly in Mandeville Park Road, knowing
nothing, naturally, of Ernest's Will.

"You wouldn't have liked," she ended, lying back on
her cushions with the glimmer of a smile, for somehow
the atmosphere had lightened, "having two of us on
your hands, would you?"

"But did she know it was all you had?" Fred asked.

"Well, she knew I'd got——" Milly's eyelids quivered
and drooped—"all of you," she finished.

"Yes," Fred reflected. "Yes. Still, you know, to take
every penny a woman possesses——"

"But she didn't. I've got my jewellery," said Milly,
raising her eyes again and looking at him. "I told you
I want to try and sell it soon. I think it's quite valuable
—don't you?"

"Still, you know," persisted Fred, not to be deflected
from his consideration of Agatha's conduct, "to take
every penny a woman possesses——"

Milly was a fool to have given it to her, of course, but
what sort of a creature could she be to take it? Well,
he knew the sort of creature she was; out of the distant
past the old scandal came back quite clearly to him
again, and his mouth took on an expression of distaste.

Milly guessed what he was thinking. "I made her
take it," she said. "And naturally she thought it didn't
matter, because I was going to be m——"

She stopped with a small gasp. Had he noticed?
If this talk went on long enough she would be sure to
let out what at all costs the Botts didn't want definitely
to know. Oh, she was too weak for an interview like this.

She ought to have been given a lot of meat, or something, before Fred came up, to put some strength into her. Just then, in her anxiety to protect poor Aggie, and having nothing but beef-tea and milk puddings inside her to steady her, she had been on the very verge . . .

Fred, however, hadn't noticed. He was still deep in unflattering consideration of that sister.

"You hadn't heard anything of each other for years, had you?" he asked after a moment. "Never since she——"

"Ran away," Milly finished for him; and saying to herself that here at least was something she could talk openly about, that she could confess, now that it was all over and didn't matter to anybody, she told Fred how they had written to each other during the whole time. She knew it was a deceitful thing to have done, she said, but she had loved her sister, and couldn't endure, she anxiously explained, her eyes on his face, to be cut off from her for good and all.

And again she had that feeling that if only she had had a tonic, or some meat or something, before this interview, she would have managed it better.

"He forbade you to write, didn't he? Ernest, I mean," said Fred, who had listened intently. "I fancy remembering his telling us he had."

"Yes. And I disobeyed. Wouldn't you have, Fred?"

He grinned a little. "I don't know," he said. "I don't quite see Mabel forbidding——"

A tone of friendliness, as distinguished from his first awkward heartiness, was warming his voice, crept into it at the point where Agatha had entered the conversation, and increasing as he talked. Great was his relief that at least it wasn't that fellow who had got the money, and that it was her sister she had been with in

London. One blot at least, and a nasty one too, had been removed from Milly's character. Also, it now seemed possible that the secrecy of her journey might be explained by a desire to evade the certain hostile criticism of the family if they had known what she intended doing. They would have been mightily and properly shocked to think of Milly's meagre inheritance going to that sister. She well knew how much they had all objected to the sister, and how painful the whole story had been to them. Natural that, determined to see her sister and help her, she should have run off without a word. And he had always liked poor little Milly, and it was exceedingly difficult for Fred, sitting with her and talking, and seeing her looking so good and sweet in her plaits, and hearing her sounding so much too weak to be able to tell anything but the truth, either to remember or believe that she was a deceiver and a bad lot—in fact it was getting more difficult every minute. While as for the money, what was the loss of fifty pounds or so a year, compared to the comfort, the relief, of knowing Milly wasn't quite so wicked after all?

Then a thought struck him. He leaned forward. "Did he ever find out?" he asked quickly. "Ernest, I mean. About the letters," he added, for Milly was looking frightened, and as though she didn't understand.

"I—don't think so. Why?"

"But he may have without your knowing, mightn't he?"

She hesitated. "Yes—he *may* have," she said slowly, remembering that which he had indeed found out. Since Ernest was such an expert at finding out, why should he not also have known all about the letters?

"And he never would forgive you if he had, would he?" asked Fred, with curious and unusual eagerness.

"Oh, *never*. I can't imagine Ernest ever——"

"Nor can I," Fred agreed. "No, I'm certain he wouldn't have."

He was leaning forward, staring at her with an odd expression in his eyes, and his sallow face was red.

"My dear Milly," he said after a moment, stretching out his hand across the dish of grapes, and closing it tightly over hers.

She shrank back, but he held it fast.

"My dear Milly," he said again, his eyes fixed on her face, "anything we any of us can do to make up——"

A hot flood of still brighter colour rushed into her already flushed cheeks. She knew what conclusion he had jumped to. She tried feebly to pull her hand away.

"But, Fred," she began in consternation, for here she was being whitewashed with a vengeance, being forced to take in poor, kind Fred really, not just playing her part in a game of pretence they were all joining in. "But, Fred," she began, trying to draw her hand away—and who knows what she wouldn't have said next, if at that moment the door hadn't opened, and Mabel, who had been fuming and fretting downstairs, and at last couldn't endure the idea of Fred being alone up there any longer, hadn't appeared.

She stopped when she saw them, and stood rooted. Even a person who wasn't a wife would have had the feeling of intruding on something very like a love-scene, they were both so red and obviously agitated, and he leaning over the grapes and the violets and everything, so as to hold her hand.

Mabel's puckered face was a study in amazed, indignant misery. Edith's words came crashing into her mind. Taken in indeed she was; taken in all round.

She stared at them, rooted. She couldn't have believed it of Fred—the very first moment he was left alone with her. And Milly—Milly, of whose innocence she had been so sure, whom she had nursed so devotedly, who had seemed like a grateful baby.

"I suppose you know," she said slowly, trying to keep her voice from going up and down in squeaks, "George is waiting for you all this time on the links?"

§

Fred was now to discover what Mabel could be like when roused.

He hadn't had an idea of her possibilities; nor had he dreamed how small a part reason played in her make-up. He now was to find out. For, as he hurried downstairs to get his clubs and be off to old George, who must have been cooling his heels for the best part of an hour—"By Jove, yes," he exclaimed, looking at his watch—she caught him up, and said in a voice he didn't know, "I wish to speak to you. Please come into the study."

"Not now—after tea," said Fred, seizing his cap.

He did, however, go into the study; he found himself in it, apparently of his own free will, and the door shut; and there he became, for the first time in his married life, really acquainted with Mabel.

Just as she, upstairs, had had difficulty in believing that that was Fred, so he, in his study, had difficulty in believing that this was Mabel. Yet she looked like Mabel; she had on her clothes. And also she looked like an ordinary, reasonable human being—with a face, that is, and a forehead, and all that. How could he answer her? What could he say to someone who consisted entirely—he had never suspected it—of violent possessive emotions, uncontrolled by any, or the very smallest amount of, intelligence?

He looked, and listened, dumbfounded. They had jogged along the years together, no demands made on her mind beyond housekeeping, and he had done the thinking, and she had done the rest, and done it quite nicely; and if, sometimes, he had thought her a little silly, he had supposed that all women were, sometimes, a little silly, and it hadn't disturbed him.

Now he discovered that silliness, an inability to understand, even to listen and try to, was her usual condition, had always been her usual condition, hidden only by the want of occasion for exercising sense.

"If what I've just seen," said she, her voice trembling with fury, her whole body shaking, "is your idea of talking business with Milly, let me tell you I won't have it. Do you hear, Fred? I simply won't have it."

And, as he stared at her, really at first not understanding, she flung up at him, "What were you doing, holding Milly's hand, and your face all red, and you pretending to me it was business? Business! A nice sort of business. I shall know what you're up to next time you tell me you must do business."

Mabel speaking to him like that. Mabel.

Calm in the face of such monstrous excitement, Fred tried to explain what he had discovered—that they had all been wrong about the unfortunate Milly, that there wasn't a man in it at all, and Ernest had cut her out of his Will for nothing whatever except disobeying his order not to write to that sister of hers; and Mabel, she just laughed at him—loudly, strangely, derisively, her hands pressed against her sides.

Such sounds as these he had never before heard proceeding from her whose mirth, when there was any, expressed itself in small titters; and, still not understanding, his blood a little chilled by the unaccustomed noises she was making, on his asking, "What on earth's the matter? What has happened to you?" her amazing answer, jerked out on a shriek of laughter, was, "You're a fool."

A fool. He. Mabel telling him so.

Then Fred settled down to it; settled down to his melancholy realizations. He tried, before quite giving up hope, to regain some control over her, to sober her by calling her My dear—"Don't call me names, my dear," said Fred, who had only addressed her as his dear once before in their life—years ago, when in spite of having been told she wasn't to, she drove his favourite mare and let her down and broke both her knees, and the effect of this endearment, used in the particular tone he was again using, had been devastating. But now it passed over her like water, because Mabel, born all heart and no head—she began, he slowly realized, from the chest downwards, and above her chest, though she appeared to have a head, there seemed to be nothing really but a strange little box, full of a litter of disconnected flimsy odds and ends—Mabel, having been born like this, couldn't concentrate, didn't listen, intent only on what her injured heart felt, which was that she had been made a fool of, and shamefully taken in.

Slowly Fred, as he listened to her, realized this—that he was, in fact, talking to a person with the mind of a child and the enormous heart of a woman. What a combination, he thought; perhaps more frequent than he knew. He had only not found it out sooner because of the uneventfulness, the plain sailing, of their life. And it considerably depressed him, for a man, he thought, likes his wife to have a head as well.

It did, however, this realization, keep him from getting angry and saying things no Bott husband had yet said, and he was very sorry for his poor distracted little wife, making herself so miserable about something which hadn't happened, when, her sense of injury, of having been taken in by the husband to whom she had devoted her life, and by Milly in whom she had come to believe, overwhelming her, she burst into a wild flood of tears.

Then he took her on his knee. She was a child; a kind, unreasoning child, he said to himself, feeling suddenly lonely, as if something he had supposed was there had gone out of his life, and she would never be anything else. And because he hadn't sat her on his knee since the early part of the first year of their marriage, Mabel was so much overcome by this action that her fury melted, and with her arms round his neck, her wet cheek ruining his tie, she asked him, sobbing, why he had been like that with Milly—why, why—so dreadful of him when she had been such a good wife to him—and loved him, loved him——

"Why?" said Fred. "Because I was so ashamed of myself, and ashamed of all of us, for having at once believed what we have believed about her."

"But Ernest——" sobbed Mabel—"he wouldn't have —not for nothing—just for letters—oh, Fred—as if he would!"

"Wouldn't he?" And Fred, remembering Ernest, repeated with conviction, "*Wouldn't* he."

"You'd rather believe your d-dead brother has——"

"Much rather. What do you think?"

"I think," said Mabel, dropping from sobs into plain despair, "you're very fond of Milly. Fonder of her than you ought to be."

And Fred couldn't go and take counsel of old George, he couldn't tell anyone his troubles, because she was his wife, and the Bott tradition shut his mouth.

✻✤(*XIV*)✤✻

WHILE this was happening, the Alec Botts, at Brighton, were enjoying sea breezes, mild sunshine, and complete immunity from worries. They had been doing this for over a fortnight, their time filled up by morning strolls on the front, afternoon drives along country roads, evening repose in a corner of the lounge watching the other sojourners in the hotel but not speaking to them, and regular and excessive meals.

The family didn't write to them; the family was annoyed with them; and accordingly they were steeped in peace. Alec stroked his beard, and congratulated himself. Ruth, thankful to have escaped Milly, couldn't do enough for him who had saved her, and, happy to have her husband exclusively to herself, said at frequent intervals that it was like a honeymoon, with which Alec, though his idea of a honeymoon was different, politely agreed.

At first he felt peaceful and pleased, not only because he was clear of Milly but because of the comfort of having a virtuous and devoted wife; but, as early as the second week of peace and comfort, he began to notice a good deal of sameness about Ruth when one was with her without stopping, and by the third week he was wondering, as he stared out the window at the illimitable sea, whether being alone with virtue and devotion couldn't be overdone. That his wife was delighted to be alone with him was evident; and this, to which he was indulgent at first, being rather pleased by it in fact, presently cloyed him. Never since their honeymoon had they gone off by themselves and not a soul to speak to, she reminded him, with a kind of meek exulting which he bore in silence. She asked nothing better, she assured him, than not to have a soul to speak to except him, unless—but this she didn't say aloud—it was that he shouldn't have a soul to speak to except her; and she inquired—foolishly, it seemed to Alec staring out of the window, for she well knew it was impossible, even if they had really wanted to—"Why can't we always live like this—just you and me?" And he, avoiding a direct answer, confined himself to correcting her grammar and telling her she shouldn't say me, but I; which she accepted with meekness, submitting herself in all things to her husband, according to the directions of St. Paul.

Meekness, devotion, virtue, accompanying his every step—what could a man want more? He didn't want more, he wanted less, Alec said to himself, after being shut up with these attributes for a fortnight. And by the end of another week he became aware that he was secretly glutted with Ruth.

Shocked at this, he grew very quiet; and the quieter he grew the more she plied him with devotion, and he was more glutted than ever. In fact, at last he could hardly bear it. Then one evening, when their *tête-à-tête* had gone on for nearly three mortal weeks, and Alec in his dinner jacket, the garment Ruth admired most, and said he looked such a gentleman in—didn't he look like a gentleman in the mornings, then, and wasn't he anyhow a gentleman? he asked himself, glutted—was thinking, as he settled down opposite Ruth in her black beads to his nightly struggle to keep his beard out of the soup, or, alternatively, the soup out of his beard, that there were worse things in the world than the worries he had dodged, and was wishing, though he knew vainly, that

Ruth were somebody else, anybody else, really anybody else at all, if only for a few hours, one hour, half an hour, five minutes—who should walk into the dining-room but Fred.

"Fred! Old *man!*"

In his pleasure, in his relief, Alec didn't at first grasp the significance of such an arrival, but Ruth did; Ruth was good at grasping unpleasant significances, and knew at once that it could bode, as she put it to herself, nothing but evil, and her heart, after a most uncomfortable stoppage, sank like lead. What was he doing there by himself, and why had he left Mabel alone with his disgraceful guest?

Strange as his appearing like that was, and ominous, and agitating, Ruth was yet able to find room in her sinking heart for surprise that Alec should seem so much pleased to see him. After having been out of sorts the last week, with a touch of liver he said, and not wanting to talk, here he was suddenly quite bright and perked up because Fred, of all people, had arrived. Had they not come to Brighton on purpose to get away from Fred, and his distressing plans? You would have supposed, thought Ruth, darkly watching the brothers thumping each other's backs, that they hadn't met for years. And she felt Alec slipping away from her, away from the closeness, the almost sacred intimacy, there had been between them during their blissful little holiday.

She felt it still more, this slipping away, when Fred, apparently in high spirits but with harassed eyes—oh, she noticed them at once—ordered a bottle of champagne, and Alec, who had been having only barley-water lately because Ruth, who lost her meekness when it came to his bodily welfare, wouldn't let him have anything else while his liver was upset, and told him lovingly and earnestly and before the waiter (making him

look like a fool, thought Alec, glutted) that he knew it
was poison for him, when he didn't know anything of the
sort, was obviously delighted. Slipping away from her;
at once; after all they had been and meant to each other
for three blissful weeks. . . .

"I'm with you, old man," cried Alec. "Let's have a
drink. Waiter!"

"But, Alec——" began Ruth, her heart like lead.

"Waiter! Bring the wine list," cried Alec, out of
hand.

Withdrawn into her jet beads, Ruth sat stricken.
Why were men so different, such changed creatures,
when they got together? And why had Fred come?
What could be the object of so sinister an interruption
to her and Alec's quiet happiness?

She soon got an answer to the second question, for,
studying the wine list, the waiter bending over him and
Alec making expert suggestions, Fred said casually, as
though it were the most natural thing in the world,
"Milly's here."

Milly?

Ruth sat back in her chair, stunned. Before the
waiter—on purpose before the waiter, Fred had sprung
it on them, so that they should be gagged, and couldn't
do anything.

Alec, one would have supposed, would be stunned too,
but, strangely, he wasn't. On the contrary, he looked
round quite vivaciously, and said, "Here? Where?" as
though expecting to find the dreadful woman at his
elbow.

Perhaps, however, it was a good thing he could conceal his real feelings so completely, Ruth was able after
tremblingly sipping a little champagne to reflect, for the
waiters were listening, and the people at the next table,
to whom they had lately begun bowing, could hear every

word; perhaps he was only being very wise and diplomatic, hiding the extent of his anger, hiding what he thought of Fred for playing such a disgraceful trick on them, till they should be by themselves. It would be just like him if he were, Ruth said to herself, recovering her trust and pride in Alec. But what of his brother? What was she to think of his brother, foisting Milly on them by a trick? Not as an honourable man, certainly, could she ever, she feared, think of him again; and, about to sip more champagne in search of strength, she remembered it was he who was paying for it, and pushed away her glass.

"She's gone straight up to her room. Number nineteen. On your floor. I asked which floor you were on, and got her put near you," Fred was saying very loud in answer to Alec's question, and everyone could hear him.

Of course. That was his intention, that everyone should hear him, Ruth was sure. She and Alec were being exploited. Her blood boiled.

"She's been ill, you know," Fred went on, turning to Ruth.

She couldn't speak. She couldn't even look at him. How completely she had been mistaken in Fred. And there were the waiters listening, and there were the people at the next table, to whom they had lately begun bowing, able to hear every word.

"Indeed? I'm sorry," said Alec, concealing his real feelings.

"Yes. She's had a breakdown. And old Wilson said Brighton was the place for her to pick up in. So I brought her along. She isn't quite herself yet," he explained to Alec. "Needs a little cosseting still," he explained to Ruth. "But a few days here with you will soon set her up," he explained to them both.

Cosseting? And the waiters listening, and the people at the next table able to hear every word, so that they were committed, positively committed, to—dreadful word—cosseting. That, of course, was Fred's intention. How would she ever be able to think of him as decent again?

But Alec, wiser and more self-controlled than she was, bless him, said, "Of course we'll do what we can——" and Fred, talking very loud and fast, explained that he wasn't staying that night himself, but was going back by the ten-fifteen—"Just time to have a bit of a chat with you both," he said, spuriously cheerful, Ruth was convinced, "and then back to home and bairns."

"Why didn't you bring Mabel along too?" Alec asked; how well he kept it up, Ruth thought, through all her consternation and anger admiring him.

"I did think of it," said Fred, tossing off another glass of champagne, and having tossed it calling to the waiter to take up half a pint of the same brand and a grilled sole to number nineteen—"Must feed her well, you know," he said to Ruth, who gazed at the table-cloth, noting how he slid off the subject of Mabel. "You'll see to that, won't you."

And again he told them that she needed cosseting, and again Ruth doubted whether she would be able in the future to think of Fred as honourable.

Afterwards, seeking out the most private corner of the lounge—"You should have had a sitting-room," Fred said. "We don't throw money away," said Ruth—and drawing his chair as close to them as it would go, before Alec could begin, as Ruth was sure he was about to, to express his indignation and disgust at Fred's behaviour, Fred, in hurried undertones, hurried because he hadn't much time, and undertones because of the people sprinkled near, told them of his discovery

of Milly's innocence, gave them the real explanation of
Ernest's Will, and informed them how, in his opinion,
she had been used more badly than any woman he had
ever heard of.

Alec leaned forward surprised and flushed, his hand
buried in his beard. Ruth listened in silence, her head
bowed, nervously playing with her coffee-spoon. Again,
she thought, this terrible topic. The mere mention of it
made her feel quite ill. Innocent or not innocent, Milly
hadn't *seemed* innocent. St. Paul said, *Avoid the very
appearance of evil*. Milly certainly hadn't done that.
It behoved everybody, especially women, most carefully
to obey this injunction. And what proof had Fred that
what she said was true, and that she had really run away
only to her sister? Besides, that awful sister . . .

Ruth shuddered; and however ready and anxious
she was to see good in everybody, the case against Milly
didn't seem one less whit black than before.

"I tell you," said Fred, "I'm more pleased about this
than I've been about anything for a long while."

"So am I," said Alec, taking a long sip of brandy—
sheer poison, Ruth's eyes told him, but he didn't look at
Ruth's eyes. And he repeated, with increased conviction
as he put down his glass, "So am I."

"I'm sure *you* must be, Ruth," said Fred, determined
to get some sign of gratification out of the silent figure in
the beads. She of all people, being so pious, ought to be
glad there should be one sin less in the world. And he
remembered, much ashamed, the way he had abused
poor little Milly to Ruth that day he went to quell the
rebellion of the servants at Ernest's house. "It just
shows," he went on, "how careful one ought to be before deciding people are guilty."

"And perhaps," said Ruth, "before deciding that they
are innocent."

Fred looked at her. He wondered what Alec made of a wife like that.

"What does Mabel say?" asked Ruth.

Fred was taken aback. Commend him to women, he thought, for putting their finger on one's raw place. Mabel at that moment was his raw place. It had been like ploughing the sands, trying to get her to be reasonable, like beating off flies—such unending, such useless effort. He had had to take her on his knee so often that his very trousers were losing their shape, and it hadn't helped a bit either, because the minute he put her down, thinking he had brought her round to being sensible, she began at exactly the same point where she had been when he took her up, and she had refused to go on looking after Milly, turning her over to the housemaids, and discomfort had settled on his house like a pall, and the butler and the cook had both given notice, scenting, with the infernal flair of servants, that there was a row and that Milly was in it, and at meals it was most awkward, with the boys pretending they didn't notice anything, and, in short, it was because of Mabel and her folly that he was there. The *power* of wives, he had often thought these days, astonished; the wearing-down power of wives. . . .

"Mabel?" he repeated, trying to look at Ruth with the care-free face of the contented husband. "What should she say? She's delighted, of course—I mean, she's been devoting herself to Milly and has tired herself out, so she's gone off for a rest to the old lady."

"Really," said Ruth, manifestly considering this from every angle. And she added, having done considering it, "That'll be very nice for her."

Clear it was to Ruth that Mabel had been having a bad time; but her conjectures as to what she had prob-

ably been going through at once gave place to conjectures as to what she herself was about to go through
—highly unpleasant conjectures, painful ones. For
Mabel and Fred evidently had quarrelled because of
Milly; was it possible that she and Alec, her own Alec,
her husband whom she so much loved and in all things
till now had submitted to, might be brought to such a
state of difference of opinion about her that they quarrelled too? Oh, not quarrel—never quarrel; but be
separated by an inability to agree. Sad days, she
feared, were ahead for her; difficult days. For why,
exactly, had Mabel and Fred quarrelled? Was it because Mabel, like herself, was unable to accept without
proper proofs Fred's story of Milly's blamelessness?
Or was there—she shivered—some other reason?

"Cheer up, Ruth," Fred said, startling her out of
these dark thoughts. He was getting up. He was going.

"It's natural," he said, holding out his hand in fare-
well, "that you should feel down in the mouth, like the
rest of us. One feels a bit ashamed, having judged poor
little Milly as we did. But you'll have lots of opportunities now for making it up to her. Taking it to heart, she
is," he said, turning to Alec and jerking his head towards
Ruth—she was very certain now she could never think
of him as decent, as even possible, again—"but you'll
find it quite easy," he continued to her. "Milly doesn't
bear us any ill will. There's no grudge about her, I'm
thankful to say. Good-bye. Look after her well. Coming
with me to the station, old man?"

Yes—Alec was coming with him to the station, was
coming with alacrity to the station.

"Your overcoat, Alec," Ruth moaned after him.
"Your *overcoat*, dear——"

§

They walked, so as to talk more comfortably. Directly
they got away from Ruth, everything seemed simple
and natural. Fred had noticed that before—how,
directly one got away from women, difficulties disappeared, and it was quite easy to discuss and arrange
calmly. A silent wave of understanding, of sympathy,
washed between them, very soothing, very lulling, and
both felt how real, after all, and in spite of sometimes
being forgotten, was the bond of brotherhood, and
neither mentioned their wives. Alec was sorry, for
more reasons than one, and much ashamed, that he
should have come away to Brighton so as to shirk his
share of Milly, and being an excellent man he not only
rejoiced that the family had after all escaped dishonour,
but was heartily glad he could now once more think of
his sister-in-law as good. Of Ernest's conduct they
didn't speak, the subject being all too painful, but Fred
had a suggestion to make, and Alec at once fell in with
it, that they should ask George and Bertie to join them
in paying back the thousand pounds that fellow Jenkyns
had advanced to Milly. Fred said it was a slur on the
family that Jenkyns should be allowed to help her when
there they all were. The money had already gone,
Alec heard with concern, to her sister, but this didn't
alter the fact that Jenkyns must have advanced it, and
would be out of pocket till the Will had been proved
unless they paid him. Why, asked Fred, should the
fellow be out of pocket on their behalf? Why should
he lend money to their family—which was what it
amounted to? Why indeed, echoed Alec, briskly
stepping out; confounded impertinence, it was. They
would only have to put up two hundred and fifty
pounds apiece, the four of them; George and Bertie

would be certain to agree, said Fred; it wouldn't hurt any of them much; and it would just show Jenkyns.

Alec was entirely with him. After his three weeks of cut-offness, he was ready to coöperate in almost anything. He had a natural reluctance, concealed from Fred, who had it too and in his turn concealed it, to part with two hundred and fifty pounds, and much disliked the idea that it was really Milly's shady sister who was getting it; but greater than this reluctance and this dislike was his objection to that fellow Jenkyns's insolent assumption that if he didn't help Milly nobody would. Fred felt precisely the same; they didn't need words, they were brothers. And Alec went back to Ruth so much cheered by Fred's visit, and his news, and his unspoken understanding, and his not being a wife, that he felt quite reconciled to her company again, and was sorry, now that the time in Brighton alone with her was over, and in another week they would be going home to their customary occupations and salutary separations, that his thoughts hadn't been more kind.

"Are you awake, dear?" he asked, putting on the pyjamas she had hung by the fire to warm.

Yes, Ruth was awake; Ruth was always anything Alec wanted her to be.

"It's good news about poor Milly, isn't it," said Alec.

Yes, it was very good news; wonderful news.

"Been in to kiss her good-night?"

No, Ruth hadn't been in to kiss her good-night, because she thought she might be asleep.

Contentedly, as he got into bed, Alec felt there would be no trouble with Ruth. She would eat out of his hand; always had, and always would. A little stand-offish, perhaps, to old Fred she had been, but that was natural seeing how suddenly the whole thing was sprung on her.

Ruth took time to get going, but once under way there was no one to equal her for obedience and devotion. Didn't he know it? After all, it was a great blessing to have an obedient and devoted wife, and he was sorry he had had bad thoughts about her.

"Good-night, dear," he said kindly, that ungrateful word, glutted, on his conscience.

"Good-night, dear. Have you found the hot-water bottle? I put it your side. I do hope you haven't caught a chill."

§

But no wife who is good can look on placidly at her husband lavishing expensive attentions on another woman. To be able to do that she must be bad, with her own particular and regrettable irons in the fire. Ruth was the best of wives, and therefore when Alec, moved by a creditable desire to make up for the family's unjust judgments of poor Milly, liberally interpreted Fred's injunction to cosset, though she looked on, being obliged to, she didn't do it placidly. If he had cosseted —the word afflicted her—with effort, as a duty which went against the grain yet must be honourably discharged, she wouldn't so much have minded, though still deploring his excess of zeal; but there was no evidence at all that it went against Alec's grain—on the contrary, there was every evidence that he liked it. And indeed Alec, after the extreme boredom and idleness of his time alone with Ruth, would have flung himself on a far less important opportunity for activity.

Nothing was too good for Milly. Inclined to parsimony where his wife was concerned, on behalf of Milly he spent his money—surely Ruth's money too, the marriage service said so—like water. Pints of champagne appeared as the usual accompaniments of both

lunch and dinner, and since Milly didn't drink them—
Ruth would have disliked it excessively if she had, yet
thought it ungrateful of her not to—Alec did, paying
no penalty proper to having taken poison, as she for-
lornly expected, seeming on the contrary in better
spirits after every pint. Special dishes were ordered
daily. Oysters became commonplaces. A private sitting-
room was engaged, and in it the fire, as also in Milly's
bedroom, blazed from before breakfast till bedtime.
And he went out each morning and bought her papers,
and magazines, and even flowers; and he insisted on her
having a bathchair, walking himself beside it as if he
were her husband.

Nothing, in fact, was good enough for Milly. Yet,
thought Ruth, secretly thought Ruth in her outraged
heart, was not everything really too good for her? That
story of Fred's, unauthenticated by any proof—how
could Alec so easily believe it? Mabel was the person
Ruth at that moment most wanted to see; she could tell
her much. The first thing she would do when she got
home would be to go over to Denmark Hill and have a
talk with her, somewhere away from the old lady, whose
ways of approaching serious matters, almost of pooh-
poohing them, was so very trying, as well as being sad.
But it would be a week before she could hope to meet
her—an endless week, she feared it was going to be, and
all she could do, while it dragged along, was to watch
and pray.

But she found they excluded each other—watching
she couldn't pray, nor praying could she properly watch.
So she reserved her prayers for the night hours, concentrating in the daytime on attentiveness, and withdrawing into a silence which at last became so complete that
Alec noticed it, and injudiciously asked her before
Milly—everything now was said and done before Milly,

there was no more privacy, no more intimacy, except at night in their bedroom, and even then there wasn't any, because he was either asleep or not being intimate —what was the matter.

The moment the question was out he recognized its injudiciousness. A man, he had long known, should never ask his wife what the matter is, in case she tells him. But Ruth only said she thought she had a touch of liver—at which Alec began to draw his fingers through his beard, looking at her sideways. However, it was easiest, he decided, to accept this explanation as true, for he wanted no trouble with Ruth, being determined that nothing and nobody should stop him, during the one week at his disposal, from doing all he could for Milly.

He needn't have been so determined. Nobody tried to stop him. Ruth didn't attempt to, and Milly seemed dazed. Between these two almost speechless women he went through the week in an orgy of spending—at last, it seemed to him, all by himself. Since he couldn't do it in words, material luxury was the only way he had of apologizing for the atrocious conclusions his family had jumped to, and of which, thank God, owing to Fred's insisting they should all behave to their unhappy sister-in-law as though nothing had happened, she wasn't aware. Gladly did he lavish; but he did think there might have been some response. Well, not response, perhaps, but some sign that what he was doing was being appreciated. Well, not appreciated, perhaps, but noticed.

Nothing seemed to be noticed by anybody except the waiters, who certainly leaped about him in a furious zeal. Ruth, he soon suspected, was ignoring on purpose, and Milly continued dazed. He kept it up, however, his voice, as he made determined cheerful remarks at meals,

coming back on him like an echo out of emptiness, and
it wasn't till quite the end that he began to flag. Not in
expenditure; that remained at the same dizzy level the
whole time; but in spirits he flagged, a feeling at last
taking hold of him that he was bursting himself to be
the life of a party which was composed of two sponges—
wet ones; filled, really, not with water, but with ink.
On one side of him Milly, who seemed dazed, and though
he was ready with every excuse for her, poor, stricken,
ill-used woman, yet she did make heavy going, and on
the other Ruth, with her silence and her alleged liver—
what could a man do, placed like that, but ultimately
flag?

He deemed it useless to try to cheer up two sponges.
And the unaccustomed champagne he had had at every
meal at last telling on him, his thoughts about Ruth
became bad again. Ruth, he considered acidly, might
have helped him more, and not been such a sulking
dummy. He knew quite well, none better, what an
alleged touch of liver really meant. She had let him
down in a way he hadn't expected of her. If this was
all she could do for him after he had given her what
she herself had called the happiest three weeks of her
life, then he didn't think much of her—frankly he
didn't. Let him, thought Alec, his views distorted by
high living, face facts: Ruth had failed him, and not only
failed him, but neglected a splendid opportunity of
showing what a believing Christian could do. Here was
Milly, positively flung at her by Providence as an occasion for exercising pity and compassion, and what
does she do? he asked himself, tugging his beard. Writes
letters all the time; sits writing letters, as though her
life depended on it, to a pack of children and grandchildren who didn't want them. Nothing but an excuse,
he knew, for not talking to poor Milly. He was ashamed

of her. He had had enough for the rest of his days of Christian women. And on the last night of their stay in Brighton, inflamed by his diet and his grievance, for the first time in his life he quarrelled with her.

§

They were in their room, going to bed; or rather Ruth was going to bed, and Alec was already there. In it he sat up, bony and vengeful, his long beard flowing over the chest she was so much accustomed to, and suddenly began to tell her what he thought of her recent conduct; and she, very pale now that what she had dreaded, yet not believed possible, was upon her, but continuing un-abatedly patient and loving, for the ultimate cause of his outburst, back behind the excess of food and drink, was, she knew, Milly, listened. Milly, said Ruth to herself; Milly alone was the cause that her Alec, after more than forty years of unclouded married harmony, was speaking harshly to her. She called it speaking harshly; as a fact Alec, doing the thing thoroughly, was roaring.

"I was afraid this would happen, dear," she said gently, when, for want of resistance on her part, he at last petered out into a kind of smoking silence; and with the idea of helping him back to his real self, of restoring him to being her own dear, good Alec, she softly assured him that he was out of sorts, and that it wasn't her husband speaking but all that nasty champagne. What she really wanted to say was, "all that dreadful Milly," but champagne was more tactful and would do, for it was the result of Milly—it was Milly, as it were, at one remove.

At this Alec, bursting out afresh, declared he had never been more himself in his life, and what he was telling her had nothing whatever to do with champagne,

but only with her own intolerable behaviour. "I'm perfectly well, thank you, and perfectly in possession of my
faculties," he loudly and angrily informed her from the
bed.

"That's what people always think, dear," Ruth said
soothingly, "when their systems are a little poisoned.
You'll be better in the morning. You must try and get
some sleep."

Sleep? Alec didn't want sleep. What he wanted was
a wife who behaved herself; a decent helpmeet was what
he wanted. Sleep? Was that the way to talk to a man
with a legitimate grievance? As if he were a fool? Or a
child?

Violently he asked her which of these did she take
him for; and pale, but obstinately soothing, Ruth said,
finishing plaiting her meagre hair, "Hush, dear—don't
try to talk. Just get off to sleep, and I'm sure you'll be
quite yourself in the morning."

"If you think you're going to muzzle me——" began
Alec furiously.

"Hush, dear—I want to say my prayers now," interrupted Ruth, kneeling down meekly on her side of the
bed.

"Well, whatever you do don't pray for *me*," cried
Alec.

"Ah, dear," said Ruth, shaking her head, level with
the bed, sadly at him across the counterpane, "you can't
prevent my doing that."

And closing her eyes, and folding her hands, she withdrew out of his reach; for he couldn't pursue with argument a woman praying. And he was left to solitude,
impotently tugging at his beard.

⁑(XV)⁑

It was Nora's—George's wife's—habit, when in more than usually high spirits, to tell such of her sisters-in-law as happened to be present that she had no time for stick-in-the-muds. The implication estranged them. Much about Nora estranged them. She was, they considered, remarkably unlike a lady. She enjoyed, for instance, food and drink, and said she did; her observations on the subject of love-making, when, in spite of watching, it somehow got into the conversation, had to be interrupted at once; and her whole attitude towards the physical and material sides of life was unpleasantly suggestive—they hated saying it—of one who is smacking her lips. Vulgar, undoubtedly, Nora was; very. Some of the ladies of the family went further, and called her gross. And they all invariably spoke of her husband as poor George.

Milly too, in Nora's view, had been a stick-in-the-mud, and, though they had been perfectly friendly, the friendliness Nora felt for her was not much different from that which she felt for a tame mouse or a pet rabbit if and when she came across one. Just about the same, Nora thought; there was just about as much go in Milly as that, just that sort of pleasant, unenterprising softness; and it had been the great thrill of her life to know that she was wrong. What a triumph, thought Nora, dazzled, what an *artistic* triumph, to behave like a mouse, a rabbit, and a stick-in-the-mud, and all the time be leading a secret life of ardours and ecstasies!

Fred's ridiculous story that there was no man in it at
all, and only her sister, Nora impatiently brushed aside.
Too burning was her faith in the existence somewhere,
if one could get away from rabbits and mice, of warmly
throbbing human beings engaged in happy amorous
activities, to believe that such skill in deceiving everybody for years on end should have been practised only
on behalf of a sister. Enthusiastically she was sure it
wasn't with a sister Milly had hidden herself in London,
nor was it because of a sister that Ernest had cut her
out of his Will, nor had a sister got her thousand pounds.
The facts were far too divinely fishy for so silly a theory
to hold water. Sister, indeed! How well she could imagine giving the man one loved all one's money with a
great, splendid gesture, and all one's everything else, if
he wanted it. Stuff to pretend, as Fred pretended, that
no man would take money from a woman. A man would
take anything—at least, she fervently hoped so. She
hadn't proved it herself, not being the sort of woman
men had ever wanted to take things from, but for the
honour of vitality, of full-bloodedness, of all the jolly
things which were the opposite of death, she fervently
hoped so.

In this spirit of tiptoe excitement she prepared for
Milly's visit, which was due the day after Alec tried in
vain to quarrel with Ruth in the Brighton bedroom;
and she welcomed her on her arrival so enthusiastically,
with so much of the clamour, as well as of the gesticu-
lations, of delight, that Ruth, who witnessed the meeting from the window of her car, her painful task having
been to motor down from Victoria alone with Milly, and
hand her over to Nora on her way home, was much
shocked. She could only suppose Nora gave credence to
Fred's story of Milly's innocence, though even before
that absurd story had been put about, she remembered,

she had been ready to gush over her. Why? No doubt because she was coarse-grained, and didn't mind what form excitement took so long as she got it. Shivering, Ruth refused all offers of hospitality and caused herself to be driven away as quickly as possible, shutting her eyes and trying to forget the scene on the door-step—and trying, too, to forget Milly altogether, and Brighton, and the swift descent from peaceful happiness to wrongs and injuries, and Alec not speaking a word to her since the night before, and the hotel bill being simply appalling.

"Well, Milly, you *do* look peaky!" cried Nora, left alone with her guest and twisting her round by the shoulders to the light—wonderful to Nora, thrilling in the highest degree was it, that, known to be inwardly a raging fire, Milly should look so exactly like a rabbit that has been out in the rain. Nora's eyes danced over her. Vitality streamed out of them. "What has Ruth been doing to you?" she asked. "Giving you a rotten time, I bet. I can see she has. Well, what can you expect? I always say that in spite of her children and grandchildren, Ruth's nothing but an old virgin. Let's go upstairs, shall we? Come up and take off your things. Would you like anything before lunch? Milk, or something? It's at one. Sure you can hold out? Oh, I'm so *thrilled* at getting you here! Your trunks came this morning. Fred sent them. You know Mabel's gone to stay with the old lady? Funny of her, isn't it, to go off like that and leave Fred. Here's your room—near mine, you see. If you want anything you've only got to shout. Look—we've put your things through here, in the dressing-room. I'll unpack them for you—yes, I will, I'd love to. And then we can talk. I'm *dying* to talk— have been, ever since everything happened. You *will* talk, won't you—you're not going to stay all corked up?

Oh, but don't you look *ill*, Milly!" she broke off with sudden compunction. "I believe you ought really to go to bed at once, and not bother to come down to lunch. Wouldn't you like to? Oh, do—and I'll ring for a hot-water bottle."

Kindness; warmth; every appearance of affection. The change of temperature was so abrupt that it took Milly's breath away. Only that morning she was still, as it were, being whistled through by an icy north-easter, and now at lunch-time the atmosphere was hot enough for alligators. Here was high summer; here, for the moment at least, was a life-giving, tropical sun.

She blinked a little, blinded. The free and copious chatter, after Ruth's frozen silence, poured over her numbed spirit like warm oil. Wasn't this too good to be true? Could it possibly last? Then into her dulled mind came the recognition that it is the women of a family who make the temperatures, and that in this house she need fear no sudden drops. Slowly she began to relax, to thaw, to give herself up to the atmosphere, to have a feeling as if, after being interminably on her feet, she now for a while might sit down by a fire, and rub her stiffened joints, and rest.

Without more ado Nora undressed her and put her to bed; and when, having fed her, she bent down and gave her a hearty kiss and told her she was to go to sleep till tea-time—sleep off Ruth, Nora said, with one of those loud laughs which made the ladies of the family wince—Milly with a deep sigh of thankfulness for this interval of comfort, this blessed respite before proceeding to what she dimly felt would be the rigours of Edith's hospitality, murmured gratefully, her eyes shut, her body relaxed, snuggling down in the pillows, with Nora's kiss warm on her cheek, "Angel."

"Who—me?" exclaimed Nora, with another of the

laughs. "Ask George. But I tell you what *you* are, Milly—you're the one real live woman I've ever met."

"Who—me?" said Milly in her turn, opening her eyes, and looking up at the face bending over her, in wonder. "Me, Nora?" And she added, with a small, tired gesture of the hand lying on the quilt, raising it a moment and dropping it again, "Why, I'm dead. I think you must know I'm dead."

"That's where you're so wonderful," cried Nora, red with enthusiasm for so admirable a piece of acting. "You manage to look dead, and are really the only woman in the family who isn't. You'll never believe it, but for years I've been putting you down in my mind as a sort of rabbit. Really I have. Doesn't that just show? Fancy *you* a rabbit!"

And on Milly's staring up at her in silence, she went on, "Do you know, I'm simply bursting with admiration for you? Yes, I am—you're so talented, Milly, you've got such complete mastery over yourself. And I dare say you'll laugh, but I'm bursting with respect into the bargain. There," she finished, stooping down quickly and tucking her up, "now you're to go to sleep. I'm off till tea."

And blowing her a kiss, with vigorous movements, Nora hurried out of the room.

§

Milly lay in the bed dumbfounded. Admiration? Respect? What words were these? After the iciness of Ruth at Brighton, after the bewildering last days at Mabel's, when, suddenly handed over to the care of obviously unwilling servants, she had been left to guess at the reason as best she could—and she had guessed it very soon, but it had taken a long while before she could believe it—they sounded strange indeed.

What could Nora mean?

Milly's mind groped about. It hadn't been much use to her lately, her mind hadn't, having fallen, before leaving Mabel's, into a condition of blank bewilderment, but it was beginning to work a little now, warmed by the brightness of her welcome. What could she mean except that, passionately believing her innocent, she passionately admired and respected her for—Milly turned a dull red with shame—her patience in bearing such grievous wrongs?

This must be stopped, she thought, sitting up in the bed. It would be the last straw that she should be looked up to as a saint. That was what Nora would be doing next—reverencing her. She stared at the grotesque picture of herself on a pedestal, being reverenced by Nora. Down what gulfs of hypocrisy was she being forced? It was hardly decent of Fate to be so vindictive. That Nora should love her—and she had every appearance of loving her warmly—was an unexpected development in her wretched situation, and to go on deceiving in her own house someone who loved her as well as believed in her, to accept her admiration and respect and not say a word, would surely be as base as anything she had done. Oh, she didn't want to be base any more —she didn't, didn't want to be base any more, Milly cried to herself, twisting the sheet in her fingers. Yet how stop it, except by telling the truth? Nora would be terribly upset by the truth. For all her way of talking, of saying things the rest of them never dreamed of saying, she hadn't in her life *done* anything that wasn't strictly proper, and at heart was every bit as conventional, Milly was sure, as the others. Besides, the truth couldn't be confined to Nora. It would spread. Nora would have to tell George, and George the others, and the family's peace and honour be after all destroyed.

"No, no," thought Milly, "they couldn't bear it. They mustn't ever know. It's got all, all to wash over me——"

And looking round the gay bedroom without seeing a thing in it, not a single one of those bright-coloured objects in which Nora expressed her flamboyant personality, not even noticing that the sheet she was twisting in her fingers was, like the rest of the bed, orange-colour, she said to herself, "I do think I'm being punished very *much.* . . ."

§

The maid appeared, and asked if she should bring tea, or wait any longer for her mistress's return.

Tea? Milly gazed at her, hardly taking this in. It seemed only ten minutes since Nora had left her. How deeply lost one could become in the agonizing puzzles of which life for her now consisted.

"It's past five, m'm," said the maid, who looked pleasantly at her—not like the maid at Mabel's, who wouldn't look at her at all, nor like the butler at Mabel's, of whom her last glimpse, as Fred took her away, had been a nose held high at an angle of sternest disapproval.

"Mrs. George said she would be back to tea," hesitated Milly.

"Yes, m'm—at half-past four. But it's nearly a quarter past five now. Hadn't I better bring it up?"

Milly was doubtful. Nora had made a point of having tea with her. Where could she be so long?

It was brought up, and when it had stood till it was cold, and there was still no Nora, she got out of bed and began to dress, and by the time she was dressed it was half-past six, and there was still no Nora.

What could have happened? She went downstairs, wondering; and going into the drawing-room found

George there, standing in front of the fire looking worried, and the moment she spoke to him she knew that George, whatever Nora might do, didn't respect her.

His manner was most chilly. He was quite different from what he had been the last time she saw him, that afternoon he had come across her at Victoria, and brought her home. Then he had been agitated, and embarrassed, and human; now he was as heavily cold as lead. And when she said, "Oh, are you home, George?" —somehow expecting he would be like Fred and Alec, and welcome her as Alec had welcomed her at Brighton, naturally expecting it, seeing the extreme warmth of his wife, he said, his face like an empty church, "How do you do. Where's Nora?"

That was all. Just, How do you do, and then at once, Where's Nora? and no attempt to shake hands.

She stood uncertain of everything except that George didn't respect her—did, apparently, the exact opposite, in spite of being Nora's husband. Well, that oughtn't to surprise her, she told herself; look at Fred and Mabel, and look at Alec and Ruth. Still, in this house, full of Nora's personality, she had somehow been sure. . . .

"Yes—where is Nora?" said Milly, confused and timid.

George, however, seemed to disrespect her so much that he couldn't bring himself to say anything more. Looking at his hands, turning them over and examining them on both sides, he appeared to decide that they needed immediate washing, and without more words he walked heavily past her and through the door.

Milly stood looking after him, feeling as she had felt when Jenkyns suddenly turned from ingratiatingness to ice—as if she had been whipped. Could she stay in a house where the host wouldn't speak to her? And what was the matter with George? He was the last person she would have imagined taking a line different from his brothers and his wife. Why had he let her come there, come to stay a whole month, if he was only going to be rude? It was his house. He could have refused to have her. Better, surely, to refuse to have her than to let her come, loathing her so much that he couldn't even speak to her?

She sat down miserably by the fire. Wherever she went, was she to be raked on one side by cutting blasts while on the other she was being basted? And she had been so thankful, so grateful, to have got into what she had thought was going to be a shelter.

She sat, her spirit blown out again, staring into the fire. Where was Nora? Why didn't she come home?

But listen as she might for sounds of arrival there was nothing but silence in the house, and the clock on the mantel-piece ticking away the empty minutes, and outside the window a loose bit of leafless creeper ceaselessly banging against the pane.

§

George stayed up in his dressing-room. It was safer than his study. Milly wouldn't be able to walk in on him there, and nothing would have induced him to come home so early if he had known Nora was going to be out. But he had caught an earlier train on purpose to be alone with her a little, before dinner forced him to meet his guest, for he was worried; much worried; worried out of his life; and wanted the comfort of Nora's irresponsible cheerfulness. He wouldn't tell her, he couldn't tell her, what was worrying him; he simply had a great wish, strange and unusual in him, to feel her propping him up with her jolly optimism.

Just his luck, considered George, that they should find out the true story of the thousand pounds on the

very day he was to start having Milly in his house; and
his opinion of his luck in everything that concerned the
woman became even poorer when he got home to find
himself facing her alone. He needn't have gone into
the drawing-room at all; he could have gone straight
to his study, and sent a servant after Nora. But he was
so much distracted by the need to be with her at once
that he went to where she always was at that hour, and
for the second time, without anybody to help or advise
him, ran into Milly.

He found he couldn't speak to her, in spite of knowing
he ought to. Perhaps he would be able to by and by,
helped by Nora; but for the life of him, he being a plain
man not used to hiding his feelings, he couldn't do it
at that moment. What was he to think of this latest
development in her wretched affairs? Alec and Fred
didn't know what to think either. In Fred's office that
morning—Fred had rung up and asked them to come
round—they had sat nonplussed. Bertie? It wasn't
that he should have advanced the money; that, they
agreed, was a decent, praiseworthy action, which they
regretted not having thought of themselves; but that
he should have done it secretly, have kept quiet about
it that night at George's when they were all so much
surprised, and have told Jenkyns, they were now aware,
not to let any of them know. This was it, this evident
fear of being found out, which worried the brothers.
They didn't say so, but that they were much worried
was implicit in their silence, in their avoidance of each
other's eyes, in the way Alec held on to his beard.

Fred hadn't been able to get into touch with Bertie,
who was in Birmingham on business, so as to ask him
to contribute his share towards the paying off of Jenkyns,
and unwilling to wait longer, and sure he would agree,
as Alec and George had agreed, had that morning rung

up the fellow to say he was sending him a cheque for the amount he had advanced to his sister-in-law, Mrs. Ernest Bott—kindly advanced, Fred amended, cold and polite. And then Jenkyns cold and polite at the other end, who had been in a state of fuming fury with all Botts and their connections and transactions since Bertie's and Milly's and Agatha's visits to his office, said he had not had the privilege of advancing the money himself, and the cheque should be sent—kindly sent, he amended—to Mr. Herbert Bott, who had merely made use of the firm of Jenkyns and Rowe as the instrument of his thoughtful generosity.

Mr. Herbert Bott. That was Bertie. Fred was so much surprised that he lowered the receiver in order to think.

The voice at the other end, however, went on speaking. What was the fellow saying? Fred picked up the receiver again, and attended.

The fellow was saying that he hoped, on second thoughts, he had not been guilty of an indiscretion, for he now remembered what had momentarily escaped him—the particular request of Mr. Herbert Bott that the matter should be kept private. No doubt, however, he could rely on Mr. Frederick Bott—it was Mr. Frederick himself speaking, was it not? Yes, quite—to do so.

"Private from Mrs. Ernest, I suppose?" said Fred into the telephone.

"I gathered," said the smooth professional voice at the other end, "Mr. Herbert was also anxious it should not be mentioned to his brothers. Nor, presumably—" there was a pause, and a clearing of the throat—"to his wife."

Fred had told Alec and George all that Jenkyns had said—no use not to, no use trying to keep it to himself—and they sat silent, worried, not quite knowing what to think. It was plain enough what Jenkyns believed, but then a scoundrel like that would believe anything. Dead against them, he was; dead against the whole of Ernest's family—they saw that the day he read the Will. Still, dead against them or not, in the minds of all three insisted on creeping a paralyzing thought: Jenkyns would have first-hand information from Ernest, and didn't need even to believe, because he knew.

Each in turn carefully stamped out his thought. Nothing at all had happened, they said to themselves, except that Bertie had been secretly generous and they had found it out; and it was mere accident that before Fred's eyes should pass irrelevant visions of himself, ashamed of his foul suspicions, anxiously begging Milly's pardon that day in her room, of himself going round to the others trying to make them be sorry and ashamed too, of being forced into repeated scenes with poor old Mabel, of being at last so angry that he couldn't any longer keep his anger in, and she, scared and weeping, departing to seek sanctuary with his mother. Mere accident, too, that Alec should suddenly remember Brighton, and all he had done there, his efforts to proclaim his belief in Milly's wrongs and innocence in terms of expense, his quarrel with poor old Ruth, to whom he hadn't said a single word since, and the staggering nature of the bill he had had to pay that morning. What had this to do, each asked himself, trying to put these visions and memories aside, with their present discovery? But, chancing to glance at Fred, Alec found Fred was glancing at him, and both their glances were rueful.

Only George was spared irrelevant visions, not having yet begun with Milly. He, however, though he was accordingly unable to look backwards ruefully, could and did look forwards ruefully, and sat outwardly stolid, and inwardly dejected. Milly would be at his house

when he got home; what was he to do about it? No one
had been more glad to hear from Fred than George that
she was after all virtuous, but now he was hanged if he
knew what to think. These things keeping on happening
upset a man. A thousand pounds from Bertie? And not
a word said about it by either of them? George was much
worried. That it should chance to be his turn to have
her for a month just at such an unexpected crisis, appeared to him downright cruel. Fred or Alec would, he
hoped, soon say something suggesting the line for him
to take. He was blest if he knew one himself. He would
far rather, far and away rather, neither see nor speak
to the woman ever again, and here he was going to be
her host that very day. Somebody certainly ought to
give him a lead. He supposed they would all have to go
on behaving as though nothing had happened. He didn't
see what else they could do, now that Bertie was mixed
up in it. Poor old Bertie—she had got round him, thought
George, having successfully stamped out that first
paralyzing thought. He was such a good-natured chap
that he would fall an easy prey, thought George. "Don't
let her try any of her tricks on *me*, though," thought
George, squaring his shoulders.

Then at last Fred did give him a lead. He suddenly
pushed back his chair, got up, looked at his watch, said,
"Well, I'm for lunch," and while he fussed round locking
up things, declared that he thought it jolly decent of
old Bertie to have done what he did, and if he didn't
want it mentioned why should it be? Humour him, they
ought to; back him up in his idea of not wanting his
left hand to know what his right hand was up to—doing,
Fred meant to say. "It has cost him a thousand pounds,
anyway, poor old chap," said Fred, taking down his
hat. "All gone to that sister. And what I say is," he
finished, turning and looking them in the face, his hat

crushed well down over his eyes, and speaking slowly and emphatically, "what I say is that it would be a shame to rub it in. Least said, best for everybody. And for heaven's sake don't tell the women."

With anxious, with almost servile unanimity, Alec and George agreed. And tell the women they didn't; but by that same evening the women were telling them.

§

Nora heard about it at Denmark Hill, at the old lady's, whither she hurried on leaving Milly so as to get exercise, so as to blow off some of the steam she was so uncomfortably full of, and at the same time have another look at Mabel, at whom she had already had several since she so mysteriously left Fred, without yet having made out why she had done it. Her chief reason, however, for choosing this particular walk was because there was a nice long stretch of uphill at the end of it on which she could let herself go; and though it had often struck her as a poor fate for a woman only to be able to let herself go on a hill, on this occasion she blessed the hill, for it was really the cause of her happening to be present at the best family crisis anybody could possibly wish for. She hadn't been in the house ten minutes before it began to develop and to it she remained glued, absorbed, with time become as nothing to her; so that she not only wasn't back to tea, but hardly was she back to dinner.

To begin with things went, as Ruth would have said, their usual gait, the old lady quietly shaking in her chair by the fire, a mauve woollen shawl round her, her small feet on a footstool—"Ah, my dears," she would some-times say, drawing attention to them, "they don't make feet like these nowadays"—just as she had been ever since Nora could remember, placidly glad to hear about Milly, as glad as Mabel obviously wasn't, who sat not saying a word, and looking like a sick monkey, and as if her fur were coming off in patches, thought Nora, eyeing her eagerly and wishing to goodness she would up and tell them what the row with Fred had been about. And Ruth presently came in and joined them—part, too, of the usual gait, for the women of the family were always coming in and joining each other at this hour of the day, especially when they were, as now, in mourning, and unable to join anyone else. And there was no indication that there was going to be a crisis anywhere visible.

Ruth seemed taken aback at seeing Nora—this too was quite usual—who concluded that she seemed so because she was, and cheerily called out from the hearth rug, where she was standing with her legs not at all nicely together, observed Ruth, and also observed the old lady, who, however, condoned what legs did so long as hearts were kind, though of course she would rather they behaved like the legs of ladies, "Hullo, Ruth, here we are again——" just as if, thought Ruth, ignoring her, they were a pair of rough and tumbles in a pantomime.

"I thought," said Ruth, looking away from her to the old lady, "I would like to have a little talk with Mabel, mother."

"Oh, *do*," encouraged Nora, in a most uncalled-for manner, Ruth considered, ignoring her. "By all means, if you can. She hasn't uttered a single word since I've been here, but you may have more luck."

Poor George, thought Ruth, ignoring her; and Nora, her bold bright eyes dancing over Ruth's dim respectability, thought, Poor Alec. For the Bott wives readily pitied each other's husbands.

"Do you mean somewhere by yourselves, my dear?" asked the old lady. "Well, there's a nice fire in the dining-room—would you like to go in there together, and have a cosy chat?"

"*That's* put the wind up Mabel!" cried Nora; and indeed Mabel's expression was that of one averse from chats.

Before Ruth had had time to do more than ignore this remark, the door opened and Edith came in.

"Oh, Lord—I'm off," said Nora when she saw who it was, hastily picking up her gloves from the sofa where she had flung them; and even the old lady found Nora's implications trying.

"Not just yet, my dear," she quavered. "Sit down, won't you? And rest yourself a little. Such a long walk. And wouldn't you like a nice cup of tea before——"

"No, thanks, mother—I must get back to Milly. I promised——"

"Perhaps you'll take your guest a message from me," Edith cut in like an icy knife.

"Yes—do, Edith, my dear," quavered the old lady. "Do send poor Milly a nice message. And come and sit by the fire, won't you? It's quite chilly again to-day, I think, in spite of all the pretty spring flowers everywhere."

"Tell her," said Edith, addressing Nora, "to drop me out of the list."

"What list, my dear?" inquired the old lady.

"I think it's time," said Edith, looking round at them, "that we took the gloves off about Milly."

"What gloves, my dear?" inquired the old lady. "Mabel my dear, will you ring the bell and tell Jenny we would soon all like our tea? There's a fresh cake been made to-day that you girls will enjoy, I'm sure."

"I may stay, I suppose, mother?" said Edith, advancing into the room. "My things are in the hall."

"Stay, my dear? Do you mean for the night?"

"Nights," said Edith shortly; and it was at this point that Nora drew up a chair, sat down, and prepared to enjoy herself.

"Nights, my dear?" repeated the old lady. "Well, of course if you want to. That makes two of my sons' wives here staying nights, what with Mabel as well. Still, you'll be pleasant company for each other. And there's a roast chicken for dinner, and I daresay a nice cauliflower. I fancy I smelt it just now. Mabel my dear, will you tell Jenny?"

Edith walked to the fire, and stood waiting till the elderly servant had been in, received her orders, and gone out again, before saying anything more. Her nose was pinched and sharp, the nostrils drawn flat, and her mouth seemed to have gone into a single thin line. Nora was a little subdued by the unusual look of her, and Ruth, her legs beginning, she was sure prophetically, to give way beneath her, sank on to the end of the sofa, and bowed her head to receive whatever new unpleasantness should be poured over it, while Mabel, huddled by herself in a corner, looked drearily out of the window.

"What I always think," said the old lady, directly the door was shut behind the servant and before Edith could open her mouth, "is that there's a great deal more fuss made over everything than there need be, my dears —a very great deal more."

"You don't think anything matters very much, do you, mother," said Edith, hardly unlocking her mouth to let the words out; upon which Ruth, bowed on the sofa, thought, "I'm glad Edith said that. Very glad——" for it had often seemed to her tragic that anyone so old, so inevitably near eternity, as her mother-in-law, should still apparently not have made up her mind on the great simple questions of right and wrong, good and evil. Indeed, sometimes it actually almost looked as if the head of the family didn't—only of course this couldn't be possible—believe in sin, or, believing, didn't—this of course couldn't be possible either—mind it. Therefore Ruth was glad of Edith's words.

The old lady, however, said nothing in answer to them, and merely sat shaking her head, which with her, naturally, didn't necessarily mean disagreement, and looking all-embracingly benevolent.

"Perhaps, though," Edith went on, "you'll think what I've come to tell you this afternoon is important, mother."

"Yes, my dear, I daresay I shall. Especially if it isn't about somebody's wrongs. We all have our wrongs, and I find the only ones I can enjoy now are my own. Won't you sit down, Edith my dear? It's nicer sitting down, I always think."

There; that was mother all over, thought Ruth with a sad movement of her bowed head. And one couldn't do anything with her because she was so old, as well as so obstinate. But—what was Edith saying?

Ruth became suddenly prickly with attention, though still apparently lost in a detached contemplation of the carpet, and Mabel at the window gave a convulsive start, while Nora's eyes came farther out of her head.

Edith was saying, holding on to the mantelpiece with one hand to steady herself, that she knew who the man was.

"The man, my dear? What man?" asked the old lady. "There are so many men, I find."

"Oh—*mother!* " exclaimed Nora, in an agony of impatience. "Milly's man, of course. Yes, Edith? Yes?" she cried, leaning forward eagerly, trying to drag the words out quicker.

But Edith was having difficulties. She seemed for a moment unable to go on.

"Milly's man?" repeated the old lady. "Has poor Milly got a man after all? I thought you all decided she hadn't. Dear, dear—poor little Milly. They're such a worry. But I daresay he won't last."

"Mother——" began Ruth, raising a shocked head. But what was the use? She bowed it again. Everything slid off the old lady like water.

"I didn't mean to tell you—not to-day," said Edith, the words seeming to force themselves out. "I only came to say I'll have nothing to do with Milly. I won't, I can't. But you'll know soon enough—oh, you'll all know anyhow, and the whole place will know, and all the children and servants——"

Rage and shame choked her.

"Dear, dear," said the old lady. "Dear, dear, dear. We'll have to be extra kind to poor Milly, then. Nothing but trouble, one has with men. Still, they pass."

This on the brink of eternity. Ruth could only shiver.

"I hope you'll find it easy to be kind to her, mother," said Edith, "considering he's one of your own sons."

"Oh, my goodness! Oh, my goodness!" burst out Nora, starting up. Remembering herself, she put her hand to her mouth. "I mean, how too awful," she finished, sitting down again quickly. Then, struck by a tremendous, a breath-robbing possibility, she leaned forward and said awestruck, "It's not George?"

"George!" Edith glanced at her contemptuously. George? That slug?

"*In all time of our tribulation*"—Ruth began murmuring, taking hasty cover in prayer, fleeing away from this room, away from the dreadful words being said in it, and those still more dreadful ones that were coming next. Which son? Which? Not George—then which? Was it possible—no, it wasn't possible—*In all time of our*—still, the champagne, the fuss, the wild extravagance, the things he said to her in the bedroom because she too hadn't made a fuss, because she had remained dignified and aloof—"*Good Lord deliver us, deliver us, deliver us,*" murmured Ruth feverishly, over and over, so as not to hear, so as not to remember and think, so as to fend off. . . .

Mabel, in the window, had begun to cry.

"It's Fred," flashed into Nora's mind. "Of course. That row they've had. Oh, my goodness—and I who've been thinking the lot of them stick-in-the-muds!"

"Don't cry, Mabel my dear," soothed the old lady. "Mabel's a good girl, and very kind—there's nothing for her to cry about, is there, Edith my dear?"

"Mabel!" said Edith, in scornful wonder. "I should think not. You don't imagine it's *Fred?*"

And there followed that which had never yet happened in the whole annals of the family—the open denouncing of a Bott husband by his wife.

The words, once loosened, flowed in torrents. The room seemed instantly to become awash with them, and the listeners to bob up and down helplessly. All Edith's bitter wrongs swirled round them, and they were so much tossed about that they weren't able to see looming ahead the rock the family was being driven towards. Even old Mrs. Bott didn't see it, and sitting shaking in her corner only thought pityingly of these poor distracted children, and of how sad it was for women that their wrongs should have the effect of setting one against them. The more wrongs they had the less, somehow, one liked them. Look at poor Edith now, for instance—full of wrongs, and only put at a disadvantage by them. She didn't remember ever having seen poor Edith to less advantage. And it really was hard, because it was bad enough having wrongs, without becoming less likeable than usual at the same moment.

Edith did seem to the old lady ever so much less likeable than usual. Was it her way of saying things? Was it the way she put her story? Or was it the story itself? The old lady, shaking her head, and nobody could know if it was in disapproval or sympathy, listened attentively to poor Edith's story—how she went up to town that morning, and before coming home thought she would look in at Bertie's office—

"Why, my dear? Bertie is still away, isn't he?"

That was just why, said Edith—because she knew he wasn't there, and she had been uneasy about him for some time—oh, she had had good reason, she could assure them—and wanted to have a look round and see what she could see——

(Well, well, poor children; they got suspicious of their husbands occasionally, and so, the old lady supposed, they couldn't help trying to find out things. But finding out things never made anybody happy yet.)

—and there, on the table, was a letter sent by hand, and marked private, so of course she opened it, and it was from that solicitor of Ernest's——

(Not a very nice man, the old lady was afraid.)

—apologizing for having forgotten till too late Bertie's having asked him to keep it from the family that he had given Milly a thousand pounds—"Why, only the other day," cried Edith, white with her wrongs, "he told me he couldn't afford something I, his wife, particularly wanted!"—but assuring him there would be no unpleasant consequences, as he had carefully impressed on Fred that it was to go no further, and especially that it was on no account—Edith choked—to reach the ears of his wife. So of course she went round at once to the solicitor himself, and questioned him, and though he had been guarded and reserved, he had said quite enough to convince her that it was because of Bertie Milly had been disinherited by Ernest.

That, as far as the old lady could make out through the torrent of words, was Edith's story, interrupted once by the arrival and arranging of tea, which nobody touched except herself—such a pity, and that beautiful fresh cake, too—and resumed and continued with ever-increasing volume—poor Edith, making her seem so unattractive—for a very long time afterwards. But once a poor girl gets really started on her wrongs, who shall stop her? thought the old lady. There isn't much reason in a poor girl with wrongs—not much reason, and not much idea of consequences. All very well being angry, but after all one's husband existed, and one had got to live with him, and it didn't make it any easier being angry. Well, well—poor children. Edith would have finished some time, was bound to be quiet presently. What a good thing it was that everyone was bound to leave off talking sooner or later. And it just showed how one oughtn't to open somebody else's letters. The whole trouble came from that—opening poor Bertie's letter. Once, she remembered, her attention straying a moment, and wandering off down the years, she had done that herself to one of poor Alexander's; not opened it, because it was open already, but she had read it as it lay overlooked on his desk, and it hadn't been meant for her to see, of course, and it had made a good deal of trouble between them at the time, because in those days she didn't yet know how all such things pass.

"Such a pity you opened the letter, my dear," she remarked, when at last Edith's story reached the state of quivering off into a panting pause. And when they all looked at her open-mouthed, even Edith dumb be-

fore this failure to grasp essentials, this failure once more
—or was it unwillingness? lamented Ruth—to distinguish, she went on, "And perhaps, my dear, it isn't
nearly as bad as you think."

"What? Not so bad that he has committed——"

"Oh, hush—oh, hush!" gasped Ruth in agony.

"And it was only very nice and kind of Bertie to
help poor Milly," continued the old lady, determined to
have her say.

"What? Nice and kind to give our money, mine and
the children's, to his——"

"Oh, hush—oh, hush!" gasped Ruth, wringing her
hands.

"And anyhow, Edith my dear, it will soon pass."

Then Edith was beside herself. "Soon pass?" she
cried, loosened once more into fury. "Soon pass, mother?
Yes—it soon will. I'll see it does that. I'm going to
divorce him."

§

Divorce.

The word fell on them like a stone. Even Nora was
stunned by it. This, she thought, was going too far.
Having fun, having secrets, blowing off one's steam,
wasn't after all very thrilling if it ended in atrocious
scandal. Besides—a brother-in-law. Better be good,
thought Nora, much subdued; far better, really, just
be good, and put up with being bottled up and bored.
Divorce? No one in Titford, she said to herself, ever was
divorced. It simply was unheard of. One wouldn't get a
servant to stay with one. And fancy the leading family,
the very top of the Titford tree, being the one to start
it, and getting cut in the streets!

"But, Edith——" gasped Ruth. This was too much,
too awful. They would all be in the papers. Edith must

be stopped. It meant black ruin for everybody. Didn't
she see?

"Why, my dear—why, my dear," quavered the old
lady, "what grounds have you? Why, you have no
grounds at all."

But Edith, deaf to reason, indifferent to consequences,
out only to smash—smash everybody, herself too, if at
the same time she could smash Bertie, assured the
stricken assembly that she would soon find all the
grounds she wanted; and the old lady trembled into
silence, for she remembered how much struck she had
been on the afternoon of Ernest's funeral by the skilful
noiselessness of the way Bertie had opened and shut
the bedroom door. It had occurred to her then that he
must be practised in such entries and exits. Indeed she
feared Edith might find grounds if she set to work, and
perhaps more than, and different from, what she had
bargained for.

Ah, let be, leave it alone, she almost begged—and
would have begged if poor Edith had been in a condition to listen. What would the unhappy child get out
of it but misery? Such a mistake, such a mistake,
thought the old lady, to start digging about in what
one's husband did in his private moments, behaving as
if they were the most important things in life, those
stray and fleeting moments of foolishness. It seemed as
if these poor children had no sense whatever of proportion. They wasted their short time in making much of
what was little, and little of what was much. Well, they
must settle their own affairs.

And looking at Edith, distorted by her emotions,
convulsed, blinded, she found she couldn't wonder much
at poor Bertie. Only—was one woman better than another, in the long run, to get mixed up with? Didn't
they all, however different they seemed at the begin-

ning, during the course of the affair become alike, and
end by going equally curdled? Well, there was nothing
to be done.

"You don't think Milly will have waited for her tea,
and be waiting now for her dinner, do you, Nora, my
dear?" she asked with a sigh, for she was tired, and the
clock on the mantelpiece said half-past seven.

. An astounded silence fell on the room. Milly's tea;
Milly's dinner. Was it possible to think of such things,
after hearing what Edith had been telling her?

"George will be getting hungry," continued the old
lady. "And there's Alec, too—won't he be wondering
where you are, Ruth, my dear?"

That was it: second childhood; complete inability to
grasp. They oughtn't really to mind anything she said.
Entirely negligible she was, really. George getting
hungry and Alec wondering, when life, as they had
known it, threatened to be shivered to atoms at their
feet!

The old lady held up her withered little cheek to be
kissed. "Good-night, my dears," she said, waiting. "I'm
tired." And negligible or not, in her second childhood
or not, Ruth and Nora found themselves taking their
dismissal, and getting up and crossing to her chair and
kissing her.

"You too, Mabel my dear," she said, when they had
done, still holding up her cheek. "You'll be wanting to
go home now, won't you, to Fred?"

"If you don't mind, mother," said Mabel, shame-
facedly coming out of her corner, her one longing being
to fling herself into Fred's arms and beg him to forgive
her. Awful, of course, about Bertie, but how thankful,
how thankful . . .

"Mind, my dear? I like it. I always think it's nice
when people go home. Edith won't, of course, because

she's angry, poor child, so she and I will have a quiet little dinner by ourselves. There's a rhubarb tart for dinner, Edith my dear. You'll enjoy that. So nice, I always think, the first young rhubarb."

The door was shut behind the departing two before Edith recovered her speech. Then, she said, very bitterly, "Rhubarb!"

"Yes. And cream," nodded the old lady.

There was a silence. Then Edith, looking down at the figure in the chair, said with icy scorn, "You haven't much sense of proportion, have you, mother?"

And the old lady said, "Well, my dear, perhaps I haven't." And asked, after a moment, "Have you?"

⁜(XVI)⁜

No BOTT went to bed that night till the small hours, nor did anyone who was married to a Bott. Disaster, staved off so carefully, lately indeed regarded as out of the question, was at last full upon the unhappy family; and much worse disaster, of course, than that which they had been staving off.

Laden with their dreadful news, Ruth and Mabel and Nora hurried home, and in each of those three homes, where there had been merely a worried man before, there was now an overwhelmed one. Bertie? Their own brother? The whole thing going to be dragged into the courts by Edith? In that case the family was ruined. Socially, if this happened, it would certainly be ruined. In Titford it could never hold up its head again, and there would be nothing for it but wholesale migration, and scattering.

Unless Edith could be stopped, that is—but who can stop a wronged woman, maddened not only by the discovery that somebody else has got her husband, but has also got a substantial slice of his money? The wrongs of such a wife go up with a shout to heaven, and she doesn't care a straw who hears them; as if the life of a whole family, its diligently built-up position, its reputation and honour and all its happiness, were as nothing compared to the avenging of what one member of it had done in his odd moments.

The brothers were overwhelmed; and Ruth was so deeply horrified by the idea of a divorce in the family, with all its accompaniments of scandal and publicity, that she didn't even wish to remind Alec how sure her instinct had been about Milly, while Mabel was much too thankful it wasn't Fred to think of anything but craving his forgiveness.

Mad of Edith, of course, Fred at first blustered to the abjectly agreeing Mabel, trying to reassure himself, to suppose she could do anything with that letter of Jenkyns's; the only proof to be got out of it was that Bertie had been kind. But the letter, he knew beneath his bluster, was fatal, because it set Edith off on a track at the end of which, he now was quite sure, would be Milly. Jenkyns knew. Ernest, obviously, had told Jenkyns all about it. The whole of Jenkyns's behaviour had been that of one who knows. And Fred was so much submerged in consternation that he hadn't even the breath to say what he thought of that tight-jawed scoundrel.

In each of these three homes that night was consternation; and by the time the small hours had been reached, five more homes had become filled with it—the ones, that is, inhabited by those who had married Botts. For presently, coming a little to the surface of the tumultuous waters, Fred began telephoning, and his voice was so anxious, as he asked the still unconscious members of the family if they wouldn't come round and have a talk, that in spite of its being very late for Titford, and most of them beginning to think of bed, they did go, the brothers-in-law dutifully accompanying their wives. Milly, of course; Milly again. They were only too sadly sure that this invitation of Fred's meant more Milly.

The one thing to be done, they agreed with him when they had got over their first incredulity, was to go and see Edith as soon as possible—proceed *en masse* to Denmark Hill, and by the pressure of their united weight

try, at least, to stop her further explorations. She must
be brought to reason. She must be made to see the
frightful, the fatal results for the family if, having got
her proofs, she persisted in divorcing Bertie. How easy,
how almost pleasant, they now realized, had their deal-
ings with Milly been, compared to what it was going
to be like trying to restrain Edith. These virtuous
women, the brothers-in-law silently felt, were the very
devil once they got on the warpath.

It was too late to do anything that night, but they
arranged to meet at the old lady's house next morning
directly after breakfast, and there talk the whole thing
over with Edith as calmly as possible—point out, im-
press, enlarge. By that time she would have had leisure
to think, and might be more open to argument than,
they understood, she had been in the afternoon. They
ought all to go, the husbands said—their wives as well,
because not only was it now impossible, they realized,
not to acknowledge the flair, insight, intuition, or whatever the unpleasant thing women had was called which
enabled them to be right when decency and charity
would prefer that they should be wrong, but the wives,
every one of them, would be dead against any divorcing,
and their pressure should also be brought to bear on
Edith.

Then there was the pressure of her grown-up children.
She must have forgotten them. She couldn't possibly
have thought of them. For surely no woman could be
so blinded by fury and the desire for revenge that she
didn't care what her children would suffer by her satisfying it? They would remind her of her children; they
would talk much to her of them; they would do everything in their power to get at her softer side. But had
Edith a softer side? Doubt lay leaden on the husbands'
minds. If it had been Milly now . . . Milly, they were

each privately sure, was made up entirely of softer sides
—things you could appeal to, things you could get
round, things, in short, no woman should be without.

In the small hours each went home to bed, but not
to sleep; and through Fred's mind, as he got into his
comforted, to some slight extent, by the fact that
Mabel, restored to him and penitent, was in it too—except that she kept on being penitent, just as she had
kept on being foolish, and he had to spend a good deal
of the time needed for collecting his wits in keeping on
forgiving her—passed Milly's image, with, beside it,
Edith's as Mabel had described her that afternoon.

He stared at the two in the darkness, comparing
them; and he wondered for a moment, being worn out
with worry and fear, and accordingly not quite himself,
whether perhaps sinning made a woman soft and kind,
educated her, helped her to wisdom and understanding,
—the sort of sinning, he meant, in which, in some form
or another, as there must have been in Milly's and
Bertie's, there was love.

But when he realized what he was thinking he was
much shocked, and dismissed it sternly from his mind.
Was he, in his anxiety, losing his sense of moral values?

"Yes, yes, old girl—that's all right. Of course I
know you didn't mean it. . . ."

§

In those same small hours Nora, walking home with
George and holding him affectionately and encourag-
ingly by the arm, gave it a little squeeze every now
and then, and said, "You've always got your Nora,
Porge——" to which he made no reply.

He made no replies to anything she said; not even
when, having got home and both gone upstairs, she informed him, just to test him, for his silence was rather

frightening, that she was going into Milly's room to wish her good-night. Good-night at three in the morning? And to the person who ought, in George's view, never to be wished anything good again? Nora did think this would bring him back to life. But it didn't. He remained dumb. And she began to be afraid that what had happened had broken poor Porge's spring—such spring as he had ever had.

This sobered her still further. The consequences of vivid and daring living, what with George gone speechless and Milly found out, seemed pretty poor fun. She supposed the great thing, in the interests of everybody, not only of oneself, was never to be found out; and Milly, in spite of her startling cleverness and amazing histrionic talent, hadn't been able to avoid that.

Poor old Milly. Nora wanted badly to go in and kiss her—just give her one little kiss before the next day should be upon her, and all its trials and distresses.

She stood hesitating in the passage, sorely tempted. It wouldn't do anybody any harm, she thought, and there would be one more kiss in the world. If the world were fuller of kisses there'd be less room in it for such a lot of quarrels, thought Nora, hesitating in the passage. Edith, for instance, would probably be quite quiet and contented if some vigorous philanthropist, intent only on helping, started really kissing her. Let one kiss while one could, thought Nora, not at all sure how long she was going to have Milly in her house. They had been saying things to George about it at Fred's, and though George hadn't answered, because of his spring having broken, she was afraid he might get mended enough in a day or two to start turning Milly out—or else the others would come and do it for him.

Besides, she had rushed away and left her without a word directly after dinner, being obliged at once to take

George into his study and tell him about Edith, and
dinner had been awful, having to sit down to it the
minute she got home, with George looking as though he
had swallowed a broomstick, she supposed because she
had kept him waiting, and little knowing what tremendous reason he really had to look like that, and
Milly being the most marvellous impersonator of still
life—a perfect masterpiece, positively behaving as if she
were nothing more alive than a bunch of grapes and an
apple on a plate, instead of being a force so violent that
she was blowing the family to atoms, and she herself,
agonizingly bottled up and bursting, trying to hide from
them both, by chatting as usual, that the heavens were
falling about their ears, and then, when Fred telephoned, leaving the house with George at once, quite
forgetting in the excitement to go and say good-night or
anything to Milly, who had been left alone in the drawing-room—just disappearing.

So that, apart from everything else and whatever the
time was, oughtn't she, as a duty, to go in now and give
her a kiss?

She was sorely tempted, but she resisted. Better resist, thought Nora. Better go to bed, and let poor Milly
sleep. If she went in, she might be led to blurt out something best not blurted, and the poor soul ought at least
to be allowed to sleep on this night before catastrophe
was upon her.

So she went into her room, softly shutting the door,
and undressed and lay down by the side of the inani-
mate George, where she tossed for the rest of the night,
with him taking no more notice than if he had been a
corpse.

§

In those same small hours Milly, sometimes in bed,
sometimes walking about the room, sometimes sitting

by the remains of the fire, was telling herself that she couldn't stay in that house, that it was the worst of any, and that George was the last straw.

She was nearer indignation than she had yet been in her life. Really there were things a woman oughtn't to be required to bear, whatever she had done, she thought. George's hostility was far more difficult to endure than Mabel's or Ruth's had been, because it was so entirely unlike him. Flat, downright, shrivelling contempt in one who had always been the least important of the family, the slow good-natured one, the one who didn't matter, who was to be relied on to follow suit and do what his brothers did—why, it was as unexpected and as humiliating as if a dog should suddenly begin openly and utterly to despise one. And he was her host. Much worse, she now knew, when a host was hostile than when a hostess was. He paid. It was his food, his house, his everything. George's food choked her. His very fires—this one, this one in the bedroom—she hadn't even been able to bring herself to poke, though she was growing colder and colder.

Ridiculous position. And so sinister, because one couldn't in the least understand it. While as for Nora—what was she to think of Nora? Her behaviour was even more incomprehensible, the way she had gone off promising to be back to tea, and then staying away till dinner, and going out again without a word of explanation, not only for the evening but for nearly all the night. Soon it would be quite all the night. What did it mean? What was she to think of the gulf of difference between the Nora who left after lunch, and the Nora who came back, flustered and unnatural, to dinner? And where had she gone afterwards with George, where was she during these endless hours, each added one of which made her absence more mysterious? Nora, so frank and open, beginning to hide, to disappear—who could stay in a house where the hostess took to disappearing?

Oh, impossible, impossible, thought Milly, to endure these visits. Each seemed worse than the last. They were torments to everybody. There was only one house where . . .

Suddenly she was quiet. She was in bed at that moment, got back into it again driven by the cold, and she lay motionless, her hands, which had been nervously pulling at the frills of the sheet, quite still, wondering why no one had thought of it before. The house on Denmark Hill. The one place in the family where she might yet find comfort. Mother's house—mother's, who didn't seem to mind things as other people minded them, who had always been uncritical, incurious, kind.

But—would mother be kind now?

Milly didn't know. She began turning her head from side to side on the pillow and pulling at the frills again, because she didn't know, and it was so important.

Perhaps, she said to herself, her restless fingers twisting and pulling, when one was so old, so old, it was more difficult not to be kind. She had finished, mother had, with the heat and burden of life. She had withdrawn from the clamour, she could take a bird's-eye view of the fighting going on down where people still tormented each other, and be pitiful, and be patient. If mother were able to be kind to her now, or even if she simply took her in without being either kind or unkind, what a refuge it would be, her house! In that one house she would be safe from crushing aversions and reluctances and equally crushing efforts to make much of her. There she would stay quietly, if mother would let her—oh, but wouldn't she let her? Wouldn't she? If she knew it was her last hope?—till the family decided the time had come when she might go away for ever.

Each minute she saw clearer: each minute what she saw seemed more desirable. Really astonishing that nobody had thought of it. With mother she would be out of everybody's way, yet still visible to Titford, and able to be produced at a moment's notice if necessary. George would be relieved of her, Nora wouldn't have to disappear, the looming visit to Edith, which made her go cold to think of, would be avoided. How could anyone possibly object? The most it would do would be to upset the family's plans—and not even upset, merely defer; for always later on, when the Botts were more unanimous as to what they really wished, she could resume the rounds. . . .

She threw back the bedclothes, and got up again. Now she was in a tumult of impatience for the morning, for the moment when she would see Nora, and explain and insist that it was the only thing to be done.

As she got out of bed a distant church clock struck three. That was St. Timothy's; and there, a second after it, so solemn, so slow, booming across the sleeping fields, was St. Jude's at West Titford. She knew them both. She had heard them for years. All the hours of all her grown-up life they had solemnly, the pair of them, tolled off one by one.

She pulled on a dressing-gown, and went to the window. Starlight and quiet. The night seemed deep in thought. Where was Nora, in this huge silence?

She turned her head, listening. At last there were sounds in the dead house—the front door being opened, and then carefully shut; footsteps on the stairs; cautious footsteps in the passage, hesitating, stopping. . . .

She padded across the room on her bare feet, and

stood with her ear to the crack of the door. Was someone standing just outside it? Didn't she hear heart-beats? Or were they only her own?

"Is that you, Nora?" she whispered; and after a pause, anxiously, "Nora—is that you?"

No answer. Nobody was there. A distant door shut softly.

§

And the same thing happened next morning—no answers; nobody there; Nora not coming near her.

When, having waited with what patience she could for George to have had time to eat his breakfast and be seen off by Nora to the City, she still didn't come up, Milly, trying to be reasonable and allow wide margins, told herself that now she was probably with the cook, ordering the day's meals, and would be with her in a few minutes. But she wasn't. Minutes passed, and still Nora wasn't with her. They stretched into half an hour, into an hour, and still she wasn't—the reason being that she and George were in one of a procession of cars, all full of heavy-eyed Botts, proceeding in the direction of Denmark Hill.

For Fred, afraid of Nora's careless and indiscreet tongue, had telephoned before she had finished feeding the passive George, telling her to hurry up and bring him along, that he himself and Mabel were just starting, and nobody must on any account be late and give Edith time to do something irreparable.

"You'd better not go near that guest of yours," he said, "till we've met and decided what we intend doing. It's important we should act absolutely together."

"She won't be awake yet," Nora answered, thankful now that she had resisted the temptation in the early hours to go in and kiss her; and Fred at the other end of the telephone, for the first and only time in his life lashed by his bitter cares into epigram, said, "Let lying Millies sleep——" immediately hanging up the receiver, and leaving Nora open-mouthed.

So that by the time Milly's patience came to an end and she started out of her bedroom in search of Nora, both she and George were well on their way to Denmark Hill.

§

She went along the passage, and leaned over the banisters and called.

As in the night, no answer. The house seemed deserted; empty of everything, except sunshine and the April wind. Windows and doors stood wide open. Nora's bed was airing, the mattress turned back. George's Jaeger pyjamas hung over a chair in his dressing-room, their limp legs flapping in the draught. Everywhere a smell of soap and toothpowders struggled with the smell of the wallflowers blowing in through the open front door. The only sound, apart from garden sounds, was a noise of plates and knives from somewhere where the servants were having breakfast.

She went downstairs, looking into all the rooms, even, cautiously, into George's bleak study.

Nobody.

She went back to the drawing-room, and rang the bell.

The maid said her mistress had gone out. No, she had left no message. And this was so queer of Nora, such a culmination of queerness, that Milly had all the sensations of a worm turning, and made up her mind then and there to go at once—not wait to explain and suggest and if needs be insist, as she had meant to, but just go.

She had had enough. Not an hour longer would she
stay in George's house. Straight would she go to Denmark Hill, leaving her trunks to be fetched when she
knew whether the old lady would take her in. And, if
she refused to, she felt she would do almost anything—
sleep on mother's doorstep, sit up all night on a seat in
the playing-grounds, or on a straw-bottomed chair in
St. Timothy's, rather than come back to George and
Nora. Who could have believed Nora would behave
like this? Who could have imagined her capable of such
swift changes, of such unfairness, and unkindness?

Her eyes full of indignant tears, she went upstairs
and once more packed the little bag she had had with
her at Brighton; and arriving by means of two omni-
buses and a tram at Denmark Hill soon after eleven, she
went straight to the old lady's bedroom, where she knew
she would find her still in bed, went straight to it unhindered by Jenny, who was too much startled on seeing
her to utter a word, and opening the door, after knocking and hearing the old voice quaver "Come in," found
herself staring into the faces of the assembled family.

§

The room was black with Botts. In astonishment she
gazed at them. Crowded into the not very big space
were sixteen of them—seventeen with the old lady,
whose voice she had heard, but who was invisible in the
bed behind the clustering figures; and every face was
turned to her as she stood motionless on the threshold.

What were they all doing there? And so quiet, as she
came up the stairs, that she hadn't heard a sound.
Nora—that's where she was, then. George too—not
gone to his office. And Alec, and Mabel, and—but
everyone of the generation she belonged to except—
no, she couldn't see Bertie.

She gazed round in such surprise that for a moment she forgot she was the family outcast.

Haggard, from the depths of the exhausted silence that had fallen on them, they gazed back at her.

Milly.

After their prolonged struggle with Edith, trying to bring her to what they called reason and she called their cowardly desire to save the family at the price of her humiliation, after the exasperations of the last hour, the anxiety, the efforts to propitiate, the constant being driven back by her flinty determination to be avenged, it was, the husbands felt, curiously refreshing to see Milly. So easy to manage, so pliable and ready to be convinced. Every one of the baffled brothers-in-law felt this secret, and they feared reprehensible, relief when they turned from Edith's destructive virtue, and beheld the soft sinner in the doorway.

Milly; the cause of all their troubles. Yet at that moment they had it in their hearts to forgive her, simply because, the exhausted Botts felt, she was the opposite of Edith. Wrong, wrong, all wrong, they knew, some of them, wiping their foreheads, said to themselves; but it was Edith's personality driving them. Virtue shouldn't be so violent. It shouldn't scold. It shouldn't force one to dislike it. Above all, it shouldn't ruin a whole family. And even into the women's hearts, friable now from fear, even into Maud's, even into Ruth's, trickled the confusing feeling that if Edith had been a little more like Milly everything might have been avoided.

There she stood, blankly staring. They, in silence, stared at her. And the invisible old lady in the bed, who for once had been finding her knowledge that these troubles would soon be over, soon be fallen into dust and forgetfulness, not enough to keep her calm, unable to see who it was that had come in because of the crowd around her, immediately felt a different quality in the silence, and asked, a little petulantly because of being so much hemmed in, "Who is there?"

No one answered her. The eyes of the absorbed assembly were watching Milly as her glance, after travelling round the room, reached Edith and stayed fixed.

Now was the moment when they expected her guiltily to shrink back and disappear again; but she didn't. Her face, on which had been nothing but wonder, when she saw Edith took on an expression of surprised concern. That was all—just surprised concern.

Edith was standing at the foot of the bed, in the middle of everybody, but not much crowded upon, and she looked so extraordinarily unhappy, so desperately tormented, that anybody who hadn't been alienated, as they had all been alienated for the last hour, by her vindictive unreason, would have shown concern—anybody, that is, one might have thought, except Milly. Milly oughtn't to. Her showing it, felt the Botts, was hardly in the best of taste.

But they were not given time to consider questions of taste. Edith, her blazing eyes on Milly, was saying so evenly, so quietly, that it seemed impossible she should be using the words, "I wonder you dare show your face here——" and there wasn't a man in the room who didn't wish on this, wish with all his heart, that he were somewhere else. Two women, one injured and the other injuring, meeting and going to have it out—what man wouldn't, if he could, from such an occasion slink away?

"It's Bertie," thought the old lady when she heard Edith's remark—poor Bertie, being spoken to like that by his wife. "Come in, Bertie my dear, and shut the door," she called out, unheeded. "No use making draughts."

"But I'll do you this justice," went on Edith. "You didn't bargain to run into *me*. Even you aren't as shameless as that."

Dear, dear—talking like that to her husband. Annoyed, of course, at seeing him, when she had been making up her poor mind never to see him again except in the divorce court, as she had kept on telling them all —such an unpleasant place to see one's husband again in, the old lady tried to point out, but no one had listened. Still, annoyed or not, it was a pity to talk in such a way to poor Bertie.

"Bertie my dear," she quavered from the invisible bed, "don't mind her. Mother's here."

Milly, her eyes on Edith, groped for comprehension. What was the matter with Edith? What had happened to make her look so ill, and let loose such—wasn't it hate?

"I—don't understand," she faltered.

"Why, it's Milly!" shrilled the voice from the bed. "Well now isn't that a pleas—— a surprise. Come in, my dear, and shut the door. Some of you get upset by husbands, but what upsets me is draughts."

"If she comes in," said Edith, "I go out."

"She's feeling a little sore about Bertie, my dear," explained the old lady, in so loud and hurried a quaver that they were bound to attend. "It'll pass, though. If you dear children could make a little room now, so that I can see poor Milly—yes, that's better. Thank you, my dears."

"About Bertie?" repeated Milly, her eyes and lips showing such complete surprise that into the dark hearts of the Botts straggled the faintest ray of hope. "Why? What has happened?"

"Oh" said Edith, at that, through her closed teeth. "Oh, you accomplished liar."

The room winced.

"Now, now, Edith," expostulated Fred.

"No use calling names, Edith my dear," expostulated the old lady, visible at last between the pressed-back figures, and apparently as complete in her cap and shawl and ribbons as if she were dressed all over, instead of only down to where the counterpane began. "I should have thought anybody could see poor Milly doesn't know what you are talking about."

"Oh," said Edith, looking at her scornfully, "you poor, deluded old woman."

The room started. Talking to mother like that? Calling her an old woman?

A storm of protest rose from every corner. The sons made angry movements towards the defiant figure.

"Look here, Edith—you keep a civil tongue in your head to mother," said Alec in high indignation.

"How dare you talk to mother like that?" threatened Fred.

"A brawl, a brawl, a public brawl," Ruth was heard to gasp over by the window.

"Poor child—so unhappy," explained the old lady indulgently.

"Absurd you are," was all Edith said to the menacing faces, waving them aside, and striding towards the door, against which Milly stood frozen.

"Let me pass, please," she ordered.

"No, no, my dear—you're not to go away," cried the old lady. "Fred, find Edith a chair—on her feet, poor child, so long, and being annoyed and all——"

"Let me pass," repeated Edith, directly addressing the frozen Milly.

"You can't disobey mother, Edith," remonstrated Fred angrily, laying a detaining hand on her arm.

"Can't I? Can't I?" she answered, turning on him; and suddenly burst into wild, violent weeping.

The room was appalled. Nobody had ever seen Edith cry before. The effect was overwhelming. The old lady's head wagged faster, and Milly's eyes, dark in her white face, were fixed on Edith's, so close to hers, as she shrank back against the door in horror.

"Oh, Edith—what is it?" she stammered. "What's the matter?"

"She thinks you've taken her husband from her, Milly my dear," explained the old lady hurriedly. "Such a pity, I always think, to think a thing like that, because if it's true it only leads to trouble, and if it isn't it's not a very nice thought to have had. Much better," she went on as nobody spoke, and Edith's bitter weeping was the only sound, "not worry, and just wait. They always come back, husbands do, if one just waits—and sometimes that isn't very nice either. Mabel my dear, give poor Edith the smelling-salts. You'll find them in the cupboard behind you."

"But——" said Milly, her astonished eyes on the convulsed Edith, "taken her husband? Do you mean Bertie?" And with a helpless glance round the room she asked, idiotically, "Where to?"

"Yes, my dear—that's what poor Edith believes, and whether she's right or wrong it's very sad for all of us, because she's going to try to divorce him. And that, you know, will disgrace us all a good deal, I'm afraid—especially as it's because of you, his sister-in-law. Nora my dear, just come and tie this ribbon better. No use not looking one's best, I always think."

Milly's bewildered eyes appealed to the nodding figure on the bed. "I don't understand, mother," she said.

"Why should Edith—what has her divorcing Bertie to do with *me?*"

"You see, my dears?" quavered the old lady. "The poor girl doesn't know anything at all about it. Edith thinks, Milly my dear, that you've—well, it's no use not saying it, is it, when you dear children are all thinking it—she thinks that you've committed adultery with poor Bertie."

The room held its breath to hear her answer.

It was merely to repeat, in a whisper, the terrible word, "Adultery"?

"Yes, my dear—adultery. What people commit," explained the old lady a little irritably, as Milly's face continued blank. "Some, that is. Such a pity, I always think, for it only seems to lead to worry. But fortunately it doesn't last."

Milly looked round at them in amazement, her hands spread out behind her against the door.

"With—*Bertie?*" she whispered.

"Yes, my dear—Bertie. My son, and your brother-in-law. Not a very nice thought for Edith to have, is it? However, she insists that it's true, and the family will be a good deal dragged down, I'm afraid."

"But——" began Milly, staring round.

"Do you dare," burst in Edith, pushing aside the smelling-salts Mabel tremblingly offered, and trying to control her twitching face, trying to stop the humiliating tears at least while she asked this one question, "do you *dare* stand there, Milly, and say you haven't committed adultery?"

"Oh, how terrible—oh, I can't bear this!" gasped Ruth.

"Answer the question, Milly my dear," quavered the old lady. "Answer it like a good girl, and set all our poor minds at rest."

And Milly, looking round at the crowding faces, her

hands spread out behind her against the door, her face frozen into a mask, said slowly, as if each word were a drop of her blood, "But it wasn't—with Bertie."

§

Faces, faces, faces; crowding so close to see her shame. Or was it—she caught her breath—her release?

It was her release. Suddenly she knew it. Here, in this room, she had reached freedom; here she had got to the end of all her torment.

An extraordinary sensation of being healed came over her; and something in a poem Arthur used to read aloud stirred in her memory as she stood, still pressed against the door, her eyes on the faces but no longer seeing them, and the room and everybody in it gone hazy—*Then clear, unburdened, careless, cool*, it went; and it was about what it was like after one had died.

That was what one felt, that was what one was, when one had finished with being afraid. Clear; unburdened. How lovely. What depths of—peace.

"Give her the smelling-salts," said somebody.

"No, no, my dear—Milly doesn't want smelling-salts," said the voice from the bed.

Slowly she became aware of the faces again, the crowding faces—Edith's with red eyes, incredulous, as if she weren't going to believe.

But she must believe. This one service Milly could do the Botts before she passed out of their lives for ever—she could force them to believe, save them from tragedy by telling the whole truth.

"No," she said, leaving off pressing back against the door and taking a step forward—towards them now, instead of shrinking away, wonder on her face that she should no longer be afraid, "it isn't smelling-salts I want. It's to tell you everything."

And then and there she was going to—going to strip herself naked before them, pick off all her lying shred by shred, tell them everything except only Arthur's name, give them such details that they couldn't but be convinced, when a loud quaver arose from the bed.

"My dear, I shouldn't do that," vehemently protested the old lady.

They all turned to her. They hadn't ever heard mother speak so loud before. Supported by the heaped-up pillows, sitting in the bed as on a throne, she was wagging her bead with awe-inspiring violence. Her cap, its mauve ribbons shaking with the rest of her, had gone a little crooked, and the crookedness only made her the more impressive. She had raised a trembling hand. She was imposing silence. Her old face was flushed with determination.

"We don't want to hear anything more, Milly my dear," she announced authoritatively. "You've told us what we wished to know, and taken a great load off our minds, and I'm sure we're all very thankful and glad, especially poor Edith. But I always think long stories should be kept for winter evenings and rainy days and when we're old, my dear—no, no, don't speak—that's the time for telling everything, not now when it's spring, and we're none of us nearly as old, I'm sure, as we're going to be. Besides, it's getting on for lunch-time. We don't want to stay all boxed up here together on a nice bright morning when it's getting on for lunch-time talking about what's finished and done with, and the boys anxious to be off, I'll be bound, to their offices, and the girls worried, I'm sure, about not having ordered dinner yet."

She paused; but her eye was on Milly. If Milly had so much as begun opening her mouth, the old lady would instantly have interrupted. No more of that, she was determined; no more nonsense from anybody. They didn't know how to manage their lives, didn't they? Well, she would manage them for them. They had talked quite enough, the poor sillies, about what the others had done or not done, and what they were going to do next, or not do, and she wasn't going to have Milly making a fool of herself too.

But Milly stood quite quiet, not attempting to do anything, and the old lady, seeing this, ceased to hold her with her eye and looked away at the others. Considering that her head was shaking, it was remarkable how pointedly she managed to look at them.

"I'm tired," she announced briefly.

There was a movement, notably among the sons-in-law squeezed together over by the windows.

"I'm tired, my dears," she repeated, encouraging the movement. "I always think," she went on, as it showed signs of subsiding, "that offices in the City are such a comfort, because then people go to them."

The movement became more pronounced. With curiously abashed faces, on which was yet relief, the sons-in-law began disentangling themselves one by one.

"Are you going, Walter Walker my dear?" asked the old lady approvingly, as her eldest son-in-law appeared from behind the dressing-table, edging his way carefully to the door. "That's right. And my Noakes son-in-law too. Katie, of course you'll want to go with your husband. My dears, I'm tired," she said again, looking at her own sons, who stood jammed together with their wives, not quite sure what they ought to do.

The movement became general. Waistcoats were straightened, and bags picked up. The old lady, her eye on them, checked any tendency she observed to linger by saying with increasing insistence, "I'm tired, my dears——" and when Maud, her eldest daughter, a woman not easily removed from such places as she wished to stay in, began to protest, she was cut as short as if she were still in the nursery, and briefly told to hold her tongue.

After that the daughters went very quietly, cowed by hearing one of themselves, a woman of sixty-two, bidden hold her tongue and seeing her obediently holding it. Besides, mother's face was dangerously red. Suppose she had a fit, and died then and there? What would their consciences feel like then?

"I'm *tired*, my dears," repeated the old lady, annoyed by their slowness, the red of her face deepening alarmingly.

They began to move more quickly. The sons, intensely relieved at being let off, anyhow for the present, further scenes and explanations, grabbed at their wives and drew them along with them towards the door. Mother was quite right. Much best stop Milly getting things off her chest. They had had enough, first and last, of Milly's chest. Besides, what did it matter now, her exact form of sinning? The great thing was that old Bertie wasn't in it, and that they were all saved from any beastly divorcing. One or two of them would have liked to have shaken hands or something with the poor creature, who stood at the foot of the bed as if she didn't know whether she too was expected to sheer off or not, for after all she had got them out of no end of a hole, and Nora and Mabel both wanted to kiss her; but every time anybody showed signs of lingering, the old lady repeated commandingly, "I'm *tired*, my dears."

Edith got away one of the first. Her departure was watched from the bed with approval.

"Edith's gone," the old lady remarked, encouraging the others to follow so excellent an example. "Sensible of her. She'll be better next time we see her. We'll all be better, my dears—and rested."

The room grew lighter. Presently Milly, still uncertain, her hands on the rail of the bed, had quite a large empty space round her.

Lighter and lighter grew the room, larger and larger the empty space round Milly. At last there was nothing but space, and light, and herself, and the old lady.

Except for the birds in the garden, very busy that fine morning, and the rumble of traffic on the road beyond, the room was quite silent.

They looked at each other—Milly, at the foot of the bed, her white face framed in the thrown-back crape veil against the bright window behind her, the old lady in her quivering mauve ribbons, propped up on the pillows at the other end.

"Then," said Milly at last, her eyes on the flushed old face, her voice very low, "then—I may go?"

"Yes, my dear. Upstairs, to take off your bonnet."

Silence; except for those birds, and the distant banging of the doors of cars as Botts departed.

"You can't keep on your bonnet for the rest of your life, can you?" the old lady, after a moment, pointed out.

Cleared of blocking black figures, the windows were streamed through by warm sunshine. Light washed round the room, flooding the face on the pillows.

"Do you mean——" began Milly.

"Come here, my dear," interrupted the old lady in a commanding quaver, "and kiss me good-morning. You haven't yet, you know, and we must keep up our manners, mustn't we, as we're going to live together. Besides, Milly my dear"—she held out both her unsteady hands—"I want to bless you."

THE END

Persephone Books publishes the following titles: